APPLES IN THE DARK

John Alex Taylor

Troubador Publishing Ltd
Unit E2 Airfield Business Park,
Harrison Road, Market Harborough,
Leicestershire. LE16 7UL
Tel: 0116 2792299
Email: books@troubador.co.uk
Web: www.troubador.co.uk

ISBN 978 1805144 342

Cover painting by Louise Ryder
Typeset in 11.5pt / 15.2pt Minion Pro by Leigh Forbes,
Blot Publishing, blot.co.uk

British Library Cataloguing in Publication Data.
A catalogue record for this book is available from the British Library.

Printed and bound in Great Britain by 4edge Limited

For Fiona, Lucy and Simon
And in memory of my loving, caring parents
Charles and Nancy Taylor
And for anyone who lives with a hidden disability

1

DEATH RAYS AND SHOCK-STOPPERS

Alice

No rabbit holes or tea parties were involved. This Alice's adventures started on a Cardiff bus. That's where I met the first adult who truly understood the weirdness of being an undergrown girl with an overgrown mind.

It was a hot Saturday morning in June and some girls from my class were playing football on Roath Park playing field. I would have joined in, but the class nerd wasn't welcome. Shopping with Mam was safer.

I led Mam to a seat near the back of the bus, and I couldn't help looking at the woman in the seat behind. She had her hand clutching the side of her head, like she was holding it on. Her dark fringe covered her eyes, and her hair was as tangly as mine. Was she hiding from someone? Or was she an assassin, waiting for her chance to take out that man by the far window in a white hoodie?

'Nosey,' Mam said, and so I looked out of the window at the crowds in the playground by the library. Kids who didn't know the climate was burning up. The woman behind was squirming around. Had the man got her first? Now she was rubbing the side of her head. Poisoned dart?

Probably not, on a Cardiff bus.

I tried to ignore her and started drawing on the window with my finger. No mist on the windowpane, but I could just see the mark from my sweaty finger. I wondered what poison woman would make of it and gave her my best smile. 'Guess what it is!'

'Um…' She stared at me, and then at my invisible picture.

Mam shook her head at me. 'Don't bother her, Alice.' And she turned round to poison woman. 'Sorry.' Mam's always saying sorry about me.

Poison woman gave a sort of smile and looked at my drawing again. 'How about a galaxy? A distant galaxy.' Her voice came out in a hurry, like mine.

'It's a velociraptor,' I said. 'But a galaxy's better – tidy, like. An invisible one with invisible aliens.'

Her big brown eyes peeped out from under her fringe. She couldn't have been poisoned because she smiled straight at me. 'Plenty of galaxies have invisible x-ray sources,' she said. 'Some, immensely powerful.'

And I liked her straight away. This was lush – people on buses don't say astronomical stuff. I stroked my finger in a spiral around my velociraptor. 'There, it's a death-ray veloci-galaxy!'

X-ray woman was rubbing the side of her head again.

'You alright?' I asked.

'Just a twinge. It'll go.'

Mam's good with twinges and things, but she was busy texting. Probably Dad, about not sending my money this month.

The bus rattled along Albany Road. X-ray woman was still smiling, and I tried to think of something astronomical to tell her. We lurched across the junction into Richmond

Road, and she had her hand on her head again, looking twitchy. I tried holding my head, but my brain wouldn't twitch.

She touched the glass with her finger and began to draw. Adults don't do that stuff – maybe she was a teenager in disguise. Her drawing had big swirls and tiny swirls.

'Another galaxy? A universe?'

'It's a stegosaurus,' she said.

Mam smiled, back from text-land. 'Someone else who likes dinosaurs, Alice.'

'Ever since I was Alice's age,' nice woman said, and I liked her even more.

I wanted her to know that I took dinosaurs seriously. 'Primitive dinosaurs, stegosauruses were. Tiny brains, they had.'

'Stegosauri?' she said, pulling a thinking face.

'Nah, stegosauruses sounds better,' I told her. It does.

'Stegosauruses it is, then,' she said. 'Maybe we'd better tell them at the museum.'

'Cool! What's your name?'

'Rachel – I'm Rachel.' She gave her head another little rub, but leaned forward and opened her eyes wider. 'Alice, my stegosaurus has a massive brain. She's from the Alpha Centauri system, plays the xylophone… ac mae hi'n siarad Cymraeg.'

And now I knew. Rachel had a cool brain stuffed full of ideas like mine. 'Speaks Welsh?' I said. 'Not Stegoic?'

Mam joined in. 'Cymraeg – the language of dragons.'

'I'm sure she was speaking Welsh last Tuesday, out by Alpha Centauri,' Rachel said and leaned her head from side to side, sort-of bothered.

'You sure you're alright?'

'Just a false alarm,' she said. 'I thought… No, I'm fine, now. Finer, for meeting you.'

Mam gave her one of her soft smiles – the kind I'm not so good at. 'Alpha Centauri, you say? Do they have Tuesdays out there?'

Trust Mam.

'Mam! Don't be silly.'

'You'd have a job proving they don't,' Rachel said.

Okay, then.

'I bet every day is a Tuesday on Alpha Centauri,' I said.

But I didn't get to find out what Rachel thought because the bus was juddering to a stop in town and she was sorting her bag. I'd missed the boring bit of the bus ride along Newport Road – I was four light years away at the time.

Mam and me got up and Rachel stood up behind us. She looked a bit shaky and I was bothered for her. I wanted to tell Mam that Rachel would be safer sticking with us, but was too shy about it. Bad mistake. And Mam didn't seem to notice.

'Bye! Nice to…' Mam headed for Queen Street, and I had to follow, but Rachel was looking down with her fringe over her eyes again. I waved and she raised her hand a bit and then other people got in the way and I needed to catch up with Mam. For about five minutes, I'd had a real friend. I hadn't needed to hide being intelligent and weird. And I would never meet her again, ever. Well, not for another five minutes, anyway.

Mam needed to go to Boots, and Queen Street was too crowded for me to wait outside. After the long queue to pay, I said, 'Market, alright?' Mam hates shopping as much as me, but we both love the market. So, we headed along Queen Street towards the castle, and that's when I saw her.

She was standing bent forward over one of the metal benches, with both hands clutching the back of it. 'Mam! It's Rachel.'

Rachel staggered away from the bench, held her head, lurched back, crashed onto it and curled up tight. I heard a loud screech and people were looking and pointing. Mam raced over and sat with her arm around Rachel's shoulders. The other people turned away, and now it was just Mam and Rachel on that bench under the statue of Nye Bevan, the Health Service man. But he had his back to them.

Now Mam was stroking Rachel's head in her lap, but I was stuck behind a litter bin. Was it okay for a kid to help an upset adult? Some sort of gravity pulled me over to Rachel and I sat up close behind her. She was still curled up tight and her face looked red and she had a scared, sweaty smell. More kid than adult.

'I'm here,' was all I could think to say, and put my hand on Rachel's shoulder next to Mam's. Touching Mam's because it felt safer. 'I'm here, Rachel.'

'Rachel's had a shock,' Mam said. 'We might need to sit with her for a bit.'

Rachel glanced up at Mam. 'Sorry.'

'No worries. I'm Beth. And you're safe,' Mam said.

'Safe,' I said, and stroked Rachel's shoulder. Her skirt was tucked up, showing her tights, and I pulled it free and smoothed it down for her. 'That's better. You upset?'

She struggled to sit up, holding onto her head, and Mam helped steady her. 'Thank you,' Rachel said, shading her eyes. 'Bit of a mess.'

'No one's looking,' Mam said. 'It's still Tuesday on Alpha Centauri. Can you tell me what's wrong?'

Rachel took slow breaths, and her lips were moving, like she was counting. 'Sorry,' she whispered. 'Panic attack. I thought a seizure was coming.'

'You get seizures?' Mam sat back, like it was scary, but I know seizures.

'No worries,' I said, stroking Rachel's back. 'Girl in my class has seizures. Epilepsy. I help her. Other kids treat Shareen bad. Make a fuss. I time them for her with my teacher. Talk quiet.'

'I didn't know,' Mam said.

Rachel reached for my hand. 'Thank you, Alice.' And now she could talk, she talked quick. Mostly stuff I'd heard at school. Low probability of anything serious. Number of false alarms. Instructions in her bag if she were to have one. And then stuff Shareen had never told me, but I'd guessed. How Rachel's body went into automatic panic whenever she felt anything odd. She'd felt it when she got on the bus at the stop before us, further up Ninian Road. But doing dinosaur and galaxy stuff with me had calmed her down.

She pursed her lips and then took some more of those counting breaths. 'I'm okay now.' But she still smelt hot and panicky, and I shook my head.

Mam stroked Rachel's hair out of her eyes, like when she tidies me up. 'You should have someone with you, Rachel. God, this place is noisy – can we get you somewhere quieter?'

Rachel wiped the back of her hand across her eyes and looked down. 'It's more the bright light and people rushing around.'

And I knew. 'Rachel needs shock-stoppers, Mam.'

'Good thinking, Batman!' Mam said. 'Rachel, do you have shades with you?'

'In here.' Rachel fumbled for her bag, down under the bench, and I held it for her.

'Alice calls hers shock-stoppers,' Mam said. 'She's sensitive – wears them when too much is happening. Goes into overload.'

'I know that feeling.' Rachel smiled at me, slipped her shades on, and moved her hands back a little way. I saw more of that counting with her lips and then she relaxed her hands. 'Magic! You're right, Alice – shock-stoppers – they really work!'

I fished my rose-tinted shades out of my rucksack, put them on and framed them with my fingers. 'Yeah, don't forget. Shock-stoppers.'

'I'll remember – thank you. They look smart.' But Rachel turned away, sort-of rushed, like she'd gone shy. 'I must get on down to the office – I'm over it. Thank you for stopping – you're both very kind. More than that – you're... People don't...'

'Just being friendly,' Mam said and shook her head. 'You're really not over it, Rachel. Your office can wait – let's get you a drink. I'm not leaving you in a tizz.'

Rachel tried to stand up, but she was all shaky, and Mam took her by the arm. We usually have a drink in the market, but Mam took Rachel across and into the nearest coffee bar. I sat up close to Rachel, and Mam came back with two teas and a hot chocolate with sprinkles for me.

Rachel lifted her shades and parked them on top of her head, but she kept her hands there for a few moments.

'Not dizzy?' I said.

'No – it's gone. You two… If I had medals to give… Just… Thank you. I feel almost normal.'

'I'm never normal,' I said. 'Normal's boring.'

Mam smiled at me. 'You're so right, Alice. Normal is overrated.'

We sat with our drinks not saying much. I could tell Rachel was thinking stuff, because she started twiddling with her hair like I do when I'm thinking. But we'd run out of stuff to say, and I didn't want to stress her. Shareen likes quiet when she's had a panic or a seizure.

When they'd both finished their tea, Mam poked at her phone. 'Drink up, Alice. We mustn't be late for Granddad.' But hot chocolate with sprinkles is only best ever for about three gulps, and then it tastes of sick. I could make my fortune inventing not-sick hot chocolate. But I did want to see Granddad, so I drank it, like a princess drinking poison and pretending to enjoy it. Because.

'Granddad Joe's not normal either,' I told Rachel. 'Calls me his apprentice.'

We stood up and I stuck close to Rachel. 'Shock-stoppers on!'

'Thank you for the idea, Alice. Really. I'll get some rose-tinted ones like yours.' She thanked Mam for the tea and all her care, and then smiled the best smile at me. A best smile, but a sad one, like she didn't want to leave us. 'Is it still Tuesday on Alpha Centauri, Alice?' she whispered.

'Not on the third planet. It's November there. They only have months.'

'Thank you for looking after me.'

'Shock-stoppers,' I said.

'I bet they stop the death rays from your veloci-galaxy.'

I tapped the frame of my shades. 'That's why I wear them.'

She reached out to my hand, but looked nervous again, so I reached for hers with both of mine and pulled her close. 'You take care.'

And then Mam was hugging Rachel and so was I and I felt all teary, which was weird because I didn't really know Rachel. Saying goodbye was hard, and I think Mam felt it too.

Rachel walked off towards her office in Newport Road, and I kept watching until she disappeared into the crowd. Odd – she was heading in the other direction when she panicked.

'Mam, we should… I don't know. Be friends.'

'We should have swapped phone numbers, shouldn't we?' Mam said.

It was too late, and there must have been hundreds of Rachels in Cardiff. How would we ever find her again? I just hoped Rachel's shock-stoppers would keep out the death rays.

2

AN OCEAN BETWEEN US

Rachel

I'd planned to go shopping but headed for safe loneliness at work. Stressed sky-high by meeting lovely, curious Alice and comforting Beth. Longing to turn back and stay with them forever. And knowing I would die of embarrassment if I saw them.

Five floors above Newport Road with tinted glass to keep the world away, I put on my invisible cloak and became Doctor Bothwell, senior scientific consultant. Not lonely and small. In charge.

And slowly joining the dots. I could have predicted this morning's panic. Dad. Yesterday, I had summoned the will-power to catch a train to London and support Mum at Dad's funeral. And I knew I should have been there for her sooner. A lot sooner.

Had Dad controlled Mum in the way he controlled me? I was just thirteen when he explained that my frightening new condition was psychosomatic. And I half believed him. I was still a student when I woke up to the pattern and cut my ties. With Mum as well – I couldn't find another way. She'd never blamed me, but how had it been for her?

For the rest of the day, I tried to concentrate on statistics in a world where I didn't need shock-stoppers because I was the one directing death rays at other people's work. And I drew a little stegosaurus on my scribbling pad, wondering whether Alice had enjoyed shopping with Granddad Joe. I hoped he was an exciting granddad.

Three years in the science division of an anonymous multi-national had been harmless, well-paid therapy after the research I loved consumed me until I was burned to a shell. I'd known what was happening but couldn't let go when it mattered. Everything in this job was safe, predictable, and like the corporate logo, grey.

It was nearly six o'clock when my phone beeped.

> Back home cooking supper.
> You still down the office?

Cai, the only man I'd let in far enough to share my insecurities. Not that he'd got as far as sharing any of his in our safe, semi-detached relationship. Earlier this year, Cai had revealed that he'd been offered a job across the ocean, and my guilty first response was relief. He would be leaving for New York next Wednesday. Life would continue with an ocean between us.

I walked home, trying to sort through the muddle in my head. Cai waited until I was settled with dal and chapatis in front of me before extracting my admission of panic in town. I played down the parent connection and told him instead about Alice and shock-stoppers and veloci-galaxies. But I couldn't keep my eyes away from his travel documents on the dresser and neat piles of clothes beside the ironing board.

When I went to bed, I tried to disengage my imaginings from life without Cai. I would have no compulsive tidier to keep my house and life organised, no cook, no one to pick me up and tuck me in after a seizure, no bass player to share my violin practice, and no one but my rag doll to talk to. Stop it, Rachel.

That girl with a big bunch of golden hair, racing along the bus to the seat in front. The woman shuffling in next to her with the same hair fighting to escape, a shade or two darker. Alice and Beth – people I could relate to – have fun with. Somewhere nearby – they got on the bus further down the road – but would we meet again? Sleep took time.

In the morning, I snuggled into my dressing gown and headed downstairs, only to meet my life reduced to a list in a spiral-bound notebook. Rachel, defined by what she hadn't done and a shortage of toilet paper. I added painkillers to the list: I needed them.

'You know you had one last night?' Cai called from the kitchen. 'Two o'clock.'

My symptoms in Queen Street had been real after all. 'Sorry. Did I disturb you?'

His voice came closer and softened. 'No more than any other screaming banshee. I tucked your leg in – you were half out of bed.' He shook his head and flopped onto the sofa. 'I suppose I'll miss all this,' he said. 'You managing?'

At what level? Not answerable. I shrugged.

I settled next to him, wondering what to say. Nothing fitted.

He examined his fingernails. 'I'll never forget you – us – escaping together.'

I'd felt lucky to land any job at all after my Cambridge career went to pieces, let alone one that more than doubled my salary. And Cai had been sleepwalking towards an exit from his endless round of lecturing for years. A pair of escape artists? Hardly.

'We'll always be friends,' I said, feeling stupid. We had coexisted, but my clothes and books and coffee cups on the floor had sent Cai running to the back bedroom within days of our experiment at sharing a bed. And sex was a failure we didn't talk about.

I was already missing a man who had never seemed entirely present, and automatically cuddle closer, squeezing myself against his side and hoping to blot out conflicting feedback from my body.

'Are you sure, Rachel?'

No, it wasn't meant to be an invitation – how dumb am I?

'I'm not sure, no. I'm… I need you, now.'

'Loneliness is the killer, isn't it?' he said.

Yes. The cushions slid off the sofa and we slid with them. An uncomfortable coupling seemed inevitable and would at least mark our parting.

He smiled and took my face between two gentle hands. 'The morning after a seizure? I can see your headache from here. Let's take the next few bars as read, Rachel. We don't need full brass and timpani.'

I breathed out. It wasn't just my headache: each moment of intimacy was a reminder of past encounters with men who hadn't been so understanding.

Cai diverted my attention towards some artefacts from the dark interior of the sofa: his library card, a takeaway menu, a button, one pound twenty-six in loose change, and a green sock we both disowned (mine).

'You don't know how wonderful you are, taking me as I

am,' I said. 'Over there – promise you won't retreat into your shell – you will tell me if it gets too much?'

'Isabelle has friends over there. I'll be okay.' Cai was relocating to follow Isabelle, his senior editor at an academic publisher. Maybe they would find some magic together, but I didn't like Isabelle much. Surely this wasn't jealousy?

'I'll just have a shower,' I said, still puzzling out the jealousy thing.

'Wait. We need a way to say goodbye. Let's share it.'

'No... yes.'

We hadn't showered together since I bought the house, but Cai's idea worked. Peeling off our pyjamas and sharing a gentle, intimate wash let me show how much I cared for this dear man who had put up with my... being. As if I was washing away my mistakes and clumsiness and unthinking self-centredness.

We softly towelled these familiar, separate human bodies, and without words, Cai grabbed some clothes and led me into my bedroom. For the first time ever, we dressed each other, a little clumsily. One garment at a time, we put each other back together. I could feel the fabric holding me; containing me; protecting and reassuring me. Cai was Cai; I was Rachel, and we were both whole.

In a perfect universe, he would have donned a flying jacket and kissed me; vaulted into a convenient biplane; roared down steep Morlais Street; zoomed up over Roath Park, and banked around with his red scarf trailing out behind him. Then he would have waved and disappeared into the setting sun on his way to the New World.

But he wouldn't be travelling until Wednesday and rushed out in a hurry, late for a goodbye lunch with his writing friends. When he wasn't editing books on obscure and extinct languages, he was an author of grim, dystopian SF. His books had a cult (equals small) following in America. And yes, I worried for him.

What his American fans would make of Cai, I wasn't sure. His doctorate in ancient languages might surround him with an aura of mystery, but what about the vase of cut flowers that he maintained on his desk, a reminder of the transience of all things? They knew Rick Vega Jr., author of planetary death and destruction, not a shaggy-haired Welshman with a permanently puzzled smile. A smile as annoying as it was attractive. I would miss it.

I woke up on Monday morning with my rag doll's hair wrapped around my finger. Unconscious Rachel had needed her Molly. I headed for the kitchen and played a few morning arpeggios on my violin while Cai dug out some muesli. He kept glancing at me and looking away. 'Rachel…?'

'What've I done now?' came out in F# major and my bow shrieked.

'Are you sure you'll be alright?' he said, concentrating on opening a carton of orange juice. 'I was serious about you joining me. There's room in the apartment.'

Abrupt halt to arpeggios. I didn't want to be alone. I did not want to be alone. The most selfish reason to tie him down when he could so easily take flight. 'You need a new start, Cai. Don't spoil it by looking over your shoulder.'

'Just don't let your next lover near my comics.'

Yes, I would be storing his comics, his LPs and double bass until he had decided where to settle. But next lover sounded close to a joke. I was late now and rushed to loosen my bow and put my violin away. Just time to munch through a banana and rush upstairs for a shower.

Mirror next. Apply office war paint. Put on confident face. Adjust it for approachability. Bag – keys – phone. Time for work, Doctor Bothwell.

My day in the office passed with predictable greyness and some awkwardness with Tom Richards, PhD. Older than me, my new junior consultant was a mystery. Shyness or reticence? His or mine? I couldn't help feeling that he'd arrived here by mistake. His abrupt change of career echoed my own three years earlier, but I hadn't been a merchant ship's officer. Odd.

A Celtic warrior with a shock of wavy bronze hair, he would make a perfect pirate captain. I looked up his thesis: interesting. And his age: forty-four. Nicely mature. Stop it, Rachel – why waste time figuring him out? Even sitting on the bus home.

The house was empty when I walked in. After Wednesday, empty would be my new normal. And something unwanted from my old normal was happening. Something I'd noticed on the bus but preferred to distract myself with pirate Tom.

My horizon was going askew and tinged with rainbows. The kitchen tasted of tinfoil. The spider on the window had precise hairs down its legs, each in painful focus.

Right, Rachel, deal with it – do it on your own – you can. I threw some coats on the kitchen floor. Lay down. Felt silly. False alarm. No…

Awake. Who? Who am I?

Rachel – that's me. Where's the rest of the information?

Onion. Onion? Kitchen floor. Needs a wash.

It's… Monday night? God, I've had one. Bugger.

A small one. Only a few seconds of disorientation, not much headache, no bitten tongue. And I hadn't even been afraid to deal with it.

Shit, yes, I had.

Don't lie to yourself, Rachel, it's a bad habit. You're going to be alone every time. Alone. Every time the world keeps turning without you.

3

I FELL OVER

Alice

I couldn't tell Miss in class. Miss hated having an Alice who was too clever for Year Five. Who wasn't one of the girls and needed extension work. And asked chopsy questions because she couldn't stop her mouth doing it. No, I couldn't tell Miss.

'I fell over, Miss.'

Was tripped over and kicked in the jaw in the toilets. Again. With an audience too scared to say a word. Because they would be next.

Justice, the Evil Twins called it. They are the class Justice.

'I fell over, Miss.'

And I would not. Ever. Cry. Not in front of the Evils.

Maybe I could have told Rachel. Had a laugh with her about death rays melting the Evils so that their flesh dripped off. Dripped off enough to stop them ever growing up to be influencers. Class influencers, they called themselves, when they weren't being Justice.

I had other words for them. A whole dictionary of words I had stored up from Dad when he was off his head. Not that he ever remembered saying them. Dad was sort-of like me. More victim than bully. And never around.

'I fell over, Miss.'

I couldn't tell Dad, even if he was around. He was stressed enough just being human every day.

Rachel.

Maybe, if I found her, I could tell her.

Miss sent me to the school nurse, who sent me to casualty.

'I fell over, Nurse.'

Nothing broken. Got painkillers.

Then I had to face Mam. The one person in the universe I never wanted to worry, ever. Who fought to keep me happy and cared-for. Who loved me. Who was the best artist in the universe. Who was hurt each time Granddad had to pay for stuff. Who cared for EVERYONE, even Dad who never paid my allowance.

'I fell over, Mam.' And I got that look. Like she didn't believe me, but she didn't want to say so.

It hurt, lying to Mam. Like it was eating me inside.

Because of my jaw, Mam took me to the dentist. 'I fell over.' My teeth were okay.

Rachel. I could tell Rachel. She would understand.

How did I know that? Telepathy? Mind-cloning? Human wi-fi?

And to tell her, I would have to find one single Rachel in a city full of Rachels.

Rachel

Cai had gone. Our goodbye was badly rehearsed and brief. Would he really manage New York? Wednesday was lost in unfocussed worry, with no comforting messages. Then on Thursday, I got home from work to an empty house and still not one message. But neither were there any headlines about missing Welshmen or air disasters.

You okay? I sent.

Last week's to-do list lay on my desk, written in the Cai-and-Rachel era, but he wouldn't be reading my life over my shoulder any more.

— Frankfurt? Call again. Do they really mean FULL figures for the bid?
— Toilet paper, tissues. ?Cai do big shop before he goes?
— Wellfield Rd > pineapple, coffee, prescription. PAINKILLERS.
— Call Mum.
— Has he remembered to cancel his rent?
— Find man – eye candy – mustn't write SF or eat chocolate.

Yes, Cai had done the big shop for me, but he still hadn't cancelled his rent. And a regular supply of chocolate would be simpler than another man. I avoided the time bomb hidden safely in the middle of the list. Call Mum. Another time.

You liar, Rachel.

The pineapple pieces and coffee on the list used to fuel me through late nights of research on the ragged edge of sanity. Now that I was a comfortable hired brain, I kept a pretty glass jar of pineapple pieces on my desk. A relic from a life with ideals and purpose that had expired before I was thirty-five.

I didn't get to sleep until about three in the morning and then triumphant Verdi from my radio alarm made me grab for my rag doll. Molly was my only housemate now, and we had just about negotiated two nights alone together.

Dressed and ready for work, I stepped out into the noise and presence of Cardiff waking up to another Friday. A beeping van was struggling to reverse up our dead-end street and a spicy aroma hung in the air. Lots to decode. Even in the small universe of this smallish city, I've always felt such a miniscule presence that it takes me time to insert my consciousness into the great continuum of existence around me.

I pressed my palm against the green wall tiles in the front porch. Traced the black-and-white floor tiles with the tip of my toe. People had passed through this lovely porch for over a century before I walked in and knew I'd found home the moment I stepped inside. It must have been the easiest sale the estate agent ever made. I needed the feeling of security and stability this house gave me, halfway up a steep, leafy dead-end street and just a stone's throw from the park.

A liquid arabesque of song drifted down from the tree in the street. My friend the blackbird, staking out our territory. I ran my fingers around the carved stone edging of the porch, feeling its coolness and solidity. Now I was ready to face a new day.

New day – new worries. As I walked down towards the bus stop in Ninian Road, I was puzzling out how to frame an advert for a new tenant. How could I warn them that those screeches in the night every couple of weeks were due to faulty wiring in my brain, not the Grey Lady of Roath? And how would I know which prospective tenant could be trusted with an unconscious woman?

I wouldn't be waking up with vague memories of Cai stroking my forehead any more. And if a seizure really did its worst, not even a tenant as good as Cai would hear. Dead people don't make a lot of noise. You have a road to cross, Rachel. And work.

Work. I didn't want to pressure Tom, but he spent the morning carefully applying precise mathematics, just when I needed speed. My approximations for the Frankfurt bid seemed to spook him, as if I was doing something slightly naughty.

What could I say when my results turned out as accurate as his? Oops? 'Sorry, Tom. My freaky brain came bundled with a quantum calculator.'

Pause. Deep eruption of bass-baritone laughter.

At least that broke the ice and gave me one person in the office happy to share more than the weather and celebrity gossip.

Home, Rachel. And at last, late on Friday evening, I had a message from Cai.

> Good diner on the corner
> for pancakes. Coffee
> terrible. Air conditioning
> saving my life. You good?
> xxx

> Been worried stiff. Thought
> you'd been mugged or
> something.

> Sorry – busy x

I swore and bashed the wall with my fist. Then I went to bed and informed my rag doll that Cai could stuff his pancakes. What if I had easier friends? Friends who could share galaxies and dinosaurs and wonder. Who wouldn't think it odd that I still told Molly everything and needed her woollen hair around my finger. Or that I needed a nightlight in my room and was still afraid of the dark. No, that was beyond odd.

Not ready for sleep, I wrote out a plan, determined that thoughts of Cai wouldn't ruin my weekend.

— Wear your shock-stoppers and walk the length of Queen Street.
— Discount any and all symptoms.
— Pretend you're a grown-up who can go shopping without getting scared.
— Then go to the market and buy lots of chocolate.

I even kidded myself that I might meet Alice and Beth.

4

AN ADULT IN DISGUISE

Alice

I'd been thinking about Rachel all week – well, Rachel and the pain in my jaw and Miss hating me and how to stop the Evil Twins and how stupid it is to be not yet eleven and exactly what Dad's swear words mean and why no search engine ever answers my questions and WHY nobody cares about global warming.

And how to draw melting flesh.

I asked Mam to catch the bus at the same time as last week, and RACHEL WAS ON THE BUS, looking out of the window in her dark shades.

Maybe she didn't see us. Mam said, 'Don't disturb her,' and we sat on the other side near the front. I wasn't going to disturb her anyway. Rachel needed her shock-stoppers, and that meant Do Not Disturb.

It felt different when we got off the bus. Like my inside was a giant magnet pulling me after Rachel. I followed her, a little way behind, and Mam didn't stop me. Rachel walked along Queen Street in a straight line, like she was on a track, not looking around. 'She's nervous,' I told Mam. 'I wonder where she's going.'

I was getting nervous too, and put my shock-stoppers on. Following Rachel wasn't like being a detective. It was real and she might turn around and hate me. And that sweaty-scared Rachel feeling was inside me.

Then Rachel did an Alice. What I would have done if I was nervous. She turned up past the church and into the old market. The safest place in town.

Rachel stood inside the arch looking at the fishes laid out on their stall like an old oil painting. There was even a shark. I look every time – she WAS being me!

Seeing her being me made me brave enough to put my shock-stoppers away.

'You okay? It's safe in here – you can take off your shock-stoppers.'

'Alice!' She lifted her shades.

'I've been a detective, tracking you. No, not really. Bothered you might get a shock.'

'Were you on the bus? I kept looking out of the window for stuff to distract me. But I did hope… I wanted to say a proper thank-you to you and Beth.'

Mam turned up, out of breath. 'Alice! Don't pester the poor woman.'

'No, it's fine,' Rachel said. 'I've been trying out my shock-stoppers.'

'I guessed, from the way you were walking – you looked like you were on a mission. I didn't want Alice to disturb you – I'm sorry.'

'No, I'm sorry for all the fuss last time. If I'd worn shock-stoppers then, I might not have panicked.'

'Let's have a wander round,' Mam said. 'It's our favourite place.'

'Yeah, no bright lights and hard colours,' I said. 'I need shock-stoppers for the big shops – not here.'

'It's like walking back into an old film,' Rachel said. 'The market can't have changed much in a century.'

We went through the doors into the main market hall, all jumbled full of scents and colours and people chatting and shouting. And Rachel just stood there smiling.

It looked like an experiment. Trying out a smile to see if she could. And I needed to ask her. 'Are your seizures REALLY scary? Shareen in my class never says. Won't talk about it.'

'I never managed to talk about it much when I was younger. I've had epilepsy since I was a teenager, but I've never got used to it.'

'Shareen bites her tongue when she has one – blood and gob and stuff comes out.'

'Me too, but that's not much bother. Losing control scares me. Your friend Shareen... Just be there when she needs you.'

'Yeah. Like, not going on about it? Not like the others?'

'You've got it. I hated talking about it at school. Ugh.' She folded her arms tight.

'Yeah.' I wanted to put my arm around Rachel, but that never worked with Shareen. 'You want tea, Rachel? Mam has tea when she's stressed. Up on the balcony. We call it the toast café.'

'Your mam will have plans–'

'Nah – just boring shopping.'

Mam smiled and touched shoulders with Rachel. 'It looks like we're having tea whether we want it or not. Is that okay?'

Rachel glanced at me and back at Mam. 'I could do with a mug, actually.' Maybe she said it to please the kid. Adults do that.

We headed up the steps to the balcony and I saw Mam take Rachel's arm at the top. Careful, Mam. She needs her space.

Past all the racks of second-hand LPs. I love to look at them, but need Mam to tell me which ones sound good. They're more fun than streaming. And Mam won't let me have a phone anyway.

'Hiya, Elvis!' Mam patted the plastic statue in the corner on the arm.

'Poor woman can't help it,' I told Rachel. But I like Mam when she's happy, and put my arm around her. Rachel looked sort of lost or left out, but I could tell hugging wouldn't work. I went and sat at the long counter and pulled out a chair for her.

She smiled and sat down. Her dark blue nail polish looked smart. 'Nice colour.' I reached out towards her hand, and she touched my fingertips, looked at me and looked down. And it was like telepathy – I knew. 'You're not used to kids, are you?'

'You don't miss much, Alice! You're right – I don't know any children. How old are you? No, that's a daft question – it doesn't mean anything.'

'Ten-and-a-half. Years older when I'm thinking. Years younger when I'm a pain. That's what Mam thinks.'

'When did I ever say that?' Mam said.

'How old are you?' I asked Rachel.

'Thirty-eight-and-two-weeks. But yes…' She rolled her eyes. '…about four when I panic.'

'You're WAY younger than Mam!'

'Forty-five. Past it,' Mam said, still standing behind Rachel.

'Past what, Mam?'

'Past thinking up a clever answer. I'll get some tea and toast.'

Mam went to the counter and me and Rachel looked at each other. And I couldn't help my hand covering my bruise. Me thinking I could tell Rachel was just stupid.

But she gave me a sad look. 'You don't want to talk about it, do you, Alice?'

'No.'

'Okay.'

'I lied to Mam about it.' I glanced over at Mam, in the queue.

I didn't know I was going to tell Rachel that.

'I lied to Mum when I was at school,' Rachel said. 'A lot. Protecting her.'

I reached out my hand and she just brushed it with her fingers.

'Don't worry about not knowing kids,' I said. 'You know me. I'm an adult in disguise.'

'I hated it when adults talked down to me,' Rachel said.

'Yeah, like, "ISN'T she clever?" Yuk.'

'I got that all the time. Being an intelligent kid is hard.'

'I love drawing, but I never draw at school. Mam's an artist and… it's just easy, but I don't want the others to see me not drawing like a kid.' I showed Rachel my sketch pad in my rucksack. Ready to draw Granddad Joe and Nana Siân again this afternoon.

Rachel had that sad look again, and I could tell she was still bothering about my bruise. She gave a sort-of made-up smile. 'No kids here. You could practise drawing me. I won't make a fuss – promise.'

And that was magic, here in the market. 'REALLY! You won't mind?'

'I don't remember anyone drawing me – ever,' she said.

'Wow! Mam draws me all the time.'

I took a nice soft pencil from my tin, and looked at Rachel across it a few times, getting the shape of her face. She stayed perfectly still, not like fidgety Granddad Joe. Then I traced in a centre line, an eye line and her eyebrows and mouth, and worked on from there. Mam was coming back with a plate of toast when Rachel said. 'You're right – you don't draw like a child – I would never get the proportion as accurate as that.'

Mam looked over my shoulder. 'You've got her eyes peeping out behind her fringe – big and soulful.'

Rachel didn't go on about me being a kid. 'That's a first,' she said. 'I've never been drawn before. Could I look at your other drawings?'

I passed her my sketchpad, and she leafed through sketches of the stray cat that sits on our wall, my REALLY rough picture of Granddad Joe and some insects. She smiled, turned the page and stopped. My pastel drawing of Mam.

'This is special. I'm not praising you as a kid, Alice. I'm praising you as an artist.'

It felt warm and special, but I'm not that good. 'Not an artist like Mam.'

Mam hugged me close. 'I've had years of practice. Trust me, Alice, Rachel is right. You see things your own way – no need to compare yourself with me.'

'Beth-a-ny Howells,' I said. 'Should be famous. But no-one really calls Mam Bethany.'

Mam lifted one eyebrow like she does. 'I'd hate to be

famous and Alice hates Bethany. I like it – I'm called after my great-grandmother.'

Rachel gave Mam one of those shy glances – being me again. 'I'd love to see your pictures,' she whispered.

'I don't paint much nowadays,' Mam said, and now she had a sad look. A look that told me she didn't paint because she needed to earn money to look after me.

A pigeon fluttered across inside the glass roof, and I wondered what a bird's eye view of the three of us at the counter would look like. Rachel knowing my secret, Mam worrying about us both, and me in the middle, wondering stuff.

Rachel and Mam could be two different species of human. Rachel all neat and tidy in her dark skirt and tights. Professional, they call that look, but I call it boring, like school uniform. And it doesn't suit her. Mam with her favourite faded Stereophonics t-shirt, leather waistcoat and jeans. And Mam bigger and cosier, with her rosy cheeks and that funny plastic Alice band Dad gave her. Rachel, a bit shrunk and sad.

Mam was looking at Rachel's clothes, too. 'On the way to work again?'

'I get more done on Saturdays when the place is quiet,' Rachel said, holding the counter with one hand and looking away. Tense.

I needed to relax her. 'Mam and me are going round the arcades. Just mooching. But I've got a craft workshop at Chapter this afternoon.'

That made Rachel smile. 'I love Chapter,' she said.

'We're making a dragon out of bamboo and stuff. We'll get lunch there, and then my group can make a mess – some of the kids are hopeless, but it's fun. And Mam chats and eats cakes ALL afternoon.'

'Alice! One cake.'

Rachel smiled again. 'I go for the chocolate brownies. And the veggie lunches. I like to see the indy films at Chapter cinema.'

I wanted to say we could meet there, but Shy Alice shut me up. The sneaky Shy Alice I hate.

Mam told Rachel we could have done our shopping around Albany Road and got Granddad Joe to drive us over to the workshop, but I'd wanted to come to town. Actually, I'd wanted to see if we would meet Rachel, but I didn't tell Mam that.

Mam was in full chatty-Mam mode now. 'I've noticed you sitting on the bus a few times,' she told Rachel, leaning around me. 'Sorry, it's a habit – I like sketching people when I'm on the bus.'

And I knew Mam would go on and say the wrong thing. And she did.

'I've only ever seen you on your own. Have you someone to go back to?'

Rachel gripped her mug, and I was dead embarrassed for her. 'Not now,' she said. 'My housemate has just moved to New York.'

'It must be a big change for you.'

'Mam,' I mouthed, but Mam was on her friends-with-everyone mission, and I couldn't stop her.

'Do you have people to talk to. We could…'

I screamed, inside. NO, MAM.

And Rachel stumbled on, lost already. 'It has been hard – getting used to being on my own.' She twisted a finger in her hair. 'I'm a bit of a loner, really. Never mind…' She looked away. And I wanted to hit Mam.

Mam's hand reached across in front of me, I gave her a frown, and at last she caught on – badly. 'Rachel, I didn't mean to intrude.'

Rachel looked down at her hand, gripping the greasy counter.

'You don't have to tell me anything,' Mam said, but I knew anything she said would make it worse.

And I couldn't think of anything to make it better.

'I'm sorry…' Rachel's voice was all dried up. 'I must let you get on with your day. Thank you for–'

'Rachel, it's okay. Don't feel…'

STOP IT, MAM!

Rachel turned, stood up, wobbled a bit and walked off. Mam stood up, but I made her sit down again. 'Too late.'

'Was I being too friendly?' Mam said, like a little girl asking her mam.

'It's… she's not like you, Mam.'

I could only find one way to explain. 'It's… Listen, I got kicked at school. Kicked on the floor. I lied to you because it hurt to tell.' And now tears were happening, and I didn't want them and sat back from Mam with my hand out to stop her hugging me. 'When people try to get close about stuff like that, it feels they're getting inside me. It hurts.'

'Oh, Alice–'

'No, Mam! Stop thinking about me – think about Rachel. Rachel's like that, Mam, but Rachel's like that ALL THE TIME. Letting stuff out hurts. Like she's being kicked – all the time.'

'Are you okay, though?'

'I had to tell you because of Rachel. I'll deal with it at school. Tell them if it happens again. Rachel will deal with her stuff. Needs to.'

'How do you know all this about Rachel?'

'It's like I can feel her feelings – Rachel's like a grown-up me.'

'She is – you're right – in so many ways. You could be friends, and I made a mess.'

'Not your fault, Mam. You're just too nice.' And I hugged her, and it was okay to hug her and I didn't hide the tears. Mam's always too nice. No one knows how nice she really is – only me.

Mam looked at her phone, swore and covered her mouth. 'I still haven't got Rachel's number.'

'We'll see her again, Mam.'

'Do you think?'

'We've got to.'

5

AN ARTIST OF HER TIME

Rachel

Why run away? Alice knew – I could tell from her expression. I've never coped with sympathy: the complete absence of it from Dad had wrecked my sympathy-receptor at an early age. But there was something else with Alice. The current of fellow-feeling. The knowledge that she had been bullied for her giftedness. It hurt in a very tender place. I could so easily help her – or at least offer solidarity. If only.

I bought a coffee on the way to the office and punished myself by adding a salad that I didn't want. And settled down to work, trying to deaden the might-have-beens.

Bethany Howells. She liked the name Bethany. No one asked her to care for me. No one dictated how she looked. And what of the girl not yet eleven who could draw my likeness with the finesse of an adult and needed shock-stoppers?

Doctor Bothwell, stop it, you have work to do.

Alice had deflected my praise of her drawing onto her mother. Who was Bethany Howells? What windows on reality had her artwork opened?

Doctor Bothwell…

Shit, Rachel, find out. None of this data is time limited.

Bethany Howells. It felt creepy prying into her affairs, but

I did find the answer I was looking for. Beth was an abstract artist and art therapist. Respected, judging by her list of exhibitions. At least, she had been.

A website was clearly defunct and looked as if it had never functioned properly. It gave her therapy qualifications and a list of exhibitions. She had exhibited in London, Copenhagen, Amsterdam and year after year in Cardiff. Some shared installations with Iestyn Corbett caught my eye. A street photographer and social activist, I'd been to a couple of his exhibitions: street photography had been my thing for a while.

All record of Beth's artistic career dwindled away a decade ago, and I wondered how motherhood had treated her. A recent reference in a business directory mentioned a gallery, but gave no clue whether Beth owned it, exhibited there or worked there. I scribbled down the address – almost on my way home. Well, a roundabout way home.

No, don't look. Beth could remain the kind woman who helped me through a panic attack, and if we did meet again, I would remember to thank her. The one adult not repelled by a screaming woman on a bench. The mother of…

Stop it! She was nice. She was friendly. She was sympathetic. And you know other nice, friendly, sympathetic people. People who are still around if you could steel yourself to pick up the phone.

Nobody in my office world. Tom was another square peg, but we had yet to find much in common besides being outsiders. And I had trouble admitting that the rumours about my salary were true: Ian, the domineering sleazebag of a local manager earned less than Tom, never mind me, even before the bonuses that kept falling into my lap. Tom and I answered only to headquarters in Zurich.

I'd tried to befriend the women in the general office downstairs, but either there was a strict caste system, or they didn't like me. Maybe they saw my occupation of an upstairs office as a travesty without a silver Porsche to certify me as corporate management. Instead, I had four pairs of expensive-but-comfortable boots, claimed off the transport budget to make the point that active epilepsy altered my transport needs.

My nemesis was Mrs Jones the administrator, the only surname in the building. I was one step sideways, 'Doctor Rachel.' As the only other woman in the top office, I had to field her stream of memos on washrooms, printers and inappropriate-use-of. 'The men will never remember.' Not if you never tell them, Mrs Jones.

I wasn't ready to face the world but got up, stretched, and reached for Mrs Jones's laminated instructions for closing down the office. 'IMPORTANT – read thoroughly.'

Yes, Mrs Jones.

Everything off that should be off – check.

Everything on that should be on – check.

Taps off, washroom light off – check.

Remains of human finger behind dead plant on window ledge – check.

One last look around. I took care not to set foot past Mrs Jones's partition: it was probably booby-trapped. Ian's huge desk asserted managerial pride under a golfing calendar and a framed photograph of his fake-tanned daughters on horseback. Arguing, probably – I was sure they didn't know it was Tuesday on Alpha Centauri.

Gentle giant Tom's desk looked comically small by comparison, hidden from Ian's view in my territory. My paper cup stood defiant on the desk in my comfortably cluttered corner. The cleaners had been and gone, my new white bin liner dared me to spoil it, and if I didn't remove the offending item, I would face the horror of a tidied desk on Monday morning. I saved the cup for the bin in the lobby.

Now for the alarm, Mrs Jones's ultimate test of credibility. 'You're a scientist for heaven's sake – you can remember a few numbers!'

No, Mrs Jones.

I'm a scientist. A different species. A scientist would never flunk a digital alarm. A scientist is a rational, motivated being, and has a memory like a computer. Welcome to the movie, Mrs Jones, where scientists make astonishing discoveries daily and never need a hug. A real scientist wouldn't run away from sympathy, would she, Mrs Jones?

I dug out the slip of paper Mrs Jones must never see. My fingers hovered over the alarm keypad. A code as simple as DNA. Deep breath.

Bee-eep. Bup-bop-bip.

Agony.

Beep bip.

Breathe out.

Five floors down, I waved to my mate Carlos the security man, pushed open the smoked glass door, and set out on the long walk home.

Still clutching that paper cup. Sod you, Mrs Jones, why do you frighten me?

'Home,' I told the cup. 'Take me home.'

Treacherous cup. I didn't plan this detour – sex, mystery and kebabs – three shops in a row surrounded by decaying terraces of bed-sits, on a street lined with wilting trees and skips that seemed to have taken root. According to my scribbled note, the middle shop was an art gallery. It wasn't as if I wanted to check up on Beth, but my paper cup led me this way.

It did. I'd spotted the bin opposite.

Really, Rachel? Oh well…

The gallery windows were as blank as those of the sex shop next door, although I could see spotlights shining above the white panels. A patch on the wall showed where a sign had been removed, as if the gallery had seen me coming and decided to hide. Was there a protocol about entering such a place? Did I need an invitation?

An attentive young man sprang up when I was barely through the door. Downy beard, expensively vague t-shirt and skinny charcoal jeans. 'May I ask who you represent?' he said.

I reached for one of my cards, but his presumption changed my mind. 'I represent me. I'm curious.'

'Oh, of course. We don't get many casual visitors.'

'Well, the gallery isn't very visible.'

'The plaque? The owner has new ideas. A more contemporary image.'

'You do sell paintings?'

'Naturally. Would you like to view our latest acquisitions?'

I followed him up a few steps and around a corner but was distracted for a moment. A second person had read my office clothes today. Why did it bother me? If I stood in front of one of Beth's paintings, who would it see? Would it see anyone?

Curious thought.

My guide had left me behind and I hurried after his footsteps, images along the walls drawing my eyes left and right, leaving me dizzy.

You are not having a seizure.

Nothing dizzied me in the upstairs front room. The paintings and engravings suggested the expensive, monochrome décor of our office. And if these were works of art, then art was a precise, insensitive, masculine creature. Not one image invited me in. 'Do you show local artists?' I asked, certain that Bethany Howells didn't belong here.

'I'm sorry – there are other galleries in Cardiff. We have an international outlook.' Maybe I didn't look sufficiently impressed, because he carried on. 'The owner does support chosen local artists. We don't currently display… Follow me.'

Beyond a tiny kitchen at the back was another room. The assistant's face suggested the possibility of a dead cat as he walked in. A blaze of colour leapt out to meet me. I felt the presence of Bethany Howells before I could register a single individual canvas. It was as if all the colour in the gallery had been sucked into this back room, along with every other human sensation. It tasted of life.

'These are all by Bethany Howells?'

'Yes, the owner was at art school with her. Very much an artist of her time – not easy to place in the market. Frankly, if this were my gallery, I would lay them to rest. They're sweet, but not exactly relevant.'

I kept my voice even. 'I'm interested. May I spend some time with them?'

He didn't blink. 'I suggest you take expert advice. Even in this lower price range, I can show you exclusive prints that will become future-proof investments.'

And you, sir, have just sold me an original Bethany Howells.

The deal was done before I'd stood in front of a single canvas. It served me right for blaming my paper cup: now I was an art collector.

But where to start? Intense life greeted me from each canvas. The same warmth and open honesty I had met in Beth. Abstract, these pictures might have been, but they felt intensely personal. Beth was here, opened up and vulnerable, drawing me in. But how could I choose from these rectangles of intense colour and emotion? Which one could I let into my empty house? The house where no one lived but me and my rag doll.

I wanted the biggest one.

I imagined Cai beside me, carefully examining each canvas, proclaiming himself 'no expert' as he always did, a statement somewhere between modesty and a lie. He would be referencing numerous artists I'd never heard of. Yes, I wanted the biggest one, despite what my imaginary Cai might tell me.

When my bitching attendant discovered he'd made a sale by accident, he overflowed with praise for Beth's unique attributes. And he supplied the information that she job-shared here with him. 'She'll be pleased. Hasn't made a sale in a while.'

And his name was Graham, and the hand I shook reminded me of raw meat, the reason I'd turned vegetarian. How come Beth didn't paint 'sweet' paintings 'of her time' now? He was happy to deliver my picture at closing time, and he even held the ladder for me while I removed Cai's vintage comic book poster and manoeuvred the light but unwieldy unframed canvas onto the fixings above the fireplace. Then he left in a hurry, as if I had triggered an allergy.

Cai's poster of a woman with pointy breasts and x-ray eyes went to join its fellows lining the front hall. Too awkward to cross the ocean with him. As was I.

My new prize fitted well, thanks to the lofty ceiling of the Edwardian terraced house, but the more I looked, the more confusing signals it triggered. A tangle of half-formed limbs, it spoke of complete, ecstatic abandon. Toned in earths, oranges and deep reds, Beth could hardly have painted a better challenge if she had tried. Where was the tangle of intimacy in my life? The warmth? The energy?

A curious thought from the gallery came back to me, and the timing of it, before I'd even met Beth's work. Would her painting see me at all?

I now shared my space with a painting that could well unpick every lock and throw open every door I'd closed around my inner life. And I felt a strange yearning for it to prise me open and spread out all my urges and contradictions for the world to see. Not that I expected the world to show much interest.

6

MY SUMMER HOLIDAY

Alice

Operation find Rachel didn't last long. Operation find Dad took over. I even forgot about Rachel for most of the summer. I might have had a brain the size of a minor asteroid, but I was only ten and concentration wasn't my skill.

One of Mam's really big paintings sold, which was fortunate, because Dad disappeared, and we'd had no money from him forever. And Mam hated it when Granddad Joe offered to pay for stuff. Granddad might have been Dad's Dad, but he was retired, just did odd jobs, and Nana Siân said he was too soft to charge much.

Dad was famous, sort-of, but not famous-as-in-rich. Iestyn Corbett, photographer of boring stuff they put in galleries. And a permanent wreck. I don't ever remember living with Dad, but we did when I was small. And Mam kept on caring for him – caring like it hurt. I hated him, mostly. Every time he let Mam down, I hated him. But he was fun to have around. When he was around. And when he wasn't around, I hated the way it kept hurting Mam.

I wanted a normal dad. Any dad would do, as long as he was around. I wouldn't have to share a room with Mam. I would have money and holidays. And most of all, I wanted a happy Mam. A Mam who didn't have to run art classes at all hours and then stress about leaving me with Nana Siân and Granddad Joe too much. I liked it with them – they were always the same.

School summer holidays started, and still no Dad. Some holiday. Ten-year-old girls are meant to be out playing with their friends or watching TV in the holidays. Okay, so I'm not normal and don't have kid friends and prefer research on Mam's old tablet to TV, but most ten-year-old girls don't have dads like mine.

I found Dad after about a month of looking. By then, we'd had the police searching because he'd left no message. Even the kids up the street knew – I don't know who told them – Dad lived on the other side of town. I hated everyone knowing.

I wasn't expecting Dad to turn up dead this time. It had happened too often. I'd expected him to turn up dead before, and he'd always come back.

This time, I just carried on doing me-stuff. We finished the dragon at Chapter, and a bunch of us took it on a parade through the park with lanterns. And I kept on helping Mam with her special needs art group – I love those kids and they love me. Nothing nasty, like in school. And I took online classes about global warming – because it matters.

When we didn't hear from Dad, Granddad and me started checking all the old places. And about the fifth time I checked it, I saw Dad sitting in the Gorsedd circle outside the museum. Exactly where I'd found him the time before. I told Granddad to let me out of the van, and he went off to park it.

Dad was shivering on a hot day. I knew he'd been taking stuff.

'When did you last go home, Dad?'

He shook his head.

'When did you last eat?'

Nothing.

'Where've you been?'

Nothing.

'We need to get you looked after.'

He turned away.

'Mam's upset – it's not fair. It's not fucking fair.'

'Don't you swear, Alice.'

'Oh – you can talk, then. Granddad's parking the van. We need to get you home.'

And Granddad came, and we walked him to the van, and I called Mam. Granddad didn't want me inside Dad's flat, so he took me home first. And just as I was going to get out of the van, Dad said, 'I got some good photos.'

'Is that all you care about? Good photos?'

'I need… sometimes I need extreme.'

'What about Mam?'

'I don't know why she bothers. Or you. Why do you bother, Alice?'

'Because you're her father,' Granddad said. 'And because she's a caring person, like her mother. You don't deserve them, Iestyn.'

'I'm sorry, Alice,' Dad said. 'This isn't fair on you.'

'Why do you keep doing it then?'

He shook his head.

'You don't like it – being like this,' Granddad said. 'I know you don't. So why do you do it, every time?'

'Pressure, I guess. It gets to me. People wanting something new. Always something new.'

'Mam says that about painting, Dad. They need her to shock them into looking – that's what she says – and she hates doing that. But Mam doesn't do drugs or run off without telling anyone.'

'She's stronger than me, Alice.'

'You think.'

'She has a strong little girl.'

'I DON'T WANT to be the strong one all the time. And being little isn't working. I'm having to fucking well grow up. AND I HATE IT.'

I jumped out of the van and straight into Mam's arms. Arms that needed me as much as I needed them.

And that's when I remembered Rachel. Because being grown-up was hard for her, too.

Dad said he was going to do rehab. Again. Like that would last.

My summer holiday.

There and then, I bet myself they would ask me to write about it in Year Six.

7

THE MADNESS OF RACHEL BOTHWELL

Rachel

I didn't know the nightmare Alice was enduring over her father. I didn't know that my buying Beth's painting made the difference between her keeping some dignity and being bailed out again by Iestyn's parents. I lived in a comfortable house on a more-than comfortable salary in a world where no one would have admitted to taking drugs.

On the Sunday morning after buying Beth's painting, I stepped outside the back door. Fresh air, sunshine and a good crop of swelling green apples on the lovely old tree in the middle of the garden. Would I be used to a solitary life by the time they ripened?

I'd lost a chance to show my humanity. That bruise on Alice's chin – it was as if Alice had bruised me. Bruised my inadequacy. Above the garden wall, I could see houses all around me – houses full of people I had never tried to get to know.

I shivered on a warm summer's day and headed back into the cool of the house, expecting more shivers. But in the front room, I found something that was anything but cold. Beth's painting seemed to be looking at me. Asking a question.

I gave it one of the blank stares I'd perfected for meetings with corporate men. 'I don't want to talk about it.'

Silence from the painting.

'Okay, so I'm a mess. A fucking mess. What else do you want me to say?'

Talking to a painting. The madness of Rachel Bothwell beginneth here.

Or my freedom? Had I really lost that chance? Could it still be Tuesday on Alpha Centauri?

Silence from Beth's brushstrokes again, a more powerful silence this time. But I knew a voice was there somewhere, if only–

What was this sudden joy?

I grabbed my shoulder bag, went out into the front porch and shut the door. No one in the universe knew I was there. No one expected me anywhere. I was free to do what I liked – to imagine what I liked.

Heading down the street, I felt a spring in my step, but I'd forgotten the aggressive tendencies of the tree on the corner. It had caught me before, not to mention engulfing a pillar box, and I promptly stumbled on a root. Embracing the trunk with force, I felt like a cartoon figure – one of Alice's cartoons?

Not much harm done beyond a scrape on my palm. I patted the trunk. 'You can't have me. You've got the pillar box – the Victorian listed pillar box – what greater sacrifice do you want?'

And now I was talking to trees.

I crossed Ninian Road, wandered into the gardens opposite and found a vacant bench. I could feel my tense muscles relaxing one by one. Time to myself. Could I ever be as lazy as the people around me, sunning themselves on the lawns? They didn't look bothered about their embarrassments, their silliness or their to-do lists.

My list – ring Mum. We didn't talk. Mum, always on the list. Never ticked off.

No – this would not be a good time. I needed to get over these mood swings before facing Mum. Dad's funeral could stay tucked away for now. Silent and uncomfortably present, like a lump in the unexplored past. We didn't talk.

Damn – I was sitting upright on a perfect, lazy afternoon. I didn't want to speak to Mum. Yes, I was sorry for her, but what was there to say? Dad had withheld his approval from first to last. I'd never found a way to be acceptable without conditions attached. And we didn't talk at the funeral.

We didn't talk.

I needed to get back to the house and sort out the muddle with… Oh, not with Cai. With Beth's painting?

My street was deserted. No witnesses to my return – not even Dad. I stepped cautiously into the silent house. Was the picture asleep? My voice sounded unnaturally loud. 'Painting, it's like I said. I'm a mess.'

Talking to oil on canvas, again. Idiocy. Run with it, Rachel. You talk to your rag doll often enough. 'I don't know how I'm ever going to manage.'

Rachel? A light woman's voice from nowhere. Not from me and not comfortable.

'Who…?'

You could let the anger out. No one will complain.

I looked around, saw no one, and swayed on my feet. Molly never answers back when we're tucked under the duvet. Rag dolls don't. Was this some kind of dissociative episode? Whatever it was, it was my choice. I had initiated it by talking to the painting. Run with it. 'Anger? Me? I'm rubbish at anger. Let's talk about what I can change. I could try and make new friends. Join something, maybe?'

Anger, Rachel. It's there. It was there in the park. It's always been there.

'Fuck.'

That's not anger.

'FUCK.'

Mere irritation. Where's the real anger? Where's it sitting?

'That's not fair. There's you, whoever you are, all confident, analysing me. And… and invisible me with five blue office skirts.'

That sounds like anger with yourself. What have you ever done to deserve anger?

'I don't even like navy blue,' I said, as firmly as I could.

You didn't ask to have epilepsy.

Where was the voice leading me now? 'That's… I can't change that.'

You loved research. The play of it. The excitement of it.

'Stop it! You know I couldn't cope.'

But how could a voice from a painting know that about me? This really was madness.

I tried covering my ears, but the voice didn't stop. *You blamed yourself. He taught you that. Get a safe job. Do the rational thing. What he would have wanted.*

'He's dead. I can't change that, either. He's DEAD.'

You never told him how much it hurt. His sarcasm. His indifference. That's his fault, never yours. He's the one who took away your confidence.

Dad. Always Dad. Why did I even go to his funeral? I

turned back towards the painting, but couldn't look up and sank to my knees.

'I hate being me,' I whispered, and curled up tight.

More and more hurts were piling up with each memory of Dad.

That's right, get it out. There's more to you than you imagine. There's a person you could live with comfortably. A loving Rachel who is easy to love.

'If only. Who would love me? I didn't even help Alice. Maybe if I started small. Stopped hiding in navy blue.' And stopped curling in an inadequate ball on the floor.

How often do you over-think things, Rachel? A bit more bravery and you could stop hiding altogether. Would admitting your vulnerability hurt more than running away from people who want to be friends? People like Bethany and Alice. You have helped Alice already – just by being yourself. No need to hurt yourself further.

I stretched out, lay on my back and let those swirls of colour have a long look at me. The painting seemed warmer, friendlier and not so challenging. And I imagined a warm hug from Beth. Needed it.

You're still the helpless little girl who wished she felt loved. There's no shame that it shows. Not for you – the shame is and should be your father's.

Gentleness in the voice now. I imagined Cai's gentleness – Beth's gentleness. Gentleness was both my need and something I could offer. But in what kind of relationship? Yes, I'd had crushes on assorted men and women all my adult life. The next step was always where doubt set in. 'I keep running away.'

You've been surviving. Protecting yourself. Don't punish yourself for it.

This felt like real comfort. 'What am I talking to? Your source, or your effect on me? Have you got a name?' I propped myself up with an elbow and examined the picture. *April 2011 #3* was pencilled up the edge of the frame. 'Not new, then?'

I don't think you'll find me in there. Now, the voice seemed slightly apart from the painting, as if examining it.

'You're not in the painting?'

I don't know where I am. If I'm anywhere. The voice sounded puzzled. And it definitely wasn't my own voice. *But I am your friend. I trust you. You can trust me.*

Trusting a disembodied voice. I crawled onto the sofa, felt a wave of tiredness and dozed off. When I woke up, maybe half-an-hour later, I felt refreshed. Had the whole event been some kind of seizure? It didn't feel like it.

That unhinged conversation in front of a painting was so far outside my definition of sanity that I decided just to let it go. It was me having a moment. But strangely, a much happier week at work followed. Tom seemed to be less defensive, maybe because I tried not to be so fearsome and monosyllabic. We could talk, and did, often.

And I kept up the insanity, sharing my thoughts in front of the painting each evening. Did I even need another tenant? I'd found a tenant inside my own head.

The voice seemed to come from a space in front and to one side of the painting, as if someone were standing there. But not always the same side. She seemed to know a good deal about me. But also, and this still linked her with the painting in my mind, she knew Beth, who she always called Bethany, and she knew Alice.

She wasn't frightening: she was a welcome presence, a

kind of madness I could accept as necessary for my survival. No substitute for Cai when it came to doing the housework, of course, but my invisible friend gave me the confidence to turn my nightlight off and accept that nights were dark and that mornings would follow. Provided I survived.

Over the next three or four weeks, each Saturday, I caught that same bus to town. I had no more panics or seizures, but I didn't see Beth and Alice. I wanted, needed to repair my rushed departure and give Alice space to share her troubles. To be a vaguely human creature who could share friendship. But how to start?

At work, I expanded my repertoire of office clothes beyond navy-blue conformity. Sitting watching Tom twiddle a pencil at his desk, I wondered whether he had noticed the change in me – or the madness.

No, don't stare at him, Rachel. Think of the years he spent working on his PhD while travelling the world on container ships. And you've got him sitting at a desk doing routine statistical analysis. Not that he ever complains. Give him something – trust him – give him the Franco-German bid, that's safe enough.

And stop your dreaming, Rachel. He's probably a lousy cook anyway.

I was still wondering whether I could find the courage to attempt real friendship when I noticed the text on my phone.

> Sorry I didn't manage at the
> funeral. Are you okay?

Mum – what could I tell her?

My personal life had never intruded into my office world, and this knocked me sideways. I'd only discovered that Mum could send texts at all when she sent me the funeral details. I told Tom I was taking some work home and rushed out before Mrs Jones had a chance to interrogate me.

The pavements radiated heat, leaving me wilting by the time I came face-to-face with Beth's painting in the front room. I don't know what I expected, but the picture looked startled, and no voice welcomed me.

After a shower, I got a coffee and crept back into the front room. This time, the voice was ready for me. *Talk to Gaynor.* My mother.

'Have I got the courage?'

You won't find out if you never try.

'Okay, I'll try.'

One step at a time. Now I was sure her gentle, compassionate voice came from outside the painting. From a woman I couldn't see.

I took that step. I called. We talked.

Nothing complicated – no blinding revelations. We both knew the hurt Dad had caused. But I shared a conversation with the woman who had given painful birth to me; sat patiently feeding me; washed me and changed my nappies; who blew my nose and wiped my chin; endured my temper tantrums and answered all my questions; who taught me to walk, to read, and to ride a bike; who endured taking me to casualty and the doctors and the dentist; who sat with me reading, bought all my clothes for me, patiently encouraged my early violin and piano lessons, and, and...

And when I turned thirteen, this woman had to adjust to her only child waking her with a scream at any time of night, and to finding her writhing in bed, or on the floor, unconscious and often bleeding from the mouth.

A daughter who stopped breathing in hospital and had to be resuscitated. Who went into status epilepticus and needed a controlled coma to recover. And who did her maths A-level at fourteen and would purposely play her violin slightly behind the beat to avoid being hailed as a prodigy. Never off-key: that would have been too painful. A daughter who would cut her wrists just to make sure she could feel pain.

All that crushing load, and this woman still had to face up to her husband.

And I had ignored her ever since I left home. I had never managed to think of Mum without that other presence that I feared. Dad.

Eventually, I managed to let out words that had lodged inside me for all those years, present, true and uncomfortable, but never spoken. 'I love you, Mum.'

'I love you too, my love. I always have.'

We talked, but we didn't arrange to meet.

8

A HOLIDAY INSIDE ALICE HOWELLS

Alice

Dad was more himself towards the end of summer. After Mam had been in and cleaned out his flat, and Granddad and me had helped him develop the plates from his ancient camera. And helped him tidy his studio. We found some good photos Dad had forgotten and some dead embarrassing ones of me in the bath when I was tiny. Once we got him talking, Dad wasn't even rude to me much, and I heard him thank Mam for sticking by him.

Best of all, he sold some of the photos he'd taken on his trip to nowhere. We never did find out where he'd been, and extreme closeups of drains and scaffolding and piles of litter didn't give any clues. I don't think even he knew where he'd been, but the photos sold, and he paid for Mam to take me to a caravan at Tenby for a week.

Tenby is where Mam's favourite artist Gwen John grew up. And it has houses like a box of pastels, a pretty harbour, lots of clean, sparkly sand and rocks and rock pools and good cafés. A perfect seasidey-sort-of place. But I didn't find any fossils. There wasn't a lot to do when we'd mooched around the harbour and the cafés and poked around in rock pools and played games in the caravan. We'd done being on holiday.

Maybe that's why Gwen John left – because there wasn't a lot to do. Gwen spent most of her life painting and modelling in France, a century or so ago. Me and Mam love Gwen John's girls, the paintings in the museum in Cardiff. Each one is herself, not what some artist thinks she should be. That's the magic of them, Mam says. Gwen knew how to use the softest of colours to let the person be herself in paint on canvas.

I like the idea of not turning people into something they aren't. I like Mam as she is. And Granddad and Nan. Even Dad wouldn't be Dad if he wasn't so freaky. And I don't want to be turned into someone else. I want to be Alice.

I finished my course on global warming before we went to Tenby, and I wanted to talk about it with someone apart from Mam. Dad was good at science, but Dad was Dad. And Granddad Joe said he learned most of his science when Dad was growing up, because Dad never stopped asking questions. Just like me. So, Granddad's science was too old for global warming. And that's when I thought of Rachel again.

We hadn't talked much, but Rachel knew about astronomy and dinosaurs, and the way she talked about them, there was bound to be more. It was like I could see all the sparks of thinking inside her. She must have known something about global warming because it's such a big subject.

Rachel worked in an office; I knew that. And I'd met Mam's friends from the university where they did science and stuff. None of them dressed like Rachel. But Rachel hadn't looked comfortable in her office clothes. I couldn't make her fit in with anyone I knew.

And sitting on the beach at Tenby, I began to wonder about Rachel's epilepsy and how it must feel to be a grown-up and frightened to go out in case you panicked. Or had a seizure. Being scared like that would be a lot worse than me when I saw the Evil Twins at school.

They weren't real twins but looked like each other and were IN CHARGE of how all the girls in my class thought. Influencers with menace, controlling half the class. All the girls but the chopsy freak called Alice. Who was beginning to be proud of her bruise, even though it had gone.

Forget the Evil Twins – I planned to make it better in year six anyway. Think Rachel instead.

Rachel. Did she have any friends? She told us her housemate had left, and her voice sounded hurt when she said it. I hoped she wasn't alone. Why hadn't I thought of her all summer? Dad, that's why. Dad had stolen my summer.

Was Rachel another Dad? An adult who needed to be rescued every so often? And did she have anyone to rescue her? I started to wonder whether that would be my job. I've got form when it comes to rescuing adults. Even Mam.

Mam quite a lot, actually.

And thinking about all that turned my holiday in Tenby into a different kind of holiday. I told Mam I just liked sitting playing with the sand between my fingers while she did her sketching. But really, I was having a holiday inside Alice Howells. Figuring out me. And Mam didn't interrupt – she's good like that. I think she knew something was happening that mattered – maybe that's why all her sketches were of my face.

I'd discovered a part of being Alice that I hadn't known was there. Not all kids notice what it's like to be other people.

Not all kids want to. But I do. Other people are amazing, once you get inside them.

And that's what makes me Alice. I get inside people.

I knew what had made Rachel run away. It was like Mam pulled her down into a big pool of friendliness and poor Rachel couldn't swim. Not without endless space and time to get her used to the water. And thinking about that pool of friendliness made me realise that I knew quite a lot about being Rachel.

Part of being Alice is being Rachel or Mam or Dad or anyone else around me. That part of being Alice is like Gwen John choosing just the right shades of colour to suit people on the inside as well as on the outside. Getting inside them and feeling what it's like.

Even being Dad when he's out of his skull. I've been there and it's as scary as anything I've ever known, but I know the feeling, and that helps me talk to him. And swear. I swear more than is healthy for a ten-year-old, that's what Nan says. And then spoils it by going, 'Ych a fi!' like she does. Swearing in Welsh doesn't seem to count.

Maybe having a dad like mine has made me the kind of person who can cope with all that inside stuff. I've seen his nightmares, and I've put them in a box marked Dad with all the swear words.

Most kids at school see adults as different. There's kids and there's adults and adults are boring and not worth thinking about unless they're superheroes or celebrities.

I don't think like that at all. Everyone is interesting – even the Evil Twins – I can see chopsy nerd Alice through their eyes. Not many of the adults in my life are big and strong and separate from children. Sometimes they're like big children. Mam is, a lot, and often we're more like two sisters. Granddad is a big kid, a lot of the time. Nan, not so much. She looks after everyone, even Granddad. But I never knew my Nan and Granddad Howells, Mam's parents. They both died before I was born.

I love Mam as she is. If I was Gwen John, I would paint Mam as she is.

I know lots of things that frighten Mam, and one of them is not giving me a perfect childhood. She wants me to have things. She wants me to be happy and play like other kids. And I keep telling her that playing like other kids just isn't me. I'm an explorer and a scientist and an artist, and that's my playing.

There's something else about Mam. When Rachel said she had epilepsy, it really freaked Mam. So much, that I asked Dad about it. And his answer freaked me, because if I was going to rescue Rachel, I would have to do it on my own. Mam's father died when she was about my age. Not epilepsy – it was his heart – but anything serious freaks her, because she was with him when he died. And she had never said a word about it to me.

Maybe Mam was one person I couldn't quite get inside – not all the way. And that thought freaked me. I shared a one-bedroomed flat with a mystery who snored every night and farted in her sleep. I knew everything about Mam but what mattered most.

9

ALONE

Rachel

My invisible friend made up my mind for me. I would find Alice and Beth again. But there was an interruption – an interruption I knew only too well.

I think having a fit in public in Roath Park and wetting myself marked me as a Cardiff girl. I hoped so, anyway.

We moved to London when I was still a toddler, and Dad cut all contact with our Cardiff relatives. As far as I knew, none were still living. I escaped from London to Cambridge, but even after my research attracted attention, I half expected Dad to turn up and say I was there under false pretences. And for them to believe him. Now that I lived in the city of my birth and Dad was dead, I did have some sense that I might fit in. Eventually.

I was thinking about calling Mum when it happened. We hadn't spoken again, and I needed to pick up the conversation. The seizure crept up on me unnoticed, masked by the panic I always feel when I think about Dad. There was no mistaking my epileptic aura: I knew this would be a big one.

I clung to the railings edging the path. No one in sight. The big trees around me were turning slowly, each individual leaf edged with rainbows. And I stopped panicking. What

60

was the point – I was going to die anyway. I knelt down on the edge of the nearest lawn under the trees. Trees getting impossibly green and radiant.

You're safe. I'm here.

My companion's voice was with me in this glowing, enchanted forest.

Glowing and darkening.

Glowing and darkening.

Pulsing.

Pulsing.

…

Taste… earth.

…

Dark.

A voice. 'It's all right. I've got you. I'm here.'

Oh. Here.

Alright… Here.

Here?

…

Ow! A feeling.

Hurting. All hurting?

…

Bright light. Eyes hurt.

…

Can't see. Must be shut. Where am I?

I?

…

Words. 'Shit, I haven't done first aid in years. You'll be okay. Please? Please, God?'

You? Me? WHO AM I?

…? A pulse of rootless terror.

Where? WHERE IS THIS?

…? Another pulse.

When? AM I GROWN-UP?

…? And another.

Lost. LOST. No bearings. But I know this terror – I know these three shocks. I've had a seizure.

I recognise this life. I'm…

I just don't know. How old?

I'm lying down. Am I?

A quiet voice again. 'Rachel? Are you back yet?'

Rachel. I must be Rachel.

Are we in the playground? Has Mummy seen me?

I need to speak. How?

Breath: that's what I need.

'Oops.' Oops, I've had a seizure.

'You're back. Are you? Rachel?' A stranger's voice – an older woman? Close to my ear. Real. Not Mum.

Concentrate. Speak. 'Had one. Be fine.'

'That was… Never mind.'

Where are we? In the lab? No. I broke my wrist that time. The May Ball? That was a bad one. Was. Not that one. That's a memory. This is another one. Where? When?

My knee hurts. The floor's damp… wet… puddle… Oh God, it's me! The big girls. What have they done? Not the classroom – PLEASE, GOD, NOT THE CLASSROOM. No, that's a memory too.

'It was a long one. Take your time. I hope you don't mind – I looked in your bag. Got your instructions here, Rachel. What to do.' That woman – not the big girls. 'A man's called 999,' she says. 'They should be here soon.' She strokes my arm. 'I saw you from over by the bridge. You'd started convulsing by I got here. Not so fast on my pins. I knew someone who had seizures, years ago.'

Another voice. Man. 'Ambulance is on the way. God, has she wet herself?'

Dad. FEAR.

I know this fear. This is real. It's Rachel's fear.

I can't see. Is he coming?

Eyes. Have I used them?

Open – no focus. One blurry face. Woman. Grey hair. Am I old? Is this my funeral? Where's Dad?

Or is it a photo in a book? The woman looks upside down. Screen's getting fainter. Is it a screen? I need to ask.

'What's happening?' No, my voice didn't work this time.

Eyes are shut. I thought I opened them.

Try again. Oh, I'm lying on some muddy grass beside a path. I'm soaked – it's raining. Or I've wet myself. Or both. Both – I can feel the warmth below and the rain on my cheek.

Do I live here? God, where are my feet?

My feet…?! No!

Oh… under the bushes. Stupid Rachel. And grey.

Whose hand is that: that's not mine. Beth? Alice? Like that time in Queen Street? No, it's the woman's hand.

Stop thinking.

Stupid Rachel, stop thinking, you can't do it yet. Talk – you can do that. 'Hello…'

'Hello yourself. You've taken a while coming round.' She strokes my forehead. Gentle.

That's my knee over there: it hurts. That's my leg. And I've bitten my tongue.

'Hello… sorry… bit of a mess…'

She's behind me – warm – leaning close, holding me in the recovery position with one hand. There's a streak of mud across her face and drips of rain are curling the hair in front of her ear. There was a man's voice, but I think he's gone. It's this strange woman and me in the whole universe.

'I'll be… soon… thank you… sorry…' Moving my mouth up and down is too much. And, and… In a painful rush, my world falls into place. I am me, here at this moment in the continuum of time and space, with my past and my future. It's Saturday, I'm in the park and I've had a seizure.

Somewhere at the bottom of this flood of information, all the stuff of my consciousness, sits a tiny grey bundle of thoughts. I'm the bright kid who has fits and harms herself. Dad wanted a gifted genius and got me. I'm not good enough. Never was. Never will be. I don't deserve love from anyone.

And inside that grey bundle is another, greyer one, the fundamental emptiness of me. I'm Rachel and I'm an accident. I'm a freak coalescence of particles and forces and coincidences that will soon dissolve away into oblivion. I shouldn't have happened in the first place: I overheard daddy say that when I was small. And now that I'm here, there's no escape from being me, alone.

Alone. It doesn't matter from where or when I look, and it doesn't matter how many states, dimensions or universes I look through, I'll still see me, separate and alone.

I don't want to be here. I don't want to know this.

I don't want to grow up. I want my Molly.

I want her hair round my finger.

'Molly…?'

'Who?'

10

GOBSMACKED

Alice

Term started when we got back from Tenby. Time to face the Evil Twins and all their hangers-on again. I didn't expect anything physical – they were seen kicking Shareen on the last day of term – but they had sneakier ways to hurt me.

My new teacher was Miss Akoto with her beautiful bright clothes and her headdress thing. Like she stepped out of Africa and into my classroom, bringing the sunshine with her. But the best thing about Miss Akoto was that at last, I had SOMEONE who could answer my science questions.

She started slipping me extension work without telling the others. Sometimes it just meant asking different questions about the same stuff. My last teacher ranted at me in front of the whole class about educational giftedness. Telling me it's no excuse for sloppy work on the boring bits. Miss Akoto didn't mention the 'G' word once.

But even with Miss Akoto on my side, there was another science person I really wanted to find: Rachel. I looked at the picture I drew in my sketchbook, way back before Dad did a bunk. And the picture brought the feeling of being Rachel back – even that sweaty, nervous smell. And the way she hid behind her hair was like she didn't believe we would want to see her.

I was sure Rachel needed a friend. Me? No, probably not a chopsy almost-eleven-year-old nerd. And Mam would be too freaked by her epilepsy to be much use. But I decided it was time for Operation Find Rachel anyway.

It was scarily easy, but I did it on Granddad's computer in his workshop so as not to disturb Mam. 'Rachel' and 'Science' and 'Cardiff' and 'Office' found a website with a little picture of her on it, along with some other people. Senior Scientific Advisor, Doctor Rachel Bothwell, formerly head of a research group with a name that was a long string of initials at the Cavendish Laboratory, Cambridge University. YES!!! Previous research projects – and there was a list with dates, mainly about fundamental particles.

FUNDAMENTAL PARTICLES!

But then I looked at the rest of the website, and it was all business stuff about handling contracts and the corporation's global reach and terms of business and a lot of words that didn't mean anything at all. There wasn't even much clue about what the corporation actually DID. Just a flashy picture of the headquarters in Zurich.

Senior Scientific Advisor sounded big and expensive. So, what was Rachel doing on the bus in the first place? Why not in a Mercedes or something?

That didn't need much thinking out. Epilepsy. She couldn't drive.

And I couldn't visit her at work. It was one of those big office blocks in Newport Road, and they would never let me in the door. The website didn't even give a contact number or e-mail for Rachel. It was like you had to be a company before you were allowed to talk to her. I had a little fantasy about founding my own dinosaur fossil-finding company, but that was just silly.

Operation Find Rachel could have succeeded on the first Saturday of term – nearly did – but me being a kid with kid-shyness made a mess of it.

Mam had a meeting with some art people at Chapter, and I was hanging about in the café, playing a board game with some older kids I didn't much like. They'd been on my dragon-building team and knew I was good at strategy stuff. But it was one of those crap medieval games where luck mattered more than strategy, and I had my head chopped off in a dungeon.

So, I went for a wander until they started a new game. And there, sitting at a table, hunched over her laptop with a coffee in front of her was a woman with straggly dark hair. Even from behind, I knew who it was by the way she was sitting. Not relaxed. And I couldn't go near her.

It was like Rachel had a force field all around her table. She was doing some stuff on her laptop with one finger and twiddling the handle of her coffee mug with her other hand. The screen in front of her wasn't like any screen I'd seen before. It was just lines of numbers and symbols. Computer code, I suppose. She could have been on another planet, she was so far away. Like a projection of Rachel, here in the Chapter café.

She didn't look up and I couldn't see past her hair. I stayed safely behind, feeling more shyness than I ever had in my whole life. MAXIMUM shyness.

Why, Alice?

Because Rachel looked more busy even than Mam when she's painting, and Mam HATES being interrupted.

And interrupting busy adults is where kid-Alice kicks in and scientist-Alice doesn't have a chance. I turned into jelly-Alice and stood in the middle of the room in everyone's way, because I couldn't move.

I must have looked at my feet or something, because the next thing I knew, Rachel had folded her laptop, put it in a briefcase and stood up. She stretched and looked around, a bit like a criminal hoping not to be seen. But I don't think she saw me. Whether she did or not, she headed away from me and out of the big doors at the front. And jelly-Alice didn't even follow her.

The boys at the game were calling me, but then Mam appeared. Which was fortunate, because I was in no state to have my head chopped off again. Mam looked at me. 'What's wrong? Did you lose?'

'I'm just a stupid kid.' And saying it, all tears came out, and Mam took me in the cloakroom to wash my face.

'What's wrong, chuck?'

And I had to tell her.

'Rachel was here. You know – that Rachel. The special Rachel who ran away. And I wanted to talk to her and I was too shy, and then she went, and I don't think she even saw me. And she's a scientist, and she's special and I think she–' It sounded stupid in my little girl voice. 'I think she needs me.'

Mam hugged me tight. 'I think so too, chuck. I more than think so – I know so. I've had a shock. Just now, in the meeting. Graham from the gallery gave me this.' Mam fished in her bag and pulled out a sheet of paper.

Three large abstracts by Bethany Howells.
Purchaser: Doctor Rachel Bothwell.

'That's the biggest one-off sale I've made in twelve years. And that other picture I sold – I got him to check – that was Rachel as well. She's throwing her money at my stuff. Why would she do that? Because she ran away? We've got to stop her.'

Mam didn't usually leave me gobsmacked. But my gob was so smacked, nothing came out.

11

A SPACE AGAINST MY SIDE

Rachel

Julie Cook was my consultant neurologist and played lead cello in the Sinfonietta, sitting opposite me every Tuesday night. A friend, distanced in a way appropriate to a doctor who knew the shape of my brain waves. But not so distanced as I had thought.

Julie spent ages sitting beside my bed calming me down after the Roath Park incident. In hospital on a Saturday when she wasn't even on duty. Telling me all the stupid things I needed to hear. That I was a real human being who deserved friends. Who didn't have to be alone. And that wetting myself in seizure didn't make me an outcast, despite memories of it happening twice in front of my whole class at school.

If she wasn't already, Julie turned into my hero that day. And with no other candidates around, she was my closest friend on this side of the Atlantic.

After some thought, I found a way to thank Julie and to help Beth without her even knowing – or so I thought. If I spend a lot of money, I feel guilty. Dad, I suppose, looking over my shoulder. But this purchase defied Dad. It was my money to spend, and the pictures were going to the neurology department, to soothe the waiting room.

I reserved three large paintings that seemed aspects of

the same concept and told Graham I would need to confirm with the recipient. Thanks to orchestra, I had Julie's personal e-mail address and got an instant reply. 'Rachel, I love you for this. Bethany Howells! I haven't seen her pictures in an age. Those prints in the waiting room give me mental health issues. Can we do it while our administrator is in Mallorca? They were her idea to brighten up the place.'

The following Monday, a cloud of perfume announced the arrival of Mrs Jones at my desk. She handed me an envelope and kept standing too close above me. 'This was left for you at reception downstairs.' The tone of her voice suggested that only contraband arrived by hand.

For the attention of Doctor Rachel Bothwell. Open if you are who I think you are.

Beneath the writing was a tiny impression of me, with straggly hair over my eyes. Not so accurate as Alice's drawing in the market, but vividly expressing my embarrassed fear. I thanked Mrs Jones, placed it upside down beside my keyboard and got on with my work. An irritated glance was necessary to send her trotting back to her own territory.

I had planned to trace Beth, however scary the prospect, but now she had traced me.

Back from Tenby to a big shock. That's FOUR paintings altogether. I wondered which collector had taken an interest, but that name – Rachel Bothwell – I could only think it was you. Alice told me she had already looked you up and gave me the address.

There's no need to feel bad about the way you left, or to keep buying paintings. I've been worrying about you ever since.

Then Alice saw you in Chapter on Saturday and was too nervous to approach you. She was in tears when I found her. We need to break that barrier and meet. And please don't go on a guilt trip spending all that money. But thank you. Stop now.

B x

An e-mail address was scribbled on Beth's note but no phone number. I wouldn't have managed to call her anyway, and it took me a while to compose a reply. I desperately didn't want to upset Alice again and I didn't want Beth worrying about me. The only sensible plan would be to meet and, as the voice in my front room kept reminding me, not to hide my vulnerability.

This is no guilt trip, Beth. That first painting is helping me sort out my life. I bought the other three as a thank-you present to the neurology department who keep me alive and functioning. Their waiting room desperately needs something you can look at for more than ten seconds.

I'm nervous about messing up again, but I'll try not to run off. Tell Alice I'm just a shy little girl, really.

Toast café, 11.00, Saturday?

R x

We met, but not before I experienced a minor panic on the way from the bus stop. (Sorry, make that a major panic.) This time, my shades just about saved me. So predictable.

As was the way I arrived ten minutes early in the market, hanging in the corner with Elvis, flexing up and down on tiptoes and staring along the balcony. I was shaking and sweating by the time Alice dashed into my arms from the other direction.

She didn't say anything – she just held on tight and buried her face in my chest. But after a few moments, she looked up. 'You don't mind? Me hugging you?'

'I need hugs, Alice. Really need them. But I'm rubbish at asking for them.' I put my arms around her. Actually holding another human being.

She smiled up at me. 'You're shy. Like me. Need your shock-stoppers.'

I took off my shades off in time for Beth to envelop us both in her gentle warmth. 'Found, at last,' she said. 'Meeting you keeps coming back – like it matters.'

'To me, too. I've been hoping… Alice is right. I'm too shy. And too stupid.'

'The word is sensitive, Rachel, not stupid. Now – I'll get some tea and toast. You sit down before you fall down.'

I collapsed into a chair, and the relief felt like… Say it, Rachel, while you have the courage. 'You two – it feels like – I don't know…' I did know, but couldn't get the words out before my tears started flowing. It was a precious kind of relief I had never once experienced in my childhood.

It felt like coming home.

Alice took my tissue from my hand, stood close beside me and mopped my streaming eyes. 'Yeah – we're proper friends now.'

When Beth brought tea and toast, I tried to deflect the conversation away from me. 'You're an art therapist. I've been pushed that way a couple of times.'

'I don't take people who are pushed. I take people who jump.'

'That might be where I'm at now. Ready to jump.'

Alice gave me a serious glance. 'Mam's painting is helping you. I saw your message. Most people don't understand Mam's stuff.' She put her head on one side. 'And Mam isn't behind with the rent anymore.'

'Your Mam's painting is worth a lot more to me than money. I guess I've been doing art therapy on myself.'

We were back talking about me again, but maybe that voice was right about sharing vulnerability. I told them as simply and honestly as I could what made me run off last time.

Of the way I saw my younger self in Alice.

'You see?' Alice grabbed Beth's arm, and Beth nodded.

Of my fear that my seizures would upset Alice. 'Mam, more like,' she said and rolled her eyes at Beth.

Of the way sympathy triggers feelings of unworthiness.

'Dad's like that,' Alice said. 'And me, a bit.'

And I told them about my struggles to patch up some kind of relationship with Mum, and the real skeleton in my closet – Dad.

'You're angry with yourself for not noticing he might have treated her just as badly, aren't you?' Beth said.

'I knew things weren't right. I could have done... something.'

'That's all in the past. You'll have time to work through it with your mam. You know, I'd rather not be your therapist. Why can't we just be friends? I'm hoping we already are.'

'I… it's always a surprise. Friendship.'

'You don't expect it, do you? That's your father again. Anyway, you're talking to a sometime art therapist. Right now, I have no official clients at all.'

'Cutbacks?'

'And some. There's no budget for it – that doesn't mean the clients don't need it. I fit in a few long-term ones. Running art classes pays. And I work you-know-where.'

'With that sodding Graham?'

She laughed. 'Poor Graham! Sharing his hours helps. I hardly ever see him.'

'I looked you up,' Alice said. 'You're a scientific consultant. What do you do?'

'Boring stuff. Whatever they throw at me – feasibility studies – reports. Statistics for contract bids. The small print.'

'Why? Why not discover stuff?'

I couldn't stop my eyes wandering, but tried my best. 'I did research, once upon a time. I did discover stuff about the structure of – stuff.'

'It mattered to you a lot, didn't it?' Beth said.

I couldn't lie. 'I had to give up – It got too much for me. Sold my soul to the corporate monster. It's remarkably painless.'

'Painless? I'm hearing bitter.'

Yes, and I thought that had gone. 'Not any more. Old wounds.'

'But in a perfect world?'

Beth was leading me where I didn't want to go, but Alice put her hand on my arm. 'Don't tell Mam. I don't want you running off again.'

I took an extra breath. I could go there after all. 'Some bad memories, but I'm okay with it, Alice. I used to be a high-energy physicist, working on fundamental relationships at the smallest level imaginable. Where normal physical rules fall apart.'

'That's quantum stuff – weird stuff – I saw your list of papers.'

'Are you sure you're only ten?'

'Some of me is.'

'I think we have more in common than you know.'

'Alice knew the very first time we met,' Beth said. 'A stranger on a bus talking about x-ray sources in galaxies. Making silly imaginative leaps to match hers. When I heard you talk, it was like listening to Alice.'

'Educationally gifted. Freak.' Alice spat out the words that had clung to me throughout my childhood.

I reached for her hand. 'I wore that label. It's no fun.'

Alice gave the slightest smile and squeezed my hand back. 'Yeah, you and me.'

'We don't push it at home,' Beth said. 'Alice pushes herself hard enough. Her Nan and Granddad say her father was just the same. He's a photographer – a good one.'

Alice blew a raspberry.

Beth looked to the heavens. 'We'll save Iestyn for another time.'

'Iestyn Corbett? I know his work.'

'I have to keep reminding him that his greatest work has two legs and deserves some attention.'

I didn't pursue the subject. 'Alice, don't think I'm some kind of genius. My brain's not up to it anymore. Do you know what burnout means?'

'Going faster and faster until you go kersplat?'

'That's why Alice needs her shock-stoppers,' Beth said.

'Adults aren't so flexible. I really can't do what I used to do.'

Beth twisted her mug around on the counter and didn't reply.

Alice gave me a worried glance and I hurried on. 'I've had a few years to get my head together. But I'm no example for Alice.'

Alice jiggled up and down next to me. 'Better I know – better you tell me.'

'She's right, I suppose,' Beth said, picking a flake of paint off her finger. 'Alice has seen what pressure has done to Iestyn. He's a wreck, half the time.' She took out her phone. 'Graham passed me Sir's invoice. I haven't sold any of the big paintings in years. But without Alice and her techie skills... I'm not sure I'd have had the guts to trace you. Okay to share numbers?'

I dug out the phone-with-embarrassingly-few-contacts. Was I ready to take another step? Yes, I could open the door this far. I told myself that Beth might not even call, but I knew she would. And I expected them to go on their way after we'd exchanged numbers, but maybe friends don't do that.

We wandered around the balcony under the market's great iron and glass roof, meditating on mysterious old electrical components, tropical fish (Alice did an impression of a bored neon tetra) and a drab stall displaying an odd mixture of unlovely small objects. Beth said they might keep the real stuff under the counter, but we couldn't decide what the real stuff might be.

At every second moment, I expected Alice to get bored. But she seemed to fit naturally against my side, under my arm, in a space I hadn't known was there. An Alice-shaped space she seemed in no hurry to leave.

Back for more toast, more tea, and more unwinding. Beth gave passers-by imaginary private lives for fun: the kind of game I thought no one played but me. Then Alice showed off some number tricks, at home in the language of mathematics. And we swapped drawings of each other in her sketchbook. 'Mam! Rachel's good.'

'Just cartoons.'

'What's wrong with cartoons?'

I suggested a visit to the old-fashioned sweet stall, but Alice led us to one that sold Turkish Delight in all kinds of flavours. 'Mam and me like mixing them up and not looking when you pick one.' Then she helped me choose a batik skirt to match the ones they were wearing, although I couldn't imagine wearing it at work.

No, that was yesterday's response. 'I'll wear it at work to remind me of you.'

The morning had passed by the time we parted company, and this time, I knew we would be back together soon. Maybe we'd do some science at Techniquest. Or not bother. We could just be us. Alice's hug felt so natural I almost managed it without crying. Until I saw tears stream from her eyes and we both burst out laughing.

I put on the skirt for a trial run at work in the afternoon. I even gave Carlos the security man a twirl. He nodded. 'Yup.' A man of few words.

A couple of hours later, chimes from my mobile disturbed me. I switched on my automatic, sing-song, 'Science Division, can I help you?'

'Can I speak to Doctor Bothwell, please.' Beth's deep, breathy voice.

'It is me. Sorry, I'm on office autopilot – there's no one else here – I am the science division.'

'Fancy meeting up tomorrow?'

With the distance of work between us, this felt more of a challenge. I needed a gulp of cold coffee. 'Don't expect... I'm not much fun for Alice.'

'So why has she not stopped talking about you since we got home?'

And why was I still noticing that Alice-shaped space at my side?

'We seem to have made a connection.'

'Seem to? You've been connected ever since that first bus ride. Anyway, Alice is with her father tomorrow. I meant you and me. I get nervous when she's with Iestyn.'

And at last, it sank in. Friendship went two ways. Beth had needs of her own.

This Beth was not the Beth I had been imagining for weeks – the confident artist who painted with deep insight and had stopped when I panicked. This Beth was a flesh-and-blood human being with complications in her life. And it was common knowledge that I was a walking accident when it came to dealing with real human beings.

12

BIG REVEAL

Alice

Dad, drunk. Granddad to the rescue. Again. And me stuck with Mam, at work in the gallery. I was sitting on the floor with my head between my fists thinking of the best ways to torture Dad when the door chimed and Rachel turned up. At last.

Mam was slumped over the desk, but jumped up when she saw Rachel. 'Thank God! I thought you weren't coming.'

'Sorry, I… What's wrong?'

'He came. He'd been drinking. He left.'

'Iestyn?'

Mam nodded. 'His dad handled it.'

Rachel did that goldfish thing with her mouth. 'His dad?'

'Iestyn's going through a bad patch,' Mam said, in the biggest understatement of the century. 'Granddad Joe won't let him take Alice out unless he's sober.'

'I wanted to go with Granddad.' I couldn't help the whiny kid words slipping out and had to wipe my eyes.

'Sometimes he needs a rest, Alice.'

'Nothing to do.' Also whiny kid words – what is it with me?

'I know, love. I wish I didn't need to work Sundays.' Mam folded her arms and squirmed. Rachel was looking lost. How could I explain that this is our life?

'I know what, Alice,' Rachel said. 'Why don't you show me around the gallery? I haven't a clue about art.'

That was unexpected.

I stood up and did my best Graham impression. 'May I show you our latest acquisitions? We pride ourselves on our discerning selection.'

'Discerning?' Mam had to hide her face.

'Graham said it, Mam. That time we were at his launch party.'

'That time you necked a whole glass of champagne when no one was looking?'

'NEVER, EVER AGAIN. It's like piss.'

Rachel smiled. A real, proper Rachel smile. 'The first time I found the gallery, I had to persuade Graham to let me see your work, Beth. He said I should take expert advice. Buy his boring grey prints.'

Mam sighed. 'That's what he's paid for. I would have given you much the same spiel – it goes with the job. Graham's a sculptor. A good one, actually.'

'But he managed to be nice about you and more insulting at the same time. He said your paintings had a certain charm. And it sounded as if he was holding his nose. Why do you put up with it?'

Mam flopped back into the reception chair and rubbed her eyes. 'I know what he says, and he's fundamentally right about one thing. I haven't had an original idea in years. I'm too busy surviving.'

I couldn't help running across and hugging her. 'Hard work, being my Mam.'

Mam nuzzled into my hair. 'Worth it.'

'Could you sell anywhere else?' Rachel said.

'I've nothing new worth selling.'

'Waiting for inspiration to come back?'

'It's not like hatching an idea. I'd need to let it take over my life.'

I hugged Mam tighter. 'You could, if Dad wasn't so crap.'

'Don't blame your father for everything.'

'Give me ONE reason?'

'Alice, Rachel's here. Don't… Life's tough for him right now, and he did pay your allowance this month. And for the holiday.' Mam gave Rachel a 'sorry' look, and I wanted to tell her not to keep apologising for Dad. But two men in smart suits walked in. Mam painted a smile on her face like nothing had happened.

'Rachel?' I led her to the room behind the kitchen where most of Mam's paintings were in quarantine. But that's when I noticed: some had escaped. Two big pictures lit up the back gallery and three small ones were in the corridor. 'This is you, Rachel. None of Mam's pictures were up last time I was in here. You've done it – broken her out!'

Rachel smiled. 'I love Beth's pictures. I hope she sells some more.'

'She'd be able to paint more if Dad wasn't…' And I couldn't help the words coming out. 'He's not a proper dad. He's shit at it.'

'Oh, Alice…'

But I didn't want to think about Dad. I had Rachel to myself in the gallery. 'Let's talk pictures. You've been doing therapy with Mam's picture.'

'It feels as if it's talking to me. I actually… It sounds crazy, but I hear words. Not really from the picture. I think they're in my head.' And she was talking to maybe the one person in Cardiff who understood.

Perfectly.

'You REALLY do? Me too – I hear them. I thought I was loopy, the first time it happened. Not Mam's pictures. It's some portraits of girls in the museum. One of them talks to me every time now, but I'm not sure which one. And I've only ever told Mam.'

'The voice I hear around the picture feels like a person,' Rachel said. 'She gave me the confidence to talk to my mother. And she told me not to hide my... do you know what vulnerability means?'

I nodded. 'Mam talks about it a lot. Gwen's girls in the museum say the same sort of stuff to me. Like not worrying about being different at school. But I do worry. Like, if there's something wrong with me because I don't like children's games.'

Rachel nodded, looking sad. 'There never seemed to be time to stop and play when I was a kid. Mum and Dad had me doing so much extra work.'

'I make up my own stuff,' I said. 'Games no one else gets.'

'Playing – I don't know any children, Alice. Didn't when I was your age.'

'I'm not sure whether I count as a kid. But I'm here.' I tried a smile to see if it would fit, and Rachel gave me one back.

We could have gone on talking about feeling different, but Mam turned up in the doorway. 'They've gone. Bought the most uninspiring print going. I'm guessing it matches their wallpaper.'

Rachel smiled at all the pictures stacked against the walls. 'Beth, you really are my favourite artist.'

Mam shook her head. 'How many paintings have you really looked at? Find your own way to relate to them and you could have a lot of favourite artists.'

'You teach, don't you? Would you teach me?' Rachel put her hand over her mouth, like she hadn't meant to say it. Or maybe she had surprised herself. I do that all the time – say stuff and catch up later.

Rachel still had her hand over her mouth. 'Drawing, I can manage. The last time I picked up a paintbrush must have been at school.'

'Alice can teach you all you need to know about art appreciation,' Mam said. 'The rest is a matter of taste. I could teach you the mechanics of painting. But I would rather share my way of seeing – if you would share yours.'

Rachel looked at her, eyes wide.

'I'm guessing you haven't used it much lately,' Mam said, looking straight back.

And by some miracle, Rachel didn't look away. And I WISHED I'd had a photograph of the two of them.

Rachel's voice came out quiet, like she was in a trance. 'You're talking about a different person… Before I cracked up.'

'Okay… And if I'm looking to recover a different person too?'

Rachel and Mam stood looking at each other, a couple of paces apart. But beneath the surface, another Rachel and another Bethany stepped forwards and joined hands. I was watching it all happen in the space between two motionless, silent adults.

I counted to ten. 'Big reveal!' I said, and the three of us burst out laughing.

It turned into the best of afternoons. Mam needed to stay until closing time, but Rachel and I wandered around the gardens along Roath Brook, in no hurry to go anywhere or do anything. I stood on a footbridge for a long time, watching the sunlight sparkling on the water, and Rachel stood next to me. 'It's nice with you,' I told her after a while. 'You don't interrupt my thinking.'

'Because I remember another girl who used to stand watching the water forever and ever and ever.'

'I bet she was called Rachel, and she did a load of thinking.'

'Sometimes, I just emptied my mind because it was too full.'

'Me too,' I said. 'Going on the swings helps.'

'I haven't had a swing in years.'

'Come on, then!' And we walked up to the park.

And the two of us whooped so loudly on the swings that a pair of mothers shook their heads and raised their hands in the air. And we didn't care. We were ACTUALLY playing.

Rachel's phone beeped and we went back to meet Mam. As we walked down the road, me close against Rachel's side, she put her arm around me. 'Alice, there's been this space here, right next to me, all my life. And I didn't know it was there until you fitted right into it.'

And that's one of the nicest things anyone has ever said to me.

Dad being drunk didn't matter anymore. We really had found a friend both for Mam and for me. Saying goodbye was tough, and Mam and me watched Rachel walking up Ninian Road until she was out of sight.

*

Rachel

Now I was on my own, walking up to Morlais street with an empty space at my side. From the street, my house looked dead. A big, empty shell. Walking up from work each day, I had stepped around sleeping bags, duvets and cardboard on the pavement down near Newport Road. And I would open the door and let these lonely, vulnerable people in, if I didn't feel so scared.

Grow up. You can manage on your own.

Fumble with key, pulse racing. Slight dizziness starting.

Breathe. Get a grip. You're not having one.

The front hall tiles echoed emptiness back at me. But I knew where I would find life. In the front room. I sank onto the sofa and watched a movie, but kept imagining Beth, comforting and challenging, standing beside her painting. Wholly different, and yet sharing a deep empathy. No need for words – no need for disembodied voices.

Empathy. That was where it always used to start. Would Beth consume me in the way I had been consumed so many times before? I had treated my recurring problem by embracing corporate life. By becoming a woman in a suit. But now?

Who had control of my boundaries? Not me.

Beth? I'd never been strongly oriented either way and I'd begun to embrace asexuality: it explained my absence of sex drive and washed away a lot of unnecessary guilt. But I'd hoped that identifying as asexual would cure me from falling head-over-heels in love with people, ideas, images – anyone and anything that would accept my surrender. Beth.

Stop it, Rachel. Bedtime. Important meeting tomorrow. The Franco-German bid: Tom's work. Tom, my pirate captain.

No, Rachel, you're doing the same trick with Tom and Beth.

That green sock was still on the arm of the sofa. Cai.

Don't start again, Rachel. Bed.

Bed. Beth.

STOP IT.

Bed. It is your bedtime, Rachel.

I headed upstairs and tried to empty my mind.

No one here but me and my rag doll. 'Sort me out, Molly,' I said, and arranged her on the shelf – within reach if I needed her.

The shape and angles of the bay window caught my eye, and I found myself imagining the air in the room as a solid shape. Beth.

Could I stop myself jumping into her life?

Did I want to?

Stop it. Think Cai – that story is safely over. Think Cai.

I tiptoed into Cai's room, trying not to disturb sleeping memories. Putting one hand on the body of his bass, I moved in close, intimate with the instrument. I thrummed the fingers of my other hand across the strings. Out of tune. The bass moved slightly against the wall, and gave a hollow creak. Sorry, Cai.

I crept away. Bed.

But as I pulled the duvet over me, I found I wasn't alone.

No need to stop yourself. Your father isn't looking. Be yourself.

And yes, her voice was a shock, but she still gave me a smile. 'Night-night,' I said to the darkened volume of air in the room, and to any other presence who might or might not be there. 'Night-night.' And without one worry about the dark, I fell fast asleep.

13

ATTACK OF THE EASELS

Rachel

Getting a phone call each night was at first puzzling and then charming. Who knew that friends like to talk? On Friday, I was out of the house early, happily strolling up and away from the bus stop. It was a shorter walk to work this way, and I needed freedom for a while before I was cooped up in the grey office block all day.

In my first attempt to step inside Beth's world, I carried a new, unused sketch pad in my bag. But I'd been putting off using it all week. People I passed became imagined drawings, each with an individual posture and gait. Clothes moved against bodies, revealing curves and angles and volumes. And hopes and fears and boredom. Was I staring, or simply using a faculty I'd ignored?

I stopped for a coffee, the magical first coffee of the day, and found I could fill a page with people-shapes easily enough. But my default skill was cartoon, not reality, and at work, I dared myself further, trying a truthful sketch of Tom. He was sitting hunched over his desk, far from the glamorous pirate I'd first imagined. Mrs Jones caught me in the act. Oops. 'I'm going to art class tonight,' I told her. 'First time.'

'I can't draw for toffee,' she said, and handed me a pile of post. No comment on my effort. Maybe it didn't deserve one.

Back home, past more real people, each one subtly different. Sketches without limit. The Cardiff I thought I knew had filled with people, each one filled with possibilities. Each one stepping inside my boundary, breaking it down. I had no defence anymore. But did I need one?

Beth's life class was in a community hall, an awkward double bus ride away on the other side of town. I got there early, found the upstairs studio, and helped Beth fetch easels from a preparation room. 'My people all end up like cartoons,' I said, expecting a reassuring answer.

'Are you comfortable with this? You look anxious.'

'I don't know. It's as if I've never looked at people properly. It's shaken me up.'

'You don't often meet my gaze.'

Easels are not logical. And this one needed all of my gaze. It was fighting back.

'You've seen what I'm like around people,' I said, from beneath a tangle of wooden legs.

She rescued me from my assailant. 'When are you at your most comfortable?'

Not now. I rolled my shoulders in the way I did when I was warming up for... Yes, warming up for the time when I really did relax. 'Playing my violin is comfortable – I lose myself in the music. Piano, too. Improvising – playing out my moods.'

She smiled. 'I thought you might be a musician.'

'I'm in the Sinfonietta – we're not bad, for amateurs.'

'The word is good, Rachel. Good. Leave it there, have a walk round the word, and own it. Good – I know, because I've heard you. Come to think of it–'

'We have some ex-professionals.'

'Your summer concert – that piece by Grace Williams had a gorgeous violin solo. So peaceful. The player's face was hidden in a tangle of dark hair. I recognise that hair.'

'I borrowed it for violin. It's written for trumpet.'

'No confidence with people, but you can play like that in public?'

'Not really. To me, it's the violin that's the performer. I'm supporting it, animating it. I've played in public since I was tiny. Don't think I'm not shitting myself beforehand.'

'Welsh women composers – that wasn't the average amateur programme.'

'We're more about exploring than performing.'

Beth gave me a more penetrating look and raised one eyebrow. 'You've been struggling to contain your inner explorer, haven't you? She keeps peeping out.'

'It's actually scary, letting her out. Memories of not coping. With school. With university. With research. With Dad, I suppose.'

'No one here knows. You don't need to cope – that's what I'm here for.'

I gave a self-conscious shake of my arms and legs to prove I was relaxing.

Beth smiled. 'I'm not that strict a teacher.'

We heard voices downstairs, and she took both my hands in hers. 'Go on – dare yourself – use your musicality in your drawing. What ends up on paper doesn't matter. It really doesn't matter, Rachel. Your pencil plays the music and then it's over.'

The other artists began to file in. Ages twenty-five to eighty-five at a guess, women and men, and from their clothes, every walk of life. And they all seemed to know each other: this felt more like a club than an evening class.

An older woman stopped, her eyes staring through me. 'About time we had some fresh blood,' she said, moving on and leaving me thinking of vampires.

A spotty young man cleared his throat. 'Sorry… you're new?'

'Rachel – friend of Beth's – just trying it out.'

He glanced at the vampire, now unpacking a large wicker basket, and grinned. 'I'm bottom of the class. Stanley.'

I picked an easel next to him, with Beth's words playing through my head. 'You don't need to cope.' Stanley's head swivelled on his long neck like a friendly-but-nervous ostrich. Miss X-ray eyes took the easel on my other side. Oh well, vampire bites couldn't be that painful.

Looking around the others, with boxes of charcoal, pastels, oils, watercolours and acrylics, I decided I must be in big class now. Stanley followed my eyes. 'She told me to ignore the big boxes of kit. Some people need to feel prepared. Or to look the part.'

That made me feel better with my three pencils. I'd become a minimalist. Stanley was another, with pencils in a Spiderman pencil case. I was sure I had a Winnie-the-Pooh one somewhere.

Beth asked if everyone was ready, but a couple of older women ignored her while they debated different schools of thought on… something. The model, George, appeared from the other room in a white robe. And Beth explained today's session. Three-minute poses: just long enough to get an outline and move on. The two women sighed in unison and dug for something else in their boxes.

'Proportion, energy and a sense of movement,' Beth said, and walked round the ring, having a few words with each artist. Stanley and I were last. 'Just go for it,' she said. 'Stanley, remember that nobody's looking. The sketches you sent from your office were brilliant. I could imagine every person.'

He shrugged, and I managed an encouraging smile. Solidarity.

Beth told the whole class not to worry about quality and comparisons. This would be our impression of this figure on this day in this place. Then she gestured to George, who took off the robe and sat on a stool facing me.

I saw two prominent knees, a bulging paunch, an almost hairless chest, two arms hanging loose, and a face – he could have been Cai's older brother. Same high cheekbones, bushy eyebrows and shock of dark hair.

Dressing Cai. Smoothing his shirt down his back.

George was in the next pose. There was nothing on my paper.

He was standing sideways on to me, with his paunch hanging over his genitals. Skinny chest and legs. I marked the paper for head, torso and legs, remembering some children's TV programme where they made proportion seem easy. The body I drew had a sticking-out bottom that wasn't there. I ignored his paunch and added an arm. It was too long. Legs. Too short. A head. Too big, with his neck seated above his shoulders like a stalk. Hair. That wasn't too bad. Eye – sideways was difficult. Nose. And...

George had moved on. He was lying on a rug, and I hadn't finished the other one. My hand had clamped around the pencil and my other hand balled into a fist.

Beth came close behind my shoulder and spoke in an undertone. 'Okay, relax and shake your hands out for a moment. Get rid of the tension.'

I managed to put the pencil down and give a self-conscious shake.

'This is your first time, Rachel. Let it be your first time. Imagine you've never, ever picked up a pencil before.'

I closed my eyes for a few moments, and tried to imagine that, and to ignore the feeling that everyone must be looking at me. And the feeling that it was too hot in here and I was wearing too many clothes.

'Now, all I want until we break for tea is a sheet full of waves,' Beth said. She took down my muddled George and gave me a fresh, big sheet of paper. 'Just waves. Forget George. Imagine you're pulling the pencil across the paper. Make a ballet dancer's hand, and let it flow with the waves.'

'Forget George,' I whispered, looking straight at him.

'Well, try to,' Beth said, and moved on to Stanley.

I became a ballet dancer with a pencil. Waving. Until I broke the lead. Keeping an even pressure wasn't easy with a dancing pencil.

Second pencil. Relaxing and ballet dancing and ignoring George (who was sitting upright on the floor with his legs splayed apart) and keeping an even pressure on the paper and waving up and down and... my pencil flew, ricocheted off the edge of Stanley's easel, bounced up and hit him on the chin.

'Oops – sorry.'

He poked out his tongue and aimed his pencil at me. 'Detention after school.'

Third pencil. Waves. Sine waves? No, think art class. Japanese waves? I couldn't even visualise them. Little Welsh waves off

Cold Knap beach in Barry. I could do these. Wriggly waves, Cai called them. When was our last trip to Cold Knap? May?

Broken lead.

I held up my last pencil, feeling about six. 'Please Miss, my pencil's broken.'

George, lying flat in the middle of the room, gave a bellow of laughter, and his paunch rippled. Heads turned. The little girl in the corner's eyes started leaking. Mine.

Beth came and stood close beside me. I turned away from the group and poked at the tears on my cheeks. 'Why?' I didn't know why.

'Does there need to be a reason?' Beth whispered. 'Back in a mo.' She walked into the middle of the room. 'Thank you, George. Let's have an early break and then some longer poses. I know you painters are itching to get going.'

Beth came back, took me by the hands and kept me facing away from the others as they filed out of the door. 'You've been on quite a journey this evening,' she said as I wiped my tears. 'First George puts you off, and then you're thinking at a thousand miles an hour and tense as a spring.'

'George reminds me of Cai.'

'I thought maybe your father, from the look on your face. That wasn't all, was it?'

'I'm not... I'm just not used to... Oh, I don't know. I need to grow up a bit.'

Beth held my arms, anchoring me. 'Why not go home before they come back? We can do some artwork together away from the class.'

'No, Beth. Please? I'm really getting this – the whole process. And being outside my comfort zone. It's good. I need it.'

'If you're sure.'

'And I like Stanley. He's not bottom of the class anymore.'

'He needs an ally. Stanley was petrified on his first day. I didn't think he'd want to come back, but he kept sending me drawings over the summer.'

'I didn't find the serious ones so easy.'

Beth smiled into her chest. 'You mean, the ones who need to be seen as serious?'

I found myself smiling back. Just thinking about this little group was helping.

'They're all lovely,' Beth said, with a sigh full of affection. 'Lovely people who need affirmation. Just a bit fierce, some of them.'

'You take Stanley as seriously. I can be his understudy.'

'If you like. But that drawing would have worked if you'd dared to leave your first attempt visible and gone on refining it. I stopped you because you're the kind of person who would need to rub out every slip.'

'I suppose I am. Covering my tracks.'

'If you stay, people will see you've been crying. If that bothers you, go now.'

How important was my dignity? Here, where Beth had read me like a book? I hated this person who needed to rub out every slip, for fear of an imaginary grown-up. I wanted to conquer her. 'It's okay. I guess I'm ready to come out as someone who makes mistakes, sheds real tears and moves on.'

Suddenly, tears filled her eyes as well. 'Thank you. Thank you for the trust. Oh God, I...' She hugged me tight. 'It's tough, sometimes.'

I stayed. No one commented on our freshly scrubbed red faces. I drew some wispy George-like figures, hardly daring to touch the shape of him with my pencil. As if the tip could inflict pain. As if a single detail would kill him.

Beth stood watching me for a long time, her silence doing more for my confidence than words. I could have drawn George all night, soaking up Beth's silence. At nine-thirty, a rattle of easels and an absence of George brought my reverie to an end.

A low whistle of admiration from Stanley did me a lot of good. And what I found on his easel arrested me. His style was childlike and simple, but each drawing was filled with essence of George. Stanley most definitely had his own vision, and I said so.

'Next week?' he said.

'You bet!'

I meant it, but sitting on the bus, trying to make sense of the swirling emotions of the evening, I found myself shaking. And later, I needed a strand of Molly's woollen hair around my finger as I tried to relax into sleep.

14

HEADS AND TAILS

Alice

I wasn't sure about Rachel and Granddad Joe. Granddad is the opposite of an office person – he's a maker. And his workshop is my favourite place for making stuff. But he's touchy about letting just anyone in there. I did tell him that Rachel's a scientist and bound to be good at stuff.

The workshop is over the other side of the railway bridge, a long walk from our flat, but much closer for Rachel. And we met her there on Saturday morning. Granddad was standing outside smoking, but as soon as he saw Mam, he dropped his cigarette into a rusty oil can, quick. If Mam told Nan, Granddad would be in big trouble.

The workshop has a small wooden door that's been cut in one of a much larger pair of grey doors that I've never, ever seen open. With those faded white letters over the top, like an arch, *Corbett Quality Components*.

Granddad worked for his dad, and his dad worked for his dad, and his dad worked for his dad, who built the workshop. But Dad came along and spoilt it all by turning into a photographer, not an engineer. Nowadays, it's an engineering club for Granddad's retired mates. Strictly no children allowed – unless they're me, and know all the safety stuff, like wearing a hairnet.

Anyway, Rachel and Granddad together WORKED.

Rachel used to make robots when she was a teenager, and she can do soldering and everything. And she didn't put Granddad off by talking. But he dug out of her that she'd spent a whole year smashing particles at CERN, and then he was doing the talking, big time. He wanted to know EVERYTHING. I think he's turned into her number one fan.

But why hadn't she told ME first? She actually worked on the Large Hadron Collider and I know EVERYTHING about the LHC.

Mam was behind the window in the little office talking to Dad on the phone. I could see she was upset and had to keep checking on her. And then Rachel and me working together was not what I expected. It was actually scary.

We decided to make a stegosaurus from Alpha Centauri, because. And when we'd swapped sketches, my plan was to do it with brass rods that bend easily, with Rachel soldering them together. Then we could coat the frame in paper and goo.

We got the banana-shaped body all right, with me cutting rods to run along it and bending them, and Rachel soldering them to some rings she'd made, dead neat. Granddad even came over and said that's a mighty fine banana. Daft. And Mam was still on the phone, and she had a tissue out.

The legs were where the stegosaurus went wrong. I bent them to fit, but then Rachel bent them a different way when she soldered them. And it looked wrong, and me and Rachel got cross, because she couldn't see what was wrong, and I could, and I picked it up to bend it back and the whole thing broke in half.

I broke it, and it was ours.

And then I wasn't an engineer. I was an angry little ten-year-old banging the bench with my fist. And Rachel was standing way back looking shocked. And Mam was still on the phone and I could see tears and that gave me more tears.

'SHIT! SHIT! SHIT!' And I banged the bench so hard I got a bruise and everything jumped.

Rachel came a bit closer. 'Maybe I didn't understand. Show me your way.'

'WON'T WORK.'

I didn't want Rachel, I wanted Mam. And she was still on the phone.

Rachel looked at Mam, and back at me, sort of scared.

Granddad scratched his head. 'Calm down, chuck.'

But I wasn't ready to calm down because it was Mam and Dad, AGAIN.

Rachel went back to the bench and soldered the stegosaurus back together again, but she left off the legs. 'Which bit next, Alice?'

I had to wipe my face, and Rachel reached out to me, but I didn't want a hug. 'Shit,' I said. 'SHIT.' And I cleared my mind of Dad and Mam and concentrated. 'This bit, for the front legs.'

'Oh…' Rachel's mouth went wide. And then she looked over her shoulder at Granddad. 'We've gone heads and tails!'

I'd thought the head was at one end, and Rachel, the other. 'Yes! That'll work,' she said.

And when I got over being all shaky, and had a long hug with Granddad and a glass of water he got me, we made a whole dinosaur with a head and a tail my way. I snipped armoured plates for her back out of thin brass sheet, and Rachel soldered them on, and then Steggy was ready for her coat.

Mam came over and tried to put her arm around me, but I stood back.

She looked at Granddad and back at me. 'Sorry, love. Really, I am,' she said. But I didn't think anything was sorted between Mam and Dad, and Granddad just twitched his head, like he does. What Rachel thought of us all, I couldn't guess.

Mam shaped her hands around Steggy. 'This is GENIUS. You are so clever!'

'I lost my temper with Rachel, Mam. Me being stupid.'

'Me too,' Rachel said. 'Just as stupid. We're not used to being a team, are we, Alice? But we could be.' She explained our head-for-tail Steggy. 'I needed to look at her through Alice's eyes.'

'I bet your Steggy was better,' I said.

'Maybe we should have drawn a plan.'

Mam sighed. 'Maybe your mother should have picked a better time and place to argue with your father,' she said.

Granddad put his arm around her. 'That son of mine!' But he nodded at Rachel and me. 'Engineering's a good cure for brain ache.'

And when he'd taken Mam to the office and put the kettle on, Rachel whispered, 'Do you think he would be my Granddad too?'

'I bet he would. He likes you.' I'd seen him watching Rachel soldering, and she was dead neat and quick.

And me and Rachel want to make a maze-solving robot, like the ones she used to make that won competitions. And maybe we need to practise not arguing.

I bet no one else noticed the bit of the morning that mattered most to me. When Mam came out of the office, Rachel went and put both her arms around her and held her forever. And I know that isn't a Rachel thing to do. The longest hurt I've ever had started melting away, because I've wanted Mam to have a real friend forever.

And then Rachel and Granddad Joe had a long chat in his office while me and Mam tore up newspaper and dunked it in goo and spread it all over Steggy, like putting her skin on. And when we had finished, Rachel and Granddad were still talking, and laughing as well. And that was just fine by me because Rachel needs friends too.

15

LOOK AROUND

Rachel

That morning in the workshop taught me a lot – and not just about the need to subdue my ego when sharing with a child. Alice's constant checking over her shoulder was graphic evidence of the strain her parents' relationship put on her. More surprising was how much Beth relied on Joe, Iestyn's father.

I wanted to help Alice and Beth, but how? I had qualifications to spare, but what use were letters before and after my name if they didn't prepare me for the messiness of engaging with the human beings around me. These messy, wonderful human beings I now cared for so much, it hurt.

On Sunday, Alice went for a boat trip around the bay with Iestyn and Granddad Joe. She called me twice on Joe's phone to tell me in worried tones that her father was very quiet. I listened with what I hoped Alice understood to be heartfelt sympathy. But I couldn't think of anything helpful to say. Beth was working in the gallery all day, and so she couldn't even treat herself to a proper rest while Alice was out.

A surprise gear-change at work interrupted thoughts of becoming a helpful human. On Monday morning, my phone was full of messages from HQ in Zurich, all implying that I should have been in the office and available at 7am.

Mrs Jones was flustered when I walked in, because Ian the boss had vented his anger about that Bothwell woman and flounced out to a game of golf. And Tom needed the situation explaining quickly because we had serious work to do.

Last year, I had alerted the LA office to flaws in their data for a green energy bid. They'd ignored my advice, submitted it unchanged, and had it rejected on sight. In my final findings on the LA bid, I had added the nugget that the competing bids were equally flawed. I heard nothing back from HQ until seven o'clock this morning, when I learned that my figures had found their way to the State of California Energy Commission six months ago, and as a result, they had re-set the bidding process.

Now, Global HQ in Zurich were planning to submit a new bid based on my work. I would be senior advisor, and LA were out of the loop. No pleases and no warning, but I wouldn't have expected them. Run with it, Rachel.

As soon as America woke up, my inbox filled with indignant denial, and I had to field a series of irate but satisfying transatlantic phone calls. Who was this Bothwell woman, working for a little Cardiff company the corporation had inherited by mistake? Was she for real? My interference on HQ orders last year had incensed them. And now, their anger knew no limit, questioning my competence, nationality, and gender.

I didn't care – I had a trusty pirate captain at my side with my list of their mistakes at his fingertips. It was the most fun I'd had since I took the job, and with Ian out of the building, most of the women from the general office abandoned their posts and came upstairs to cheer us on and sort through the irrelevant statistics LA kept firing at us.

My mind was still racing over work when Alice phoned in the evening from Joe and Siân's house. Beth was out modelling for a friend's life class at the Art School. Steggy's newspaper skin had dried, and Alice had painted her green and red and white.

'You sound fuzzy,' she said. 'Like, miles away.'

'A lot on my mind. I've got a big new job at work.'

'Tell Mam's painting.'

'Oh.' I hadn't heard that voice all week. 'I haven't talked to her for ages. I've got you to talk to.'

Would I ever hear that voice again? Now I noticed its absence, I missed it. Maybe I wanted to believe in the phenomenon. Maybe I did believe in the phenomenon.

Alice kept silent for a while, as if she knew I was thinking it through. Then she said, 'There's the portraits in the museum – they listen when I'm full up with stuff. And I think they talk to Mam. She wasn't shocked when I told her I could hear a voice.'

'Who's best for a chat, then?'

'Gwen John's girls, but I'm not sure which one talks.'

'Okay, I'll go and have a listen in my lunch break if I get time.'

I did have time on Tuesday, because the American side of the corporation was still absorbing the reality that a scientist in Wales (where the heck's that?) had constructed a more sustainable bid than the mighty LA finance team.

The marble halls and massive bronze doors of the National Museum dwarfed the paintings, but the place was full of light, and my footsteps echoed through an almost empty gallery. I had to ask for directions to Gwen John's early twentieth century portraits: they didn't jump out at me.

Girl in a Green Dress was sombre, with her hands clasped

in her lap and an impassive, round face. The girl in the middle row at high school, perhaps, desperately hoping no one would notice her. Not interested, defiantly uninteresting, and she clearly had nothing she wished to say to me. And yet I already knew so much about her. I could almost smell her nervous sweat.

I didn't want to keep disturbing her and sat down to ponder how the artist had given me so much information about such an uncommunicative subject. I supposed that in keeping a respectful distance, she had let the girl be herself. Alice had said I would need to listen hard, but this girl simply wasn't talking. My guess was she had period pains and I couldn't offer painkillers to a portrait.

In a corner, beside a larger portrait of a nun, a small, pale picture caught my eye. 'Girl in Profile' seemed to have been painted off into the distance. 'Oil and chalk,' the label said, and at first glance, the chalk had almost flattened her into a greyish pastel pattern, although gentle brush strokes and subtle hints of colour took her far from the precise masculine greyness that had repulsed me in the gallery in Roath.

The painting drew me in, but only so far. While the other girl had nothing to say, this girl wilfully ignored me. Her nose in the air implied that whatever wisdom she had to share was not for the likes of me. And yet I couldn't look away. I stood for so long that an attendant offered me a folding stool. But I needed to get back to the office.

After work, I met Beth and Alice in the coffee bar, and Alice told me about her school trip to Techniquest, radiating enthusiasm. 'Miss Akoto got all excited about the experiments. Real science! And we went in the planetarium.' I let her enthusiasm wash over me and didn't ask if she wanted any science explaining.

A twilight trip to the swings seemed natural, and we left Beth catching up with messages over her coffee. I didn't mention my visit to the paintings until we were swinging next to each other.

'That painting stuck her nose in the air and ignored me.'

'The one in the corner? She's my favourite. Needs her shock-stoppers, she does. I think she's the one who whispers when I'm not looking.'

'I'll go and have another listen.'

A bunch of girls passed the railings, talking loudly. Alice looked away. They didn't call out, but a loud 'Miss Akoto's pet' was answered by giggles.

Alice stepped off the swing, and we headed back to Beth in the coffee bar, with Alice walking several paces in front of me, head erect and rigid. She stopped me in the doorway with a finger to her lips. 'I can handle them. Mam's got enough worries.'

In the absence of news from America, I went back to meet Girl in Profile next lunchtime. I got a nod from the same attendant and accepted a folding stool. This time, I was armed with my sketchpad, but my pencil didn't touch it. Was Alice right? Did she need her shock-stoppers? Was that why the artist had veiled her in chalk?

Voices and laughter from a school party echoed through from the next gallery. What these paintings must endure, every single day! I thought of Beth's painting, comfortably resting above my mantelpiece. What if she were here, in the stark, public light of the gallery? Such an intimate painting, even though she was bursting with life and energy. I didn't like the idea of streams of visitors staring at her. It felt wrong.

I let my eyes rest somewhere above Girl in Profile, trying

to feel her presence without staring. A dignified young woman, with her hands in her lap and her eyes half-closed. Fully herself, safe behind her layer of chalk and oil.

Look around, Rachel, she whispered. *Look around and you might find yourself.* Shock, terror, or joy? All three at once. I knew this voice. It was the same woman's voice I had heard at home, with the same concern and personal insight that kept spooking me. The same hint of an accent, which I now recognised as French, but also with something Welsh about it. I had little doubt that the girl in the painting and the voice at home were one. And I also knew that all this could be happening in my head.

Look around and you might find yourself. I had to sit for a while and collect my wits. Yes, I would trust her voice. In no way was she threatening me, and all I'd heard had been positive and affirming. Whether she was real or the workings of my subconscious, I could leave for another time.

'You are the same person who helped me at home, aren't you?'

I know you, Rachel. And Bethany. And Alice. Myself... I'm not so sure.

I didn't push her to explain. I gave her a thankful smile, whispered, 'Au revoir,' and left swiftly, not entirely sure whether I wanted to share what I'd heard with Alice. That Wednesday evening, Alice had art club anyway, helping Beth with a group of children with learning disabilities.

Look around. I sat down under the painting in the front room and tried to draw Alice in that profile pose. My sketch ended up looking like me. *Look around and you might find yourself.*

Thursday, still no news from America, and my third appointment with Girl in Profile. And I found something in those whispered words before I even reached the corner. Something that gave us a personal bond. Her erect pose wasn't haughtiness at all. She was a violinist like me; in a playing position absorbed in her bone-memory through hours of lessons. All I'd needed to do was shift my perspective. *Look around.* She was a sensitive girl, lost in music, and the genius of the artist had been to avoid exposing her.

Now, I could see life and colour shining behind that opaque surface. The girl was shielded from public gaze by an artist who genuinely cared. Gwen John knew all about invasive stares: she had made her living modelling, a lone Welshwoman in Paris in the nineteen-hundreds. And she had found her own way to protect her subjects.

Bethany Howells and Gwen John. Now I had two very different favourite artists. And I shared that shift in perspective with Alice and Beth after work, in the coffee bar. 'She did talk to me, but I'm still working out what it might mean.'

'You realise that kind of work doesn't go away,' Beth said. 'Welcome to real engagement with art. It'll keep you busy for the rest of your life.'

I was about to ask Beth whether paintings talked to her in words and sentences, or simply in ideas. But it felt such a silly thing to ask that I just gave her a vague nod. We didn't visit the swings this time, and we didn't talk about the decision. Alice had my solidarity.

And on Friday evening, Stanley had my solidarity. I even felt relaxed and at home behind the easel with my more-than-three pencils in my Winnie-the-Pooh case. I'd almost become one of the group – although I was still half expecting a vampire bite.

Look around, Rachel.

16

MAM AND HER HURTS

Alice

I had a new friend and new stuff to think about – lots of new stuff, mostly from my new pet science encyclopaedia. Rachel and me still argued over making stuff, but it was fun-arguing, not in-a-temper arguing. And we made a lot of stuff in Granddad's workshop.

Mam and me often went to meet Rachel in the coffee bar after her work. But some days, she worked on into the evening and we had to talk on the phone instead.

Several happy weeks passed when Rachel had no more seizures and neither did Shareen at school. I told Shareen I had an adult friend with epilepsy, but Shareen didn't want to talk about it. Didn't want to talk at all.

Actually, they weren't happy weeks.

They were shitty weeks with happy bits when I was with Rachel. Mam never ever stopped worrying about Dad. He stayed out of trouble, mostly, and he was getting an exhibition together. But the money had dried up again, and Mam was running more classes and looking shattered, every night. I didn't complain about the number of takeaways because Mam always looked guilty, not having time to cook.

School was the shittiest place of all. The Evils started a thing where saying anything at all to Miss Akoto was banned. Which made the gobby class nerd stand out a mile. I couldn't not talk to my favourite teacher.

One day, Kamala came and stood next to me and said, 'Don't let them bug you.' Kamala was a new girl who came from another school. And she had a sort of air about her – like she was above the Evils.

Easy for her. She was the biggest girl in class and sat with a boy called Jake who had hair like he was in a band. It was like Kamala and Jake had a cool zone of their own, because they both looked about fourteen and didn't care about the boy-girl thing.

Then there was that other zone I was beginning to notice. The Random Boy Zone. Most of the boys were so random in the way they behaved that talking or not talking to Miss Akoto wouldn't bother them. And personal hygiene definitely didn't bother them.

So, the class had zones, and tiny little Alice's mission was to escape from the Evil Twin zone. Which seemed much smaller, now the class had three zones – four if you counted Shareen in an Untouchable zone. But Shareen got embarrassed if I talked to her, and I didn't smell like a Random Boy, and no way was I cool enough for Kamala and Jake. I was in the Evil Twin zone by default, like they had me under a curse.

Rachel was in a zone, too – the Pill Zone. She looked more relaxed with us now, but it wasn't quite real. It was the pills. After her big seizure in Roath Park, she'd joined a pilot scheme to test a new epilepsy drug, and her cello-playing friend Julie asked her to write down any side-effects. Rachel asked us to tell her what we noticed. 'Weirdly normal and relaxed,' was my best guess. Rachel told Julie, and Julie said I would make a fine diagnostician. I liked that word.

I asked Rachel if she'd told Doctor Julie about disembodied voices, and Rachel said NO WAY, just in case she put her on a whole different set of pills.

All the way through September and October, we kept on meeting and being best friends ever, but not once did Rachel ask us round to her house. I wanted to see it, but Mam said we shouldn't ask. And I was sure that was because if we went round there, then Mam would have to invite Rachel round to our flat. And she COULDN'T do that, because our flat was a dump.

And the more I thought about it, the more serious that problem got. I knew Mam was dead embarrassed about how we lived. And I knew Granddad and Nan wanted to help, and she wouldn't let them.

Rachel showed us some pictures of her apple tree, and the apples she had picked, and even gave Mam and Nana Siân some bags of apple puree to make puddings. I wanted to go there and hear Rachel playing the violin, but I was good and didn't say a word. I didn't tell Rachel that Mam couldn't afford my piano lessons anymore, because I know Mam and stuff like that. It hurts her, not affording stuff.

Mam had lots of hurts – especially on a Friday after life class – she always looked terrible. I was bothered in case someone there was bugging her – there'd been a stalker on the news. So, one Friday when she'd paid my babysitter and asked why I was still up, I said something. 'Every time you come home; you're hurting. What's wrong?'

And that made Mam crash down into her beanbag. I got her a glass of water and waited. At last, she said it was

Rachel, mainly. And someone else called Stanley who didn't want Mam to talk about his stuff. She could never praise Rachel's drawings in front of the others. If she did, Rachel just turned away. She was sure it was to do with Rachel never getting praised when she was a kid. Like her dad had done something to Rachel that couldn't be mended.

'I want to make Rachel better, Mam.'

'I think you're doing that, just by being you. But it might take years – there's a big hole in her life.'

I was ready for years of it. Every time I saw Rachel, it felt like she needed love but was too shy to ask. But my biggest worry wasn't about Rachel. I was sure that the person in my life who got hurt most wasn't Rachel or Dad. It was the person who felt every hurt everyone ever had. Mam.

17

PHYSICIST, UNDRESSED

Rachel

October turned to November in Alice's half term, and we managed a couple of days working on our first robot in Joe's workshop. Everything kicked off in California on the Friday afternoon, and Joe and Alice drove me straight to the office in my jeans, with flakes of glue all over my fingers. I waved madly from my fifth-floor window – whether Alice could actually see me through the tinted glass didn't seem to matter.

The California Energy Commission were seriously considering our bid and I'd hardly sat down before two technical questions came in. I stayed on into the evening with Tom, double and triple checking each answer and running it past HQ in Zurich.

We had sandwiches and coffee delivered to the office and it almost felt as if my old research days had come back. I was even wearing the same comfortable old jeans and fleece, gaining a strange look from Ian. Either he didn't approve, or he was attracted to my bottom – or both.

We finally got the okay, sent off our revisions and flopped back in our chairs. Job done, and we should have California's final decision by the end of next week. Breathe.

I was late for Beth's class and Tom offered to drive me there. A call from Carlos in security downstairs interrupted my awkward refusal. 'Taxi for my special girlfriend.' I thanked Tom for the offer and rushed out for my taxi to the community centre.

Beth was in the doorway, staring at her phone. She saw me, smiled briefly, and shook her head. I followed her in, and the room went quiet. 'I must apologise for George again,' Beth said. A groan passed around the room. 'He has flu. Again.' One or two stifled chuckles. 'This will be the last time. It was his last session anyway.'

'Do you need a volunteer?' Stanley asked.

Beth turned to me, tipping her head in a silent question about my late arrival.

'Just work,' I said.

'Let's try a little experiment.' She turned to the whole group. 'Rachel and I have been sharing each other's view of the world. My reference is visual, and meanings grow from there, but Rachel can imagine and bring to life a reality where visual reference isn't possible. The interplay of particles and fields at a quantum level.'

Eleven pairs of eyes turned towards me and I realised that these familiar people knew nothing about me. And also, that I knew nothing about them – not even Stanley. From the looks I was getting, I had transformed into a female Stephen Hawking (with floppy hair like Brian Cox, of course).

Beth turned back to me but kept her voice loud enough for everyone to hear. 'If you sit in the middle, you'll have a unique view of artists at work. No need to undress. Just be yourself and watch us – not many people get that view. I model regularly, and it always feels like a privilege.'

I nodded. 'Okay – why not?' At least I wouldn't have Morwenna close beside me with her braided silver hair, silk scarves and fierce eyes. Each week, her easel seemed to have edged closer. Maybe it was the scent of my blood.

Beth glanced at Morwenna. 'You will feel concentrated gaze. Keep a check on your feelings – if you get uncomfortable, I'm sure Stanley will take your place.'

Stanley gave me an encouraging smile. 'It felt good, last time.'

'Back in a moment,' Beth said, and took me in the other room. I fingered the model's white robe, hanging over a chair.

'You won't need that. Five-minute poses. Keeping still will be hard at first, but if you have to move, you move. Don't apologise – you're in charge.'

I sat on the chair and practiced sitting still for Miss in primary school.

She smiled. 'You don't have to be rigid! And as long as you keep your head still, you can look back at them. I'll move you around, so you get to see everyone in the circle.' Her hand touched my shoulder for a moment. 'Remember how stressed you were, coming to that first session? Look at you now – I'm so proud of you.'

'I'm just–'

'Just a star.' She headed for the door. 'I'll fetch you in a couple of minutes when I've gone over a few things from last week.'

The door shut behind her. A star? Proud of me? She was being kind.

No, that was my self-image speaking. I knew what I had achieved, just by sticking with these classes and becoming one of the group. Almost one of the group.

Look around. Look around and you might find yourself.

Look around – artists all around you. You've become one of them now, the model. Gwen John was a model, alone in Paris, taking her clothes off for strangers. And yet she protected Girl in Profile with all that chalk.

I've needed a few layers of chalk over the years, but I've always felt comfortable in my body. It's a nice body. My trouble has been the faulty brain that came in the same bundle.

I wondered how it might feel to blow away some layers of chalk, and I took off my fleece. No feeling. Unbuttoned my work shirt. More exposed.

Okay then, Rachel – take it off. You can always put it on again.

My bra looked worn and laundry-grey. Not so good.

Right, it's off or fully dressed. Your decision, Doctor Bothwell.

No answer.

Beth models at the Art School, and she's older and quite a bit larger than me. George and his wife Jean must be twenty years my senior, and it doesn't hurt them to model for us. Gwen John thought of herself as much a model as an artist.

Rachel, do you want a life of grey office-ness at work and laundry greyness at home?

That was the kick I needed, and I took off my bra. Chilly, but it would be warmer in the other room. Maybe I wasn't so good looking, but to stop now seemed wrong. I took my boots off: somehow, just as much a commitment as the bra. And then my comfortable jeans and knickers in one go. Oh, socks too – not green ones. And there I was, as born, no wrapping.

A quick check revealed a couple of small bruises. I was a bit sweaty, but didn't smell too bad and the marks from my bra straps looked quite faint. And Beth was in the doorway, staring at me. 'Rachel – are you sure?'

'Oh.'

I had just taken all my clothes off in a public room. Madness.

'Sorry...'

'No problem. I just didn't expect...'

A little late, I covered myself with my arms.

She smiled. 'You look good, by the way, but there's no need for you to do this.'

'I don't know why I did.'

'Trying how it feels? Why not?'

'But I just... did it. I was miles away.'

'Don't worry, there's time for you to get dressed. Clothed models are just as much a challenge for them.'

And I would have been half-daring. I stopped protecting myself and stood straighter. 'Can I go ahead?'

'If you walk out there; this will be their image of you from now on. They won't un-remember it.'

The idea was a shock, but I wanted... I wasn't sure what I wanted, just that I might miss this one chance.

Look around and you might find yourself.

'Beth, my body is the part of me I like. I know I'm not bad looking.'

'You are a wonder!'

'I'm winging it. I had no idea I was going to take my clothes off. I was thinking of Gwen John. She covered everyone except herself. She was brave.'

'Most people with image problems can't look at themselves.'

'Most of them aren't waiting for the next seizure.'

'Okay, so image isn't a surface thing for you. Do you know that in terms of classical proportion, you're the best model they will have seen?'

I looked down and patted my well-filled tummy.

She smiled. 'You're my kind of model. Human.'

That was a nice thought, but her gaze shifted to the old white scars across the inside of my left arm, far enough above my wrist to hide. I clasped my arm across my stomach.

Beth looked away for a moment, and then handed me the robe. 'There's reason enough for you. History. Go for it – walk in with the robe on. It's your call for each pose I give you. Robe on, falling loose, or take it off.'

'I don't want to shock them.' I put on the robe.

She tipped her head. 'For all they know, high-energy physicists work in the nude.'

'This one prefers comfy pyjamas and woolly socks.'

'You can keep the robe on. If it helps, imagine yourself at your comfiest and cosiest. I hate models who strike attitudes.'

I could keep the robe on but knew I wouldn't. I walked in smiling and sat down as directed, chin in hand, elbow on knee. Then I pulled the robe off my shoulders and down my arms. One side slid off my leg, and I lifted my elbow to let the other join it. I was exposed, and remarkably comfortable. Maybe I was Gwen John.

No, Rachel, you are yourself.

This time, her voice was welcome and not in the least scary. I was ready for her message and silently thanked her for it. Yes, I could be both comfortable and myself.

People were looking and measuring. Curious, holding pencils or hands out to give them proportions. Busily sketching and glancing back and forth between their easels and my cosy, non-pyjama-clad body. And I just sat and absorbed all this attention.

Beth drifted round, quietly commenting here and there, usually drawing a smiling response that I'd been too nervous to notice from behind my easel. Even an unexpectedly shy smile from Morwenna. Beth was playing the group like an instrument, and I could see the whole performance.

Another pose, twisting round, and harder to hold still on a backless stool. Another, crouching without the stool, felt spooky. I had to look at the floor for five minutes and could hear rustles and murmurs focussed on me. But the worst was the simplest: standing with the gown on. As if in the queue for meds from Nurse Ratched. I didn't like this gown, and for my next pose, sitting upright, I abandoned it and draped it over the stool. Now I was comfortable. I felt in charge.

Break time, and they headed downstairs for a drink. Beth's eyes were full of questions as she dug out a flask. I was still relaxing in my pose and felt serene. For the last five minutes, I had imagined playing second solo line in the slow movement of Bach's double concerto. Not a piece I had attempted since I left Cambridge, but in harmony with Girl in Profile, here alongside me, anything was possible. Just look at the pair of us now, Girl in Profile.

'You can relax,' Beth said.

'I'm comfortable like this.'

'You are, aren't you? Peppermint tea?'

'Please.'

She washed up a spare mug. 'Have you done this before? You have poise.'

'It's my stance when I play the violin. I guess I've learned to relax upright.'

'Ah – all I need is to sketch in the violin and bow.' She gave me a curious look. 'Most amateurs grab the robe the moment the others have gone. Change of dynamic.'

She handed me a mug. Do naked people drink tea with fully dressed friends? It was beginning to feel like an act, and I put on the robe. Why hadn't I reacted? Because she was a friend? No, there was something more.

'You know me properly naked, Beth. Screaming down Queen Street. Running scared from the market. I don't think I've got any more nakedness to show you.'

'I suppose so.'

Her continued puzzled look suggested I'd triggered other thoughts. She didn't share them and so I had a wander round the easels. Eleven sets of five sketches, as seen from eleven angles around the room. A 360° view of a genuinely beautiful body, captured in all sorts of ways: simple ink line, shaded pencil, smudged charcoal and different kinds of pastel. Some stylised, almost schematic drawings, some so faint that there was the merest hint of a body. And all but one of them had something in common. This was not me; it was a model. The complex curves of a woman not far off forty. No attempt had been made to capture the detail of my face and some even dispensed with hair.

One face was present in a set of childish pencil drawings. The calmness I had felt was perfectly captured. Beth shook her head. 'Stanley can never resist personalising his pictures. And I can never bring myself to point him another way. He's a one-off.'

Beth suggested I dress for the second half and feel the difference.

I did, but clothes just got in the way of people seeing the

shape of me. That long, unbroken series of curves from my hip to my thigh to my knee to my calf to my ankle and around my instep to my toes had been more than attractive, naked. In jeans and boots, it got confused with seams and angles and wrinkles.

Had I turned into a narcissist, falling in love with the shape of me? I wanted to stand up and tear all my clothes off. But it was time to go.

Stanley was talking to Beth at length, I had a bus to catch, and it was beginning to rain out there. I waved to Beth. 'Call you tomorrow. Lots to think about.'

'Me too,' she said. 'A lot.'

On the way home, I managed to get drenched walking from one bus to the other. And so I warmed up in the bath with my newly-intriguing curves for company.

In bed, comfortably without pyjamas, I smiled up at the print I'd bought of Girl in Profile.

Now you understand, she whispered. *You can bear to be you. Love to be you.*

I wondered whether the artist's greatest feat had been to set her free. Set free to see her own beauty, and to escape other people's expectations. Set free as soon as Gwen John put down her brush. With thoughts of the mysterious girl behind the portrait, I went happily to sleep, with no need for Molly to leave the shelf beside my pillow.

18

FIRST FROST

Alice

It poured down on Saturday. And I soon got sick of documentaries about climate change – all doom music and soft voices saying nothing new. I needed to ask Rachel about the real stuff. She was busy at work in the morning, but we went under Mam's big umbrella to meet her at the coffee bar in the afternoon. Mam left me with Rachel and went down to the gallery to help hang some new paintings.

Rachel got us both peppermint tea, my new grown-up treat. 'Tell me about climate change,' she said, and relaxed back in her chair.

Me tell HER? I just did a fish-mouth.

'I know you're angry about it,' she said. 'And you're as much a scientist as me.'

Me, a scientist? No way. I felt like a stupid little girl. Was one.

'Alice, you said on the phone about documentaries repeating the same old doom set to music. Tell me about that.'

And once I started, I couldn't stop. All my anger about people turning real stuff into a side show. Getting frustrated because people WOULD NOT listen. Being scared ALL THE TIME for the future of the planet. I don't know how long I talked, but Rachel finished her tea and got another one, and I hadn't even started mine.

At last, Rachel reached for both my hands. 'I'm sorry,' she said. 'Sorry for the mess my generation has left. You have every right to be angry with me – I'm part of it. Sorry I haven't managed to do more. I will try harder.'

'It's not you!'

'It is, Alice. You know who I work for. They're not as green as they tell the world. I'm trying to change that, but I don't have much power. And it hurts.'

'Why do you work for them, then?'

'I ask myself the same question every day. But I didn't have much choice of jobs when I left research. Not many came up when they saw my health record.'

'So, you took a job that didn't ask?'

'I took the first one where I made it to interview.'

'And you hate it.'

'That's why I said you're just as much a scientist as me. You've shifted the way I see things. Made me look much more towards the future.'

'At work – can you say what you think?'

'I do – I do. Sometimes they even listen. But money talks louder.'

I stood up. 'It's ALWAYS money people. Greedy people. I hate them.'

'And your generation will inherit our mess.'

'My generation KNOW! What about climate strikes and things?'

Rachel looked straight into my eyes. 'You're right. Teenagers today are learning how not to be fooled. They're getting smart, and they give me real hope. You give me hope – children of your age are getting the same message. But it shouldn't be like that – my generation should be dealing with it right now.' Rachel shook her head and looked at her hands. 'I should.'

She was so sad and helpless that I stood against her chair and hugged her, and she held on tight, like she needed it.

'You're one of my generation, really,' I said. 'Don't let them shut you up.'

'Thank you, Alice. For understanding. It's just so… big.'

If Rachel felt small, I was a lot smaller.

But my brain was doing tricks again. Maybe I was just a smaller scientist. The smallest scientist? Whatever, I was still gobsmacked that Rachel wanted to listen to me.

On Sunday, Mam had the day off while they re-hung the upstairs gallery. We set off early to meet Rachel up by the lake and have a drink in the Terra Nova.

Out in the street, it was bright and dazzling. Saturday's puddles were still everywhere, but all the car roofs had white threads like spiders' webs – the first frost of the year. I love to feel signs of changing weather in the air – cold and dry on my cheek today. But I still felt all that anger from yesterday – warming climate – November before frost found Cardiff.

I stopped to look at the tree eating the post box at the bottom of Rachel's street. Mam said the post box was Victorian – even older than Rachel's house. And suddenly, I was Rachel, opening the front door and needing my shock-stoppers, dazzled by the glinting sunlight on each leaf and cobweb. And feeling dizzy.

'Mam – Rachel – the light–'

And Mam's phone rang and I heard Rachel's voice. 'I've called 999 – can you get here?' And we were running.

I'm quicker than Mam, and when I got up to Rachel's house, she was convulsing on her doorstep, and a man was kneeling next to her, looking scared. 'Don't panic,' I said. 'It's epilepsy. She's called 999.'

'She shouted, then screamed. I thought she was being attacked. I'm from across the street.'

And I got my coat and he helped me get it under Rachel's head, but she was still thrashing around and her mouth was bleeding. And I remembered the timing thing. 'How long since it started?' I asked him.

'A minute at the most.'

And just as Mam turned up, Rachel went limp. I got the man to help me turn her on her side. Much harder than getting Shareen into the recovery position. 'She's breathing okay,' I said. But Mam was sort-of sagging in the doorway, all white. 'She'll be fine, Mam.'

'How do you…?'

'It's all normal.'

And Mam slipped down against the wall, like in a film. 'Oh, Mam!'

And now there was a woman from across the street. 'Rachel's okay,' I said. 'Can you help Mam? Glass of water, or something?' And Rachel's door was still open, so the woman went in and got water. And she sat with her arm around Mam, giving her sips of water, and Mam was shaking, still all white. And I had my arm around Rachel, still out of it, but breathing steadily. And then we heard the siren.

Alice is with you, Rachel. Do not be afraid.

Rachel

Pain. My head. Bright lights. Noises. Swaying. Siren.

'She's stirring.' A woman's voice – not one I know.

'Rachel, can you hear me? You've had a seizure.' Alice's voice.

I've had a seizure. This is an ambulance. My face: I'm wearing an oxygen mask. Okay.

I'm not afraid. Girl in Profile told me Alice was with me. Told me not to be afraid. And I'm not. I must have believed her. Or my hallucination of her.

Give up thinking it out – try speaking.

'I'm back,' comes out with a wobble.

'Phew!' Alice.

And another voice. 'She's been brilliant. Your daughter? She took charge. Take it easy now. The woman is following on. Had a bit of a turn.'

'Beth? What?'

'You've been unconscious a long time. Lucky we were just up the road.'

Ambulance stopping. Squeaky brakes. A&E entrance – yet again.

Alice? My daughter? Beth? Had a turn?

'Don't worry, Rachel. We'll sort it out when your brain's in gear. You're safe – Mam's okay.' Alice, telling me all I need to hear.

I'm rolling in on a trolley. And my head hurts. But Alice is with me and I'm safe. The next bit will be a long wait behind some curtains.

I didn't have to wait alone.

'Rachel, you are so WICKED, making Mam faint.'

'What happened?'

'We were down looking at that tree eating the post box, and then it was like I was you, opening the door and dazzled and dizzy and then you called Mam and we ran. And you were lying in the porch and this man helped and Mam came and she sort of sagged over in the doorway, all white.'

Granddad Joe appeared with his arm around Beth. 'There, you see. Rachel's fine.'

Beth dashed over, took my hands and looked me in the eyes. 'I thought you were dead.'

'The fuss I cause.'

'Alice checked your breathing, got you in the recovery position, did all the right things. I just sat there. The ambulance was double quick, but I don't know how long–'

'All sorted, Mam – I timed it.' Alice wrinkled her nose at Granddad Joe. My brain was too muddled to interpret that look, but he grinned.

And safely surrounded by the people I needed, I dozed off.

All three were still rooted by my side when I woke up. And I was more-or-less sensible – barring the usual hangover – when the duty doctor arrived. He discharged me on condition I checked in with Neurology next morning.

'Do you want to come over to ours?' Joe said.

'I'll be okay now.' I didn't manage much conviction.

'We could stay over with Rachel,' Beth said.

Someone to hold my hand. No – that wasn't fair. 'I've shocked you enough for one day. And you'll have things to do.'

'Don't be silly – we'll come over – it's what friends are for.'

Feeling smaller, I managed a guilty, 'You're okay to stay?'

'Yeah, we'll look after you,' Alice said.

'You'll have to be very quiet,' Beth said. 'Rachel will need a sleep.' She stroked my hair out of my eyes. 'We have sleeping bags.'

'No need. Cai kept the spare room made up. It'll need airing out. But are you sure?'

Joe stepped forward. 'She'll only worry more if you send her home.'

'So right!' Alice hugged her mother.

Here was I, unable to cope on my own and putting all the weight on Beth's shoulders. A woman with enough responsibility already. It wasn't fair, the way I kept disturbing her. And worse, Alice had needed to look after us both. What was I doing, letting them step in?

But as I thought of the alternative, of going home alone, I heard a distant echo of Dad's voice after a seizure. Many times, after many seizures. 'Nothing wrong with you, young lady. Don't think you can dodge school that way.' And I recalled the dizzying days that followed, sitting in class, unable to process the voices around me.

Once seizures were over, they were over, for him. More than twenty years too late, I had Alice and Beth to help me back into a functioning relationship with the world. But it felt wrong. I should not have been relying on them like this.

19

A KEY TO THE GATE

Alice

I got nervous stepping inside Rachel's house and hid behind Granddad in the kitchen. He waited with us until Nan turned up with a bag of our stuff for the night. Then they both went, and it was just us and Rachel. I couldn't hide behind Mam because I think she needed to hide behind me.

Rachel's house was as big as the gallery where Mam works. There was even a piano in the kitchen – A PIANO – and the kitchen was as big as our whole flat.

Rachel saw me staring and asked if I wanted a look around.

'We haven't got an upstairs. Can I see… upstairs?'

'Rachel needs a rest,' Mam said.

'Later,' Rachel said. 'Let's go exploring, Alice.' And I wondered whether the house might have other dimensions to explore, maybe in different universes. And whether I might need GPS to get around.

We left our bag in the small spare room at the front. Small equals bigger than our bedroom. Then we were in Rachel's room, and it was ma-hoo-sive – so big I could spin round in the middle. So I did. And it had a lovely bay window with a tree outside in the street and a blackbird looking in at us.

'My friend,' Rachel said. 'He sings to me.'

I wished and wished we could have a tree with a black-bird. No trees down our street.

On a shelf, I found a photo of a younger Rachel in a hard hat with hair right down to her bottom. She was standing inside a giant metal thing. 'Is that CERN?'

'It's the ATLAS detector, before it first ran. A student visit. I didn't know then that I would do some work there. You know, Alice, one of the other detectors–'

'A. L. I. C. E. I know. It means A Large Ion Collider Experiment.'

'I pity Miss Akoto,' Mam muttered. But I can't help knowing stuff.

Even the toilet was big enough to have old comic posters and a bookshelf – books to read while you poo! And next to it was a big bathroom with a shower, a bath, and a sink. We had one tiny room with a shower that got the floor wet and a sink and a toilet – and no room to get dry.

Mam went crazy over the bathroom, because Cai had decorated it like something out of a fairy tale. He'd painted stars on the ceiling and all the pipes were different colours. 'Pretend William Burges,' Rachel said. The man who turned Cardiff Castle and Castell Coch weird and special.

The back bedroom was locked. 'Still full of Cai's stuff – he's coming over to fetch it soon,' Rachel said. That made three bedrooms for one Rachel. We had one bedroom for two us. I was NOT going to get jealous, because Mam couldn't help it, but sometimes I hate Dad A LOT. And I'd missed a door. There was a smaller door, up one step, between the two big bedrooms. 'Cupboard?'

Rachel opened the door, and I could see dark stairs going up. She switched on a light. 'Have a look.'

Maybe I was right about another dimension. 'SCARY! You got a ghost?'

'They told me a housemaid lived up there. I'm sure she'd be a friendly ghost.'

'Like, with an apron?'

'Yes, over a hundred years ago.'

Rachel led us up the steep wooden stairs. Into the ROOF! There was wooden floor and roof all around us with sticky-out bits going into shadows. And a window, sloping with the roof. 'Best room in the WORLD,' I said, and couldn't help it – I lay flat on my back on the floorboards and spread out my arms like an angel.

'It's my favourite room, Alice. My playroom.'

'What's with the drawings?' Mam asked, pointing at some long strips of paper stuck to the one wall that went straight up-and-down. Little round cartoon people were dancing along, done in felt pen with lots of complicated lines between them.

'It's people for particles, isn't it?' I said.

Rachel stared at me for a moment. 'Good guess – it's the theory I burned out on.'

I wanted her to stop – now. I could hear her getting tense.

Not Mam. 'I love the flow of the drawings. Unfinished business?' Mam said.

Rachel swallowed. 'I've been looking again. It's the first time I've been back to it. It's not provable. I really was going loopy – or desperate.'

'You haven't left it behind, have you?'

'Mam!' I mouthed, and this time, Mam noticed.

'Sorry, Rachel.' Mam said 'Not good timing.'

'I will talk about it sometime,' Rachel said. 'Alice... Have a look in the housemaid's room: it's tiny.'

There was a little door I hadn't noticed, and I jumped up and ran, and—

CLANG!

I banged into a water tank. It was in a tiny room with a window in a bit that stuck out of the sloping roof.

'Careful!' Mam said, and she squeezed in next to me. 'Just enough room for a bed – imagine living here. I guess the tank came later.'

'The really old tank is above the bathroom, but this one's far from new,' Rachel said, slipping in so that the three of us had our backs against the tank.

'Look at this patch of wallpaper,' Mam said. 'This is old – original? It's beautiful – would they do that for a maid?' There were birds and flowers, like an old storybook.

'It could have been a child's room,' Rachel said. 'I thought of tracing the family – never got round to it.'

I turned into a girl from a century ago, in a long skirt. 'I'd love it,' I said. 'A little room in the roof. Cosy and private.' And Rachel smiled at me.

Mam wasn't listening – she was back at the window in the playroom. 'Your apple tree – it's lovely.' And then I knew there was more magic to find. I ran down lots and lots of stairs, through the kitchen with the piano and out of the back door.

It was getting dark, and the garden wasn't big or fancy. It had walls all round it and some straggly grass, but right in the middle was the BEST TREE IN THE WORLD, because it was real, and it was Rachel's tree.

I put my arms around the apple tree and listened to the trunk to find out what it would tell me. Rachel and Mam came down at adult speed – slow.

'You ate her apples – she told me.' I stroked the trunk.

'Well, you ate some of them in the apple puree Rachel gave us,' Mam said.

'I picked them in September,' Rachel said. 'Before the wasps could get to them.'

'She wanted to give me an apple.'

'There's still some apple crumble in the fridge.'

'Apple's more real.' I listened to the trunk again. 'Next one's mine – she says so.'

'They're not very sweet – better cooked,' Rachel said.

'When can I pick one?'

'Next September.'

My brain went FIZZ. Next September, I would be in a different world. 'That's AGES! I'll be in high school.'

Rachel put her hand against the tree trunk and stroked it. 'She needs time.'

'Why? Why so long?'

*

Rachel

Before I knew it, I was explaining the life cycle of the apple tree to a listener more receptive than any student I had taught. And as I described the smell and feel of a freshly picked apple, I realised how much wonder I was bursting to share.

Alice had been beaming at me, but her face took on a serious, wistful look. 'It won't be so exciting next year. This stuff gets boring in high school.'

And suddenly, I was in her shoes, ten years old and never wanting to grow up. Hating being the brightest kid in school.

At Alice's age, I'd known some of the chemistry that gave the apple tree its energy and already regretted the passing of a childhood I'd never really experienced.

'You saw my drawings upstairs. I know I said I haven't played much, but I do play all the time in my head. And you know I love a go on the swings. You don't have to grow up all at once.'

'Suppose so.' She didn't sound convinced, running her hand regretfully across the tree trunk. 'First apple's mine – remember!'

'I won't forget.' And there was no reason why Alice shouldn't witness the wonder of it growing. 'Does your flat have a garden?'

She shook her head. 'Just the bins and a load of junk.'

'There's a spare key to the gate from the back alley. You two could have it. We could share the garden.' And here was I, letting them further into my life when I should be discouraging them.

Alice plodded around the edge of the rectangle of grass, gave me a look that suggested I'd gone mad, then smiled and hugged Beth. 'You'll say yes?'

Beth beamed back at her. 'It's a lovely idea.'

One annoying, impulsive part of me was desperate to say more. To ask them to come and live with me here and fill this big empty house with new stories. But I would have needed to say more. To admit that I couldn't help loving everyone – everybody – so much that it hurt, but usually ended up ignoring people because I couldn't cope with more than one life.

Warning lights were flashing before the shock effect of my epilepsy came into the equation. I stuck to the reasonable. 'You can check on the tree each time you walk up to the park. Watch for the apples. They do take time to grow, but that makes them special.'

Alice went looking for bugs amongst the pile of old paving in the corner. 'Done mini-beasts at school.' The garden was her territory already.

Watching her explore set off poignant thoughts that translated into loneliness on all sorts of levels. Not just the feeling of being here, alone, but the absence of... Of me. I had been a fearless explorer until I burned out at Cambridge. Well, fearless in the tiny field that I wasn't scared stiff about. I'd done precious little exploring since I ran away.

And I didn't want Alice sent so far into retreat.

Beth caught my eye. 'Your key – I'll take it – it's a lovely idea for Alice. But promise you'll ask for it back if we disturb you.'

'I really don't want to impose my mess on you, Beth. Sorry – I've been deep in my shell. Thinking of how much hiding I've done.'

'Tell me about it. You're not the only one.'

'MAM!'

Alice's voice came from the house and we both rushed inside.

'Look!'

Beth was first into the front room and stopped with her hand over her mouth.

'What is it?' I called, trying to shake my foot free from the washing basket.

No answer. Something terrible.

I found Alice, beaming up at the painting above the mantelpiece. But Beth looked as if she'd seen a ghost.

'Shouldn't I have put her there?'

'No.' Beth wiped her hand down her face. 'Yes. I don't know. It's years since I've seen my work in... in a home, in someone else's life.'

Maybe she really had seen a ghost. I hadn't thought about the painting's significance for Beth. 'It's disturbing you. I'll take it down.'

'No, don't take her down. Keep her there. You've shared yourself – let us in. I haven't – not really.' Beth didn't look at me, and as she spoke, I felt Alice's fingers working their way into mine.

We left the painting in peace and retreated to the kitchen, where Beth made soup while I helped Alice with some research for school. It almost felt as if I was part of... No, stop it, Rachel.

After supper, I was weary in the extreme and my whole mouth ached from my struggle to keep the soup on the side of my tongue that wasn't bitten. And now Alice wanted another visit to the attic.

We took some beanbags upstairs and flopped in the playroom. I pointed out the few stars we could see through the dormer window. Each star's type, distance and absolute magnitude had been filed away in my memory since I was a teenager.

'Rachel's as crazy as you, Mam.' Alice pulled a gurning face. 'Let's do stories with the ghost!'

A housemaid's ghost seemed a safer presence than the voice that kept haunting me. We squeezed in next to the gurgling water tank, and I found enough reserves of energy to get Alice to imagine being a housemaid, long, long ago, staring down at the gas lamp outside her window and dreaming of an afternoon with her beau, a boat boy on the lake in the park where bands play in red uniforms and all the fine people walk.

Would he take her in one of his rowing boats? Then they could have tea for a penny or exotic sarsaparilla for tuppence. And maybe he would take her for a trip on the brand-new electric trams down Ninian Road. Or would that be too daring?

Alice didn't think so.

20

AN EMPTY HOUSE

Rachel

In the morning, I woke with a shock. A round face with dangly golden hair was hanging over me. A pair of blue eyes gleamed in the light from the landing.

'You're alive,' Alice informed me.

My tongue hurt where I'd chewed it, but my head was clear – not as if I'd had another seizure. 'Was I…?'

'Sleeping.'

'What time is it?'

'Dunno. Mam said too early.'

'So you woke me up.'

'I didn't mean…' Her wide-open face began to close off.

It takes forever, waiting for adults to wake up. A harsh voice echoed in the back of my mind. 'You bad girl, Rachel. Go and read your book.'

'Sorry,' emerged from Alice's squeezed-shut mouth. She turned away.

I checked the time – not all that early – nearly seven on a Monday morning. It was warm in bed, and I didn't have the energy to move. 'Your turn to tell a story, Alice.'

She was up on top of my duvet in an instant, where I introduced her to my rag doll and discovered Alice's talent for the surreal. Molly had superpowers: she could draw out my epilepsy and make anybody she chose have a seizure. Even Granddad Joe.

Alice's laughter grew louder and Beth appeared. 'We're doing stories, Mam!'

I backed up Alice with a smile. 'Sorry if we disturbed you.'

'Who got disturbed first?'

'Rachel,' Alice said. 'My fault.'

'But Molly's only ever had my stories. One from Alice is special.'

Sleepy Doctor R. S. Bothwell was cuddling a faded, inanimate stuffed toy as she spoke, winding many-times-replaced mustard coloured hair around her finger. And intelligent, witty, almost-eleven-year-old Alice had wormed her way under the duvet. Now she had her thumb in her mouth and would pass as a four-year-old.

Beth patted Alice, Molly and me on the head and went down to make some tea. And I felt a tinge of relief that I had resisted the urge to invite them to live here. Children are exhausting: it's a given fact of twenty-first century wisdom. Could I cope with this invasion, this disregard for boundaries, on a regular basis?

And now, Alice was asleep up close to me with one hand around Molly's waist. She had been awake, now she was asleep, and I had missed the in-between. If there had been one. And if I hadn't collapsed in the doorway and caused her mother to faint, I would have missed these magical moments with a sleeping child I cared for, deeply. Yes, deeply. She knew me at my weakest, cared for me and trusted me. And I cared for and trusted her.

Rachel, children are exhausting. Everyone says so. And you have NO experience of living with them. And you are a fool. And you deserve the scorn of every grown-up you know. What if the LA finance department could see you now?

But Beth's face in the morning looks exhausted and sad. I'm not the only one who has been worn down. And I want to help. The two of us could pull through together – if only I could stop shocking her.

I tussled to-and-fro beside sleeping Alice, worrying that this was about me, frightened of being alone. I decided that now was not the time to say anything.

Beth came to wake Alice for school, and a moan from Alice decided me. 'Why don't I walk you to school, Alice? We could give your mam breakfast in bed.'

'Deal!' Alice sprang out of bed, wide awake.

On the way down the road, I half expected an experienced mother to stop me and accuse me of being a childless professional, who had no right to take part in this ritual.

Alice put her hand on my arm before we reached the gate, and I stopped. 'Is Mam going with you to the hospital?'

'I don't want to upset her anymore, Alice. I'm used to visiting Neurology on my own – my doctor there's a friend. Julie, the one who loved your feedback.'

'Cool. Hospital freaks Mam. Should be me with you really.'

'You can look after me some other time. School matters, Alice.'

'Oh yeah?' She walked straight past that bunch of girls we'd seen and heard from the swings, navigated the crowded playground, and disappeared inside.

Heading home, I felt a new conflict. I'd seen Alice's

bruises months ago. And I hadn't told Beth I'd heard those girls call her Miss Akoto's pet. How much could I say without betraying Alice's trust?

I kept it simple. 'Does Alice have many friends?'

'I don't think so – not at school. I'm frightened she'll be lonely, but she never says. I really don't know how to help.'

'It isn't simple, is it?'

'She knows a few outside school. But even with friends' children, she gets teased because she's so bright.' Beth looked me in the eye. 'You must know that feeling.'

Oh yes. And I'd been wrong in thinking the two of us could pull through together. It was the three of us. But still, I felt too conflicted to say anything.

Beth had arranged for Joe to drive me to the hospital, but she didn't offer to come with me, and so I had no more awkwardness to navigate. She packed their bags and we didn't say much after that. It felt as if we had already crossed too many boundaries.

Joe dropped Beth off opposite a dark alley that led round behind a long terrace of Victorian workers' houses. I got out of the van and she gave me a quick hug, but I could feel her tension and got back in again. Guilty about my beautiful big house.

On the way to the hospital, I asked Joe. 'Is their flat alright?'

'Alright as dumps go. I've offered to help them find somewhere better, but Beth… She's as stubborn as Iestyn.' He shook his head.

That idea of giving them the key. What child would want to visit a little garden with one apple tree, a patch of grass, a lot of bare earth and a high stone wall all around it? Not every child, but maybe a child who hoped she had found someone who might understand and care for her mother.

And yet I could feel another barrier which had risen as soon as they saw the house. A barrier of privilege that made me so uncomfortable I really did not want to explore it. And one further barrier with consequences I had never thought about. The inequality of freedom. Alone and on a salary, I had freedom to dictate my own path, to a degree. Beth's life was constrained by the need to keep Alice alive, fed and happy.

Any offer of help to Beth would need to be secure, and to be framed in such a way that it gave her more freedom, not less. Did I feel that brave? And was it the responsible thing to do? I did have an empty garden. And an empty house. And an empty heart, for want of a precise neuroscientific description of that bundle of emotions, thoughts and regrets.

21

LITTLE THINGS

Alice

Monday was weird. I was at school and Rachel was at the hospital. And so was Shareen. She had a seizure in the middle of the morning, and for the second day in a row, I was down on the floor holding a convulsing human being. And the other kids laughed. Kids are evil.

I was only down with Shareen for a minute or two. Miss Akoto and the class helper took over, and then Shareen went in the ambulance and my head was scrambled and at break time, my eyes started leaking. Rachel calls it leaking.

I hid in the stationary cupboard, but the secretary found me, and it was dead embarrassing. She called Miss Akoto who took me in the quiet room. And I told her about Rachel, and even about knowing Rachel was having a fit before she called Mam.

Miss Akoto believed me. 'Your sensitive about that kind of thing, Alice. It's a gift. But if it upsets you, you need to talk about it. If you're dealing with it outside school as well, maybe let other people care for Shareen. It's not your job.'

'But Shareen... the others...'

'Sometimes you need to look after yourself. Protect yourself.'

And more tears came out because it felt like I was looking after everyone. Mam and Rachel and Shareen and even Dad. But I had to explain something. 'Rachel. She's a scientist, and she makes me feel… like I matter. Doesn't treat me like a kid. So, she's sort-of looking after me, too. It's okay to be me and know stuff when I'm with Rachel.'

'You have a lot of burdens to carry, Alice. You're sensitive and you're more intelligent than any ten-year-old I've taught. Don't pretend that's easy – I was like you, and it's tough. Tell me if you need time to yourself.' And she did something teachers don't do, and it helped. She put her arm around me, and it was like a tap turned on and so many tears came out that I wondered what my tear-capacity might be. And then she called Mam and Mam took me home early, and we got sticky buns, because.

On Tuesday, I got the full Evils. I was expecting it, and I got it. 'Cry baby' doesn't hurt me. Crying's fine if you've got tough stuff to face. And 'freak' is a badge of honour. What hurts is seeing the way the others follow the Evil Twins. The way the girls stop talking to me. Don't want to sit next to me. The way they never, ever sit next to Shareen. And Shareen doesn't want to sit next to me because that stirs them up. When she's here. Not today – Miss Akoto doesn't expect her back until next week.

I sat with Ossian behind Kamala and Jake all morning. The Evils hate Ossian and some of the boys do too, because he speaks Welsh at home. He doesn't like me much because of my brains, and I don't like him much because he smells, but he's safe.

At lunch time, Miss Akoto asked me about Rachel, and I said I didn't know. Rachel had gone months without a seizure since her big one in the park, and then, BANG. But her doctor hadn't found anything on her scans that wasn't normal. 'Normal weird Rachel-waves,' Rachel called them on the phone last night, but she sounded spooked. Like she didn't think it was normal at all.

And the twins saw me talking to Miss Akoto. I sat on my own all afternoon, being Miss Akoto's pet freak, and drawing cartoons of the Evils. Miss Akoto smiled, but I covered them up quick.

It was embarrassing walking out of school, because everyone was around and Mam AND Rachel were waiting for me. I just glanced at them and walked down the street towards Wellfield Road and the coffee bar, hoping no one had noticed. But I knew something big was wrong.

I didn't ask until we were sat down with our peppermint tea. 'Mam, you look like shit. What's happened?'

Mam looked awkward and glanced at Rachel.

'Mam?'

Rachel took over. 'We've been over at the hospital most of the day – I never seem to see the back of the place. But it wasn't me. Your Dad got taken to casualty.'

'Dad.' And I guessed the rest before Rachel said a word more.

'He's okay,' she said. 'But he's had some trouble. Got knocked about a bit.'

'Drugs, isn't it? Fucking IDIOT.'

Some woman turned round and Rachel raised her eyebrows, but she didn't lecture me on language.

'He's agreed to rehab – they'll help him. The dealer pinched his wallet, Iestyn chased him and got mugged. Your Mam and your Nan have had a tough day.'

'Rehab – again.' I stroked Mam's arm. 'Oh, Mam…'

Mam sighed. 'It's so hard to get angry with him. But Rachel did it for me. Stood up and told him he should consider his daughter. That shook him.' She smiled at Rachel. 'I've never seen Rachel so fiery. I think he might stick to the treatment, this time.'

'Channelling business Rachel,' Rachel said. 'I have to turn it on at work.' She shuddered. 'You know, Alice, you have the most amazing mother, bringing up such a special girl on her own.'

'Special?' I leant on Mam and poked my tongue out at Rachel. But my brain was doing a thousand-mile-an-hour thing where Mam had Rachel to deal with Dad, and we were all happy. But Rachel looked strained. Old, even. 'What about you? I know you're still chewing that ulcer on your tongue and pretending not to. But something bad's happened.'

'It doesn't matter.' Rachel was looking at her hands.

'Bad news on your epilepsy? It fucking well does matter.'

'Alice–' Mam said.

But Rachel shook her head. 'Okay – it's not epilepsy for a change. I called Beth this morning because I had a shock. We walked up to the lake to have a talk. We were having a coffee when Siân rang about Iestyn.'

'You had a shock.'

'My mother rang. She'd been having bad dreams. Remembering stuff about Dad that I had no idea about.'

'Bad stuff.'

'I knew he could be a pain, but for me it was little things. Lots of little things. I never imagined him to be a bad man. Mum's given me a different picture. And I had no… I can say it in front of you… I had no fucking idea what was going on.

I was just so, so naïve.'

'Little things. Miss Akoto told me little things add up. Today, she said it. Tell me your little things.'

'I don't know… The cuddles I never got. A smile would have kept me going – he hardly ever looked at me. And when he did, it was like… I don't know… Like I was something he'd trodden in by mistake.'

Mam joined in. 'Yet you didn't think he was a bad man.'

Rachel had her shoulders forward and her arms crossed tight, and I wanted to give her all those cuddles she had missed, but I knew they would never be enough.

'Dad was always busy,' she said. 'I sort-of put his behaviour down to that – always being too busy for me. And the way I never got real praise. It was always conditional – telling me what I could do next. Never just praise. I didn't have the guts to tell him how pressured I felt. And when I was older, I hated myself for being so weak. I never said anything.'

'If you can't stand up to someone powerful, it's no failure of yours,' Mam said.

'I took the easy option – cut Mum and Dad out of my life – both of them. Mum had an awful time, and I never even imagined it.'

Mam stood up and stroked Rachel's shoulders. 'It's not your fault. You were as much a victim as she was. And maybe the time will come when you can help your mam.'

Rachel looked like tears were coming, but instead, she smiled up at Mam and across at me.

'I'm here, Rachel,' Mam said. 'And I'm not planning on fainting over you again.' And that was the bravest thing to say. But I still hadn't told Rachel about Mam's father. And worse, I hadn't told Mam that I knew.

'Time for a go on the swings?' I said, but I couldn't look at Rachel.

'Hang on, that's two of us who've done the sharing,' Rachel said.

'Doesn't matter.' I had to hide my face.

'What did you say to me when I said that?'

'Fuck,' I whispered into her shoulder.

'Normally it's the adults who do the coping. I know I'm rubbish at it, but I was told it's in the job description. Share?'

'It doesn't matter like Dad or your dad or epilepsy.'

'Remember what you said about little things? Anything that upsets you matters to me, Alice. Because we're friends, and because you've looked after me, and because I trust you.'

And I told Rachel the whole story of having to hide in the cupboard yesterday and Mam having to fetch me. And the cry baby stuff today and sitting on my own and no one talking to me. But that wasn't quite true. Kamala and Jake turned round, and they both said to ignore the Evils, only they called them the Celebrity Fails. It felt like a small story to tell Rachel. But I am quite small.

Rachel didn't make a big fuss, but she said, 'You are one brave girl.'

And right then, I did feel brave, thinking of all the hurts Rachel and Mam had shared with me, and what Rachel had said about trusting me. I would cope with school because I had bigger stuff that mattered more. And then the three of us went on the swings, three hurt girls together. And I was proud of Mam and Rachel.

22

CHARCOAL

Rachel

I'd taken Monday and Tuesday off, but on Wednesday I had to face Tom's worried face. I told him about my unscheduled ambulance trip, but he gently dug out more. Mrs Jones had been hinting about an office romance – maybe she was right.

Alice and Beth were running Art Club in the evening, and I had no one to talk to when I got home – the painting just looked at me and no voice came to my rescue. Was I doing the right thing by getting closer to Beth and Alice? And how could I help Mum without stressing her further? Could I call her again, or would it be a mistake? I sat and stared at a mug of tea. It went cold on me and didn't even try to answer my questions.

Tom still had that concerned expression on Thursday, and I needed to hide in the washroom a couple of times to keep my composure. After work, I put off meeting Beth and Alice in the café with the lame excuse of a headache. And then on Friday morning, I had a direct call from Global HQ with the overnight news.

We had won the California contract, with a value in the billions, spread over five years. A major coup for the LA office, according to the U.S. headlines. They didn't mention

149

that the bonus would be shared between two consultants in Wales. My nice shiny figures had stacked up perfectly where other bids hadn't.

I felt deflated. I didn't want this attention, or a bonus for winning a corporate game of chess. Our corporation was no more deserving than any of the others. Tom was all over me, and everyone in the office was excited bar Ian, the manager, who gave me a withering look. Even Tom's smaller bonus was beyond anything he might expect.

By lunchtime, I needed to get out, and headed straight for the gallery. I asked Graham not to mention the sale. Beth could find out on Sunday, leaving me two days to feel guilty over my bonus without any need to talk about it. I chose the two brightest paintings and they would be delivered to my office on Monday. The dreary grey picture of the corporate HQ on the wall above the printer could go and disinfect the men's washroom.

I dozed at my computer terminal after lunch. Mrs Jones's hand touched my shoulder and an Americano appeared, but I was running on empty.

Out in the lobby, I met Tom. 'Been out for a breather,' he said. 'It's got a bit–'

'I know. I'm finished. Off home.'

'You're ever so pale, Rachel. I could take you.'

'No, I… I…'

Stupid woman, get some words out.

'I need to walk…air…'

'Air. There's none in here. You look after yourself.' He took my hand, looked into my eyes, and I felt ready to burst into tears. I nodded and turned tail.

Fucking it up, again.

Tom? Really, Rachel?

I didn't know – couldn't know – confusion had taken over. And I loathed this Rachel who couldn't face another human being without... Forget it.

I stomped up City Road past shop after shop. The exotic new restaurant with the not-so-exotic pile of rubbish bags. The scruffy little electrician's, unchanged since the shop-keeper first dreamed his dream in the seventies. The brash new shop with a vibrant purple sign and nothing at all in the window: www.we-sell-or-go-bust? The whole of City Road was one United Nations of getting-by, and as I passed each little shop, I carried the knowledge that I could walk in and write off the owner's debts with the money I had earned in one single day.

Another Rachel to loathe. This one in her expensive boots, marching up the street with so much unfairness in her pocket.

Text from Beth.

> You still not good?

> > Managing – work a bit
> > complicated. Will call.

Tom would have given me a lift, and just to prove I'd been stupid, it rained. Gusts of the wettest Welsh rain chased me past the infinitely extended terraces of Mackintosh Place, but I never seemed to get any further. The far end was dwindling into a haze in some other state of reality, and my house was in the next universe after that. Surely this was the purgatory I deserved.

At last, I squelched my way into the front hall, peeled off my saturated coat and let it fall. I headed for the front room, saluted the painting, told her I was springing a couple of her sisters from jail; told her I might be in love with Tom, which was fucking stupid; told her I'd earned too much money today and felt shitting guilty, and asked her why she never got around to hanging up my coat for me. Then I struggled out of my boots and crashed out on the sofa.

A phone started ringing, somewhere behind shabby brown curtains. Then it fell into a cloud of fundamental particles where I couldn't plot its location or velocity. And then the phone was real, it was in my bag out in the hall, and it stopped.

Friday. It's still Friday.

Tom. Shit. SHIT! What if it is love? You'll be a jelly when you next see him.

Bonus. Shit. Well, sort-of-shit with icing and candles and a party. Shit, really: you'll never cope with the guilt.

Now. Now? The nowness of now had reached six thirty, my stomach ached, I was cold and stiff, my office tights were still damp and greyness was penetrating every cell of my body. Maybe it was the greyness of my monetary achievement. Wind and rain rattled the windows, and flashes from car headlights threw shadows across the wall. Phone – my phone had woken me.

Warming up on the floor in front of the pretending coal fire, I dug out my phone and called Beth back.

She sounded hesitant. 'I haven't seen you. Are you…?'

'Sorry, I've been a bit…' A bit what? I wasn't sure.

'Will you make it to class?'

'Yes, yes, YES! I might be late.'

'Are you sure you're alright?'

'Alright enough to get there. I'll tell you later.' I didn't want to own up to anything. Not, NOT my confusion over Tom. And not my bonus. It wasn't massive by big business standards, but by anyone else's, it was a hefty chunk of money.

Beth brought me back to the here and now. 'Stanley has volunteered. He kept his clothes on last time, but he was talking about you. We might get the full Stanley.'

The full Stanley – I liked that idea. But he was a lovely man who earned a fraction of my salary. Was I even worthy to view him naked? I had already missed the bus, called a taxi, and raced to change out of my damp clothes and clinging tights that seemed determined to topple me. I finally got them off laid on my back on the floor.

I was last to walk into the studio, drawing the eyes of that select group of people who knew me naked. Morwenna seemed curious, maybe contemplating where I'd hidden all those curves. I would have been happy to show her, if that were the extent of her interest, and half expected a quiet invitation afterwards.

Stanley emerged in the white robe, looking sheepish. Someone murmured, 'Surely not?' My solidarity was needed, and I smiled and raise two clenched fists.

Stanley returned my salute and disrobed. I smothered my, 'Yes!' and guessed that Beth was doing the same.

There was a blank sheet of paper in front of me. I had a soft pencil.

Rachel, you can do this. Well.

I looked at Stanley, a treasury of subtle curves. I delineated a Stanley-space on my paper. This time, it was one long pose, and I gave his torso and limbs weight and substance. I felt engaged with his presence in a way I never had in my cartoon days. As if Stanley was the artist and I was merely expressing him. The deepest immersion I had yet felt into Beth's world.

While Stanley and Beth had a break upstairs, I went down with the others and let Morwenna lecture me as I sipped from a cardboard cup of cardboard-tasting hot chocolate. She thought I had promise, although I wasn't sure whether she was referring to my sketches or my personal proportions. Feeling bolder, I touched her hand. 'Thank you for talking,' I met her eyes. 'I have a lot of listening to catch up on.'

She looked startled for a moment, but nodded. A lonely woman peeked out from behind her severe mask.

Part two: in which Rachel discovers charcoal.

Charcoal LOVES me. Charcoal loves my hands, my face, my pale top, and the floor beneath my feet. Some of it gets on the paper. And I love charcoal.

Smoothed out with my fingers, my charcoal Stanley looked like one of the ash casts from Pompeii. And Beth was beaming over my shoulder. 'Yes, Rachel – be playful!'

I gave Stanley another pair of raised fists. He smiled back. He was even looking comfortable. And then playtime was over until next week. I washed my hands and grubby face, blackening the sink in the process, and returned for a quick word with Beth. But Stanley had her deep in conversation, just as he had most weeks.

Beth called to me over Stanley's shoulder. 'Alice is desperate to see you.'

And I needed a dose of Alice to drive away the confusion. 'Tomorrow's fine.'

I'd reached the bus stop by the time I notice my cold neck. Scarf. It had stopped raining and the next bus wasn't due for ten minutes. The downstairs lights of the community centre were off when I got back, but a light shone from the landing. I headed upstairs, but hesitated. Stanley had kept on staying behind after the class. What if Stanley and Beth were a couple? Coupling?

Not now they weren't. Beth was talking in a steady voice. Could this be jealousy I was feeling? I walked on up more cautiously, and through the open door I saw Stanley sitting with his head on a table, arms thrown out in front of him. Weeping. A sight so unexpected, I stood and gawped.

Beth was sitting with her hand on his shoulder. She looked up, but made no move to shoo me away. 'Stanley, Rachel is here. And I really must catch that bus.'

He sat up and wiped his eyes.

'I didn't mean to interrupt… My scarf.' I grabbed it from the peg in the corner.

'Stanley has a lot to face,' Beth said. 'We talk most weeks.'

'Lifesaver,' he croaked. 'Must go.' Cold, sweaty fingers grasped mine for a moment and then he dashed out and disappeared into the night.

Beth collapsed against the wall. 'He needs a mother. And he needs a life, for God's sake.' She let out a long breath. 'Every week the same. He's fine in class. Keeps up the front. Then he just falls to pieces. It's exhausting, but I can't say no.'

'I should have knocked.'

'No, I struggle to get away from him. We've been here an hour before now.'

'What's it all about?'

'He wouldn't want me to say. But his problems are real, and none of his doing.'

Her face showed the careworn look I had seen in the early morning light on Monday, and I wasn't ready for my response of overwhelming sorrow, almost grief. I pulled her into the most secure hug I could manage. Awkwardly. I'd had no training in giving comfort and possessed no certificate to assure me that I could do this. Or was worthy to. And I was hardly tall enough.

'You can't look after everyone,' I said, kissing the side of her neck through a muddle of hair. The presence and feel and smell of her body up close unnerved me. But here and now, I was the only comfort she had.

Beth put her arms around my waist and clung on. 'How could I say no?' she said. 'I'm a bad mother to Alice and not enough for Stanley or you or anyone.'

'Right, so you're absolute crap. Let it all out before I tell you how fucking wonderful you are.'

I felt her heave and her tears flowed down my neck. 'Christ, I'm stupid. I'm a fucking stupid, fucking mess.' She leant back in my arms and a gentle smile lit up her eyes. 'You managing?'

I nodded. Yes, I really was managing. Coping with her trust. 'You're safe,' I said.

'Shit! The bus. I promised the babysitter's mother I wouldn't be late.'

I pulled her close again. 'No worries, I'll call a taxi.'

'Costs a fortune.'

'My treat. Look at the state of you.' And I held her until the taxi arrived.

When we reached Beth's flat, I was tempted to get out, pay off the taxi and wing it from there. I could have solved a lot of her problems and Alice's problems with a single bank transfer. But I didn't have the confidence.

Maybe she sensed my wavering intention. 'See you in the morning,' she said, firmly. 'Granddad's place, probably, but I'll give you a call.'

I let the taxi whisk me home and stood outside in the porch for a while, listening to the night. Back in my own little universe, where I was free to punish myself with self-destructive urges because I wasn't worrying about Alice's next meal or the state of the washing. I could afford to be introspective. Hell, I could afford a counsellor, an analyst and a personal trainer.

23

BEAUTIFUL BROTHER

Alice

Granddad had his mates in the workshop on Saturday morning, getting ready for a model engineering show. We decided to keep out of the way and went to visit some friends in the museum instead.

Girl in a Green Dress didn't want to know. 'She's in a mood again,' I said.

'Well, don't talk about her and stare, then,' Rachel said, and Mam smiled.

Girl in Profile might just have given us a glance. Rachel stood in front of her, looking at something I couldn't see on the wall above her. And her face went peaceful, as if she had no worries in the world.

Mam called her across the gallery to see Jacob Epstein's wild sculpture of the head of Augustus John – bad timing – Rachel was in the middle of something. I gave Girl in Profile a smile and said sorry. And she looked sad.

When Rachel came back, I said Girl in Profile was sad to see her turn away.

She looked at that spot on the wall above the painting again. 'I didn't mean to go so suddenly, Mathilde.'

So… Rachel knew her name. Mathilde?

Rachel was smiling with the painting, and I didn't want to disturb them.

I waited for a while and then whispered, 'How do you know her name?'

Rachel looked a bit shaken. 'I… I haven't a clue. It's… as if I'd glanced at you and registered "Alice" as your name. As if I already knew Mathilde.'

'I guess so – I knew she was sad. Maybe she's happy you know her name.' I did the looking not-quite-at Mathilde, just like Rachel had done. And I whispered, 'Hello, I'm Alice.'

And I felt a smile in the air. *I know. I've known you a long time.*

I took Rachel's hand, and we shared Mathilde's smiley feeling. No one else need know Mathilde's name. Maybe Mam, but not yet – she was off looking at something else. We stayed for ages with Mathilde, not exactly looking, but paying her attention. And by the time Mam came back from the next gallery, I knew Mathilde was one of us.

Girl in a Green Dress might just have looked up as we left the gallery, but I didn't push my luck, didn't ask her name and whispered, 'Sorry I was rude.'

We walked down to town with me in the middle, and I didn't mind being the kid with Rachel and Mam. Rachel wasn't exactly panicking this time, but she kept poking the back of her head. I didn't say anything.

Next stop, the toast café in the market. Rachel and Mam sat down and I went to get our order. Then I saw Rachel jerk back a bit and stare at a big man with his back to us, along at the other end of the counter. Maybe she was creeped by the way he was leaning over a pretty teenager's shoulder.

The girl had long dark hair like Rachel's and looked half the man's age. What was he doing?

'Who's that you're staring at?' Mam said.

Rachel had her hand at her throat. 'Um, it's Tom from work. He's…'

And from over by the serving hatch, I suddenly saw what he was doing, and went and whispered in Rachel's ear. 'He's cutting up her beans on toast.'

He was helping her hold the fork still and prompting her to cut with the knife. Her face was screwed up with concentration. Then she smiled up at him, and bright blue eyes peeped out from under her dark fringe. 'That's better, best Tom.'

I knew that kind of voice. A loud adult's voice with a kid's lift on the last couple of words.

Rachel still looked bothered, but Tom turned and noticed her. 'Rachel – fancy meeting you here!'

She stuck a smile on her face. 'Hi, Tom.' I knew why she called him a pirate. He looked like that wild sculpture of Augustus John and had a grin a mile wide.

'We love the market,' I said.

'Emily does too. We spend hours here, people watching.' He turned to the girl. 'Emmy, this is Rachel from work – and her friends.'

She got up, walked round Tom, looked at us for a second, and turned shyly away. 'Nice name,' she whispered. 'Rachel.'

'Emily's a nice name,' Rachel said.

'Nah, Emmy. Em-i-ly's boring.'

'Emmy.'

'My little sister,' Tom said.

'Not little!'

'My beautiful sister, then.'

'Me. Got beautiful blue eyes.' She was telling the truth: she had eyes like the sky on a summer's day. 'Got beautiful brother too.' Also true. I'd never met a man so wild and romantic in my life, ever.

Emmy smiled at me. 'You got blue eyes, little girl.'

'I'm Alice.'

'Alice. Nice.' She went to Rachel and leaned over to look closely. 'You got brown eyes. You got learning 'bility like me?'

Rachel looked helpless, but I'd had questions like that before. 'Me and Rachel have the same learning disability, Emmy. Too much learning stuffing up our heads.'

Tom laughed, a deep pirate laugh that would have crossed a ship in a storm. 'All that learning comes in handy at work – when she isn't in dreamland.'

'Tom!' Rachel went red.

'You 'barrassed?' Emmy said.

'Dead right, Emmy,' I said.

'Looks like you two are friends already,' Tom said to me.

'I know a few people Emmy would get on with.'

'Ah – previous.' Tom turned to Mam. 'You must be the artist Rachel talks about.'

'I'm Beth – Alice's mam. Rachel says you used to work at sea.'

'Container ships. These few months are the longest I've been in one place for years. It takes a bit of getting used to. I'm making up for lost time with Emmy. We've hardly seen each other since she was a kid.'

'Best Tom,' Emmy said, smiling up at him.

'I should have been back sooner, Em.'

'Does Emmy live with you?' Mam said.

Tom shook his head. 'Em's still with Mam. It's a headache – I should have stepped in years ago. Mam treats her like a little girl. It's not good for either of them.'

Emmy screwed up her face and crouched down beside the bar. 'Be good girl, Em-i-ly.' She clenched her fists.

Tom stood up, his face almost scared, but I knew the signs. Time to use my superpower. 'What do you like best in here, Emmy?' I waved my hand around the market stalls.

She relaxed her fists, stood up and stepped closer. 'Funny man by there.'

'Elvis? Mam talks to him.'

'Yeah, and the fish.'

I did a fish face and Emmy laughed. 'You funny girl best.'

'I like the sweet stall down at the other end. The one with Turkish delight.' I made a munching face. 'Yum!'

'Yum best!' She stepped closer again, just a pace away, up above me.

'And the doughnuts from down by there.'

'Yum, yum, YUM!' Emmy licked her lips and smiled down at me.

*

Rachel

Tom gave Beth an anxious look. 'Alice needs to move. Em can be explosive. She's not used to kids.'

'Trust me – Alice knows what she's doing,' Beth said. 'She helps me run special needs art sessions – just watch.'

And watch we did. Not for the first time, I was in awe of

this small girl. Having distracted Emmy, Alice was steering but not dominating the conversation. She let Emmy echo her words and add in a phrase or two of her own here and there.

Soon, Emmy had her arm around Alice's shoulders. Her fidgety, excited body language showed up Alice's maturity. I wondered how Emmy coped amongst strangers.

'I can see your mind ticking,' Beth said. 'Haven't you met anyone like Emmy?'

'Not to talk to.' I turned to Tom. 'How old is she?'

'Emmy confuses everyone – herself, mainly. She's thirty-five.'

That took some absorbing: even her skin and hair were childlike. 'She looks sixteen – younger.'

'Men can be a problem, but Emmy's had years of experience dealing with them. Poking a finger up her nose and showing them bogies works.'

'I must try that.'

Emmy was back finishing her plate of beans with Alice for company, but Tom was anxious to get her home 'before we have a bathroom issue.' He glanced at me. 'Unless you could help.'

'No problem.' I took instruction on escorting her to the toilet. All I needed to do was make sure she closed the door behind her and washed her hands, but I felt almost like one of those grown-ups who help other people without thinking.

Beth nudged me when we got back. 'Pushing your comfort zone? I would have taken Emmy.'

I wanted to hit her. 'I do have a few social skills.'

Tom gave the warmest of smiles. 'No one doubts that, but you must admit you need the odd bit of looking-after.' His obvious sincerity washed away my annoyance.

While Alice and Emmy had a nose around the balcony, the three of us trailed behind. I told Beth how much help Tom had been, and about being too embarrassed to accept a lift yesterday. I told Tom how friendship with Beth and Alice kept on surprising me. And I admitted my relief at finding two friends who understood that Emmy wasn't the only one who couldn't always manage the grown-up thing.

'Just hang on to your sense of wonder,' Tom said. 'Growing up is overrated.'

Alice had an afternoon workshop to get to, and Tom took a photo of her with Emmy to print off for Emmy later. I hesitated. Tom knew well enough that I wasn't needed at work after yesterday's adventure. 'Coming round the arcades?' he said, and Emmy linked her arm through mine.

Alice wrinkled her nose at me. Beth tipped her head.

'Come on then, Emmy,' I said.

Did I show my embarrassment? Probably, but I tried not to care.

The old arcades always spark my imagination, walking in the footsteps of the first owners of my house, with their maid trailing behind them. Elegant Royal Arcade first, with its lanterns, boutiques and faux-period hanging signs.

Emmy was entranced by a gorgeous window display and stood arm-in-arm with her big brother. I could picture an Edwardian Tom with a straw boater, huge moustache, and stripy blazer. Emmy might have had a frayed straw bonnet, with ribbons trailing loose and her fine dark hair flowing free. A perfect Renoir portrait, probably in a smock that had seen better days on one of her elder sisters. Perhaps Rachel, the sister who longed for an education, never married, and came to a sad end.

I wondered further about this imagined Emmy. Would her family have cherished the simple girl who never grew up? Or did an upstanding and virtuous magistrate place her in the new asylum at Whitchurch, where she would soon forget her own name? Equally probable was a history of abuse by assorted men and then death in childbirth. It must have been a matter of chance for a woman like Emmy.

Window shopping was clearly Emmy's joy – she seemed to have no interest in buying anything. Or was it that her mother had never given her the opportunity to buy for herself? I began to wonder whether Emmy had enjoyed any freedom at all. Tom pointed up at a fluorescent blue balloon, trapped in the ornate ironwork of the arcade's glass roof. Emmy pulled a tragic face. 'Poor balloon. Poor kid.'

Out in St Mary Street, the sudden bright light dazzled me and seizure-response took over as I flinched away and lost orientation. Emmy took my arm. 'Me got you.' And stability came back at once. She gently led me into the dark, homely safety of Morgan Arcade. I hadn't needed to say a word.

My favourite coffee shop was just where the arcade branched. 'My treat, Emmy.'

'Real?' She beamed at me. 'And cake?'

'Mam's not looking,' Tom said.

'And cake.' I said.

And while we enjoyed our cakes, I told them about Edwardian Emmy and Tom and their maid Rachel, going home from shopping in their pony and trap.

'Real?' Emmy's eyes were round with wonder.

'They might have done. It's a story, Emmy.'

'Best story. Tom does best stories.'

He looked down at his hands and adjusted his cuffs with

a wistful expression. 'You've got a good memory. That was a very long time ago.'

I nudged him. 'We all need stories. It's time you did some remembering.'

Emmy and I wandered along The Hayes holding hands, and I felt her satisfied smile seeping into me. Cake, the great solution to all woes.

I let Tom drive me home and multiplying my daring, invited them in. But Tom had kept Emmy out a long time, and their mother would be imagining catastrophes. 'Just a little look.' And now Emmy knew where I kept my secret stash of chocolate.

When they left, she gave me a shy, gentle hug, and I hugged her back. 'Thank you for looking after me, Emmy.'

I felt a sudden warmth from Mathilde, but no words. I knew what she meant. I'd trusted Emmy to care for me when I felt dizzy. How many people trusted Emmy? Trust could be the greatest gift I could possibly give her. Trust. I'd never trusted many people, but life seemed to be changing.

Tom looked at his sister thoughtfully. 'You're privileged, Rachel. Emmy only ever hugs the right people. She has other ways of knowing.'

'Doctor Richards?' I said, reaching for a hug. A sisterly hug, I hoped. I have other ways of knowing too, but mine get muddled up.

I found a text from Beth after they had gone.

> Ask him to come and
> pose for us.

> Ask him yourself.

24

FLAVOUR OF THE MONTH

Alice

Another Sunday in the gallery with Mam. I was going to stay at Nan and Granddad's, but one of his mates was back from a hip operation, and they'd gone over there to help out. This time, I took my sketchbook to draw some pictures for Emmy. Tom had said she liked birds. So did I, but I'd never spent much time drawing them.

I turned the display lights on while Mam sorted the alarm, and then she went to the till and picked up a couple of notes. She put her hand over her mouth and sat down.

'What is it?'

'RACHEL. The silly, silly bugger.'

'She's…? More pictures?'

'It must be her. There's been a run. They're displaying them all again. I can't… I've got nothing new. Oh God…'

Then Rachel was at the front door. It was still locked, and I undid the bolts, turned round the OPEN sign and let her in.

Mam got up and held out the note like a clue to a murder. 'This is your doing, isn't it?'

'I bought the pair of them to sneak some colour into the office,' Rachel said.

'Pair? Five have gone.'

'That's three new sales – brilliant!'

'I don't know. I'm not ready for this.'

'Mam – we need the money,' I said.

'I know, love. But last time I sold so many… It's complicated. Let's go and look – they've displayed the rest. The note's from James – that's odd – he's hands-off most of the time. Leaves it to Graham.'

Mam led us up to the front gallery. Five big pictures, all by Mam and painted when I was small. And now they were on display with no other pictures in there at all. There was a biography of Mam I'd seen before and a photo from years ago. Pure Bethany Howells, where she should be, in the main gallery.

Rachel looked at the label beside one of them and gasped. 'That's three times what I paid on Friday!'

Mam just shook her head. 'This is what happens when a buyer with influence shows up. I'm really not ready for it.' She leant on Rachel like she needed a crutch.

I had a quick look round the other rooms and soon found the rest. She was still leaning on Rachel when I got back. 'Mam, the small ones are in the top floor gallery. They've got it to themselves. And James has reserved four for his private collection.'

Rachel had her arm around her. 'Are you okay?'

'Just a shock.'

We headed back down to the front desk, and Mam didn't look happy at all. I would have been over the moon.

Rachel sounded guilty when she explained why she'd bought her pictures. 'We won the contract on Friday, and it felt… I wasn't proud of it. It was just a job, and I got a big bonus I didn't want. I guess I needed something of you in the office. Something from the world that matters to me.'

Mam shook her head. 'I suppose it's a nice problem to have, but they'll be asking for more and I've nothing. At least I can finish paying my debts and save Iestyn another guilt trip.'

A nice problem. I didn't like Mam's fixed grin. 'Rachel wouldn't want to upset you, Mam.'

'No, I know that. You were only a baby last time it happened, Alice – you wouldn't know. I've been here before – flavour of the month. They always want more than you can give, and they want it yesterday. This time, there's nothing left, so they can't have it.' She sat back on the table.

'Mam?'

'I had to keep churning out pictures, Iestyn wasn't around, and I ended up painting rubbish. Then the bad reviews started, and the sales stopped, overnight. I had a small baby. I was on my own.'

'Oh, Mam.' I ran and hugged her.

'I am just so stupid,' Rachel said. 'Not thinking through the consequences.' She sagged against the wall and her face went white.

Mam stood up and held her by the arms. 'What's going on in your head? You look petrified. None of this is your fault. None of it. It's the way the market works.'

'I'm...'

'Come out the back and we'll have a cup of tea.'

Mam nodded towards the door and I turned the sign to closed and bolted it. Mam led Rachel through to the kitchen and I could see Rachel beginning to shake. I knew what was happening and ran after them. 'Mam, get her down on the floor!'

And then Rachel was convulsing in Mam's arms and

I was holding Mam and telling her not to panic and then Rachel relaxed. Just a little one.

Rachel blinked a few times and said, 'oh.' Then she did it again. Blink – blink – blink – 'oh.' And again. And then she was properly back. 'Sorry. Been long?'

'Seemed forever,' Mam said, and I could see her shaking. 'No, a few seconds. God, Rachel, I thought you'd gone. Is it over?'

'Yeah, no panic. I'll be fine.'

I would have said the same, just to calm Mam down.

'No fucking panic?' Mam shook her head. 'Did you feel it coming?'

Rachel took a few breaths, and I could see her counting with her lips. 'Only just. I was in too much of a tizz.'

'It wasn't worth you getting upset, Rachel. I'm simply going to have to paint some pictures. It's what I do, if you haven't noticed. And NOTHING is worth you having a seizure like that.'

'Sorry, Beth. The seizure would have come along anyway. Just bad timing – it usually is.'

I helped Rachel sit up and sit away from Mam, getting her back against the kitchen unit. 'Mam, all this panic started with you, not Rachel. You talked about what happened before – not how it felt.'

Mam grunted. 'Why did you choose a therapist for a mother?' She shook her head, ignored the chance I'd given her and concentrated on Rachel. 'At least your colour's coming back. You stay down there.' Mam clambered up and filled the kettle.

'Mam, you've been keeping it all inside. Hiding it from me as well as from Rachel. I can cope.'

'Alice, it's not anything I can explain. Some things are deeper than that.'

Rachel swapped a glance with me. 'Alice is right, Beth. If you can't find the words – if it's too difficult – I'm here to pick up the pieces.' She grinned. 'Here on the floor – best place, I suppose.'

'This milk is gross.' Mam emptied it down the sink. 'I'm shutting up for the day. They've made enough out of me this weekend. Do you need a taxi?'

Rachel scrambled up off the floor, and I held her arm just in case. 'I'll be fine now – let's go and get a coffee,' she said. And I held her arm all the way up to Wellfield Road.

Mam still hadn't really talked, but now I was more bothered about Rachel. She kept fidgeting around as she sat with her coffee.

'You're having another one, aren't you?'

'Not now. These twinges and twitches are part of the pattern. I get them a week or so before the full works.'

'You were all twitchy yesterday in town. You're worse today.'

'It just happens. A prolonged seizure will come along, I'll get my scary aura, and I'll go out, big time. I'll have a hangover and a bitten tongue, and all will be fine again.'

Mam shook her head. 'I was scared out of my mind and I wasn't having the seizure. If you have one, you'll manage to get safe?'

'At least five minutes warning before a really big one – sometimes twenty. I had time to get out into the porch, call 999 and call you last time. It hurt you more than it hurt me.'

'I'll get used to it – am doing. How did Cai cope? And your parents?'

'Cai was better at medical stuff than anything involving emotions. He was an NHS volunteer during lockdown. We had to divide the house in half to keep me safe.'

'God, Rachel–'

'It worked. But Dad was something else – he never stopped going on about it, even when I'd been kept in coma for days. Telling me it was all a state of mind. That it would go away with positive thinking – his top cure for everything. Oh, and he kept on about it being "a weakness" in Mum's family. I think one great uncle had it.'

'And your mam?'

Rachel twisted her coffee cup around. 'We've never really talked about it. Mum had to deal with me and she had to deal with Dad's demands. Which were evil, and I never guessed. Or never tried. I've been blocking Mum out, haven't I?'

'You've needed to survive. Maybe now we could shift a few nightmares together.' Mam looked at me. 'But I'd prefer it without the junior therapist putting me on the spot.'

I knew more about Mam's nightmares than I could let on, from talking to Dad and Nan. This time, I pretended to be a kid not listening and balanced a table mat on edge. And kicked myself for taking the easy way out.

25

LIAR

Rachel

On Monday, Tom presented me with a drawing from Emmy. Three round bodies with an assortment of stick limbs and big smiley faces – Beth and Alice and me. All my confusion over Tom had evaporated: he was a firm friend with a lovely sister who had treated me as her bestie from the moment we met. Did Emmy treat everyone as her bestie? Tom seemed surprised we'd made any connection at all, and so probably not.

I made a quick lunchtime visit to Mathilde, only to find the museum closed on Mondays. I'd wanted to check whether the impression I'd had of her name stayed firm. Yes, even standing outside in Park Place imagining the paintings in an empty, silent gallery, I knew that Girl in Profile truly was Mathilde, the same person who had spoken to me at home. And that Girl in a Green Dress preferred to remain anonymous.

On Tuesday, I had another of those small seizures, this time at work, with Tom to look after me and Mrs Jones to panic. Two in three days was a bit over-the-top, and I mentioned it to Julie as we were packing up after orchestra in the evening. 'Cellist increases drug regime' would make a nice headline. Two, three times a day.

On Wednesday, I didn't even feel a twinge, but needed a long phone call with Beth to steady myself. The clock was ticking. She understood and kept the conversation focussed on Alice, who wanted Joe to drive her to a climate change demo at the Senedd on Saturday.

Beth thought a ten-year-old might get in the way of the teenage activists, but I said I would go along in solidarity – it was time I stood up for my beliefs. And if I had a seizure on the steps of the Senedd, there would be plenty of people to look after me.

One day at a time. On Thursday, I had a few twinges but no seizures. Beth and Alice met me in the café and walked home with me, curious to meet Cai and Isabelle, my evening's romantic visitors, over here tying up loose ends before settling permanently in New York. Yes, they were a couple now and I didn't even feel jealous. My life had changed beyond recognition in the few months since Cai had left.

Alice avoided their delicate round of pecked cheeks and ran upstairs. There was one room in the house she had never seen. A locked room is a thing of wonder, and I handed Cai the key.

'Let's check what's left to shift,' he said, ushering Isabelle upstairs.

Beth and I followed, and Alice slipped through as Cai unlocked the door.

Isabelle stepped back, looking at Alice as if she were another species. The look I might have given her a few months ago. 'Isabelle, there's a cello-no-it's-a-bass in here! Isabelle, he's got COMICS and Rachel never said. Isabelle...'

Isabelle took another dazed step backwards and Beth intervened. 'Alice, why don't you put the kettle on, so that Rachel can talk to her friends.'

Alice grew up twenty years and asked Isabelle whether she might prefer green tea, black tea or maybe a herb tea. And Isabelle's daze increased.

Cai gave me an anxious look. I returned it. What next? I was their host: it was up to me. Polite tea and chat? I would never manage, but I couldn't just chuck them out. 'Isabelle, I've never heard you play the piano...?'

Beth touched my arm and picked up on the suggestion with an encouraging smile. 'And Alice has never heard you play, Rachel.'

After a deafening silence that can't have been more than a second long, Isabelle took the bait. 'I could accompany you, maybe.' She sounded as awkward as me.

'There's a fair-sized pile of music on the piano,' I stuttered, leading them down to the old piano in the long kitchen-diner. Beth handed me my violin case with a nod towards Alice, who now sat cross-legged on top of a stool, like an expectant Buddha.

No turning back. I got tuning and Isabelle rooted through the piles of music. An album of French miniatures came out. Safe, and not too challenging.

'I haven't played these for years – haven't had a pianist around,' I said. Maybe not a pianist, but I knew the feel of a very good bass player's gentle embrace. And Alice was waiting.

Isabelle played a few figures, getting used to the touch of the upright piano the previous householder had left behind, unwanted. She smiled at me, and we eased into the caresses of Fauré's gentle Berceuse. A hesitant lullaby – we had never played together before and probably never would again.

The music began to breathe as we found our own shared rubato, and I began to fall in love with duets, all over again.

Alice's eyes were shining, and Beth leant on the piano with a dreamy smile. But as we soothed our way to a close, Alice dashed for the stairs in tears. I handed my violin to Cai and raced after her with Beth.

We found Alice squeezed in beside the water tank. 'What's up?'

'Sorry, Rachel,' she whispered. 'Like, beautiful... And piano.'

Beth looked at me. 'I had to cancel her lessons.'

'Granddad Joe SAID!' Full-on, concentrated resentment.

Beth shook her head. 'Joe offered to pay. But they pay for everything. Alice didn't understand.' She looked at Alice. 'Yes, she did. My dignity. As if I had any.'

Alice was still staring at the floor. I met Beth's eye and pointed back down towards the piano. She wiped a hand across her face and nodded.

'Alice, listen. You can practice here: the piano needs playing. And I'm sure if you can find a way to be nice about it, Mam will get your lessons going again.' I redirected her lunging hug towards Beth. She was the one giving up her dignity.

When we made it back downstairs, Cai's bass had arrived, and they treated us to some cool jazz. 'Mam? You going to sing?' Alice said, and I discovered Beth's gorgeous, throaty singing voice. Isabelle could have my bass player.

They didn't linger. Cai still looked on edge, and Isabelle... maybe the house wasn't tidy enough. Or the people.

Cai looked regretfully at his boxes of vintage comics, picked up his hand-written index and handed it to Alice. 'Look after them – they're valuable.'

Alice gasped. 'You sure?'

He pointed at a row of Alice's cartoon dinosaurs that I had framed. 'Your heritage.'

Alice smiled over her shoulder at Beth and seemed to grow as I looked at her.

'Thank you,' I whispered to Cai.

We helped them load the rest of his gear into his father's van. I didn't know how much clutter Isabelle would allow across the ocean.

As soon as they'd left, Alice got busy improvising at the piano, let loose after months without a chance, and sounding somewhere between Rachmaninov and Philip Glass. Her nose was almost down over the keyboard. Dreamy modal doodles over an open sustain pedal followed, and she leant back with her eyes shut, every inch the concert artist. Then she smiled and brought her improvisation to a peaceful close in shimmering A-major: an unexpected key shift, but then she was an unexpected thinker.

'Rachel – no room in our flat. Can I keep the comics here?'

'Of course – but don't think that'll get you out of playing scales.'

Beth grinned at me.

The twitchy feeling subsided at work on Friday and I began to relax, but I did allow Tom to drive me home. In the evening, Morwenna was our ostentatiously naked and strikingly beautiful sexagenarian model, posing with her basket. I wondered who else would volunteer to throw off their clothes. I'd started a trend.

My charcoal sketches looked as cool and remote as their subject, and I even felt proud of them, but Beth was more critical. 'There's hidden fire in Morwenna. Stretch yourself – get working under the surface.' I had met that fire, last week, and Beth had seen my partial truth. My sketches were almost lies – there was no hiding place here. And surely this cold feeling couldn't be fear, could it?

Stanley wanted another talk but Beth kept me back with a hand on my arm, telling him that today, my need was greater.

She sat me down when he had gone. 'You're twitching again, Rachel.'

'When you analysed my painting, it felt like... Dad used to lecture me on every detail of my work he thought was wrong. Just now, just for a moment – I know it's stupid, I know – but I was really frightened.'

'There's nothing stupid about reminders like that. I'm not perfect, Rachel, and I know criticism can feel like a personal attack.'

I pursed my lips, unsure what to say.

Beth waited for a moment and then spoke in a softer voice. 'You look awfully lonely when you get like this. We could easily come and sleep over.'

'I'll manage,' I said and left in a hurry.

Liar.

26

DREAMING TOO FAR

Rachel

I remember refusing Beth's offer to sleep over. And wondering why the hell I'd said I would manage.

The blank lasts from leaving the community hall until Tom and scared-looking Emmy arrived at my bedside with flowers on Sunday afternoon. I was in hospital, and I'd lost a weekend forever.

Some people prefer to lose their weekends in the oblivion of drink or drugs, but I'm jealous of my time, and resent the missed days, hours and minutes. Maybe it was my frustration that frightened Emmy. She handed me a bunch of flowers, kissed me on the nearest surface – my shoulder – and darted behind her brother.

'Thank you, Emmy. These are lovely,' I said, and she peeked out from behind him, her face flushed bright red. Tom blew me a hasty kiss as she dragged him away. Alice and Beth took their place, with Nana Siân to watch over them, and they helped me piece together the time I had lost.

Occasional blanks like this are a fact of my life – one that terrifies me. Time is not just something I live inside; it was both my research speciality and my research nemesis. The idea that I can be present without my memory recording anything disturbs both the rational scientist and the irrational infant inside me.

Beth and Alice said I talked to them briefly on Saturday afternoon and again in the evening, but they didn't know my memory wasn't doing its thing. I must have been convincing in zombie mode.

I have no memory of catching the first bus after life class, the walk between buses or getting on the second one, although I must have used my card twice. I fell off my seat convulsing on the second bus, and a stranger called 999. It was a serious delay to a Cardiff bus, but I was reported to have recovered consciousness by the time the ambulance arrived. Conscious, maybe, but my memory recorder stayed on standby.

Beth called the hospital on Saturday morning when my phone went to voicemail. While I have a vague recall of her presence and Alice's presence, and of Mathilde telling me that they were with me, I have no concrete memories until I recovered from another prolonged seizure in time for Tom and Emmy's visit on Sunday.

They kept me in overnight, but I didn't see anyone who knew my case history before I was discharged after lunch on Monday with some sedatives to add a cosh on top of my anticonvulsants. Julie was away on holiday in Prague.

Siân drove me home and stayed with me until Beth and Alice turned up after school. I expected Alice the excited child but got Alice the concerned friend, who gave me one of her mother's gentle hugs. 'You look shitty.'

I let them take over and cook a meal. And they stayed the

night, without any discussion that I could remember. And two more nights, I think. The rest of the week is a blur. I was too spaced-out to notice much. Tom went along as my guardian when I directed the Sinfonietta on Tuesday night. Julie was still away, and without her comforting presence in the cello section, I went through the motions. Tom was impressed that I could play the violin in my sleep, and he managed to persuade me to take the rest of the week off work.

On Thursday, after leaving me alone for a whole day – a day when my body finally adjusted to the sedatives and the world came back into rather shitty focus – Beth and Alice wanted to meet me in the coffee bar after school.

Laying my head on Beth's shoulder and feeling Alice's arms around my waist released tears that I neither understood nor wished to. But after they had mopped me up, fussed over me and sat me down with a coffee, I was almost myself again. Happy to let Alice tell me off each time I poked the scar on my tongue against my teeth.

On Beth's insistence, I booked a taxi to and from Friday night's life class, picking her up on the way. She had a new challenge lined up for us: she sat with modestly clothed Jade: two people in conversation. And she asked us to show more of the conversation than the people, drawing a sigh from Morwenna. I tried using ink, allowing the conversation to dribble down the paper.

Stanley was still there at the end, but I'd ordered the taxi half an hour later to allow for some Stanley time. While I tidied up the preparation room and cleared away the easels, Stanley talked and Beth listened. He glanced over his shoulder each time I fetched an easel, and I did try to keep out of the way. But Beth looked finished, and I decided to interrupt. 'Stanley, Beth needs some energy left for Alice.'

'Who's Alice?'

'Come on! Beth talks about trouble getting sitters often enough. Alice is almost eleven, and right now, she's the happiest spark in my life. Think, Stanley. Beth is a lone parent and she's a generous, caring mother. And she still never says no to people who need to talk – people like us. We should be supporting her.'

He stared at Beth. 'I never asked.'

'Don't you ever think I don't care,' she said, and he left in a hurry.

I wanted to help Beth, and I'd been frantically planning and scratching plans, but couldn't think of anything that wouldn't undermine her pride. I had to say something after all their care this week, and pointedly got out and paid for our taxi in Beth's street.

Her shoulders sagged, but she made no protest. 'I suppose it's time you saw.'

'I'm not here to judge.'

'It's affecting Alice – it hurts.' She turned away. 'All the fucking time, it hurts.' We edged round bins and stinking bags of rubbish in the passage. At the back was a cement-coloured extension. Beth knocked on a battered door and bolts slid back. A bored teenager kept playing on her phone while Beth paid her and went out to the street to watch her safely home, a few doors down.

I stood in the narrow entrance hall with interior doors at each end –all she had for a living room. Two beanbags sat against the wall opposite the outside door. Beside the door were hanging coats and a small TV. Beth came back, shut the door, bolted it, and turned a flimsy key. At one end was a kitchen hardly bigger than the hall. Beth filled a kettle. In this setting, the lovely smell of fresh bread was an alien surprise.

'Want to see my studio?' Beth opened a door at the back of the kitchen and switched on a light. A blast of cold air came from a room with bare floorboards. The smell of damp and paint made me sneeze. Canvases were stacked against the walls and a table was laden with paints, brushes and other paraphernalia. But there was no canvas on the easel.

She put her finger to her lips, took me back through the kitchen and opened the door at the far end of the little hall-way. A small bedroom had two beds, one with a mass of golden hair on the pillow. We tiptoed back into the kitchen. 'Bathroom?' I asked.

'They call it en-suite. As in student room en-suite. It gets damp even with the window open. And the drain keeps blocking.'

'How long have you been here?'

'Most of a year. Before Iestyn got hooked, he paid Alice's allowance every month. We had a better flat with a room each. Alice doesn't remember the one before, with Iestyn. Not that he was around much.'

'Right, for Alice, please let me help you find somewhere better.'

'Pound signs in your eyes – don't! It's my responsibility. I have more to spend, now my paintings are back on the radar. We'll find somewhere.'

'You know I don't want or need that bonus. I'll pay some of it to charity to ease my conscience, if it can. The rest – I do want to help. Please, Beth?'

'I've failed Alice. Should have gone for a steady job.'

'Iestyn has failed you both. You seem to be looking after half Cardiff. As well as looking after me.'

'I'm only being friendly.'

'You haven't failed Alice – failure isn't in it. She's a brilliant, caring, creative child who knows she's loved.'

That stopped her. 'Thank you. Thank you for saying it out loud. It's the one thing I need to hear, right now.'

'You both mean… the world, actually.' I was choking up. Maybe I hadn't realised just how much my life had begun to centre on their wellbeing.

'Spending all that money…' Beth grabbed a kitchen stool and sat down.

But I couldn't stay still. Couldn't stop pacing up and down in this little cage of a flat. 'Just imagine you had a partner who earned money while you painted and cared for Alice.' I added the small print before Beth could reply. 'I don't mean living together – I couldn't inflict all my mess on you. I mean a partner on paper – for Alice.'

'I don't get that at all. Really, I don't.' Beth squeezed her hands together. 'Sit down, will you?'

But I couldn't. Couldn't stay still. 'We find you a nice flat nearby. A room for Alice. A bath for you.'

'A bath would be heaven, but you don't understand. I would feel… kept.'

I struggled to backtrack and lost myself. 'I wish it was your money, not mine.'

Beth's forehead creased with worry. 'Please don't be upset, Rachel. The trouble is, I've spent years fighting for my independence.'

'I don't want to take anything away from you.'

'You might need the money – think of your health. Let's sit and talk.'

But I couldn't sit down, not after my biggest fuck-up in history. 'It's me. Dreaming too far.'

Beth wiped her hands down her face, and something switched.

Sorrow to fear. Fear of what might come out of her mouth.

I couldn't wait for the hurt to hit me. I needed to escape through that bolted door. And run, and run.

Struggling to turn the key, I heard Beth's voice – not words – pain. I slammed the bolts back and fled.

'RACHEL!'

I'd gone, frightened to hear Beth's voice, pounding the pavement with my feet.

Street.

Street.

Street.

Keep running.

I'd nearly reached home when my phone rang. I tore it from my bag and slammed it down in the gutter.

Run.

I struggled with my key, scrambled inside, caught a glimpse of Beth's painting, and fled upstairs, my heart pumping, my throat hurting as I tried to breathe.

Curled up tight on my bed, the physicality of my reaction caught up with me. Why, Rachel, why? I was shaking uncontrollably and gasping for air. A reaction from my childhood.

Fear.

Dad.

Punishment.

Rejection.

Unworthiness.

Oh, Rachel, you are so FUCKING STUPID.

Beth is not Dad.

Alice is Alice. Your commitment to them is absolute.
That won't change.

Half an hour later, I'd calmed down enough to uncurl and
lever myself up off the bed. I washed my face, went shakily
downstairs and took a flashlight up the street. I finally found
my phone fifty metres away. It still worked.

I ignored a voicemail from Beth, not ready for the sound
of her voice. Instead, I sent a text.

I'm sorry. Need time.

Will talk.

27

STEPPING AWAY

Alice

I'm sorry. Need time.
Will talk.

I was still trying to calm Mam down when the text came.

Adults! I'd transformed from sleeping child to counsellor in ten seconds after the door slammed. At first, Mam was raging about fucking it up and then she was raging at Rachel for being fucking stupid and then she was crying. Not just crying, but howling.

And all that time, I had no clue what had happened, just that the door had slammed and there had been some sort of explosion between Mam and Rachel. Rachel had been here – her old red coat was still on the kitchen stool. And I knew Mam was scared of Rachel ever seeing the flat.

'Mam – stop now. Did Rachel see this dump?'

'Not that…' Mam coughed and coughed, and I got her a glass of water.

'Okay – get your breath back. Then tell me – in order. Rachel says she needs time. The world hasn't ended.'

'People with money never understand.'

'What do you mean?'

'If something doesn't work out, they've got options.'

'And?'

'We never have. If something doesn't work out, we deal with it.'

'What's this got to do with Rachel?'

'Something isn't working – she's stepping away – like they always do. She wanted to pay for us to… to live in another flat. Keep us – like pets.'

'NO! Mam, Rachel would NEVER think like that.'

'She said it.'

'What did she say? Exactly.'

'Something about being a partner – ON PAPER.'

'What else?'

'I don't know.' Mam was shaking.

'THINK, Mam. It matters.'

'She told me I hadn't failed you… and she wished that bonus was ours. All nice stuff, but she's… Can't you see? She's standing back. Making us a charity project.'

Everything was going tight inside me. 'NO Mam! Stop it. You're scaring me – that's not Rachel.'

It felt like Mam was putting up a barbed wire fence. Making Rachel the enemy.

Mam stroked my arm. 'I'm sorry, my love. It was always going to happen. We'll manage.'

She'd given up on even trying to be friends.

SHIT.

My best friend – gone – just like that.

I had to try again. 'Mam, listen. Rachel isn't one of those people. Rachel is… Rachel. Think of all the good things.'

'I know she means well. But she was never going to stick around.'

I scrabbled to think harder, and one picture stuck in my head. Emmy linking her arm through Rachel's in the market.

Why?

Why Emmy? Because money meant nothing to Emmy? No, not that. It was about who Emmy was, and who Rachel was.

'Mam, think of Rachel and Emmy. Would Emmy trust Rachel if Rachel was like that – inside.'

'Emmy? You don't even know Emmy.'

'Yes, I do. Inside, I know her. Words don't get in the way with Emmy. I know Emmy. Emmy knows Rachel. On the inside. Trusts her.'

Mam just looked at me.

'It's nothing to do with being a money person, Mam.'

Mam shook her head, but I think she was listening.

'Now, Mam. Think again. Why did Rachel run away? I KNOW she'd not give up on us. She got a high-paid job by accident – she told me herself – that job was the only one she could get. So, think. Why else would she run away?'

'Not now, Alice. You should be in bed.'

'When my best friend just ran away from my Mam. Like that? I heard the door slam. YOU THINK I CAN SLEEP NOW?'

'She needs time – look at that text.'

'I think she means you need time, Mam. Rachel would only run off if she was hurting. Did you hurt her?'

'ALICE! Stop it. Now.'

And that's as far as I got. Crying and pain got in the way. My whole world broke.

Now I hated Mam, but I had to share a room with her.

At last, I was sick of pretending to sleep. I went and messed with my Lego in the kitchen, making Rachel detectors. At three in the morning. I knew that Operation Find Rachel would have to start all over again.

*

Rachel

Saturday. I knew it was up to me. I'd said I needed time.

But where to start? How could I build a life where Beth and Alice were not at the centre of everything?

Beth couldn't or wouldn't get closer, and I couldn't blame her. I'd seen how much my seizures scared her. And was it even healthy for a ten-year-old to choose an adult as her best friend?

I would have to start again. Raise some barriers. Be more cautious in my friendship. Save confidences for my rag doll – after all, I'd managed that for most of my life. Very early in the morning, I went outside in the freezing cold and stroked my hand down the apple tree, and that brought tears. Remembering the wonder in Alice's eyes, just here.

They love you.

'You think? I'm not worth all that pain.'

Remember – don't lie to them – don't lie to yourself. Tell them how you really feel.

'If only. I don't even know anymore.'

I will help.

I wiped my eyes with the palms of my hands. 'Thank you, Mathilde.'

A dry voice in the back of my head spoke. *So, now you're relying on an imaginary friend as well as your rag doll, Doctor Bothwell.*

Dad's voice.

28

OLD RED COAT

Alice

I slept on my beanbag because I didn't want to go near Mam. And I woke up freezing, stiff with cold and aching inside. But I needed to think, and to think hard. Rachel must have been really scared to run off like that. But I didn't think it was sympathy, like it was last time Rachel ran off.

Mam had talked about Rachel stepping away, but nowadays, Rachel is so much easier about people getting close. She soaked up our sympathy when we saw her in the café. And even thinking about that hug with Rachel made me wipe my eyes.

Keep thinking, Alice. Don't give up.

But be scientific. Rachel isn't here – you can't check out any theories with Rachel. You'll have to start with what's here. Mam and this crappy flat.

Mam looked like an extra from a zombie movie when she finally got up. By then, I was unfreezing myself in front of the electric heater, and Mam came and sat in her beanbag next to me. 'Have you been out here all night?'

'What do you think?'

'I'll talk to Nan and Granddad. Get us out of this dump.'

'Mam – that's not solving the problem. The problem is you and Rachel.'

'I scared her off. I'm sorry, Alice. But I think she was looking to move on.'

'Why do you say that? It's Rachel, the best friend we've ever had. What if this is your hard luck talking to you? If it's what you expected to happen?'

'She went, didn't she?'

'Last night, you were just as scared as Rachel. Two hurt people. And I KNOW Rachel would never want to hurt you – or me. Mam, it doesn't end here. We need to get her talking again.'

'We will – but God knows how. I'm off for a shower. Then we'll think.'

But I didn't need Mam thinking round and round in circles – I knew where that would lead. I got up, went into the kitchen – and I found my way to get Rachel talking right there. Her old red coat, still draped over the stool.

I raced to get some leggings and a top and my trainers on while Mam was in the shower, then I tore a sheet out of my sketchbook.

> *Gone to take Rachel's coat back.*
> *You stay here. She'll talk to me.*

I'd just got my coat on when I heard the shower stop. Now Mam would hear me going out.

I couldn't help that. I grabbed Rachel's coat, undid the key and bolts and ran.

Mam didn't like me going out on my own except to the shop on the corner, but Nan always let me go if I told her where I was going. And I'd told Mam. Rachel's house wasn't far, and hardly anyone was around on a freezing, drizzly Saturday morning.

I was halfway up Pen-y-Wain Road when I began to think this was a seriously BAD idea. What if Mam came after me? What if they had another scene like last night? What if Rachel didn't want to see me? What if seeing me upset her – the one person I never wanted to upset, ever? But I kept on walking.

Rachel's house was halfway down Morlais Street. The Blackbird wasn't in his tree and the house looked lonely. I held Rachel's red coat in front of me so she would see it first, and I rang the bell. And waited. Rang the bell again. And waited.

Had she gone away? Her Mam lived in London. No, frightened Rachel wouldn't go that far. Maybe she hadn't slept, like me, and gone for a walk. I wondered about going down to the park, but she might have gone the other way. She'd talked about walking in Cathays Cemetery before, with all the old monuments.

No, I sat down on the doorstep and cuddled up to Rachel's coat. It smelt of something nice. Flowery perfume that I'd smelt before when she was on her way back from work. Rachel.

Rachel cares.

'Mathilde?'

She's in the garden. Give her a few minutes.

And I did, sitting on the doorstep wrapped in my coat and now Rachel's coat on top of it and still getting cold. But I didn't have to ring the doorbell again.

The door opened. 'Alice? Mathilde said…'

I tripped over her coat standing up, but Rachel caught me.

'Your coat – you left it.'

'Come inside. You're freezing.'

And we walked in, me in my space under her arm, Rachel not looking at me. Maybe not daring to look at me.

'Does Beth know where you are?'

'I left a note.'

Rachel fiddled with her phone. 'There – I've sent a text. Said you're safe.'

I was still cuddling her coat close. 'You – Mam?'

'I've been a fool. Mathilde knows. I didn't say what I really wanted. Didn't dare.'

We were still in the front hall, but I led Rachel by the hand through the kitchen and out to the apple tree. 'Mathilde? What does Rachel really want?'

You already know, Alice.

'She wants what I want?'

Yes.

'But what about Mam?'

You and Rachel have some work to do.

I stroked my hand down the rough bark of the tree. Rachel was right next to me, and it was easy to smile up at her. 'First apple's mine. Remember?' And it was like watching the sun come out.

'Mathilde's right, Alice. We have work to do. Let's go and find Beth.'

And I handed her the old red coat.

'Mam, the coat's back. And it's got Rachel in it.'

And then Mam and Rachel were standing looking at each other in the drizzly rain next to the stinky rubbish bags.

'Inside!' I said, and they obeyed. My two big kids. 'Coat off! You sit there.' I pointed Rachel at my beanbag. 'And you sit there.' I pointed Mam at hers.

'Listen, Mam. Me and Rachel had the same idea, but Rachel was too shy to ask last night. She didn't want to stress you every time she had a seizure. It's still a problem, isn't it?'

'That's my past. Dad dying young – I'll get round it,' Mam said.

'What me and Rachel really want is for us to move in with Rachel,' I said in a hurry. 'Not this getting a flat thing she was on about last night.'

Rachel still looked nervous, and she was still holding on to her damp coat on her lap. 'I'm sorry if that's going too far. It's the way I used to be – crush after crush – falling into things, full on.'

Mam smiled at her, and I knew we'd won. 'Why be sorry, Rachel? You turn guilty every time you're the slightest bit impulsive. There's so much warmth inside you – what's wrong with letting it out?'

Rachel looked at me and looked puzzled. And I had an idea where all this being sorry came from. 'Is it your dad? Telling you to be sensible?'

Rachel sighed and stretched her arms out, letting the coat slip onto the floor. 'Yes, I suppose it is. But I… I feel energised when I'm like this.'

Mam reached out and stroked her arm. 'Impulsiveness isn't a crime.'

Rachel looked at me again. 'Maybe this is the real me – at long last. And it needed the two of you to let the real me out. Even Cai used to worry whether I was being sensible or not.'

Mam gave her a serious look. 'Cai knew you at university.

You burned out by following your impulses, didn't you? But did you ever have any real support?'

'I had enough people making me feel guilty. But they were right in a way – I do need some kind of check. It's not just people. I get serially in love with – I don't know – music, ideas, equations. Anything can grab my attention.'

'Full, fall-in-deep attention?'

'That's it! Fall in and don't care how deep I fall. I'm not proud of being like this but these last few years, I've been covering it up. Hiding.'

'Serially in love with everything.' Now Mam was sitting forward on her beanbag. 'That's about as good a description of an artist as I've ever heard.'

'Scientist too, I suppose.'

'This business of getting me a flat. You were scared of falling in love with me, weren't you? Trying to keep me at arm's length.'

'I couldn't bear to upset you or Alice.'

'So why make it complicated? Why let it bother us? I'm boringly heterosexual, but we could be sisters. We're almost a family already.'

Almost a family. 'YES, MAM!'

And Mathilde said, *Yes, Alice*! But I don't know whether Mam or Rachel heard.

I plonked myself down between the two beanbags on Rachel's damp coat, and Mam put her arm around me, but she was still talking to Rachel. 'Every time I see you, I get this urge to put you somewhere safe. To find you a nest to curl up in.'

'I've never felt settled, ever. I suppose the house here is my best effort at a nest.'

Mam patted my arm. 'You'll need some dry clothes on, Alice. And we'd better start arranging to do what you really want, I suppose.'

Rachel looked like she could hardly believe Mam. 'Beth, you wouldn't?'

'Of course! You keep the money – we move in with you. I'd feel a whole load less guilty about it.'

'But I'm… There's Alice. My epilepsy…'

'Alice cares for you just as much as you care for her. She needs to know you're safe. Building a nest together isn't just about your needs, Rachel. It's about Alice's and mine as well, and a lot of them involve keeping you close.'

Now it was me who needed to believe what I was hearing. 'Being a family?'

'When we're not running scared from each other,' Rachel said.

'Or fighting,' Mam said. 'Yes, a family, Alice.'

And I cuddled into Rachel's old red coat.

29

ABSOLUTE BEGINNERS

Alice

Mam was looking for something about our rent and giving notice. Rachel kept pacing around, flexing up and down on her toes.

'Don't pretend to be a kid,' I said.

'I'm not pretending – imagine you're me – finding where you belong.'

'Dad belongs, and he's a mess.'

Mam put a bunch of papers on the table. 'We haven't managed a proper family for you, have we, love?'

'I don't need a proper family. Got Rachel instead.' I scratched my head because this still needed sorting. 'NO WAY are you another mother, Rachel. Sorted?'

'Sorted. I'll try not to pretend to be anything, Alice.'

'You're my Rachel. Mother, daughter and...' I needed another scratch.

'Have you got nits?' Mam said.

'GROSS! No way.'

'What's all the scratching for, then? Mother, sister and daughter. How's that?'

'Nah, we're Beth, Rachel and Alice,' I said, and now Mam had mentioned the N-word, I couldn't help scratching.

And now Rachel was scratching.

'I saw that!' Mam said, scratching. 'Welcome to family life.'

Mam insisted on searching us both with her nit comb but found nothing more than dandruff and split ends, mostly Rachel's. We were simply sharing an itch.

'You need to change your shampoo,' Mam told Rachel, like she was her kid. 'And you need a trim.'

'I never get time,' Rachel said.

I poked her. 'Scruffbag.'

But she just smiled.

We ate Mam's fresh bread in front of the little electric fire – the only warm place in the flat. But when Rachel stood up, she screeched and hopped on one leg.

'Oops – sorry.' I gathered up my Lego.

'Ah – the Brick of Pain,' Mam said. 'I know it well.'

Mam started sorting clothes for the laundrette while I rubbed Rachel's foot.

'Easier to do the washing at my house,' Rachel said.

'Do you think we're in too much of a hurry?' Mam said. 'We need to talk to people. I don't know what Joe and Siân will think. And there's Iestyn.'

I rolled my eyes. 'Dad has NO say. And Nan and Granddad love Rachel.'

'Can I talk to Rachel on my own?'

'No, Mam. You'll talk her out of it – you know you will. I'm part of this – me too. Come and sit down.' And she flopped back into her beanbag.

Rachel sat on the kitchen stool. 'You're worried about Siân and Joe, Beth?'

'You're taking on a family. Not just us. Siân will be round like a shot.'

'She'll see Alice moving to a comfortable house with proper facilities and space.'

'One I can't possibly afford. Just why would a business-woman be so generous?'

Rachel opened her mouth and said, 'Businesswoman?' like it was an alien species.

'Well, you are!' Mam said. 'God knows what you earn, but it must be a lot.'

'Too much. I don't deserve it. But neither do any of the others.' She started twisting her hair in front of her face in that uncomfortable Rachel way. 'Surely, Siân wouldn't think... Not that I was trying to buy my way in? Oh God, that's... No, she's been so friendly and helpful.'

'It's Alice she'll think of first,' Mam said, and put her arm around me. 'It's taken her years to accept that Alice is better off with me than with Iestyn. I don't want them to feel we're edging them out.'

Rachel tapped the side of her head and gave a little grin. 'Okay, so we ask Siân and Joe to help us move your stuff. Make sure they're involved.'

'You know...' Mam looked out of the window. 'You might be better at Siân than me, Rachel.'

'Alright.' Rachel looked up at the mouldy patch in the corner of the ceiling. 'I'll leave you with my mum, then.'

'Obvious, isn't it?' Mam shook her head, flopped back in the beanbag, and her face filled with sunshine. 'We should have seen – we're a pair of absolute beginners.'

'That's why you both need someone sensible like me,' I said.

Mam called Granddad, and after she hopped from leg to leg forever while he talked to Nan, he told her that yes, they were free for the day and would love to help. Rachel and me packed my stuff, mainly Lego. Mam and Nan sorted and packed the kitchen, and I overheard Nan saying she would like to get to know Rachel better.

Of course she would, and I made sure she got the chance. 'Mam, if we pack the studio with Granddad, Nan and Rachel can take the other stuff in Nan's car. They'll need a few trips.'

Granddad grinned. 'Clever girl.' That's when I knew Granddad was on our side.

When we'd got most of the stuff moved, we stopped for chips from down the road – our last ever meal in our poky little flat. But Nan took Granddad home for proper lunch, whatever that was. I think he would have preferred chips with us.

Rachel told us that going back and forth in the car, Nan had needed to know about epilepsy, Rachel's work, about why she'd left Cambridge and what she did there, about her parents and her non-existent love life. And Rachel told her everything. Even that she wasn't planning on sharing a bed with Mam, and that bit made me laugh. Mam snores. And she farts in her sleep.

Nan and Granddad came back later on, after they'd a had a lie down. I was in Rachel's back porch and Rachel and Nan were in the kitchen when Nan went serious and touched Rachel on the arm. 'Beth is scared I won't accept you, isn't she?'

'Yes – Alice is your family too. We don't want you left out. That matters to Beth.'

'Awww!'

I crept into the room and heard Rachel say some words that gave me tears. 'Siân, my family were… a disaster area,

actually. I might need help to manage a family. Please, just…
be around. If that's alright?'

And Nan took Rachel by both hands and I felt safer than
I had been in my entire life. 'Any time you need me, you just
call,' Nan said. We really were one family.

And Rachel smiled, beckoned me close and put her arm
out for me to cuddle against her side. 'I was like Alice,' she
said. 'I know how it feels to want to learn everything, and
not to have a friend to share the excitement.'

'Her father, too. Iestyn never fitted in.'

'I don't want to get in the way with Alice – he is her father.'

Nan came and put her arm around me too. 'Best she has
you too, Rachel.'

And I breathed out. 'Negotiations all sorted, Nan?'

And Nan laughed and tugged my hair. 'Cheeky monkey!'

Mam and Granddad finished stacking pictures in
Rachel's workshop, and then we had one more trip to make,
while Rachel and Nan sorted stuff in Rachel's house. Before
we closed up the flat for the night, I hid one single Lego
brick – the one Rachel had stepped on. Maybe an archaeol-
ogist would discover it in a few centuries' time. The only job
left for Sunday was the big clean up in the flat – and then I
wouldn't need to go there ever again.

Back up the road, the five of us sat down in the kitchen
and munched Nan's special Welsh Cakes. I'd thought Mam
and me would be living in that flat forever, but we'd turned
into a family with our own home. I reached out and stroked
Rachel's old red coat on the back of her chair. And I whispered to it. 'Thank you.'

30

THE ROCK RACE

Rachel

Joe had built Iestyn's studio, and I soon got him fired up by the workshop-into-studio idea. I thought it best to disclose that I was under no financial pressure, and would happily pay for everything, including his time. He shook his head – I think it was my gender. 'Joe, you wouldn't let me buy you a drink in the pub, would you?'

He grinned.

'Come and have a look – there's a lot of work. The windows are all wrong for a studio, the insulation is rubbish and the floor needs re-doing. We need spotlights and background lighting. And I was hoping to put a door through into the back porch.'

His measurer appeared. We were in business, and once we were out there alone, the perfectionist engineer prevailed. I said he'd have free range in design and materials.

'Scientific consultant? You'll earn a tidy bit.'

'A tidy bit. That doesn't mean I've worked for it any more than you or Beth or Siân.'

'It must be a struggle, with epilepsy and all that.'

'Work is the easy bit. I'm a beginner at being grown-up and responsible and I've never had a family to look out for.'

He held me gently by the shoulders. 'Family. That's what Alice needs, bach. Family. And you two will make a fine job of it.' My wonderful Granddad Joe.

Beth took Cai's back bedroom, with its en-suite shower room. 'It doesn't mean I won't invade the bath,' she said, with a year's worth of baths to catch up on.

Alice took the spare room, but her dream was obvious from the amount of time she spent hunched up beside the water tank communing with the housemaid's ghost. Granddad Joe looked at the problem and showed how the pipes rose on the playroom side of the partition. The tank should have been in there, and someone's botched DIY was the reason for all the gurgles in the pipes. An Edwardian housemaid's room for Alice's eleventh birthday looked realistic, and Siân would like to decorate it.

When I thanked her, I got a full-on beaming smile that turned into a concerned look. 'You need–'

'–a trim,' Beth echoed. 'Go on, Siân. It would be good to see her eyes.' Beth gave Siân a tiny glance and fluttered her eyelids. 'Lovely eyes, they are.'

Siân slapped her arm. 'Don't you go teasing our Rachel!'

'Our Rachel' sounded so lovely, I needed a tissue.

'There, there,' Siân said, as if I were... Well, I was, now. She produced a pair of hairdressing scissors from her bag, and now I could see my family properly.

So far, so good with the almost-in-laws. When they finally left, we trooped up to the playroom and laid flat on our backs on the floor with our heads together. In our house. The giggle started with me, passed on to Beth, and on to Alice. Relief.

While we were still on the floor, I gave them a demonstration. Despite my persistent questions, my parents had never told me what they witnessed while I was having a seizure. It was painful not to know, and seizures are so varied that films about epilepsy were no use at all. Cai had seen my nighttime convulsions, and early on, I got him to demonstrate one back to me. And now I passed it on to Beth and Alice. The sudden deep breath, the arched back, the screech, the noisy breathing, and… that's all.

'WAS THAT IT?' Alice was not impressed.

'Nothing like the daytime ones, then,' Beth said.

'I hardly ever even bite my tongue. I do get a hangover.'

'We can live with that,' Beth put her arm around Alice.

'Mam means she's not scared out of her pants anymore.'

I did need to add an important detail. 'If I keep having them, and they get closer together, only a minute or two apart, call 999. It hasn't happened for years.'

'Getting closer together. You heard that,' Beth said.

Alice nodded. '999. No sweat. Easy-peasy last time.'

No sweat. Not to Alice. Beth didn't look as relaxed as I would have liked, but she had come across me in the midst of a very different seizure. I diverted their attention onto a board game that Alice had discovered while she was clearing her room. And then we settled into our own rooms in our own house.

Our house – our routine. We let it emerge gradually, and even in that first week, our family began to breathe. I was more of a morning person than Beth, and walking to school with Alice was a pleasure I didn't expect to tire of. My later arrival at the office was noticed, but I only shared my lovely reason with Tom.

By Wednesday, Joe had drawn up detailed plans to alter the workshop. He wanted to do the work with a couple of his retired mates. I wondered about making a show of professionalism and getting another quote, but the plans looked good to me.

There was something new about the house: a smell of freshly baked bread. When I was on my own, the only smell I had really noticed wasn't fresh anything. My own sweat, whenever I panicked. And there was something else new about the house. All about the house. Lego. I didn't mind. Much.

Another bit of newness was altogether wonderful. I'd waited thirty years for someone who appreciated the rock race. It began with my first astronomy book. My father had told eight-year-old Rachel that she had misunderstood the concept of relative motion. He was fundamentally wrong.

I had tried to explain the rock race to my classes of undergraduates at Cambridge. Some of them claimed to understand it. They didn't. But Alice understood it perfectly.

Two rocks were sitting under the apple tree, apparently still, but having a race. Alice and I crouched beside the rocks in the garden, watching them intently. Which one would win? It was a long race, but we could stay excited for a long time, long enough to contemplate all this.

The rocks are subject to continental drift in… that direction, Alice.

But it is… slow, yes, that's the word, Alice. They are rotating around the earth, and you know which way that takes them. And you know how fast, which is a slight surprise. They are moving round the sun and that takes a bit of working out, but no we don't need to use the astronomy app on my phone.

Of course, that's not the end of the complication, Alice. The entire solar system is subject to other influences. We are moving through the local group of stars, and I know which way, and roughly how fast, but I do need to check my app to tell you the direction. Oh, let's not bother, let's say... that way, because approximately will do. Yes, and you're right, Alice, our local group are rotating around the galaxy. Quite fast, actually. Shall we say... that way?

Then there's the local group of galaxies. Don't tell the press, but we're on a collision course with the Andromeda galaxy. It will take us a while to get there and right now, Andromeda is beneath the horizon, roughly... that way. And – oh yes, the expanding universe. Are we travelling, or just getting bigger? That's a thought.

Our two rocks are certainly not standing still in space or in time. Nothing is ever quite as it seems. After all, seen from the inside at the sub-atomic level, our two apparently solid rocks would be composed almost entirely of empty space.

We kept on watching. Had one of them moved fractionally ahead? We debated their merits. Nothing was measured. We did not consult my phone. And we never told anyone else which rock won. But Alice knew, and I knew.

31

CRUMBS

Rachel

Nothing's gone wrong yet. My first, edgy thought on Saturday morning.

Beth was in and out of my room as soon as it was light, not settling until I said it was probably late enough to phone Siân. Alice was away for the weekend with Siân and Joe: her first trip to London. Leaving two of us where there should have been three.

No, they hadn't even had breakfast yet, and Alice was... talk to her yourself.

Watching Beth talk to her daughter in whispers was magical. The wrinkles of joy at the corners of her eyes. Her hand over her heart. Her lowered eyes as she saw her worries flowing away. When they'd said goodbye, I kissed my finger and touched the tip of her nose. 'You are–'

'One special prize idiot. Of course she's fine.'

I managed to keep her chatting for a while, but she was restless without Alice around, and went off shopping as soon as she was dressed.

I'd made it downstairs in my pyjamas when my phone rang. My stomach lurched when I saw the display: Julie. For her to call on a Saturday morning, I knew it must be serious.

'I've been reviewing your notes from when you were admitted. The memory loss thing. Can you remember any aura before the first seizure? The one on the bus?'

'It was my second bus, the one from the town centre. The last thing I remember is leaving the community centre before my first bus ride.'

'So, you had no warning.'

'Not one I can remember.'

'The paramedic's notes say you fell off your seat on the bus convulsing. I would have thought you would have told someone if you'd felt it coming on. That's a real change, Rachel. I'll need you in for some tests. Have you got anyone with you?'

'I'm expecting Beth back soon.' And I explained our new household arrangement.

She sounded relieved. 'I don't want you on your own until I can see you again. We'll have you wired up on Tuesday. Any more seizures and it's 999 straight away.'

'Is it serious?'

'It might not be, but it is new. We need to know what's going on. I suppose it's not worth me saying don't panic, but don't.'

'Beth's the one who might panic. Shit.'

'Yes, it is shit, but it's shit we can deal with,' Julie said. As a stop-gap, she doubled one of my drugs. 'Expect drowsiness. You know what to record. See you Tuesday.' I didn't get as far as asking whether she'd had a nice holiday.

My first realisation after I put the phone down was sickening. I couldn't even walk Alice to school safely. I heard Beth's key in the lock. Beth's key. Our dream.

'Beth, we've made a big mistake. This isn't going to work.'

She sagged into the chair opposite, her face grave, but said nothing. 'Julie called. It's got more serious.' She reached for my hand, but I couldn't help pulling away. 'I might have serious seizures without warning. No warning – think about it. This changes everything.'

'So? We cope. Rachel, it changes nothing. We signed up to you freaking out – we both did. Alice needs you. I do too.'

'Do you know how serious this is?'

'You having any seizure is serious – do you think I don't know that?' The passion in her voice was close to anger. 'I'm here; I'm staying, and I'll keep a closer eye.'

'I don't know.' I was curled up tight in my chair and couldn't look at her.

'I'll let you settle,' Beth said, more softly. 'You've had a shock. Then we can go through the details. What I need to know.' She came over, stroked the hair away from my eyes and reached for my sketchbook on the table. 'This might help.'

We settled down to sketch each other. I had a strong sense that Mathilde was in the room, watching over us.

Simply drawing Beth's face helped me absorb her absolute commitment. I had no right to push her away. And after silently sketching each other, she echoed my thoughts. 'I'm here for the shit stuff, Rachel. So is Alice – she's stronger than you think.'

'I don't know.' I shook my head. 'We'd better go through the shit stuff, then.' I showed her Julie's charts, and ran her through my emergency procedure. Demonstrated the drug used with a dropper in my nose or cheek during a prolonged seizure. No one had thought to look in my bag in the front porch or on the bus.

'Okay, shit stuff sorted,' Beth said. 'Now let's get on with the rest of our lives.'

It was already dark when Alice called from the top of the London Eye. 'At last,' Beth had been holding back from calling all day. She didn't tell Alice my news.

And when she'd said goodnight to Alice, Beth came and put her arms around my shoulders. 'I'm with you. That time in the porch, I thought I was losing you. I'm still shitting scared about your seizures, but this is where I want to be – with you. Don't you ever think it isn't.'

We headed upstairs, and Beth gave a motherly smile. 'Sleep, now,' she said. 'I'm just next door.' I wound a strand of Molly's woollen hair around my finger, and with thoughts of those beings I cared for, and the mystery of being, thoughts of not being came back. Of not even getting a warning that I might suddenly not be.

I clutched Molly closer. Even knowing that Beth would be sleeping in the next room, I couldn't avoid the lonely tunnel of the night.

On Sunday, Beth said Graham would stand in for her in the gallery. 'No way am I leaving you alone in the house.' I had a go at sketching her in pastels while she made a batch of apple pies for Siân's lunch club, but her face wouldn't stay still.

Then Alice called and I had a perfectly still, delighted face to sketch. The smiley wrinkles around her eyes. The tiny creases across her turned-up nose as she laughed at something Alice said. The warmth that radiated from her whole face. I didn't have the skill to capture it and I felt unworthy before this loving, caring person who had let me into her life.

'Bye love – see you soon,' Beth whispered, put her phone down and came to look at my drawing. She put a floury hand on my shoulder. 'You prettify me.'

'Pretty accurate. Pretty. You are.' I was backing off, swamped by confusing feelings.

'Playing with words? I know the signs. Come on, Rachel, spill.'

'Oh, I don't know, it's a muddle. I just can't seem to relax and let go. My mind won't let my feelings take charge.'

'That's what you perceive. But you've let go at a deeper, braver level than I've ever managed. It just isn't real for you, is it? You're aware of every little letting-go.'

'Maybe I'm too used to being the one who struggles. Who needs help.'

Beth stood back. 'Let me get the list straight. Understands the physical world to a depth beyond your average professor. Tick. Plays the violin like a professional. Tick. Earns a bucket of money–'

'Stop it!'

'Double tick. Has more natural artistic flare than anybody else I've taught. God, Rachel, you even look ten years younger – if you ever bothered to look in a mirror.'

'Okay, I should be grateful.'

'SHOULD? Sometimes I want to STRANGLE you.'

I was lost. 'What've I done now?'

I got a crushing hug in reply, and she stood back, leaving flour all down my front. 'You've retreated as if it's selfish to have all these gifts. You've had a crap deal with a father, a crap deal with support and a worse deal with your wiring. You're allowed to scream. No, more – you're ENTITLED to scream!'

With Beth, who feels my screams when they're hidden deep inside?

'You rescued me when I screamed. You're with me now. I could be alone with Cai in the same room. I'm still getting my head round the reality of being together.'

'The way you talk about reality.' Beth picked up my sketch of her face. 'It shows in your pictures. You get the exact light in a way most amateurs don't even notice. You're conscious of all these different levels of reality all the time, aren't you?'

'It's not easy to filter them – sort them out.'

'Exactly. Most people have a mute button, I suppose. Something that makes reality bearable. Something that lets them take experience on trust.'

'The levels and layers of reality frighten me. I often wish I could turn them off. But they excite me as well.'

Beth examined the palm of her hand, tracing her forefinger along the lines. 'I've never faced my fears. Looking at reality through your eyes is helping me see a bigger picture – beyond my fears. How much more there is to explore.'

'Reality, okay.' And a little demon inside was waiting to stop the conversation getting any deeper. 'I'm REALLY hungry, Beth.'

Hunger wasn't the main problem. I could feel my world slowing down as the extra drugs kicked in. Concentration… Lunch. I was hungry. Eat. Go to bed and let the chemicals do their work, protecting me from… Reality?

Hello, cocoon.

Hello blackness.

Hello, 16.37 on my clock. I was on my bed and didn't remember going to lie down. I felt empty – had I eaten? Alice would be back soon, and I needed to get my system started – no way did I want her coming home to a casualty.

'Beth?'

No answer. I sat up, shakily. Come on, body.

Slippers, dressing gown. Stairs.

Beth was asleep on the sofa, with her phone just beyond her fingers. Her face looked relaxed and at peace, and I guessed that Alice had reassured her moments before she fell asleep.

Yes, your girl will be home soon.

I crept away to make some toast before the invasion. Beth's sketchbook was open on the kitchen table. She never usually left it around. A picture of me, asleep, stretched across my bed. Sneaky, but lovely. And Alice, looking up at a dinosaur skeleton. Had Joe sent a photo, or was this Beth's imagination? Reality or reality?

Coffee and toast would wake me up and fill me up, but in my semi-drugged state, making it was complicated. Victory achieved, I clutched last night's Echo under my arm and wobbled upstairs with a tray. Letting the newspaper fall, I cleared a space on the bedside table with one hand, deposited the tray and sagged onto my bed.

I had opened the paper and just bitten into my toast when loud noises downstairs warned me of incoming small human. I counted three seconds of stampeding feet and then a streak of girl rushed round the door, jumped onto the bed, and flattened my newspaper. For another three seconds, two blue eyes were so close that I couldn't focus.

'I'm back,' she said, and pinched my toast. She broke it in two, showering me with crumbs, and gave me the bigger bit as if she had made it especially for me.

'Hello?' I said.

'My Rachel! Love-you-missed-you!'

I opened my arms for a cuddle full of crumbs, sticky honey and newspaper.

Now, now, NOW! One precious moment of reality with added crumbs. No subtext. Shared delight in seeing each other after two nights apart.

Slower footsteps. Siân. She smiled from the doorway as we munched our toast.

'My Rachel, Nan!' Alice said with her mouth full.

Siân looked weary. 'How was it?' I asked.

'Joe was just as exhausting as Alice. But it was lovely – worth it.'

'What was the best bit?' I asked Alice, expecting a dinosaur-flavoured answer.

'Hotel. Not been in a hotel. Shower gel in tubes and white towels and breakfast. And watching the street with taxis going up and down.'

'Cheapest we could find, down from King's Cross,' Siân said. 'A bit noisy.' She gestured Alice off my newspaper. 'Rachel needs a lie down, Alice. Come back later?'

'Got you some pictures,' Alice told me. 'Show you later – doing my piano now – not played it forever.' And off she went.

'Wash your hands first!' I called after her.

Siân re-folded my newspaper, shaking her head at all the crumbs, and sat on the side of the bed. 'Beth told me about you needing tests. I'll take you along on Tuesday. She gets too worked up about it.'

'There's no need – I'll be fine on my own – I can get a taxi.'

'Dumb as Beth, you are. If I don't go, she will. And she'll scare herself out of her mind. I'm taking you – no argument.'

I rapped myself on the side of the head. 'I am dumb. And… thank you.'

My words seemed inadequate. I held out my arms, but Siân pulled my hands in together and leant back. 'All covered in crumbs, you are!' The warmth of her smile gave me the reminder I needed. Family.

Arpeggios from downstairs drew her away. 'I'd better go and admire.'

'Good reason, Siân. She was doing grade four before she stopped, but she's a lot better than that. I'm going to have a word with her teacher.'

'Says her proud mam.'

'It feels almost real.'

Siân's eyes twinkled. 'She sees you as a best friend, but she missed you like a mother. And…' She hesitated. 'Alice doesn't always get to see the mother in Beth.'

'You think so?'

'As often as not, they're facing the world side by side.'

Sleep reclaimed me. Several hours later, I woke up, refreshed. The immediate effect of the drug had worn off, and I got up to make another drink. Siân had gone home, and Beth was sitting on the spare bed, watching her daughter sleep. The thread between them had stayed tight all weekend.

Alone in the front room with my mug of chocolate, I had a sudden sense that I was in the wrong place. Instant warmth from Mathilde. *Follow your feelings, Rachel.*

'You're right, Beth needs…' Needs so much. She had been frightened with Alice away from her and frightened about her own inability to let go. She was more than frightened for me. Who was looking after Beth?

Upstairs, she was still watching Alice sleep. I sat down, put my arm around her, drew her close, and gave her what warmth I could. 'Cwtch up to me, Beth. Let go.' She snuggled into my chest. 'Got you, babe, got you,' I said, without a single panic alarm inside.

I let all the motherly love I could find flow into her. And I could feel crumbs down inside my pyjamas and they didn't matter, because Beth relaxed in my arms.

The word 'cwtch' had always spoken to me of tacky gift shops and sentimentalised Welsh identity. But the reality was far more real and far more mysterious. And full of crumbs. I knew that Beth felt safe and comforted. That she was at home in my secure hug. And I had found the power to open myself up that far.

I seemed to be a human being after all. 'Thank you, Mathilde,' I whispered.

Beth didn't ask, she smiled at sleeping Alice and up at the curtains. And she echoed my words. 'Thank you, Mathilde.'

32

WEIRD TOGETHER

Alice

I went to school on Monday scared shitless about Rachel. She'd had a seizure in the night – just a little one. But Mam said Rachel's doctor had called and she needed tests. Okay, tests. But Mam wouldn't let Rachel take me to school without her coming along too. That was like putting a big red flag on Rachel's head.

I coped most of the day, hiding in my little Alice world and letting school drift past me. But half-an-hour before home time, Shareen screamed, and then she was on the floor, all tangled up with her chair. I pushed past the gawping Evils, Kamala managed to lift the chair off, and then I was down with Shareen and Miss Akoto.

Shareen was coming round, but each time I looked at her, I saw Rachel. I curled up in a ball, so tight that not even epilepsy could get in. Miss Akoto put her hand on my shoulder for a moment. She had clocked that I was not okay, but was too busy to help.

Paramedics turned up and Shareen managed to walk out with them, and the rest of the class had gone somewhere else with the teaching assistant. Which left me still curled in a ball and Kamala sitting on the floor. Kamala stroked my head, like I was a puppy or something. I pulled away, and she walked off.

Miss Akoto came back. 'Kamala would be your friend if you let her.'

Kamala, the biggest girl in class? Some hope.

'Let's get you tidied up, Alice. Your mother will be here.' And we went to the cloakroom and no one was there, so Miss Akoto helped me wipe my face and tidy my hair. 'You're very brave – the way you help Shareen,' she said.

We walked to the door together, and most people had gone, but Mam was by the gate hanging on to Rachel's arm, and they both looked stressed. I rushed over to Rachel. 'No seizures?'

'Hello, Rachel would be better,' Mam said.

'Scared for you. Shareen had one.'

Miss Akoto dodged around zombie parents on phones and reached Mam. 'Alice was upset over Shareen. It hasn't troubled her before. She said she was worried about Rachel having tests.' She looked at Rachel. 'Are you Rachel?'

'Course she is,' I said, stroking Rachel's arm. Alive Rachel's arm.

'Is Shareen okay?' Rachel asked.

'Not a big seizure, but we have to follow the procedure and send her to hospital. Then her poor mother has to fetch her.'

'I've ended up in hospital a few times when it wasn't needed.'

'Is there anything I can say to Alice if she gets anxious?' Miss Akoto said.

Rachel twisted her hair, not looking at me. 'Epilepsy isn't often dangerous. But Alice and Beth have moved in with me, so she's facing it at home as well. I hope she'll get used to it.'

Words slipped out of my mouth by mistake. 'Rachel's not going to die.'

'Oh.' Rachel stepped back. 'I'm not in big danger. Is this what's upset you?'

'What do you think, pest? Pest, you are, in my head. Cos I love you.'

'Oh, Alice.'

And now she was looking at me, I couldn't look at her.

Mam was standing hugging herself. 'You alright, Mam?'

'Let's go inside,' Miss Akoto said.

Mam shook her head, but I wasn't having her hiding stuff and took her by the arm.

Now we were sitting in my classroom, and Mam looked funny on her too-small chair. One part of my brain thought she looked funny, anyway. Another part of my brain wanted to make Mam better forever. Rachel looked comfortable on her small chair, but Rachel sits on the floor a lot, so maybe that's why.

Rachel shook her head. 'This is what I hate about epilepsy. I can have ordinary seizures and upset the people closest to me.'

'Bigger seizures than Shareen – I looked them up,' I said. 'Tonic-clonic, they're called. And tonic ones at night without the clonic bit. Rachel had one last night.'

'Did I?' Rachel looked bothered.

'We both came, but you were sleeping again. Mam sat with you forever.'

'I didn't want to disturb you this morning,' Mam said. 'Because of your meeting at work – I told Tom when he came to pick you up.'

'I'll need to record it.'

'It's on your chart already. I am getting used to it. I've seen three kinds, now.'

'But it disturbs you – no need to pretend,' Miss Akoto said.

Mam closed her eyes. 'I know what's happening: we've got into a circle. I don't want Alice upset, Alice doesn't want me upset, and Rachel doesn't want either of us upset. So – we all get upset.'

Miss Akoto put her hand on my shoulder. 'Alice, why don't you stand back and let Kamala help Shareen?' She turned to Rachel. 'Alice is always the first there and helps Shareen talk about it. Some of the others give Shareen a bad time. But Kamala is a very kind girl too.'

'Thank you for helping Alice without making a thing of it,' Rachel said. 'I was a pupil like Alice – it's tough to be on a different wavelength to the rest of the class.'

Miss Akoto smiled. 'Alice says you're a particle physicist and a musician and... and make robots together...?' And from the way she said it, I wasn't sure whether Miss Akoto had believed me. But now she would have to.

'We're still working on our first robot,' Rachel said. 'I researched in particle physics before I moved here. I don't do the exciting stuff anymore, I'm afraid.'

'Alice played the piano in assembly. Do you teach her?'

O-o.

'She has a teacher, but it will be fun to play together,' Rachel said.

'Not too much in assembly – they think I'm weird already.'

Miss Akoto turned me to look at her. 'Weird? I'm from Ghana, but stayed in Wales after my PGCE because I love it. I'm learning Welsh, which my Ghanaian friends say is weird. I wear traditional Ghanaian clothes because I like them. I go to church, which my local friends say is weird. And my degree is in economics, but I chose teaching. If people think I'm weird, I don't mind. Be yourself, Alice – we can be weird together.'

Weird together?' That was the best bit of sunshine in the day. 'Yeah – you, me, Rachel and Mam. And Dad. Especially Dad. All weird and all different.'

'If you're worried about Rachel and need time, ask me.' She turned to Mam. 'Ms Howells?'

'Beth.'

'Beth. Try not to keep it in when you're upset. Alice will pick it up anyway.'

Mam shrugged. 'That's what I tell everyone else. I'm a trained therapist.'

'Not so easy at home?' Miss Akoto tipped her head like she does when I say a long word when a short one would do.

Mam shook her head, smiled and said, 'Thank you. For caring. We'll manage.'

'Sorted,' I said as we walked outside. 'She knows you're not imaginary now, Rachel.' And I skipped between Mam and Rachel all the way up the street. But I was working hard at not being worried.

Nan's car was parked crooked in front of the house. Mam rushed down the street. 'I hope Joe's okay.' Granddad must have been in the studio.

Nan was at the door, and no, there was nothing wrong a hug from me wouldn't cure. She hunted through her bag and picked out three gold-trimmed invitation cards, one of them with my name on it. First view of Dad's exhibition at a gallery down by the bay. Thursday evening, drinks, smart casual, by invitation only. Smart casual – that sounded very adult.

Mam was sort-of fizzing with excitement, wandering in and out of the kitchen. 'I didn't think he'd get it together in time.'

I linked my arm through Rachel's. 'You'll go? Mam might need you.'

'Why do you say that?' Mam said.

I mouthed, 'Wenda.' Wobbly Wenda with her sticky-out boobs.

'Because of Wenda?' Mam rolled her eyes. 'I'm glad he's back with her. She'll keep his fingers out of the drugs cabinet.' But I wanted to give Mam a hug.

'Wenda will be behind this,' Nan said. 'He owes too much to too many people.'

Granddad Joe walked through, wiping his hands on a rag. 'Guess who'll get paid back last? They call parents long-suffering for a reason. You three going together?'

Rachel put her arm around Mam's waist. 'I've barely met him – why not?'

'Siân hates do's,' Granddad said. 'We'll go on Friday. Remember, Beth, there's only one opinion on his pictures he trusts. Your invite is the one that matters to Iestyn. Not the critics, not Wenda Wonderful.'

'Wobbly Wenda,' I said, and Granddad laughed.

Nan tapped Rachel's arm. 'Hospital. I'll be round at ten. Gives me something to do apart from clearing up after His Majesty.' She poked Granddad.

'Yeah, Rachel – no getting out of it with Nan on your case.' I was thinking about the weird together thing again. Granddad had his own special way of being weird, but Nan… I couldn't think of anything weird about Nan. Maybe weird people need not-weird people to sort them out. And Nan is the best.

33

NEST OF ANTS

Rachel

On Tuesday afternoon, I went into Julie Cook's office with Siân to hold my hand if needed. I'd been through all the tests, Siân had got some knitting done, and we'd had sandwiches downstairs. I wasn't exactly scared – I'd been through the routine often enough – but I did expect some kind of result.

Or not. Julie looked worried: I could tell by her anxious flicks between screens. Normally, she was essence of calm. I was used to resting my eyes on her serene presence across the rehearsal hall, caressing her cello like a familiar lover. Strangely, she always claimed that I had the same calming effect on her. But not today.

'Serious, is it?' Siân asked after a minute's uneasy silence.

Julie didn't look up. 'We'll get there.'

'Is Rachel safe?'

'Wait a mo.'

Rather more than a mo later, Julie turned round. 'You should be safe for a few days, but I can't leave you on this dose. Your body will get used to it.'

'I'm not so tired already.'

She nodded and wrote in a box on her screen. 'Rachel, I

don't want to alarm you too much, but we have found something. It might not even be related to your epilepsy, but it needs investigating.'

'Something?'

'I've checked back through earlier scans, and it was there, vaguely. So small, no one noticed – it wasn't what we were scanning for. We need to put you through a more accurate scan. You have a small lump at the base of your brain. I can't measure any growth between scans and so it's almost certainly benign, but it might be what's skewing your seizure patterns.'

Just hearing Julie speak the words, I was already imagining the lump in the back of my head. That feeling like a nest of ants at the base of my skull I kept getting. 'You say, small.'

'Tiny – four millimetres – that's why we missed it. But it's in a sensitive spot.'

'So, what do we do?'

'We can't use radio or chemo there. And opening you up is a drastic option I want to avoid. I'm hoping the right combination of drugs might make your brain forget that it's there. But a more accurate scan is the first step. This could be a long job, but there's no reason to stop you getting on with your life while we investigate.

'So, what's the next step?'

'Scans, drug changes to get you off this dose. You know the score – we'll haul you in again. A week should do it.'

I did know the score. I would sit around in a ward for a week, alternately bored out of my mind and scared silly while I was scanned and tested, and Julie altered my drug regime. A regular chore, because my epilepsy had fallen out of any recognisable pattern as I'd grown older. But maybe Julie had found the reason it had become so unpredictable.

And whether the lump was dangerous or not, a week in hospital seemed a lot longer, now that I had a family.

Siân gave Julie a hard stare. 'You do know what you're doing?'

Julie mouthed yes but shook her head. 'Some of the time, we're working in the dark. But we do have a lot of information to turn on the lights. And don't you worry.' Julie smiled at me. 'No way do I want anyone else leading the Sinfonietta.'

I left Julie's room in a daze, and Siân sat me down on the first seats we came to. 'I wish she hadn't said anything until they'd found something definite.'

'No, Siân. Julie knows I would pick it up straight away. I'm a scientist – I know all the tests and how they work. I'm happier knowing. And it really could be irrelevant. Just a lump in the wrong place.'

'What are you going to say?'

'To Beth and Alice? I don't know.'

'Maybe leave it for a bit.'

'They'll have to know if it comes to serious intervention.'

'I'll tell Joe. That gives you someone else to talk to. Alice will take the facts when we need to tell her. It's Beth who worries me.'

I didn't like the idea of keeping anything from Beth and Alice, but they had enough to bear already. Maybe I could introduce the subject gradually.

I saw Julie again at orchestra in the evening, and she wasn't exactly comforting. 'There are quite a few approaches we can try. I've been contacting other people for similar case histories. Don't panic too much – the team are onto it.'

There was no disguising her message; I knew how many variables might affect epilepsy and how hard they were to disentangle. The lump could yet prove to be irrelevant – just a freak of human architecture – and my epilepsy would still be unstable.

But what if it was the problem? There was that nest of ants at the base of my skull. If it really was connected to the lump, it wasn't new. But I couldn't remember how long I'd been getting the feeling – certainly long before I met Beth and Alice – and my epilepsy had been growing more erratic for at least five or six years.

Any attempt to diagnose myself would be futile. My brain would keep on inventing new symptoms, and I would fulfil Dad's slur about it all being in my head. What would he have thought of a lump in my head? Would that have satisfied him?

I was going to have to trust Julie. I did trust Julie. But...

*

Alice

The new door into the studio and the floor were done, and Granddad and his mates expected to finish in a week or so. But Mam was getting itchy. Every time Mam gets stressed, she needs to paint – even when it's dead inconvenient – it's what makes Mam who she is.

And Rachel was having a week off work. Mainly because she didn't want Mrs Jones and Tom fussing over her. So, Mam passed her gallery work over to drippy Graham and got painting Rachel, up in the bathroom out of Granddad's way. And where she could paint Rachel with no clothes on without shocking Granddad and his mates.

I was happy about Mam painting Rachel – it meant I could go to school without too much worry. But Rachel told me on Tuesday that Mam was just standing there, most of the time. She had started five or six paintings and dumped them all. Not a good sign.

I was back from school on Wednesday, looking at a canvas with nothing much on it when Mam came out with the problem. 'I keep seeing Rachel in the doorway. I truly thought she was dead.'

'Okay.' (Gulp.) 'Mam, why not paint Rachel like that?'

'Alice – I couldn't!'

Rachel came through from the kitchen. 'I've never seen myself having a seizure. I always miss that bit.' And she had her scientist look on her face. Like she needed to know.

Mam dressed her in the navy suit and white blouse she'd worn when we first met and she screamed on that bench in Queen Street. 'You told me that's when I saw you naked,' Mam said. Which was a bit of a weird thing to say, because Rachel wasn't naked – not in the middle of Cardiff.

Mam arranged her on the bath mat with her arms and legs at odd angles and an arched back. It didn't look comfortable, but Rachel said it was okay.

Then Mam frowned at sketch after sketch, tearing them off and dropping them on the floor. 'Stop, Mam,' I said. And Mam ran out of the room.

'Wait,' Rachel said, and held on to my arm. 'I told her what's wrong – it only seemed fair. But she's taken it badly.' And Rachel told me about that tiny lump – so small, they could hardly see it. And which might or might not matter.

I thought about telling Rachel everything Dad had told me about the way her father's death freaked Mam. Maybe I should have told Rachel, but I didn't want to say anything without asking Mam. And Mam didn't even know how much I knew. Not just about her dad dying, but about what happened next.

34

CONJOINED

Rachel

For Iestyn's exhibition at a sleek-looking gallery down at the bay, I tried to adopt the businesswoman persona that had deserted me since I'd begun to share a desk and giggles with Tom. I let a nobody hold the glass door open for us. Accepted a flute of champagne with a distant smile to another nobody. And felt my facade drop. In this exhibition, nobody was a nobody. And beside me, Alice had her mouth wide open.

Life was everywhere. Life ecstatic, life loved, life tragic, life transient. Living energy flowed from each wall. Iestyn and photography – Beth and painting. From my first glance around the gallery, I knew how they had bonded, how they had clashed and why they kept on tussling, unable to let each other go.

I could remember the stark, gritty Iestyn Corbett pictures of old. I'd expected him to have matured into Our Graham's world. Grainy nudes, or driftwood and steel in shades of grey. Or, given his addiction, to Mapplethorpe pain. What I got was life in all its exuberance, and Beth's arm around my waist. She beamed around her, giving a whistled breath of joy at each new image. Alice rushed from picture to picture, face up close to each one, drinking it in.

Colour street photography at its most revealing made up half the exhibition, and the other half was altogether new to me. Plants and trees had been given the lighting of studio portraits in black and white. Without the green equals plant association, each showed a vibrant personality.

People hung around refreshment tables, facing away from the exhibition. Clearly, one must not look over-enthusiastic. But we were not 'one' and took our time to absorb each lovely image. Alice had been round three times before we reached the last one.

Iestyn and a woman with spiky, glossy black hair stood apart from the crowd. He was smaller than I'd imagined, and older. Short-cropped brindle hair, stubble, leather jacket, brilliant white shirt and jeans. The ageing rock star look.

It was hard to tell Wenda's age under all the makeup, but Iestyn looked far older than I remembered from seeing him in casualty. 'Beth, how old is Iestyn?'

'Fifty-four.'

'But Siân and Joe…?'

'You've worked it out. Siân has weathered well.'

Beth got a relaxed, 'Hi babe,' from them both, with hugs that looked genuine.

Alice avoided 'Wobbly Wenda' but couldn't escape her father taking her by the hand and inspecting her. 'Look at you, all grown-up and smart.'

She poked out her tongue and wriggled away.

Beth gestured around the exhibition. 'You didn't think you'd manage, did you?'

He smiled, a strange effect in a drawn face. 'It's not my worst.'

'And there was you telling me you'd worn out the language of photography. You've hardly started!'

'Rachel?' Iestyn stepped forward. 'I keep hearing good things from Mam and Dad.' He looked me in the eye. 'You'll know what a crap father I am. I have tried.'

To meet this full on, spoken in front of Alice, Beth and Wenda, left me at a loss. I squeezed his hand and kept hold of it for a few moments. One of the family. 'I've never seen anything like these,' I said.

'You really like them?' He sounded eager, almost childlike.

I gave him the heartfelt smile he needed.

'I knew Mam wouldn't come tonight,' he said.

We made another slow circuit of the pictures with Iestyn and Wenda while Alice gravitated to one single picture of some teenagers on a climbing frame in Llanedeyrn. When we caught up with her, Alice gestured to one boy at the side of the picture, almost out of the frame. 'Enigmatic, he is.'

Iestyn glanced at Beth. Beth glanced at me. New words to Alice are like sweets to other children. She will hoard them, taste their flavour and suck at them. She can never help sharing them, and sometimes, she'll gorge on them. Enigmatic.

After another wander around, we left Iestyn to his evening in the limelight. Outside, Beth shook out her hair and made a show of being comfortably herself again. 'Well then, what do you think of him?'

'I don't know what to think.'

'I never do. Contradiction is his middle name. He's a driven man.'

'He's a mad genius,' Alice said. 'And he's still a rubbish dad.' She scratched her head. 'Trust me to choose him as a father.'

'Enigmatic?' I said, and she poked me.

We walked along the old dock, gazing at the twinkling lights around the bay. I looked out at the further lights beneath Penarth head, spread my arms and let the breeze chill me, but Beth turned me back to face her. 'You understand about us?'

'You could be conjoined. No wonder you fought.'

'Still fight. I'm more comfortable with you than I've ever been with Iestyn.'

'Now she realises,' Alice said.

'Half of me wishes I could disturb you in the way he can,' I said.

Beth kissed me on the nose. 'You have quite enough ways of disturbing me.'

'Too true,' said a small voice. 'Enigmatic.'

Alice's enthusiasm for her father's pictures gave me half an idea, and when we got back, I took my camera bag out of the cupboard. 'Would you like a try?'

'That's a PROPER camera!'

'The camera isn't the whole story. Photography like your father's is all about skill and artistry and timing. I haven't used it in a while – I'll have to charge up the batteries. Fancy a go at the weekend?'

I opened the bag, and Alice ran her fingers along the lens cases. 'YEAH!'

Beth laughed. 'Iestyn won't let her near his.'

On Friday evening, Siân came round to sit with Alice. She had seen the exhibition and for the first time, actually sounded proud of her son. It was my turn to model in life class and I'd been looking forward to another chance.

I was in a longer pose and after a while, I heard Stanley talking to Beth in an undertone. 'Is she meant to look angry? I don't mean… It's fine by me.'

People were looking back and forth between an embarrassed Stanley and me. Beth rescued us. 'That's perfect, Rachel. Hold it there. Notice the shoulders, the lines of tension; the way an expression spreads from the face and out through the whole body.'

When they disappeared downstairs, Beth didn't ask. Fortunately, because I wouldn't have found a rational explanation. She just gave naked and exposed Rachel a mug of peppermint tea and a challenge. 'Could you manage to hold the same pose with a different expression? I'm not expecting happy.'

I shook out my limbs and stretched my back. 'Yes, I can do that. Tell me a nice memory. Something about Alice when she was younger.'

Beth told me all about chips and ice cream on the beach at Porthcawl while I sat back on the stool and composed myself. It was their first happy day out after Joe and Siân had finally decided that Beth was as good as a daughter to them. Tenderness filled her eyes as she shuffled through some pictures on her phone and found a smaller Alice with ketchup and chocolate ice cream around her mouth, leaning on Joe's leg.

Tenderness: it was an easy emotion to borrow for a while. I could almost imagine that I'd been there, and when the others came back, Beth carefully arranged me on the stool. She seemed to have memorised my exact coordinates in space: this was an identical pose with added tenderness. My hands were crossed in my lap, a nod to Gwen John's girls, but that didn't stop me playing my imaginary violin with imaginary limbs.

Tenderness: that Fauré Berceuse I'd played with Isabelle. And tenderness for Cai and Isabelle joined my tenderness for Beth and Alice. Tenderness: Mathilde was my accompanist, and tenderness across the years grew inside me. She was a familiar friend now, a pianist as well as a violinist, and no longer a static portrait.

My reward for borrowing a pleasant feeling was a luminous drawing by Beth, executed in primary colours with wax crayons. Morwenna lingered, asking Beth technical questions about composition. I chatted with Stanley while Beth was busy, and he told me about his parents who had upped and left when he was twenty, leaving him to care for his disabled grandmother alone. He went home after a quick hug from Beth that Morwenna clearly thought was unnecessary.

When Morwenna turned to go, she stopped close in front of me. 'I learned a lot, this evening,' she said. I reached for her hands, and her rigid body spoke of a shock I knew well. But her bony hands squeezed mine back. 'Good to know I have friends here.' And she made her stately progress down the stairs.

'I think she's accepted your right to teach her,' I said.

Beth shook her head. 'I doubt it. But maybe she's accepted that what she gets out of the class is friendship. Nothing wrong with that.'

I took another look at Beth's picture. If this image was her impression of me, she saw a serene beauty I'd never felt. 'I'm not bad looking, am I?'

'Vanity, is it, now? Get used to it: you're gorgeous.' She picked some coloured wax out of her nails. 'I've never managed this before. I've always done the finishing touches in private. Sketches, yes, but never a whole composition.'

'Honestly?'

'Don't look at me as if I'm an alien, Rachel! I'm not good in the spotlight – that's why I studied therapy.' She pointed a finger. 'You know where I got the confidence.'

'From me? No – I've just been a mess. One big mess.'

'Scientifically correct, I suppose. You have, and you've taken me out of myself. Shit, I might even undress in public one day. I've always modelled clothed at art school.' Another shock. Modelling naked felt so natural that I would never have imagined Beth having such inhibitions.

She rolled up the picture. 'You and me at our best.'

'At our best,' I echoed, and even as the words formed in my mouth, the moment slipped away. This picture was history now. But it was ours, and it was new history.

35

EMMY'S HERE

Alice

December, and proper steely greyness. Winter, but I didn't care. Not with Rachel's digital SLR and tripod to myself. Rachel explained the controls, but I soon found it easier just to experiment. I had it lined up on the apple tree and simply changed one setting at a time. With Rachel standing next to me, shivering for science.

Focus: obvious. Aperture, not so obvious, until I found that pictures with a wide setting looked cool, like Dad's arty stuff. Depth of field, Rachel called it. Shutter speed: what it says. Everything else: 'Alice, I'm FREEZING. You know enough to take pictures now.' But I still took a few more.

Granddad kept poking his head out of a hole in the workshop wall, where Nan was helping him prepare the last window. Each time I swung the camera round, Granddad ducked in again, but Rachel hid at the side of the studio and caught a picture on her phone. By then, it was so cold I was expecting my toes to drop off.

Mam rescued us from potential polar bear attack. 'Hot chocolate's ready!'

While we were warming up hurting fingers on our mugs, Mam looked at my pictures.

'Mam – don't you dare say Dad would be proud!'

'You might want to talk to him,' Rachel said. 'There's not much I can teach you.'

'Nah – I'll just experiment. Dad's bound to say I'm doing it wrong.'

Rachel looked at Mam but didn't say anything.

'Why don't you take the camera this afternoon?' Mam said. 'It might even warm up a bit.'

Tom and Emmy were meeting us for an outing, but Rachel would be going to hospital next week, and Granddad didn't want to go far in case of trouble. Mam stayed back to help Nan decorate the housemaid's room, ready for my birthday, with luck.

I knew where Granddad liked going, and sure enough, he took us to the woods where he played when he was a kid. 'Crackin' place, it is.' Rachel had never been there before, and neither had Tom and Emmy. Granddad calls the place Velindre Woods, but that's not what it says on the sign next to the old canal down the hill from Whitchurch.

Tom parked his car behind us, but Emmy looked nervous and wouldn't say hello. She kept glancing sideways at Rachel, and I wondered what she was picking up.

We trudged up the path at the top of the bank, and like magic, the sun came out, beams slanting through skeleton trees, one clinging on to its last golden leaves. Photo opportunity. STOP, Granddad.

But he didn't hear.

Another picture, with the old canal way down below us. Granddad was off round the corner, but Tom and Emmy hadn't even got going. I could see Tom trying to get Emmy to move her feet. We waited for them and left Granddad on

autopilot. If Rachel had a seizure now with just me here…
But she didn't.

A little speck of brown fluttered down from one tree to
the next and started edging up the trunk. A Treecreeper. I
raised the camera. The Treecreeper spiralled round to the
other side of the trunk. Rachel crept along in front of me
and then gently trod in some leaves – enough to alert the
Treecreeper. It spiralled back to my side of the trunk. Focus
– zoom – focus again. Steady the camera… result. And
again. And again. I'm Alice Howells, wildlife photographer.

Granddad was hurrying back to Rachel. 'Where were
you?' I put my finger to my lips and took another picture.

Still no Tom and Emmy. 'Let's not crowd her,' I said. 'You
wait here, Granddad – she knows us.'

Emmy turned her back and crouched down when we got
to the end of the path. 'Rachel scared scary.'

I patted Rachel's arm. 'Truth, now.'

'Just a bit bothered about hospital, Em.'

'Rachel bad head.'

Rachel looked at me, eyes wide. How much did Emmy
know? And how?

Tom waved us back and muttered under his breath. 'She's
tuning in. Stay clear – she might flip.' And from the frown
she gave him, Emmy didn't like being talked about one bit.
Still crouched down, she pressed her hands against the sides
of her head and beads of sweat ran down her forehead on
this freezing afternoon. I'd seen people lose it big time in
Mam's art class, but I was sure Rachel hadn't. Emmy looked
ready to explode.

Tom just stood there, big and helpless. Some use he was.
Rachel and I glanced at each other. I thought I would have

the best chance of helping and stepped forward, but Rachel held me back. 'Let me try.'

She stood in front of Emmy and looked down at her feet. 'You're right, Emmy. I am scared. I have got a bad head. Would you look after me?'

Emmy sprung up and two gentle arms wrapped around Rachel. 'Me look after best Rachel. All okay now. All best okay. Emmy's here.' And Rachel buried her head in Emmy's shoulder.

She really did need that comfort, and I wanted to hug Rachel too. But Emmy had bigger, softer hugs than me. 'She's all yours, Em,' I said.

Tom was still standing there, staring at his sister. I wondered about sneaking a picture of surprised Tom. But I decided that now was time for honesty all round. 'Tom, Emmy's right about Rachel.' And I told him about the lump inside Rachel's head.

Now, Emmy was trying to mop Rachel's face with her own tissue. Probably a used one, but Rachel was letting her do it. 'Thank you, Em,' she said, stood straighter and took Emmy by the hand. 'Will you take me along here to see Granddad Joe's woods, Em?' And Emmy led the way, not letting go of Rachel. On such a narrow path, Rachel struggled to stay up close, but she gave Emmy the best possible chance to look after her.

When we reached Granddad at the gate at the top, Emmy said, 'All better now?'

'Thank you, Em. That was kind,' Rachel said, and got another hug.

I took the chance to flip through my pictures, and Tom came for a look. 'Hey! That's some close-up. Small brown bird.'

'Treecreeper. Not like any other bird. Specialised.'

'Small brown specialised bird. Well captured.'

I smiled across at Rachel and held up the camera. 'Thank you.'

'Best birdy,' Emmy said. 'Me got best Rachel, too. And best Alice. And best Tom.' She gave Granddad a puzzled look. 'And best old man.'

'That's Granddad Joe.'

'Best old man suits me fine – it's hard work being a granddad.'

Tom was staring up into a tall beech tree. 'There's an atmosphere about this place. Peaceful.'

'An atmosphere of wild garlic in spring,' Granddad said, and rubbed his chin.

'Story coming,' I whispered to Rachel.

'When I was a lad...' I had to clamp my hand over my mouth, but Granddad was lost in memories. '...we used to come up here on our bikes. Nothing at all like this in those days. It's more peaceful, now. Settled. I'll show you what I mean on the way back.'

So far, Rachel had let Emmy guide her, but now Emmy leant on Rachel for support as we clambered down the steep slopes through drifts of old leaves to the path at the bottom. Rachel smiled at me, and I put my thumb up. She knew what was happening.

The flat trail beside the old canal would have been fun on a quiet day, but it was busy with cross-looking cyclists, weaving in and out of straggling Saturday afternoon families. I kept to the side and took some pictures of fallen trees left in the water for the wildlife.

A man on a bike skidded around Emmy, and Emmy clung onto Rachel, now her most trusted person in the universe. Tom gave the cyclist a mouthful, but he had gone.

Granddad showed me a surprise that even I didn't expect. He pointed away from the canal. Behind a wire fence, swampland stretched away under a tangle of low bushes. 'That wild enough for you?' It could have been a scene from the American South. I half expected a Lesser Welsh Alligator to stare back at me from a pool. And Granddad was back in story mode. 'When I was a lad, what do you think we came to see, just here?'

'Frogs? Herons?'

Granddad grinned. 'We came to watch the last steam trains. Just over there, where the houses are now, was a massive old factory, Melingriffith tin plate works, and behind it, Radyr yard – railway sidings.'

'And now it's boring houses, Granddad. I wish I'd seen it.'

'One of the biggest tin plate factories in the world, once upon a time. All around here were dumps of old metal. Terrible mess. But nature always wins in the end.'

'With a bit of help from people.' Tom pointed at a *Friends of Forest Farm* sign.

'We need people like that,' I said, thinking of the mess humans were making of our only planet.

'Me like people,' Emmy said.

When we got home, Mam had cooked a big pot of lentil stew. With Tom and Emmy as well, it was a tight fit around the kitchen table.

Emmy hung close by Rachel's side, and let Tom chop up her (soft) vegetables. And that reminded me of how not-helping worked in Mam's special needs art class. I nodded to Rachel, mimed cutting up and glanced at Emmy.

Suddenly, Rachel was struggling to cut up her carrots.

'Me help you,' Emmy said, took hold of the backs of her hands and helped her cut them into neat chunks. 'That's better, best Rachel.' Tom opened his mouth and shut it again. And I couldn't help a grin. Result!

Before they left, Tom took Rachel in the front room. Did he really think he was out of Emmy's earshot with that big voice of his? He wasn't out of mine.

'I've been away at sea too long – I don't know what Emmy can manage. Getting Mam to stand back is… Are you up for more looking-after?'

I didn't hear Rachel's reply, but behind me, I heard, 'Emmy's here, best Rachel.'

36

RIPPLES

Rachel

I needed more fresh air and borderless space before they confined me in the air-conditioned concrete, steel and glass world of the hospital. A good excuse for Siân to take us out from under Joe's feet in the studio. Beth's Porthcawl pictures decided Siân: she would be braver than Joe and take us to the seaside for a plate of chips.

Beth gave me a long hard look before getting in the front of the car with Siân. 'Are you sure this is safe?'

'I'm more likely to freeze than anything else.'

Alice and I crossed our fingers in the back seat and she quickly changed the subject. 'Should I show Dad the Treecreeper pictures?'

'It's up to you, Alice. I don't want to pressure you.'

She grinned. 'Yeah, Dad's got a use at last.'

'What if…' I spoke as Mathilde's idea came to me. 'The apple tree… If we mark out some stations for the tripod, you could take a series of close-up and wide field photos, spread out in time. Do it from the same stations – say – once a week, and you could make a complete record. The tree is more-or-less dormant now. You could catch all the stages until the fruit is ready in late summer. And then the leaves falling.'

'Awesome!'

'And you'd catch all the changing weather and light.' Yes, this idea wasn't from me. There was something fully-formed about it, as if it had been Mathilde's intention for Alice to explore the apple tree in depth. There was some connection there that I couldn't quite reach. I left it in the dark for Mathilde to reveal in her own time.

'Remember – first apple's mine,' Alice said. Clearly, it still mattered now, when she could step out of the door and see the apple tree every day.

'I won't forget, Alice.' It wasn't much more than a month since I gave them the key to the gate, but our emotional journey felt like years. And it had started with that small letting-in beside the apple tree – giving them the key. A small change in intention at a time when my rational mind was urging me to keep my distance.

'Shock-stoppers on,' Alice commanded when we reached Porthcawl, and put her own in place. I seemed to be the smallest member of the party today. As we walked along the freezing promenade, the smell of the sea brought flash memories. Sandcastles with Uncle Gethin – not with Mum and Dad. Scratchy sand in my sandals. Hot dogs with Uncle Gethin and Mum saying they weren't healthy. And Dad shouting at Mum – saying it was a waste of time coming all this way to see my one remaining great uncle.

'Should have brought a bucket and spade,' Beth said.

Alice rolled her eyes but gave Beth the camera bag and raced me down to the water's edge to dip our fingers in the sea.

Just the two of us where sand, still air and gently swishing waves met. The soft greys of the calm sea and sky were the antithesis of the artificial, angular grey slabs that I associated with my retreat into corporate routine and structure. These were the fluid, mysterious Welsh greys that Gwen John had used to veil her subjects. And I felt a comforting warmth from Mathilde as the idea entered my head.

Wrapped in the gentle swishing sound of the water as little ripples toyed with us, our edges seemed to blur, loosened by the natural elements.

*

Alice

Softening in the sea and air – softening into each other. We stepped back a little way and stood holding hands for a long time, staring out beyond the horizon. To infinity. I cuddled into my favourite space against Rachel's side and the last of my awkwardness and doubt vanished. 'Rachel, can you be my mother too?'

'Maybe I am already. I think I've been growing into it, Alice.'

Rachel reached up and touched the back of her head. I don't think she even noticed herself doing it, but that lump might not give us much time to be mother and daughter. I pulled her closer. Wanted to look after her forever. 'Yeah, you're my mother by magic. Not trick magic – nature magic.'

'Nature magic. The magic of becoming?' Rachel said. 'Becoming your mother makes me very happy, Alice.'

Infinite time passed. A second or two, maybe.

'You are my mother because we fit together. But I'm still calling you Rachel.'

We wandered back up the beach holding hands. And I

knew I would hold hands with my second mother even in front of the Evils. Because she's Rachel.

We crunched through the pebbles at the top of the beach, and skipped up the steps to Mam and Nan, leaning on the railings. 'Chips for Mam,' I said. 'Indoors – I'm bloody freezing. And Rachel is officially my mam too, but I'm sticking to calling her Rachel.'

Mam and Nan met each other's eyes and nodded in perfect time, and me and Rachel shared a smile – they knew we meant it.

We celebrated our family-ness with chips in a warm snack bar beside a steamed-up window. Mam smothered her chips in ketchup – she hardly ever touches the stuff at home. 'You like chips with your ketchup, Mam?'

'Only at the seaside.'

'Two seriously weird mothers,' I told Nan. Maybe I'm a weird daughter.

The snack bar didn't have a toilet, and I discovered I still had a ten-year-old's body. One that needed crossed legs.

'Come on,' Mam said.

The public toilets were freezing and smelly. Not the way to end such a special trip. I needed more nature magic before we left. Rachel took my hand for another trip to the water's edge.

Even going down the steps, I could tell Rachel was on the limit. She was gritting her teeth and shading her shock-stoppers. 'You should be getting back,' I said.

'We'll be quick,' Rachel said.

The water wasn't so far out now, and I REALLY wanted to get Rachel safe. We crouched, dipped our fingers in the water, shared a glance, and turned back. But now Rachel was leaning on my arm, seriously dizzy.

'Give me your phone, quick.'

'Call Beth. Not 999. Not yet.'

I did, and saw Mam and Nan head for the steps.

'It's 999 if you go out, Rachel. Doctor Cook said.'

'Let's just get out of here.'

Mam was already scrambling over the stones and Nan was not far behind. I wasn't managing to keep Rachel upright, and Mam took hold of her.

'I've called an ambulance,' Nan said, 'You heard Doctor Cook.'

No way would Rachel make it off the beach. I took off my coat to make her a pillow, led Mam and Rachel to a patch of sand and cleared away a couple of rocks. 'Get down here, Rachel. I've got your phone – give me your shock-stoppers.'

Now, I had Rachel in the recovery position, her head pillowed between my legs and Mam holding her. Rachel was beyond speaking, sucking in breaths, putting off the seizure, every muscle tense.

'You'll be fine. I'm with you. You can let go now.'

And I knew just how scary that letting go was. I was Rachel for a moment, feeling her grip on the present moment loosening.

'With you, I am.'

She twitched, convulsed a couple of times, let out a long breath, and relaxed. And I remembered something Rachel had said. Never seeing herself have a seizure. She was safe now, and Mam had her head turned away, not bearing to look. I took a quick picture on Rachel's phone.

Then Rachel was stirring. I stroked her head. 'You back?'

Her eyes blinked. 'Hello, Alice – sorry about that.' And she gave me the loveliest smile. 'Thank you – for being with me.'

Mam heaved a sigh. A spooked sigh.

'Cancel the ambulance,' I said.

'You sure?' Mam said.

'I'm fine.' Rachel said, but I could feel her headache by our own personal WiFi connection. And there was something else. O-o.

Nan wandered away, cancelling the ambulance.

Rachel smirked at me and I smirked back.

Mam looked puzzled. 'What?'

'Sand's a bit damp – doesn't happen often,' Rachel said.

'Don't worry – all sand's stuck to your jeans,' I said.

She looked down. 'I might get away with it.' She struggled to stand up with help from Mam. 'Are you sure you want me as a mother, Alice?'

'Want? I've already got you. No backing out now.'

37

FROZEN MOMENT

Rachel

Going home sitting on a bin bag in Siân's car wasn't a glamorous experience, especially when I discovered she kept the bin bag in there to hide under a cushion for some of her older friends who wouldn't admit to bladder problems. I'd gone from kid to elderly relative. But it didn't matter because I was Alice's mother.

While I had a shower, Beth invaded the studio. Joe hadn't finished sealing the windows or a hundred other details, but Beth needed to paint. And, I suspected, she needed space to breathe, away from me.

Alice and I had started gathering bits and pieces for tea (cereal? really?) when a distant church bell distracted me. A memory of Mum walking to Evensong skipped into my mind. I had promised to call after my appointment, and nearly had several times this week, but not got around to it. 'Alice, I keep forgetting to call Mum.'

'Forgetting?' She cocked her head. 'Yeah, I'll buy that.'

I picked up my phone, unlocked it, and there was the picture.

A frozen moment. I am laid on the beach on my side. My head and shoulders fill most of the image, with my legs splayed out behind. Beth's hands and Siân's legs are visible. My back is arched and my mouth is open wide. A pair of vacant eyes stare. Rachel Sarah Bothwell screams her absence at me.

Alice put her hand to her mouth. 'Sorry – forgot – shouldn't have done it.' She took the phone and flicked it back to my picture of Joe looking out of the window.

I needed to see it properly and swiped it back into place. This was how I looked each time. Absent.

'Sorry – I thought about you and Mam's painting – thought you wanted to see.'

'I did, you're right. It's just a shock.'

Alice pulled out a chair and got me to sit at the table. 'Meant to tell you. Forgot.'

'You did right. I do need to see.' I pulled her close and she squeezed onto my lap. 'Alice, you are one awesome girl, putting up with me. Look at the state I get into.'

'Not your fault. And that seizure was pie. I knew it would be.'

'You did. You were as calm as anything – I could feel it – I wasn't frightened. That's thanks to you. I always get frightened.'

'I took it without asking. That's wrong.'

'I wasn't exactly there to ask, was I?' I needed another looked. 'And if you'd asked Beth, she wouldn't… Maybe we'd better not show her.'

Alice frowned. 'I need to talk to Mam. About her dad, mainly. She needs to manage better.'

'You really are one special girl.'

Alice grinned. 'Should be too! I'm your daughter, nutcase.'

An odd thought made me smile. 'Yesterday, we went a couple of miles, and you got some amazing photos. We took all that kit to Porthcawl, never even got the camera out, and ended up with one picture on a phone. But it's the one picture I needed to see.'

Beth didn't appear for tea. Joe munched my rubber-textured scones and left, knowing he wouldn't get back into the studio today.

I began to worry what state Beth might be in, and sent Alice to remind her that it was almost eight o'clock.

'YOU DO NOT INTERRUPT WHEN I'M WORKING.'

'You'll have to eat sometime, Mam.'

'GET OUT!'

I had been that interrupted person. Just reaching for a tantalising connection when a housemate would shout, 'it's four in the morning, for fuck's sake,' or some other such wickedness. And my mind would scramble, and I would have to start again from the beginning. I could work through storm, club mixes and roadworks, but never the sound of a human voice. 'It's my fault – I sent her,' I called.

'WHY CAN'T YOU BOTH… Sorry, I'll stop now. Wasn't getting anywhere anyway.' She appeared in the kitchen doorway in a paint-spattered overall and bare feet. Her face was a patchy red and swollen around the eyes. 'Where's Alice?'

'Ran upstairs.'

'Fuck! My fault.'

I reached out. 'Come here.'

She looked down her front, let her overall drop to the floor, and fell into my arms.

'It's hard, getting back into the groove, isn't it?'

'I'll go and say sorry to Alice. I shouldn't have shouted.' She headed off upstairs, and I hovered in the kitchen, knowing this wasn't over. Sure enough, a few minutes later, 'YOU DID WHAT?' echoed down the stairwell.

When I got there, Alice was looking down at me from the top of the playroom stairs. She opened out her arms and shook her head. Then I saw Beth curled in a beanbag on the far side of the room with her back to us. 'You showed her?' I asked.

'Without this?' Alice patted the phone in my jeans pocket. 'I told Mam she needs to talk about her dad.'

Beth shifted around. Her face was drained of colour. 'I didn't think Alice knew so much.'

'Knew what? Please, Beth?'

'Alice knows I've only told her the pretty version. And I should have told you.'

Alice went and perched next to her. 'Nan said you'd find it hard. It's okay. I'm good about it.'

Beth sat up. 'When did Nan tell you? She should never have done that.'

'Nah – I asked Dad, way back.' She cuddled close to Beth. 'I've been talking to Nan since we moved in – about you coping.'

I pulled another beanbag up close. 'Come on, now. It's safe to talk, Beth.'

'I should have told you from the start. And I shouldn't have left Alice to find out for herself. I've been as bad as Mam. She wouldn't let us talk about Dad, and that made it worse for us all.' Beth closed her eyes. 'Me and my sister were alone with Dad when he died. I was twelve.'

'Beth?'

'I tried to revive him. He was dead by the time the ambulance turned up. His heart. No warning.'

My response was from the gut. 'You really should not be around me.'

'Rachel – it's okay. Living with you doesn't hurt in the way I expected – dreaded. Yes, your seizures shock me. Each time, they shock me. I really did not think I'd manage to stay.'

'But you did.'

'I expected pain, and got…' She looked directly into my eyes. 'You still don't get how loving you really are, do you, Rachel? It's been buried so deep inside you.'

I couldn't speak, but our long silence hurt no one.

At last, Alice whispered, 'Mam, you are the bravest person in the world.'

I laid my hand on Beth's arm. 'You expected pain and still moved in.'

'It was a harder choice than you knew, that's all. But I've used you to confront my past. I should have told you from the start.'

In no way did I feel used, but I did seem to be strangely useful. 'Beth… Oh, what is she like, Alice?'

I expected a silly answer to break the tension. Alice supplied something else. 'Mam, you're the daughter your father was proud of. You know he was. Can I tell Rachel about you and your dad and painting?'

Beth sagged back into the beanbag. And Alice told me a story so organised that I knew she had been telling and re-telling herself ever since she had asked Iestyn about it. It was her ancestral story, a story she had never felt able to tell in front of her mother. And pride of her mother, of the grandfather she had never known, and of the heritage he had passed on to Beth flowed out of her as she spoke.

Beth was the youngest of three girls but almost an only child, five years younger than her next sister. She grew up in a happy home in Canton, over on the other side of Cardiff. Her mam was at home most of the time, taking in what work she could get. Gwyn Howells was a loving father, a sign writer and commercial artist.

In his spare time, Gwyn painted in oils, and taught his little Bethany how to sketch and paint in watercolours when she was still at infants school. By the time she was ten, her portraits in oils were winning prizes and causing a stir in the local press. 'Dad showed me the clippings,' Alice said. 'Echo and Western Mail. Your hair, Mam! All cut short!'

'Mam framed the articles, not the pictures,' Beth said. 'I had to walk past them every day.'

Alice carried on with her story. Gwyn took his daughter to adult art classes and helped her develop her own style in oils. He lived long enough to see it flower, with her distinctive abstraction of energy and movement, where a crowd of people would disappear, but the life would remain on the canvas. 'Dad showed me, Mam. Amazing, they are.'

'Iestyn always rated them. I gave him the lot – too many memories.'

Alice turned to me; her face troubled. 'Mam's doing the same stuff, downstairs.'

'You mean painting in the same way?'

Beth wiped her eyes. 'Mam wouldn't let me paint when Dad died. She hated the reminders.' Anger lit up her voice. 'She threw away Dad's paints and brushes – all his kit. And mine. I wanted to paint FOR him.'

'Oh, Beth–'

'Stronger than me, she was – I shouldn't have given in. I'm trying to paint what I would have painted then. It's a part of me I've never managed to express.'

'You should have someone with you. You know that, Beth: you're the therapist.'

'I didn't want to disturb you. And I couldn't think who else I'd manage it with.'

'There's me,' Alice said.

'Alice, no! It's about Dad dying and… No, it's not. I've made peace with that. It's the way Mam covered it up – smothered the memories – good and bad. It's about squashed feelings, stuck inside.'

Alice stood up and put her hands on her hips. 'Mam, you're doing what your mam did. Not sharing it. I'm old enough to understand – I know what hurt is.'

'But I don't want you hurt.'

'You know what Nan said? About you and Rachel?'

'About Rachel?' Beth sat up and grabbed my arm.

'She said you're frightened I'll be hurt as badly as you were if anything happens to Rachel. If she dies. You've gone guilty about being here, in case it hurts me. True?'

Beth looked at me, but Alice didn't wait for an answer. 'True. But everyone dies, Mam. Everyone dies – you, me, everyone.'

'Then WHY were you taking pictures?'

'Mam, it was all normal – I've seen Shareen have them often enough. And Rachel wanted to know. She never gets to see. I took one picture.'

'It has helped,' I said. 'Helped me understand what I put other people through. Right now, your fears matter, Beth. For Alice's sake, we need you coping with all this.'

'Mam, Nan told me the best way to face death is to live. To live, Mam. And you and me and Rachel are doing that, right? Living – right? I'm good at it, Rachel's good at it, and you're good at it, but we're best at it all together. That's what Nan said.'

'Told by my own daughter. I am a silly girl.' And Alice and Siân had obviously done a lot of talking.

I took a deep breath. 'Beth, it's not silliness. You're dealing with past trauma that I've brought back by mistake. You're a wonderful, sensitive…' I didn't get any further, because Alice launched herself on top of us, and the three of us had one big cwtch.

'Best way is to live, Mam,' Alice said.

Late in the evening, Iestyn arrived at the door holding the three photographs that I'd sent, beautifully printed and framed. Two of Alice's Treecreeper and an atmospheric view across the swampland.

I hunted out some picture hooks and we hung them in a row in the front room. Beth was back and smiling. With no prompt, Alice hugged her father. 'I told Rachel about Granddad Howells and painting. But photography is more me.' She stood back. 'Not arty-crazy stuff.'

He shook his head. 'Okay – not arty-crazy. Fancy some lessons, babe?'

Just as one frozen moment had spoken to me, these others had spoken to Iestyn.

When he had gone, Alice said, 'Too much stuff – need my bed,' and disappeared upstairs. Beth went to relax in the bath. And I sat back and tried to absorb all I had learned since I had assumed motherhood.

There was the absolute loyalty of a girl not yet eleven. Alice had known the wound I had opened, and chosen to speak to Iestyn and Siân rather than to me, leaving her mother to talk about it in her own time. Only after Beth started painting out her memories had Alice decided we must talk.

Harder to get my head round was the fact that Beth had expected pain from the beginning, and still opened her heart and let me in. Why could I not get close to people without inflicting pain?

38

BLOOD ON THE CANVAS

Alice

Rachel worked from home on Monday. I think she was avoiding her office until she could be professional Rachel again. She was bothered I might not manage school, but I did – sort-of. I didn't tell anyone but Miss Akoto about my new mother. Fail: I was going to tell EVERYONE. And I didn't tell Miss Akoto about my new mother's lump, even though I couldn't help scratching the back of my head.

On Tuesday, Rachel had a meeting at work which she couldn't avoid. The seizures in the night didn't stop her, but they stopped me. I was in the room next door and heard the screams.

The first time, I went and stroked her head for a bit and she dozed off without even waking up properly. I stayed there for ages, feeling like her mam. And listening to Mam's snores from the back bedroom. Mam hadn't even stirred.

The second time was an hour later at about three, and I'd just got back to sleep. This time, Mam did wake up and started panicking. Rachel just dozed off like before, and I had to show Mam the written instructions from Doctor Cook before she gave up on calling 999.

The third seizure was just before six, and I was glad Mam

didn't wake up. But no way could I get back to sleep again, and so I sat in the chair in Rachel's room until Rachel sat up, rubbed her eyes and said, 'Hello Alice. Did I have one?'

'Three.'

'Oops.'

'Spoilt my sleep, but I only had to cope with Mam for the middle one.'

'Major panic?'

'I got her sorted – just about. Had to wave Doctor Cook's notes at her.'

'You take on so much, Alice. And you look as flat as I feel – flatter – did you get any sleep at all? No, don't answer that – go to bed. I'll tell Beth you need a day off. I'm only going in for the meeting this morning. Tom is bringing me straight home.'

When Tom fetched Rachel, Mam started flapping about me and school, but Rachel sorted her and I took my breakfast back to bed.

I felt like a dinosaur on the verge of extinction, but couldn't sleep. Granddad and his mates were hammering away in the studio and Mam was tidying up and making a LOT of noise. And I was bothered about what the girls at school would say tomorrow. And about what I wouldn't say about one of my mothers (the one they didn't know about) going to hospital. And sleep was sitting up there on the ceiling and I was down here, and it wouldn't come any closer.

Until…

You can tell me. You can always tell me, Alice. And sleep. I'm here for you.

'Mathilde?'

And all the banging and crashing in the house faded away as I told Mathilde everything. Including lots of stuff I hadn't even known was there. And I wasn't going extinct anymore and I fell asleep and woke up when Granddad brought me a bacon bap with ketchup.

'Better?' he said. 'Rachel called, worried about you. I told her you were snoring.'

'Bet I wasn't!'

'Bet you were! Rachel's going to be back later than she said. Your Mam needs to paint, so she chucked me out of the studio.'

'Painting might help Mam. Yesterday – too much stuff at once.'

He nodded and shook his head at the same time. 'I don't know when I'll ever get in to finish the studio at this rate. Anyway, I'm off home. Call me if there's any more bother. And don't worry about Rachel – we're all around.'

'Granddad?'

He looked behind him, like he always does.

'Joe?'

'That's my name.'

'Love you lots. A bit.'

He wrinkled his nose.

'More than a bit. Don't tell Nan, but you're the best Granddad in history.'

He even smiled.

When I'd finished my bap, I checked with Mathilde before I got up, calling out softly and saying thank you. But there was no sign of her. Maybe she was helping someone else.

Downstairs, I would have expected to hear Mam humming or singing in the studio – she's never quiet when she paints. But the house was creepily silent. Interrupting was a sure way to get shouted at, but I needed to know that Mam was okay, now she was painting the death stuff and the stuck-inside stuff.

The studio door was wide open. I stepped down into the porch and saw Mam's table with tubes of paint, rags, jars of brushes and other stuff scattered about in a mess of colour. The paint smell made me sneeze. If she was in there, she must have heard me. I stepped into the studio.

Beside Granddad's new window stood Mam's easel with no canvas on it. Her palette and a couple of brushes were on a tall stool next to it, but there was no sign of Mam. And then I saw the canvas, face down on the floor. I reached for it, but panicked.

Called out for Mam.

No answer.

Ran through into the front room. Not there.

Up to her bedroom. Not there. Calling.

No answer.

The painting, knocked over. What did it mean?

Think, Alice.

Can't.

Call someone.

Can't – Mam has her phone. Unless she's left it somewhere.

I ran down and checked around the kitchen and studio. No phone.

Knock on someone's door?

Bethany's here.

'Mathilde?'

The apple tree.

I ran outside and there she was, behind the tree, curled up on the ground.

'Mam?'

'Leave me, Alice.'

'Mam, you're frightening me.'

'I'll cope. Give me some time.'

'No, Mam. TELL ME. You never tell me. You were painting Granddad dying again, weren't you?'

'No – not that.' Mam sat up with her back against the tree and wiped her hand down her face. 'I've hit something different.'

'Don't keep it in – look at the state of you.'

'I don't know what to say. Rachel off to hospital is what matters.'

'Mam, you matter. YOU. Rachel's just having tests.'

Mam shook her head and brushed herself down, and that's when I saw her other hand.

'Mam, you're bleeding!'

'A bleeding idiot.'

'Mam, you're not. You've had such a tough life. You've never made a fuss about it. And you look after me and Rachel. Now, what was all that about with the painting?'

'I got angry. It hurts – getting angry.'

'That's cos you're never angry. Not with me being a brat. Not with Dad being a sod. Not with Rachel having the money we never had. You don't EVER get angry!'

'Managed it this time.' She lifted her paint-coated bleeding fist. 'Had a bit of a fight. I won, I hope.'

Mam pulled herself up against the tree trunk one-handed, I balanced her other arm, and we went into the kitchen.

'Let's sort you out first. You're still bleeding.' I held her fist between my hands, and blood trickled through my fingers. It took a while to get rid of all the paint, and then she patted her fist dry, not letting me near. A plaster wouldn't work on her knuckle, and we dug out a bandage. Mam showed me how to fasten it.

That's right, Alice. Look after her. I'm here if you need me.

I thanked Mathilde without telling Mam, but now I felt calm, and led Mam into the studio.

She picked up the fallen painting by one edge. There was a mess of colour, and it sagged in the middle, where I could see reddish brown – blood.

'So, it's not about Granddad dying?'

'It's about me. Me and Mam.'

'When you needed to paint, and she wouldn't let you?'

'That's part of it.'

'Did you even cry, Mam? Did she let you?'

'I'm always crying.'

'Not for this – it's only just come out, hasn't it?'

'Hospital reminded me – I spent a lot of time with Mam in hospital, after her stroke.'

'So, you need us to take the strain. Me. Nan. Granddad. They know hospital freaks you. They think it's your dad, but it isn't that, is it?'

She pulled her hand away, and the painting fell face-down again. 'No – it's everything I missed. By not getting angry. By letting Mam have her way. Rachel saying that about her father triggered it. Weeks ago. It's not just the hospital stuff.'

'You can be angry now.'

'That's the trouble – it's gone – gone years ago. When I looked after Mam after her stroke, and she never once thanked me. She was still blaming me for Dad dying.'

'Mam! NO. You were a kid.'

'I couldn't reason with her – it was how she was, after her stroke. She made all the wrong connections. I was with Dad when he died. And Dee. Mam wasn't. And so we were to blame. But Dee was on the other side of the world when

Mam had her stroke. I was at home, looking after her. So, I got it all.'

'And you've never let it out.'

'It's all faded away. Now, it feels like I'm playing at it. Or it did, until today.'

'Well PLAY then! What do you want to do to that fucking painting, Bethany Howells?'

Mam looked at me, and narrowed her eyes. Then she looked at the ceiling.

Mathilde said *YES* in my ear.

And Mam whispered words I couldn't hear, and stamped on the back of the canvas, grinding the paint into the new floorboards with her bare heel. And I joined in and we jumped up and down on the painting. Mathilde, too, but maybe Mam didn't notice.

When we were exhausted from jumping up and down, I led Mam to the old armchair in the corner of the studio, and she flopped down and held out her arms. And I sat on her lap, like I did when I was little.

'Mam – make this a new start – please. Don't keep stuff in. With me and Rachel, you can talk it out – paint it out – fight it out.'

'Maybe I can, now. I've always protected you – but that's what Mam thought she was doing with me after Dad died, in her own stupid way. Really, she was protecting herself.'

'Come on.' I led Mam back to the painting, lifted it up and put it on the easel. Mam waved her bandaged fist at the blurred mess on the canvas. 'First blood to us – the three of us – Rachel will get it. I won't even need to explain.'

'The three of us.' I ran my foot across the patch of paint on the pale new floorboards. 'This stays. Granddad will understand.'

39

UNPRECEDENTED OFFER

Rachel

Waking up on Tuesday morning was like emerging from a tub of sticky glue. Every part of my body seemed stuck to the bed. Then I saw Alice in the chair beside me, and realised that her night had been far worse than mine.

I felt more human after pneumatic drills finished resurfacing my brain, but I couldn't let go of all that had happened over the weekend. And seeing the state Alice was in this morning, how my condition might continue to affect her.

Tom arrived, a warrior in his grey chariot to take the queen of greyness to her office. I looked in the hall mirror and tested expressions for a woman who had stormed to success. The best I could manage was something between hungover-after-wild-party and murderous assassin. It was a day for shock-stoppers and Tom noticed. 'Those pink glasses come out on bad days.'

'My trusty shock-stoppers. I got the habit from Alice.' And I filled him in on my accidental promotion to motherhood.

'Beth and Alice have been lucky to find you.'

'I've brought them enough headaches.'

'Don't do yourself down. Ian Jacobs was going on about

you having a screw loose the other day. I said that if you've got a screw loose, pass the screwdriver.'

'That's sweet. But the screw-loose thing is… somewhat intentional. Unlike poor Mrs Jones, I have the power to stare him out whenever he looks at me. I freak him. I even like freaking him.'

Albany Road was clogged with delivery vans, and while we queued, I reminded him that I was serious about Emmy looking after me. 'It's the kind of looking-after I can cope with.'

'Seeing you together was lovely,' Tom said. 'Not many people get Emmy.'

'Emmy and I have a lot in common – struggling with emotional overload, for a start.'

'Most people wouldn't even try to find something in common with her.'

'Maybe we see each other from the inside.'

'Em hardly gets out – the day centre is about all. Mam's too afraid of her making a scene. Meeting you people could make a big difference. Alice really charms her.'

'Alice is fantastic. And eleven on Thursday.'

'While you're in hospital? That's a pain. Emmy's thirty-six on Saturday – although Mam won't let anyone tell her until the day.'

'How about giving them a joint party? Alice loves having Em around.'

'You bet! Emmy would love it.' He chuckled. 'More my style than the office party.' He gave me a worried glance while we queued for the lights at the end of the road. 'Ours isn't as bad as Mrs Jones makes out, is it?'

'Worse than a bad sitcom. You're asking for a date, then, Doctor Richards?'

'No, I–'

'Because the answer is yes. You'll be the one who needs looking after.'

He smiled. 'That was unexpected.'

Tom parked in the row of identical grey BMWs and gave me a concerned look. 'The suits are bound to make you an offer this morning. What do you actually want?'

I froze. 'They said it was about medium-term strategy.'

He stared straight ahead. 'Rachel, I think you are their medium-term strategy.'

'Oh.' Why did the realisation make me want to puke?

'They might want you at HQ.'

Beth. Alice. LOVE. Siân. Joe. Mathilde. Tom and Emmy. Impossible, wonderful Iestyn. The apple tree – the housemaid's room – HOME. Roath Park and comfortable Cardiff. Feeling that I belong for the first time in my life.

I reached for Tom's large, comforting hand. It added up. I would get an offer. It would be generous because they knew precisely how much of that success was down to me. 'I'm so glad you warned me.' I kept my specs on.

'With you.' It was all he needed to say.

We went to the coffee bar round the corner first, and I asked him whether I presented as having a screw loose. He laughed at that, but I gave him the true story of burning out on infinite possibilities. And to gently show him that our date had limits, I told him of my love for Beth and my absence of sex drive.

'You're brave to tell me.'

'I'm trying to be asexual and proud. Sort of.'

'Not a complicated date, then. I'm rubbish at complicated dates.' He smiled and led me back to this morning's problem. 'What do you really want now?'

'What I have, I suppose. My new life. Taking pictures with Alice in the freezing cold. Finding ways for Emmy to look after me. Life Class and modelling. The Sinfonietta. Even stepping on Lego bricks in the playroom.'

His wistful glow was lovely to behold. Surely, he was a demigod. But he frowned. 'I could have had a life like that if I'd been more flexible.'

'You could again, Tom, if that's what you want.'

'I don't want to mess with anyone else's life.' He studied his hands.

'That's how I feel about Alice and Beth. But we're so involved that standing back might make it worse. And... I suppose there is more. There are bigger things I don't want to mess with, environmentally. I can't do this job and face Alice with a clear conscience.'

He nodded. 'I'm beginning to feel the same way. Come on, let's see what the dragons have to say.'

As Tom had predicted, they told me I was vital to the medium-term strategy of the corporation, and that the CEO wanted me in Paris for the board meeting next Monday. I wanted me in Cardiff next Monday. Actually, and more to the point, in a hospital bed in Cardiff, but I let them make their pitch.

With Tom's reassuring presence beside me, I listened while they enthused over the 'unprecedented' offer of the handling of a series of carbon-neutral bids that would dwarf the California contract. It sounded as if carbon-neutral had been written into their script to attract me by the number of times they repeated the phrase. I would have two personal assistants (to walk all over in carbon-neutral stilettos, presumably) a riverside apartment in Zurich, and everything else guaranteed to give Ian Jacobs an orgasm.

And I turned it down.

I turned down a smashed glass ceiling in favour of the safe proximity of Mrs Jones's printer. Or more accurately, the safe proximity of my new family, the man sitting next to me, his sister and a young woman who spoke to me from a painting who could have been entirely imaginary.

This was unthinkable, suicide and the foolishness of a woman (spoken with the eyes only – these were sophisticated men). More to the point, it would embarrass my seniors at the Paris meeting.

I didn't take in the way the conversation ended. By then, I was struggling to concentrate. Three men on a screen were replaced with the corporate logo. One real human being sat beside me in the conference room, staring at me with his mouth open. 'Do you know…?' He hesitated, got up and started pacing around.

I couldn't sit still either and headed for the window. With just the pair of us in the room, I felt safe to take off my shock-stoppers. 'Go on, Tom – ask me the question.'

'Do you understand what you just turned down?'

'Yes. If I had wanted it, I wouldn't have turned it down.'

And Tom, bronze-haired demigod, lifted me clean off the floor in a cuddly hug. 'When you told them – their faces! Rachel, you are magnificent.'

'There's nothing they could have offered, Tom.'

'You've made me realise I need to stop marking time. I need space in my life for Emmy. And like you said, I'd like to make a difference. We've both got work to do.'

Tom had another meeting to get to, but he offered to visit me in hospital later in the week. 'It's not going to be easy for you, is it?'

'It is harder, now I have a family.' And a lump. I left that unspoken, but he knew. I chose Thursday evening for his visit. It was Alice's birthday, and Joe and Siân would be taking Alice and Beth to a pantomime.

Speaking to Joe on the phone at lunchtime didn't exactly reassure me. Alice had been dead to the world all morning, and Beth was itching to eject him from the studio, showing every sign of stress. But I needed more time to go through my inbox and instruct Tom and Mrs Jones on all they might need to action while I was away. It was late in the afternoon by the time I managed to disengage myself from work.

I sent Beth a text.

> Home soon. Conference
> fine.

When I made it outside into fresh air, I was so relieved that I chose to walk, daring my chemical shock-stoppers to protect me. The streets were busy enough for me to feel relatively safe, but I hadn't been walking five minutes when I got a text.

> I know you – walking home
> – silly bugger. Two pints
> semi-skim.

A couple of blocks later, I got,

> REPLY, WOMAN! Need to
> know you live.

I passed on a job in Zurich.
No Swiss chocolates for
you.

I forgot we needed milk while I wrangled with the consequences of immediate resignation. Turning back to the shop, I nearly got run over.

Concentrate, Rachel, your life depends on it.

Clutching milk and chocolate in my arms, I fiddled with the phone.

Work bearable with artist in
garret

Beth's next text arrived while I was standing on the corner, munching chocolate and getting in everyone's way.

Could be artist too. Way of
seeing faulty.

Another text came just as I set out to face the frozen north.

I've got more curves than
Tom. It's that fucking BMW,
isn't it?

Beth in text was distinctly more sweary.

I love you, woman. Tom is a
kind, very kind man

I know, softy xxx.

And then another text, like an afterthought.

He's one of us xxx

I was standing still again and tempted to talk on the phone, but the wind was cold in my face and I wouldn't get any warmer. I needed to move my feet as well as think, but this much multi-tasking felt beyond me.

How was Beth after yesterday's painful revelations? Everything this morning had been about getting me to work. How was she? Too much had happened in the last few days. I sent mental sheepdogs to round up my scattered memories while making a determined effort to make headway up Mackintosh Place.

Confused memories of Alice's awed story about Beth's father brought me to a halt halfway up the street, and I nearly got wiped out by a bike on the pavement. I said something loud, but his ears were plugged into his kill-the-pedestrians mix.

I sent,

> Don't know how you are,
> Beth. Been lost on planet
> Rachel.

Beth's reply was instant.

> Alice sorted me out.
> Taking on pain above her
> pay grade.

Pain? Beth's pain?

A long straight line of terraces stretched in front of me. The wind in my face wasn't strong, but constant and icy. I marched onwards.

The pavement wasn't particularly level. At marching speed, I was swaying.

Balance? Am I...?

BREATHE. Slow down. Run diagnostics. All systems working. Walk.

Sweating now. Scared.

Phone beep. Another text. Bugger. Leave it, I'm nearly there.

Concentrate. Getting closer – last block before the junction. Heart pounding.

Breathe. Do. Not. Panic. Breathe. Can I feel my toes?

Breathe. Nearly there. IGNORE SYMPTOMS.

Nest of ants in the back of my head DOES NOT EXIST.

Cross the road – no, stop – cars coming. Long row of cars. I want to get HOME – bugger. Wait. Bugger. Breathe. Breathe. Clear at last – cross.

Breathe. Round the corner. Almost there. Head swaying.

Breathe, Rachel, you fool. This is one stupid panic.

Breathe. Down the street.

Breathe. Beth's face in the window. Slow down. Relax.

And breathe out. Door key – fuck, where is it?

The door flew open and Beth lifted me bodily out of the porch and into the house, complete with briefcase and milk bottle. 'You crazy woman! Thought you were… You didn't answer.'

All the worry and relief in her voice. What do I do to her? 'Sorry.'

'You really are a silly bugger, Rachel.'

'I know. And I love you and I love Alice and I love… home.' Tears of relief were streaming, pouring down my face.

Home.

Beth reached to stroke my hair away – and that's when I noticed her bandage.

'Beth…?'

40

HANG ON

Alice

Visiting Rachel in hospital on Wednesday night was WEIRD. She was lying in bed with an unopened book on the covers and didn't even seem pleased to see us. Or not pleased. She didn't say anything, but pointed at one of her spiral-bound notebooks on her locker.

'On sedatives while they change my anticonvulsants. Expect zombie state. It's normal.'

I hugged her and hugged her and hugged her, and Rachel found a smile.

I whispered in her ear, 'Mathilde will look after you.'

'I told her to look after you,' Rachel whispered. And we did a not-very-high-five.

And Mam hugged her and Nan hugged her, and then we just sat. Because no one knew what to say.

After a while, Rachel seemed to wake up a bit. 'It's definite – I'm going to resign. Find some positive work to do.'

'You've done lots positive already,' I said. 'For me, for Mam, for Emmy.'

'And Tom,' Mam said. 'He told me the way you and Emmy get on has been a massive relief. He's been so worried about her. And he says it's good to have another human being working next to him.'

'But I'm leaving.'

'So is he, I think.'

'Oh, Tom… I hope that's not foolish.' Rachel sighed. 'I can afford to be foolish, for once. I'm not sure whether he can.' And she lay back on her pillow. All this talking had used her up.

We kissed her and left her to doze. Then I remembered I'd brought Molly for Rachel. She was asleep now, and I wondered about tucking Molly in with her. But what if a nurse moved Molly and she got lost. I put the bag in the locker beside her bed.

Going home to a house without Rachel was even more weird. Everything about our house was Rachel-flavoured, but she wasn't here. I went out into the dark and put my arms around the apple tree. 'Mathilde?'

But all I heard was a cat yowling, and it was too cold to stay out long.

I hoped Mathilde was with Rachel.

*

Rachel

On Thursday, I remembered last night's kisses and hugs and something about Tom, but I was completely spaced out and nothing joined up. Julie had me in for tests, but she wasn't happy with the way I was reacting. 'There's something else going on. I'm not sure whether it's the drugs or another factor.'

'The lump?'

'Maybe. Maybe not.'

'That's comforting.' Not.

'Well, you asked, and I'm not a magician. It could be anything – infection, stress, changing hormones, metabolism, diet even – or simply your neurons finding new pathways around the lump. But we will find out. For the moment, we'll put you back on the previous drugs. We need a baseline to work from, and this is no improvement at all.'

'So, I stay here?'

'It's about balancing risks. We need you more stable than this.'

'More stable than this.' I felt like the first Mrs Rochester in my garret. 'Maybe I should be the one in the housemaid's room, rather than Alice. Locked in.'

'All violinists are mad,' she said. But she was curious about Alice's room, and I showed her a new picture from Siân. Alice would be sleeping there tonight.

Alice.

Alice's birthday. TODAY. NOW.

HOW COULD I FORGET THAT?

The traces on the screen shot all over the place and Julie saw my reaction in forensic detail. She jumped up. 'What's wrong?'

'It's Alice's birthday. God, I haven't called. Haven't...'

Breathe. Breathe again. Blood pumping in my ears. Sweat. FEAR.

Fear. Fear on fear, with each remembered fear dragging more out of the past.

'Fuck, I'm not up to... Can't cope. Julie? Please?'

'Rachel, listen. Keep those slow breaths. We are keeping

you safe. You are safe. Calm down – Alice will understand. Would you like me to call for you?'

'I should. I…' But I knew my mind would wander. 'Yes, please.'

I gave her my phone. Alice was home from school and getting ready for her birthday trip to the pantomime. Julie told her I was sorry I hadn't called this morning, but I'd been too full of sedatives. And she told Alice I really wanted her to have a happy birthday, and would see her soon, but right now, the pills were making me very tired. And then Julie asked Alice if she would like to talk to me.

I heard Alice's lovely voice. She told me not to bother about answering. She told me she loved me. And she asked whether I'd looked in the bag in my locker. No, I hadn't known there was a bag there. 'Do it,' she said. And, 'love you.'

I said, 'love you,' but it was all I could manage.

'Bag. Locker,' she repeated. 'Night night, sleepy.'

I was exhausted by driving my slow brainwaves through all this stuff and collapsed into bed as soon as I was back in the ward.

Tom. I'd forgotten Tom. Here because I'd asked him.

Tom. Another forgetting. I AM NOT IN CONTROL OF MY BRAIN.

And it's nearly nighttime, and I'm frightened, because Julie thinks there's something else going on. And Tom is sitting next to my bed, not asking. I reach out, and he holds my hand, gently stroking it. And it doesn't matter – I don't need to speak.

But if I did speak, I would not be able to stop, because Tom, do you know how many hours there are in a night, when you know the drugs keeping your brain from shorting out are rubbing up against each other? The new ones that are messing me up are not yet out of my system, and others are beginning to nudge back in on the party. And they were the ones that didn't work in the first place. And I can't help them work. And the lump is still there.

Night is coming, Tom. With endless seconds and minutes and hours waiting for me. Moments and more moments beyond measure to think about not seeing daylight and not seeing Alice or Beth again, but burning in a box and being poured into a small plastic urn. Great raw chunks and blocks of time-fearing time, wasted in terror and squandered in wide-awakeness, never to be recovered; with my synapses firing in all the wrong places for sleep. Yes, Tom, the nights here are long.

Night is coming.

I don't think any of this fear left my mouth but wonderful, calm, beautiful Tom Richards kept hold of my hand. 'Hang on, Rachel,' he said. 'Hang on, Rachel.' And in his deep, musical voice, the message reached me. He was in here with me, fighting the fear for me.

Tom said, 'Hang on, Rachel,' and so I wasn't going to die.

I had so much to live for now.

I would still be Alice's mother.

Alice. She'd told me something. Bag. Locker. 'Can you look, Tom? Alice told me there's a bag in my locker.'

He fished out a plastic bag, looked inside and smiled. 'Is she important?'

I smiled back – I didn't need to answer. Trust Alice to remember.

Tom fished out Molly, straightened her clothes, stroked her hair into place, and nestled her up against my cheek.

I twisted a few strands of Molly's mustard coloured hair around my finger, comfortably at home, now.

Tom stroked his finger down her arm. 'What's her name?'

'Molly. Mum made her for me when I was tiny. Alice is a genius to remember.'

'I wish I could do more to take away your fear,' Tom said.

'You have, now.'

He bent over and kissed me on the cheek. Then he gently lifted Molly's head, kissed her, and said, 'Look after Rachel for me, Molly.'

And Molly did look after me. That night, I slept properly. But Monday's results and further tests were a long way in the future, and on Friday and Saturday, I needed Molly and Tom and Alice and Beth and Siân and Joe, desperately.

And I got them all. They took turns to make sure I did. And Emmy, who was just as scared as me and didn't manage to stay long, but she gave Molly a cuddle to make Rachel better. I only remembered that I'd forgotten to say happy birthday to Emmy after she left. She'd come to see me on her birthday, and I hadn't even acknowledged it. I hoped that Alice and Beth had remembered for me.

Then, on Sunday, Mum came.

'Hang on, Rachel,' Tom's voice said in my head. 'Hang on, Rachel.'

And I tried. But with Mum beside my bed, I was always going to fail.

We both fell to pieces.

41

JUST AN OLD BOOK

Rachel

I'd written my resignation letter in hospital – a whole bunch of them. It helped stop my mind (seated in my brain) focussing on… my brain. There was the rude letter, the silly letter, the serious letter and the heartfelt letter. And one that made no sense at all because my mind and brain weren't talking the same language at the time.

I sent off the final version before I left hospital on Tuesday, explaining that I had enjoyed solving their problems, but couldn't continue working for a corporation that paid lip-service to climate change. I even asked my consultant to check the letter.

'About time too! You're wasted there – you could do anything,' Julie said.

When she sent me home, she said just to carry on as normal. 'Try your best, anyway.' And she squeezed both my hands as if she intended an extra confidence boost. But it fuelled my uncertainty. How safe was I?

Julie was still trying to determine the factor or factors that kept skewing my results. Carry on as normal? I did not feel normal. And I had to cling on to Joe's arm when he fetched me. Beth and Alice were waiting in the porch, with Alice still in her school uniform.

When I managed to extricate myself from a double hug, I found the hallway transformed. Cai's framed comic covers were stacked against the wall. In their place, two pictures faced each other. One was Beth's lovely crayon sketch of me, mounted on white board, and the other was a small oil portrait. The artist was obvious because I recognised the sitter. Eleven years old, poised, confident and with lively, flashing eyes. Not Alice, but Beth. 'It's you!'

Beth leaned back and looked me in the eye. 'Facing a picture of the person who gave me the confidence to hang it. Iestyn kept it for me – Alice has only just seen it.'

'It's lovely. Full of…' The word 'life' didn't quite form in my mouth.

'Dad.'

'Granddad Howells,' Alice whispered and reached out to touch the frame. Reached out, not upwards. Could she have grown in a term? Yes, quite a lot.

'You're so like your mam.'

'With THAT hair?'

'Alice, thanks to you, I'll be able to walk past Dad's picture every day,' Beth said.

'Rachel did it, really.'

'You made me face up to it, and you look after Rachel.'

Alice looked embarrassed, but I couldn't help embarrassing her more. 'It's true. You remember important things, like Molly. You could be my guardian angel.'

'Yeah, angels. Tell you later.'

She scuttled up the stairs in a hurry, with Beth's gaze tracking her. 'Complicated.'

I flopped on the sofa, and Beth brought me chamomile tea. 'Alice has been deep inside herself all week. Some of it from school as well as you. And there was your mother. They made a connection – talked. Really talked, I think.'

Mum. Another situation had dropped from my consciousness. 'How was Mum?'

'She came late on Saturday – too late, really. On Sunday morning, I hardly saw her. She was up in Alice's room, and they were talking for ages. I didn't want to interrupt. At lunchtime, everything she said with me was about the past – and it was facts, not feelings. She went straight home after she saw you – didn't come back here.'

'My fault. I couldn't face her on Sunday – fell apart – had to send her away.'

'Don't let it bug you, Rachel. You can't manage everything at once.'

'Everything. Managing. It's… there's too much…' My thoughts were dispersing like petrol on a pond. In moments, my mind was blank. 'What were we…?'

'Your mam.'

I closed my eyes and took steady breaths. How many threads was I losing? No, don't think about it – keep this thread – Mum. 'Mum went through a lot with me in hospital when I was a teen. Resuscitation – induced coma – the works.'

'She said, but I couldn't get her past the facts.'

'I never have. Maybe now – if I could concentrate.'

'Let me pick up things that slip your mind. Don't let them bother you.'

'It's a nightmare.'

Beth held my arms steady while I tried to centre myself

on this present moment. This moment that would become another moment as soon as I thought about it.

Our shared point of lived experience moved on through the continuum until Beth said, 'You know too much about your own condition – you're too aware. Julie told me you'd find these tablets disturbing. Alice knows. Tom knows. Let us do the remembering for you.'

'I feel stupid.'

'You're on the previous dose plus new sedatives. You're not stupid – you're been kept stable, that's all.'

Alice hadn't reappeared. I glanced towards the stairs.

Beth shook her head. 'You talking about angels might have spooked her.'

'Mortality?'

'Something about angels she's been talking through with Miss Akoto. Whatever it is, she didn't want to share it with me.'

Beth led the way upstairs.

From the way Alice had run off, I half expected her to be crying into her pillow, but she was sitting on her new bed in the little housemaid's room, reading a book that I recognised instantly. A book that belonged on the top shelf of the bookcase beside my mother's bed. It had belonged to her mother, and her mother's mother, but nine-year-old Rachel hadn't wanted it.

And I had regretted saying so ever since.

Alice lifted the dark red book to her nose, maybe sniffing its accumulated history. 'Your mam says it's yours really.'

'I made a mistake, Alice. I told Mum it was just an old book, when it mattered to her to pass it on to me. Can I have a look?'

I sat on the side of the bed, took the book, and stroked my hand across the cover. Faded gold letters proclaimed *Alice's Adventures in Wonderland* and there was a tiny gold picture of Lewis Carroll's Alice.

Gingerly, I opened the front cover and found two decorated bookplates. One said, *For Achievement.* Two names were crossed out with neat ink lines, and at the bottom was the name Gaynor Williams, in tiny Italic letters. 'My mother, my grandmother Ruth, who I never really knew, and my great-grandmother Rhonwen.'

'I know – your mam showed me pictures. Should have your name in it.'

The other bookplate said, *This book lives with…* and was blank. But Alice was lined up and ready for me.

She smiled across at the wooden school desk with a lifting lid that Joe had found, a snug fit in the dormer window space. On it lay a dip pen with a bottle of ink and blotting paper. Alice had been practising on a notepad, and I had a go, blotting it several times. But I managed to sign my name on the bookplate.

'Impressive,' Beth said, standing in the doorway. 'But I don't think you'll make a calligrapher.'

I gave her a grin, put a line through my name, and wrote, *Alice, for a new Alice.* Alice wrote, *Alice Howells*, underneath.

'The chain carries on,' Beth said. 'I'll tell your mam – one less thing for you to remember.'

Or one more thing to fall out of my mind.

42

OPENING WINDOWS

Alice

I put Alice in Wonderland on my bookshelf, and saw Rachel begin to take in the transformed room. She had been so focussed on the book that she'd hardly noticed the full effect of the BEST BEDROOM IN CARDIFF.

We sat side by side on the new-but-old-looking bed Rachel had given me. And I smiled around the room, discovering it again with Rachel. Nan's floral wallpaper, curtains and clever paintwork. The desk, bedside table and bookshelves that Granddad had restored. A sepia photograph of Mam in an old frame from Dad – that made Rachel look – she had never seen it before. And the lace-trimmed nightdress that Mam had found in the vintage clothes shop – a bit itchy, but like a time machine for my dreams.

Best of all was the other present Rachel had never seen. I brought her out from behind my pillow. Molly's dark-haired twin, Myfanwy. Her mother had made her to Molly's original pattern – and given her a name that was in Rachel's family, way back.

'She's beautiful!' Rachel said.

'Your Mam's special.'

I couldn't help my fingers twisting strands of Myfanwy's hair, and Rachel smiled.

I wrinkled my nose at her. 'Well you do it all the time!'

Most of my stuff would never fit in here, and we had piled it up in the playroom. Granddad had plans for cupboards. I wondered if he ever woke up in the morning without plans. No – Granddad always had plans. And plans on top of plans.

Rachel was running her fingers around Nan's fancy paintwork on the window frame. 'Alice, it's all lovely. I'm so sorry I wasn't here on Thursday.'

'You didn't miss much on Friday.'

'Friday?'

'Mam can tell you.' I passed Mam a pillow, and she sat on the floor by my feet.

'You missed out on a mother's solemn duty,' Mam said, and explained about the nativity play, and my stupid panic. I was going to play Top Angel, but with Rachel in hospital I was scared about angels and stuff. So, Shareen got to be top angel – HOORAY – the first time she'd ever been anything. I narrated the play from behind a curtain sitting next to Miss Akoto. Dead easy with a microphone.

'Word perfect,' Mam said.

'Miss Akoto was there in case I froze.'

'Something to do with angels bothers you, doesn't it?' Rachel said. 'I called you my guardian angel – I hope I didn't upset you.'

I couldn't quite look at her. 'Me being silly. Miss Akoto says we entertain angels unawares. Says it a lot, and I asked her. In the stories, angels come to people, but they can't tell that they're angels. That's scary – angels coming and you don't know.'

'What do you think an angel might be like?'

'Doesn't matter – you don't believe in them.' Maybe Rachel being a scientist and not believing was the scary bit – I didn't know.

'I would never stop you believing,' Rachel said.

'But you don't.' I placed my thumb on the tip of her nose. I needed some answers, but I wasn't sure what the questions were.

And Rachel seemed to be puzzling stuff out too – I could tell by the way she was twisting her hair. At last, she copied me and placed her thumb on my nose. 'You're making one big assumption, girl. About me not believing. I believe in Mathilde, and she… well, I don't think even Mathilde knows what she is. Angelic might be one way to describe her effect on me – I hadn't thought of that.'

'Yeah, you're a scientist with an angel – it doesn't make sense – you believing stuff spooks me. It's like you're being a kid with me. Not adult enough.'

'Belief is a big worry, isn't it? It often spooks me too. Believing when I'm not sure whether I should. When it doesn't seem rational.' Rachel shook her head, still looking puzzled.

'I talked to Miss Akoto about getting frightened. She said everyone gets frightened. So, I asked her how she copes with it. She said she prays. Her faith helps her. You get major frit-frightened and you don't do faith stuff.'

'I have a lot of faith in people. You in particular, Alice.'

I took my thumb away, and so did she.

'But Rachel, Miss Akoto believes in God and angels.'

'Mum has the same kind of beliefs, Alice. And she's a scientist too. Sometimes I share her beliefs. It's a confusing world.'

'But how can you believe and not believe at the same time? It's impossible.'

Rachel sighed, a real, deep, inside sigh. 'Dad made Mum feel guilty about her beliefs, and I would never, ever do that, Alice. I wouldn't have dared tell him about Mathilde, either. He even told me off for talking to Molly.'

I hugged Myfanwy close. 'Kids in class say God and stuff is all a fairy tale. Science says so.'

Rachel brightened up. 'Oh, that narrative. They're just following what they hear. It's more complicated – things usually are. There are all sorts of ways of looking at reality. Science is reliable – scientific process works – that's important to remember. But science requires measurement. Science runs out of useful things to say when you get into areas beyond measurement. There are other ways to look at reality, and not all of them are scientific. Some admit insights we could never reach through scientific process. Are Beth's paintings wrong?' Rachel smiled down at Mam on the floor.

'Nah, they're art.'

'They're still asking questions about reality and responding to it,' Rachel said.

And that really got me thinking. I wasn't so certain now. 'Science is numbers, isn't it?'

'What about my pictures out there in the playroom? Science uses the language of numbers, yes, but scientists use other languages as well. With my theories, I was getting to the edge of what was possible with scientific process. I needed to find new languages... and didn't quite get there.'

We were sitting side-by-side on the bed with Mam wriggling around at our feet, dying to join in. 'Mam wants to say your pictures are art.'

Mam looked up. 'How do you know?'

'Cos I'm your daughter, Beth-a-ny.' I tapped the side of my head. 'Rachel, are your pictures art?'

'They express relationships I can't express with numbers. Maybe they're science and art. And some faith too – there was enough to startle me – but probably not the kind of faith Miss Akoto would recognise. I'm not sure – I'd have to talk to her.'

'So, science and art and faith are fuzzy at the edges?'

'Not to everyone. A lot of people need everything crystal clear. They see fuzziness as weakness or failure of rigour. The funny thing is, that seems to apply whatever window they look through, whether it be religion or science or law or politics or just common rumours. People like clear answers they can hang on to.'

And at last, something clicked. 'They like it easy, don't they?'

'People feel secure when they have easy answers, Alice. Usually the first ones that come along. It's always worth checking the possibilities your question doesn't address. Looking for a bigger, underlying question. And some of those questions will always remain as questions because they admit all kinds of different answers.'

'Like getting fussed about angels?' I needed a good scratch of my head, and hoped Mam wouldn't go on about nits. 'Rachel, am I really asking about the kids and Miss Akoto?'

'You are a wonder. You're more self-aware than half the students I taught at Cambridge. Go on – stretch that a bit – tell me what you think you're asking.'

'We talk about respect at school. I want them to respect her.'

'Is that a question or a wish, Alice?'

I needed another scratch. 'Is it...? You're a scientist. Do you think I'm silly to respect her?'

'Because she has faith? Respecting her isn't the least bit silly. Learning from her faith isn't silly, either. You know what I said about looking at reality through different windows? To me, it makes sense to look through every window you can possibly find. You share one window with Miss Akoto because she's someone you trust.'

A sudden thought made me grin. 'What about your window, Doctor Bothwell?'

Rachel rolled her eyes and shifted around on the bed. 'Sometimes I think I look through too many windows. I hate closing them, and I get a pretty confusing view. I think that's why I haven't tried to investigate Mathilde – I just like to let her be. Reality is awesome – no surprise it gets confusing.'

I was going to put my thumb on Rachel's nose again, but turned it round and placed it on mine. 'Me and angels and mixed-up scary thoughts?'

'People use the word awesome all the time,' Rachel said. 'But real awe is when you see the depth and height of something – whether it's an entity or an idea – and feel tiny beside it. Both scared of it and loving it. If I fully recognised an angel, I'm sure I would feel like that. Overawed.'

'Overawed – yeah – good word.'

'It's both scary and amazing to think I might have met an angel unawares, Alice. And the more I think about it – Mathilde is so much more than a ghost. She's...' Rachel's eyes opened wide, as if she didn't dare say the words.

I didn't want to say the words either, and I needed to rescue Rachel so that Mam didn't start on awkward questions.

'Awesome!' I said, and me and Rachel hugged tight and suddenly Mathilde's warmth was all around us. Rachel was still wide-eyed – I think she could feel Mathilde too.

Mam looked like she was going to ask a whole load of questions, but Rachel had that dazed look now, and I knew questions would do no good. Her drugs were taking over. Or was it that I wished her drugs would take over so that Mam couldn't ask the wrong question?

'Mam, Rachel needs a rest,' I said, and tucked Myfanwy into the crook of my arm like Rachel does with Molly, picked my book off the shelf and put a frown on my face. 'No more opening windows tonight – it's bloody freezing out there!'

But long after they had gone downstairs, I was still wondering about windows on reality and awesome angels and fuzzy edges and Mathilde.

*

Rachel

I went to my room and sat heavily on the bed, with a quick glance up at my print of Girl in Profile. Yes, it was just a print, not Mathilde herself. The only way I could think to reassure Alice about her own beliefs and Miss Akoto's beliefs and my contradictions was to teach her about scientific process and the philosophy of science. To give her the tools to see beyond people's blanket trust in simplified proofs. Was Pandora's box here, waiting to be opened, in Cardiff?

Or what about the fruit of the tree of knowledge? After all, Alice wanted the first apple from our tree. But then, was the Eden story really about falling into sin? Or was the problem that popular imagination had misinterpreted and skewed the very concept of sin? Wasn't the story more like an allegory of growing up, and the cost of taking responsibility for ourselves?

I couldn't hide knowledge from Alice, and I couldn't say that I believed knowledge to be evil. But more knowledge about the uncertainty that lies deep within our provisional grasp of reality would be confusing. Alice needed to find new stories to hold her learning and experience together, and I seemed to be the world expert at confusing them and letting them drift apart.

And letting me in.

'You've been listening to my thoughts, Mathilde.'

You've been helping me in, Rachel. Just by letting me be. Helping me become? I don't know what I'm becoming. But I do know you're helping Alice and Bethany in the same way. Might you be growing angels, Rachel?

43

WORST KARAOKE IN WALES

Rachel

I still didn't feel normal on Wednesday, and after all yesterday's talk of angels, certainly not angelic. But I thought I'd better make the effort to go to work before my date with Tom at the office party in the evening, and so I took a taxi.

I hoped to avoid Mrs Jones and Ian, who both knew about my resignation. Mrs Jones only gave me a couple of significant looks and Ian didn't seem to be around to gloat. Do people play golf in December? Even without Ian, the atmosphere was unbearably jovial with the annual orgy in prospect later, and I persuaded Tom to abandon his desk for lunch in a quiet restaurant.

'They might talk about us,' Tom said.

'Why not? Ian thinks I go home to hot bedroom action with Beth every night.'

'How's she managing, with you still waiting for results?'

Emotion caught me unawares, and whatever I was going to say came out as an incomprehensible hiss. Tom shifted his chair round next to me but didn't invade further.

I wiped my eyes and took a breath. 'Must be the medication. No, it's... I can't... None of this is fair on her – or on Alice.'

'Yes, it's tough for them. But Alice needs you – Beth knows that.'

'And if anything happened to me?'

'It won't.'

Just before I went into hospital, Tom had witnessed my will. I only needed to give him one look.

'Okay, so no one's immortal. If it makes your mind any easier, I'll look out for them.' He took my hand. 'Promise. But you'll be okay. Keep your focus on Alice – she's one amazing girl.'

'I'm an accidental mother, but I wouldn't be anything else. Thank you – really.'

Food interrupted, which helped. Even with my brain scrambled, I could think food. And we didn't hurry coffee afterwards, timing our return to the office to avoid awkward conversations before we left.

Tom drove me home and stayed as my babysitter until Beth and Alice got back from Christmas shopping. While he had a look at my portfolio from Beth's class, I wondered about calling Mum to finalise Christmas arrangements. Beth wanted her here, and to go to church with her. But as soon as I looked at my phone… I would have to leave the talking to Beth again.

When Alice and Beth got out of Joe's van, Tom headed off home to get changed for the party, but not before he'd received a high five from his youngest female admirer.

'Lush, he is,' Alice said, and sent me to my room. 'Presents in these bags – no looking!'

I had hidden in the corner wearing Rachel-drab at previous office parties, but now I was the office superstar. In the shower, I reminded myself that I looked good with nothing on. Time to try on some party clothes I hadn't worn for years.

Alice appeared in the doorway and made a big show of wiping her eyes. MAM! Rachel's gone mad!'

Beth appeared. 'You're going wear that?'

A slinky, close fitting black dress. Maybe a step too far. 'I'm too old for it, really.'

'Not to my eyes you're not, but you'd better take a pepper spray.'

'Mam, did you show your boobs that much?'

'Did I? Before I was past it, you mean?' Indignant Beth, hands on hips, gave me a flash forward to Beth and teenage Alice. And fireworks.

'No fighting, girls,' I said. 'I'll wear something safer.'

'Not when you're dating Tom,' Beth said. 'Let's have those knee boots out.'

My boots tipped it for Alice. 'Scientist in kick-ass boots.'

Beth did my makeup and Alice seemed to like the result. 'Evil woman!' But I could feel her anxiety. 'Got your emergency kit? Phone?'

'Yes, Mother.'

She rolled her eyes.

'Bodyguard?' Beth added.

On cue, my bodyguard rang the doorbell. In matching white waistcoat and trousers, he could have stepped out of an eighties mini-series. Probably the intention: Tom had heard all about the venue from me. No gold medallion, though. He looked me up and down, exchanged another high five with Alice, and said, 'Come on, let's rock the party!'

Alice whooped, Beth hugged him, and I stood with my

mouth open. I had never heard him so relaxed. And I most certainly wanted to rock the party.

Beth kissed my ear. 'Now, no over-thinking and no behaving. It's a party.'

'Mother!' said the peeved teen.

Heads turned, drinks were lowered, and phones were raised as the pair of us walked in. A red carpet would have been appropriate. But forgetting that this was the office party was not an option.

A night at Ian's rugby club was… a night at Ian's rugby club. Stuck in a time warp. Chicken and chips for the girls and fish and chips for the lads, delivered in bulk in their papers, with one concessionary veggie burger for me. It looked and tasted like pressed dog food, and I stuck to the chips. Then there was beer like piss in plastic crates, cut-price vodka and plastic bottles of blue goo. Water? But it's Christmas!

'Two waters, please,' Tom said firmly. I left him holding my glass and headed for the lavatory, returning after holding my breath for a record length of time. The single female toilet was already swimming in vomit.

I expected trial by Ian, who was usually inebriated before the party even began, but there was no sign of him. Mrs Jones was sitting alone in a corner, on her phone. And something about the way she was sitting drew Tom and I to her side instantly.

She put her phone down and looked at me. 'I should have warned Mrs Jacobs.'

'Ian? What's happened?'

'Found in his car with an empty bottle. Alcohol-induced heart failure, she says.'

'Dead?'

'He has – had – debts. Big debts. The rest of the staff don't know, but this office will be closing in February.'

I retched, choked and swallowed, my eyes swimming. 'It's me leaving. I caused it. As good as murdered him.'

Tom held my arm. 'No!'

'No!' Mrs Jones took a deep breath. 'He would have drunk as much or more at the party. Same result. It's not your fault.'

'If he had a weak heart already...' Tom tried to meet my eyes, but I studied my hands instead.

'Listen, Rachel. Listen carefully,' Mrs Jones said. 'Maybe you leaving moved the decision forward a few weeks, that's all. You're the one who kept us in work through lockdown, and before. You – you've kept us afloat, not his majesty.'

I shook my head. 'I don't get it.'

'They earmarked the Cardiff branch for closure before you even arrived. Ian knew the facts. Knew it was your string of projects that gave us a lifeline. Not that I ever heard him admit it. Don't blame yourself over Ian – the sod had it coming. Treated his wife like dirt. And the rest of us.'

'But he's dead, and I triggered it.'

'His drinking habit triggered it. And his other habits. Trust me – you don't want to know.' She stroked my arm. 'Okay?'

I nodded. 'Thank you. It's just–'

'I had a feeling he wouldn't last long. He'd been struggling to justify all that time away from his desk. I've had to cover for him enough times. I won't tell anyone about the closure until it's official – no need to spoil the party.'

'But Ian – what do we say?'

'Nothing tonight. They know Ian – they'll all think he was too drunk to bother turning up. I'll tell everyone tomorrow.'

'I suppose so. His poor wife and those girls.'

'They've lived apart for years – she sounded resigned on the phone. That picture of the girls above his desk hasn't changed in all the years I've been there. They'll be in their twenties.'

'And all this time, I'd thought…'

'Ian never talked about family. It was work and golf and money.' She shook her head. 'And sex, but I think he paid for that. And gin.'

'What will you do? When it closes?'

'New start – like you. I fancy something different.' She laid a hand on Tom's arm. 'What about you?'

'Rachel got me fired up,' Tom said. 'I'm thinking of applying for a job at Techniquest, explaining technology to children. I like that idea.'

That, at least, was cheering. 'You'd be brilliant – I'd give you a reference anytime. I suppose we'd better go home before someone asks–'

'Asks just about anything,' Tom said.

Mrs Jones looked across the crowded bar. 'They always treat me like the headmistress – here to spoil the fun. At least I'll never have my usual party job again.'

Tom raised his eyebrows.

She sucked in a breath. 'Making a list of all the women Ian needed to apologise to. I've done it at every party for the last eleven years. I'll be off home before someone asks why they haven't been harassed.'

I looked around at thirty or so revellers, drinkers and dancers. All would be without a job in the new year. Simply because I'd handed in my resignation on a whim – so as not to feel guilty in front of a child. I could afford to be unemployed. Some of them could not. And I would have to face them while I worked out my notice.

'I didn't want this to happen.'

Tom stopped me. 'There were other butterflies that flapped their wings before you flapped yours, Rachel. This lot will be making jokes about Ian's demise in a day or two. And cheerfully looking for work. Most of them are on temporary contracts anyway.'

'If it had been me dead, they would be making jokes about that screw finally coming loose.' And maybe it had. What had made me resign without even thinking that it might have consequences? And now a bottle of gin was empty and a man was dead.

That screw coming loose. The metal fixings on the bar shimmered. Coming loose.

Tom looked at me in a strange way and Mrs Jones was talking but I couldn't make out what she was saying. And Rachel the traitor was dying before them.

There was Tom's face again, and he seemed bothered, and I was looking up at him because it was easier, now that I was on the floor. My arms felt hot and the lights on the ceiling tasted of metal and I heard a microphone crackle and a woman's voice said, 'ARE YOU READY FOR THE WORST KARAOKE IN WALES?' and the world exploded in slow motion, but this present moment kept on moving through the continuum of time and space until it reached, 'ARE YOU READY FOR THE WORST KARAOKE IN WALES?' again, and the now-moment kept on moving through the exploding world and on through, 'ARE YOU READY FOR THE WORST KARAOKE IN WALES?' a different way and then my now-point was weaving crazily through the explosion and coming out backwards into sharp grey blocks and splinters of tears and blood that squeezed out and on into PAIN. But I heard that voice from another universe, right here in the palm of my hand. 'ARE YOU READY FOR THE WORST KARAOKE IN WALES?'

And then I was back in a world that made some kind of sense. 'That was strange.'

'SHE'S STIRRING,' Mrs Jones shouted, setting off fireworks in my head.

'Ouch!'

And it happened again. 'SHE'S STIRRING.'

'Ouch!'

Or had it? Time was playing tricks. Or my mind was playing tricks with time.

'Sorry,' she whispered.

Tom's quiet voice, 'You've had a seizure,' didn't repeat. Maybe the present moment was more comfortable in Tom's hands.

'Not one of mine. Strange, Tom. New.'

'Do we still need the ambulance?' Olaf said, from high above me. Olaf? Jane's boyfriend. Jane from the office. How did I know he was called Olaf? Concentrate, Rachel, he asked you a question. 'Sorry?'

'The ambulance. Are you safe without it now?'

'Don't cancel it,' Tom said.

Cancel what? Cancel me? 'Help me! Help me, Tom.'

'I'm with you,' he said. 'Not going to let you out of my sight.'

Someone was singing *You can leave your hat on* in the background, badly flat. I hoped there wasn't a stripper.

God, maybe it was me. People were looking down at me.

'Keep back! Give the poor girl some privacy,' Mrs Jones said, staring at me. A huddle of people stepped back, all staring down at me on the floor.

I was the stripper.

Olaf and Jane rescued me by standing facing them. 'You shall not pass,' their body language said.

'Tom...?' I was shaking. I've known all kinds of seizures, but this was new. And I wasn't sure whether it was over. 'Tom, this isn't me.'

'Hold on – they're on their way.'

'Tom, if anything happens – you know...'

His eyes came very close. 'Nothing's going to happen. You'll be fine.'

The singing and laughter got going again, but at last, paramedics rescued a murderer from the worst karaoke in Wales.

44

THE MOMENT OF NOW

Alice

A cubicle in A & E. Tom had stayed with Rachel until she begged him to fetch Mam. And I refused to let her come without me. Mam looked calm – too calm. And Rachel looked more scared than I've ever seen her.

I stroked Rachel's hand, and we waited.

'You don't need to be here, Alice,' she said.

'I'm in the right place. I'm the one who's seen more seizures than all of you put together. Just this once, I'm the expert – trust me.'

And Rachel smiled. 'Thank you – but they might not let you stay when they put me on a ward.'

I raised my fist at the curtain.

'I can't see them stopping her without handcuffs,' Tom said.

The duty doctor was back and gave me that child-in-the-wrong-place look he gave me before.

A small woman in a black velvet dress with a jewelled brooch stepped past him. 'My patient – thank you – I'll take it from here,' she told him.

Julie Cook, Rachel's cello-playing doctor friend. I'd only ever spoken to her on the phone, but I once saw her wearing scrubs. This time, she looked beautiful, and I could smell her lovely perfume.

Rachel sat up. 'Julie, you needn't... I've spoiled...'

Doctor Cook shrugged. 'I put a "notify" on your record, in case. You've saved me from Christmas drinks with the hospital executives and that sodding retired MP. Patronising bastard always turns up when there's a freebie.' She turned and smiled at me. 'You must be Alice, the pianist.' No comment about being a child in the wrong place. She turned that safe, comfortable smile on Rachel. 'Genius timing, Rachel, I owe you for this. Fabulous boots, by the way. Now, feedback please.'

Tom handed her some notes Rachel had dictated.

'This is different – we definitely need to investigate,' she said. And then we were heading up several floors, with Tom pushing Rachel in a wheelchair, just in case. Doctor Cook opened a door into a dark room full of equipment and turned on the lights. Something hummed as she turned it on, and screens began to light up. A young man who must have been one of her medical students trotted in and went straight to a console. And I stayed close to Rachel, holding her hand, one of the team. Mam had her hand on my shoulder, my backup.

'I do not like refractory epilepsy, jumping from one manifestation to another,' Doctor Cook said. 'We need to get you stable.'

'It would be nice,' Rachel said.

'It would save Mam panicking,' I said.

Doctor Cook looked at me, maybe measuring how scared I was. 'You're not panicking, are you?'

'Nah – got a friend at school with epilepsy. Not in Rachel's league with the seizures, but I've seen enough of Rachel's big ones.'

'Add doctor to your list of ambitions – I guess you already want to be a particle physicist like Wonder Woman here.'

'Actually, she's more of an eco-warrior,' said Rachel. But I tucked that doctor thought away for another time.

Rachel was going to stay in overnight, and Tom said he would stay here if we wanted to go home. Mam and me didn't move. They would thoroughly scan Rachel tomorrow, but for now, Julie hooked her up to an electroencephalograph (good word) with electrodes all over Rachel's head.

'Daughter of Frankenstein?' Tom said.

'Don't disturb the patient,' Doctor Cook said, pointing at a ripple on her screen. 'Or I'll send you outside on the naughty step.' Another ripple. 'Humour appears to be intact.' Another ripple.

'Focus on me for the moment,' Doctor Cook told Rachel. 'I need a steady reading.'

But Rachel's eyes were darting all over the place. 'Julie, I'm not managing. Losing my focus.' Rachel gripped my hand.

I brought my other hand over Rachel's and stroked it, and for the first time, I was really scared. Scared because I knew Rachel's fear. She had talked and talked again about the moment of now. The present moment, the precise balance point between all that is remembered and all that is yet to happen. The moment that we live in. When Rachel said she was losing her focus, I KNEW that NOW was what she was thinking about. Her living focus. And she was feeling it fade away.

I needed Mathilde for Rachel.

Stay calm for her, Alice. I'm here too.

Rachel opened her mouth a few times and then called out. 'JULIE!' And Doctor Cook took her other hand.

'I'm scared. Losing my... Losing my.... Losing my... Presence?'

'Rachel, keep that focus on me, now,' Doctor Cook said. 'On me. Think. Think of something you-and-me. Orchestra? Look at me.'

'I'm trying. Orchestra.'

'Get an image in your head. Look at me. Orchestra.'

'Too big. You – just you and your cello. Playing Bach in that dress.'

Rachel had her eyes closed, her face twitching, but then getting calmer.

'Keep focussed. Me and my cello.'

Her eyes flickered open 'You look lovely with your cello. Lovely...'

'That's because my cello has never walked out on me,' Doctor Cook said, but I don't think Rachel was listening.

'Beauty, sometimes... I need to tone it down,' Rachel said.

'Makes sense. You're hypersensitive. Let's move on from me, now,' Doctor Cook said. 'Think of something you love doing. Something that relaxes you.'

Rachel looked across at Mam, sitting behind me with Tom's arm around her. 'I model for Beth, and for life class. Play an imaginary violin. That's relaxing.'

'You look calmer, just talking about it. I can imagine you modelling – you have poise when you relax.'

Doctor Cook turned and talked quickly with her student, who rushed out for something. Then she was back up close with Rachel, but still watching the screen behind her. 'Getting further askew.'

'I'm not… not relaxing any more,' Rachel said through clenched teeth

'I can tell.' I tried a smile as I wriggled my squeezed hand out from hers and replaced it with my other hand.

'Sorry, Alice.'

'You hold on. Mathilde's here.'

Rachel nodded, but Doctor Cook said, 'Who?'

'Doesn't matter,' I said in a hurry.

'Try another image,' Doctor Cook said. 'That portrait you told me about?'

Rachel gave a real, genuine smile. 'That's Mathilde. She's here, with us now.'

Doctor Cook just nodded. 'We're going to need more intervention, now.'

I could feel Mathilde holding Rachel and me. Rachel turned her head to face me, and we looked straight into each other's eyes. Then her eyes began to lose focus, and I knew a seizure was coming. And I knew Mathilde and I had a job to do.

*

Rachel

I'm safe, now. Mathilde is here. Alice is holding my hand.
Safe.
Alice. I check with her eyes. Safe with Alice.
I check around. Beth is here. Tom is here. Julie is here.
Alice whispers, 'with you.'
Alice is with me.
Now I can let go – I can let it happen.

On a day without an end, the woman who once screamed in Queen Street and stopped Cardiff felt no need to scream.
    Julie, Tom and Beth and were with me – really with me.
    Mathilde was keeping me safe.
    And Alice was holding my hand.

45

VOICES

A warm buzzing all around. Little comforting beeps.

An Alice sound – primrose yellow, light and gentle. And a Julie sound, lower and comfortable, full and brown. Easy to live in. And there's another sound that's been around for a while, blue and solid.

Sounds. Always the Alice primrose sound, safe. Always the Julie sound, brown and caring. And there's the Beth sound, rich and loving, in reds and browns and oranges, and the soothing Tom sound, in deep strong greens and dappled light. Not now. Just the primrose Alice sound, wrapped up safe in beeps and buzzes. Comfortable.

'Rachel, you're twitching again.' That's the Alice sound, soft and close.

'All signs stable today. Does something hurt?' The Julie sound, safe and deeper.

The Alice sound flows on. 'Not pain, I don't think. You feel happy, Rachel. Easy.' Home sounds all around. Beeps and buzzes. Safe.

'Rachel?' A sound.

Don't want it. Slipping back into silvery grey singing. Silver singing, spreading to blot out the sounds.

'Rachel, you don't look happy.' That sound again, pulling against the silvery grey. Against the singing. But there's another sound in dusty pink. Calling. A voice, calling.

Mathilde. *Listen to Alice.*

'I'm here, Rachel. Your Alice. What's wrong?'

DON'T WANT that Alice sound. Want the easy silver.

Mathilde again. *Listen to Alice.*

The Alice voice.

Voice. It's a voice.

'You aren't going to answer me, so I'll tell you anyway. Good day at school. Miss Akoto let me swear when no one was around. Swear about you.'

The silver singing fades into grey. The pink and primrose fill and grow. Mathilde brings the Alice voice. Want to live in THIS voice. The Alice voice.

'Didn't know how many swear words I knew. Good day. Have you been swearing in your sleep, Rachel? Rachel?'

Words. Voice. Words.

A warm word in the Alice voice. A deeper yellow. 'Rachel.' Nice.

'Alice, look at the trace. Look at it!' The Julie sound, gone quiet.

'Did it do it?' The Alice voice, tripping through the words. 'Did it do it?'

'Did it do it?' Little ticklish words. Tickle. That's a word. A word.

Words?

Words.

In the sounds. Words. Need to tune in. Focus–

The Julie voice. 'Talk again. I need to watch this.' Voice – it's another voice.

'You're twitching again, funny girl.'

'Nothing that time.' The Julie voice, further away. 'I'll call the physio and we'll do some more exercise. Move you round – okay? Alice can help.'

Alice.

'Yes! Look at the trace. She's responding to names. Say her name.'

'Rachel?'

Rachel.

'Yes!'

Fuzzy sounds. 'You hearing me, Rachel?'

'Not this time.'

Soft sounds. Silver singing sounds. Nice.

Don't let it pull you down! Mathilde, hurting. *Listen to Alice.*

Fading… silver singing…

'Me again. Always me. Alice, come to bug you. Ra-a-achel. Ra-a-achel.'

Singing like the silver singing. Primrose-coloured singing, not silver.

The Alice voice. 'Ra-a-achel.'

It's Alice.

It's Alice. More than a voice. More…

'YES. Strongest yet.' The Julie voice. 'Alice, assume that Rachel isn't just hearing you now. She's processing. Thinking. Right, Rachel?'

Processing. That's a word. Thinking. Another word. Don't want it. Bad word.

'Of course she's thinking. She a shitting scientist.'

'No, Alice, listen carefully. I know she's in there, but she hasn't been using conscious thought. I know you've always talked to Rachel, but this time, it's a real change. Complex neural activity picking up.'

'Real stuff? Not kidding? You mean it?'

'It might take a while, but this is the most I've seen since the operation.'

'Rachel? It's pain-in-the-bum here. Are you thinking? Rachel?'

Alice speaking. She's a person. Alice is a person. And Rachel. Rachel is…?

Rachel is…?

'Yes, look Alice, it's spreading into different areas.'

Julie. She's not just a voice, either. She's a person.

'Rachel, you are GENIUS-FANTASTIC!' Alice.

'Oh, Alice, we're into the next phase. I was beginning to think…' Julie, the person, speaking with a catch in her breath. Feeling. Caring. Caring for… someone?

'Don't you dare cry, Julie.' Alice. Strong Alice.

Julie's voice, closer. 'Rachel, you are one lucky girl. Not everyone has a guardian angel like Alice.'

Rachel. That's me. Me. I. I am.

I'm a person too.

Alice, up close. 'Here for you,' she says, and I feel something. I feel.

It's more than the primrose yellow – something cuddly and soft.

'I love you – you – real Rachel, not imaginary Rachel.'

I'm not imaginary Rachel. Alice loves me. This has meaning. And Alice is a real girl. With me. Always. I'm not imaginary. A person? What am I? Just voices…

Beeping noise. 'Alice, can you stand out of the way a minute. Replace this one?' That blue voice.

'No. Function looks good. Let's see how Rachel manages.' Julie. Julie the person.

Beeping noise. 'Forget that. Level as before. Rachel, if you're hearing all this, we're bringing you back slowly. No need to panic. All the signs are good, this time.'

Her voice goes fuzzy. 'I've brought my cello again. Not much room here, but I'll try my best…' A rattling noise, then lovely warm, brown Julie-cello sounds. Sound patterns I can hear and feel. Sounds I live in. Music. Melody, carrying me. Melody? Me? Flowing, nicely in tune. In tune?

Meanings. Meanings…

Beeping. 'It's blocked. Pass me another.' Nurse voice. Nurse is a…

Fading. 'Normal sleep pattern. Good.'

Beeping. Fading.

'Look who's back. Mam told her to wait – she'll get upset again.' Alice's voice, grumpy. There's a face in my memory. A grumpy Alice face with her bottom lip out.

I have memory. Not just voices. I have memory. I remember her face.

Seeing it. I remember seeing.

'They'll tell me to leave,' Alice says. 'One visitor at a time. It isn't fair, Rachel.'

'Don't worry, Alice. It's my clinical decision that you stay.' Julie talking.

'Hello, Rachel, it's me.' Another voice, all twisted up with silvery grey.

Hurting.

I need to listen. I've missed something. Alice is talking. 'You need to tell her who you are, Nan B. I know her eyes look open, but she isn't using them yet.'

A soft touch-feeling. Touch? 'Your mam's here,' Alice says, up close and cosy. And Mam's on her way – your Beth – just been out for a sleep.' My Beth.

'Sorry, Rachel, I haven't managed much. It's a bit over-whelming.' Mum's voice – that strained sound.

'You can't help it!' Alice is talking. 'She's your little girl, Nan B.'

Nan B. Alice called Mum Nan B.

'Rachel, just… Just keep fighting.' Hurt. Mum feels hurt.

'Best leave it now, Nan B. Come back later. She is getting better – she is.'

Alice. Looking after hurt Mum. Looking after hurt me. She's been looking after me forever. I want to help her. Can't.

I CAN'T HELP ALICE.

No need to panic. I'm with you. I'm with Alice. She's safe.

Safe. Mathilde.

'Rachel, listen to me.' Julie's voice. 'You're getting agitated because you can't respond. Let it go. People will upset you. Just let it go. Relax. Your body is doing the talking for you, and soon you'll manage more. Okay?'

Quiet. A space for me to… respond? That's the word she used. Respond. How do I respond?

'Mrs Bothwell, why not leave it until Rachel has more control?'

'I don't know. I shouldn't leave Alice here on her own.'

'Don't worry about Alice. She's one of the team. And she's never on her own.'

'Yeah, Julie looks after me, and I look after Julie. Yeah, and we're winning, and Rachel's coming back. So there.'

Strong Alice.

Listen to Alice. Mathilde, in pink. But it's hard work, driving thoughts around this… this what?

Don't let it pull you down!

Too tired. Silver tired. Grey tired. Dark tired. Down dark tired. Down dark…

'Hiya, Rachel! Me and Tom today.'

'Good afternoon, Doctor Bothwell.' The lovely deep, deep green voice. That's Tom. Tom and Alice. I can picture Alice. There's more of her than the silver singing. The singing is just silvery grey stuff. Alice is a person, and Tom. No picture…

Tom. Yes, a picture. He looks like a warrior. Warrior. That's an old word. From far outside of here. Here. Here is…

I KNOW HERE! This is hospital! I'm in hospital.

'Your face looks bothered,' Alice says. 'You're thinking, aren't you? There's no hurry. You'll be fine. Tom's been upset – all wound up. What's to get wound up about my Rachel taking her time? You'll get there, when you're ready.'

'You're so much more patient than me, Alice.' Tom's lovely voice.

Tom and me in hospital. Tom and me in hospital before. He said, 'Hang on,' that time. That time in my memory. With Molly. Molly? 'Hang on, Rachel,' he said.

'Alice – look at the screen – traces filling up. Fetch the nurse, quick.'

Footsteps. People do that: they walk. I don't. I'm just… here.

Nurse: 'Definite. I'll bleep Dr Cook. Rachel, can you move anything?'

Can I? Fuzzy noises.

Alice's voice. 'Don't get too excited, Tom. She's been this close before.'

'Let's hope,' he says.

A feeling. Sadness. Greyness. The singing wraps me in silver. Silver-dark. NO. I'm scared. Dark-scared. GO AWAY, singing! HELP ME, Mathilde!

Don't let it pull you down! Stay with them – stay awake. For Alice. For Alice.

Thank you, Mathilde.

Quiet. Time passing. Time. Time does that. I'm here in time. I know about time. It's my thing. Equations that go…

Footsteps. Julie. I know before she speaks. 'Sorry, Rachel. I was busy with a patient. Don't worry: one of your guardian angels has stayed.'

'Tom's gone for a coffee with Mam.' Alice.

I love Alice. She's my… Guardian angel?

'Not every long-term patient gets this much attention,' Julie says.

Long-term patient. I'm a long-term patient. With angels.

Angels unawares. Alice said that. Growing angels. Mathilde said that.

'We are winning,' Julie says. 'Remember what we said about recovery time, Alice. No way to predict it. But we are winning.'

Julie – a picture – her eyes. Calm, warm, friendly eyes. She plays the cello. A warm, brown sound, like her eyes. Julie's eyes. Julie's chuckle when we get it wrong in the rehearsal hall. I PLAY THE VIOLIN! Have I got hands?

I don't seem to have anything. I'm a portrait, like Mathilde.

She's in a portrait. I'm not with her – poor Mathilde. I'm in hospital – I can't be a portrait, can I? Julie's got me. Julie plays the cello. Plays me. Makes me sing. Plays my strings. Not the singing dream. Julie. Her name. Her eyes. Brown. Gentle.

Julie – Cello. Julie – Eyes – I haven't got eyes. Eyes see – I can't see.

Eyes. Alice's eyes. Blue. Beth's eyes. Grey. BETH! I love Beth. I love Alice. I love Tom. I love Julie. I love Mum. More people? Siân and Joe. I love Siân and Joe. Mathilde. I love her voice inside. And Bach inside me – Bach – he's a dead composer. Bach – cello – Julie playing. Playing – me – violin. Violin and cello. Playing Bach two-part inventions with Julie.

I'm Rachel Bothwell.

Julie's voice. 'The physio's on the way for your exercises. I just need to check your scores.' Julie – physio – exercises. I have a body. Have I? I want to see it.

'LOOK what Rachel's doing, Julie!'

'Can you fetch Beth?' Julie, urgent.

'I'm going to stop one more drip, Rachel. You're right with me now, aren't you?'

Yes.

'Can you give me a sign?'

A sign. No exit. Keep off the grass. Do not flush sanitary products. A sign. It's a game in my mind. My mind. My mind must live somewhere: I must have a body.

'Rachel! Mam's here!'

Mam. Not mine. SHE MEANS BETH!

'Hello, lover.' That gorgeous, rich Beth-sound. Beth, my home.

Beth. I should shake something around. If I have something to shake.

'YES, Rachel.'

I must have done... something.

Julie: 'Yes, yes, yes, you wonderful...' She's crying. I can hear the sobs.

Alice's voice, gentle. 'Crying's allowed, Julie. You're the best doctor ever.'

'A serious wonderful genius perfect doctor.' Beth's voice. My Beth. 'Rachel, you've been... You're back, lover.'

I can feel... skin, warm, close to me. And there's something I can't feel. I can't feel the colour of her and the light of her and the shape of her. There's a feeling missing. I can't... Don't...

'Take your time,' Julie says. 'You're on the way, now. All signs good.'

On the way... Signs...

'Good? That all?' Alice. 'Ast-ro-nomically, wo-o-onderfully, fucking a-ma-zing.'

'And quite nice.' Tom says. 'Hey! Alice – stop it!' Tom, lovely Tom.

Lovely, lovely people. My people.

Lovely, lovely, lovely, lovely, lovely... I can't see them.

Must say... CAN'T.

It's dark. Scared-dark.

Can't speak. Can't move. CAN'T SEE.

Can't... Am I here?

Where's here?

When? Need...

You're nearly there. Nearly back with them. Be patient, Rachel.

No need to be scared – I'm with you in the dark. You're safe, now.

46

DELIRIUM

Rachel

Tangled. Stuck. HURTS.

TRAPPED.

Out! Need out.

'No!' A shrill voice, '…yourself!'

'Stop!' Another voice. More words, '…down!'

HURTS.

Can't see. Must get out! SCARED. DARK. Can't see.

'No!' 'Stop it!' Shouting, two voices. 'Call Doctor Cook!'

Hands, holding me. Can't see. Can't speak. Can't breathe. HURTS.

THEY'VE CAUGHT ME.

Held tight. Can't breathe. They're KILLING me.

'She's pulling at her tubes. Any damage? Calm down, will you!'

Frightened. Lost.

WHO AM I?

'Doctor Cook? Over here, quick.'

'Hiya, Rachel. I was just on my way over.' Calm, relaxed.

I'm not being murdered.

'Listen – you're okay – you're safe. Imagine you've had a seizure – you know that feeling – think confusion. It will pass.'

Feeling – touch – something cosy.

'I need you to stay calm while I check your tubes.'

It's quiet. What is she doing? I can't see. Should see. Eyes don't work.

'Tracheostomy's fine. Don't try to speak. Breathing will feel funny. We'll have it out today. You'll get your voice back soon enough.'

Quiet. Ow!

'Sorry – that one's sore. You've got the full set of drips – mustn't disturb them. Wave your hand if you understand.'

I wave… something.

'I know you can't see. There's nothing wrong with your eyes. Your sight will come back in time. Your voice will come back. But you need to be patient. Now, I've got to hurry. Beth and Alice will be in soon. Okay, now?'

I wave something again. Okay? I don't know. What's going on?

Dark. Scared. TRAPPED.

Tangled up in…

'Rachel Bothwell, will you fucking behave!' A light, prim-rosy kind of voice. 'Now, what's all the fuss about? You're in hospital, Julie and the nurses are looking after you, and you'll be fine soon.'

I'm in hospital. In hospital – it makes sense.

'Made a bit of a mess of these tubes, haven't you? We had to wait because they were taking out your breathing tube. Don't try to speak. Your throat will be sore. AND NO PICKING!'

I know this voice. Alice. I have to do what she tells me. No picking. I can't see her. I can't see anyone. I can't…

Pain. Pain. Pain. Alone. I'm alone in the dark.

Frightened. Let me out. Please?

You're not alone. You're safe in hospital.

Thank you, Mathilde.

Beeps and buzzes, I know these sounds – intensive care – I've been here before. And a fizzing air mattress. That means I've been in a while. No picking. Someone said that – Mathilde? No, Alice.

I'm not alone. I can feel a woolly, safe feeling. Molly's hair must be wrapped around my finger. Molly, my Molly. Feel: I can feel. Can I see? Not yet. I can feel my eyes. Itchy. And some hurts: arm, throat and more hurts I can't figure out. No one speaking. Must be night.

Julie Cook. I know her steady footsteps. I can't see her, but there's a blurry light.

Eyesight – that's what's been missing. My eyes are coming online, I suppose. I DON'T WANT TO SEE ME. I'm scared. What will I see? Her hand on my forehead. 'That's it, just relax, Rachel. I'm here. No worries today: you're doing fine.'

I hear her checking something. Asking a nurse. Some numbers. Then she's back up close. 'Beth and Alice are waiting to see you. You've been freaking out a lot in the last week or two. Can we manage better? Please try, Rachel. They've been through so much for you. They love you. We all love you.'

Love me. Me? What's left of me worth loving?

'Rachel, try. I know it's scary, but you're nearly into the next stage. You've been fully conscious a month. High time you moved on.'

A month? A MONTH! I can't remember... Can't ask...

'PLEASE calm down. Try. They're just coming.'

Breathe. Hurts. Breathe. Hurts. Keep calm. Voices. Moving shapes.

'I guess you'll need some questions answered,' Julie says.

Alice's voice. 'Not sure. Is she ready for it? What if she goes crazy again?'

Her voice twists something inside me. She's a child. A scared child. I know her – care for her. My child, and she's scared, like me. I'm scared.

Footsteps, and her voice again, a long way off. 'She'll get upset again. I don't want to hurt my Rachel.'

She doesn't want to hurt me. She cares. Who is this girl? Who would care for me?

'Rachel, we'll be right back. Don't worry,' Julie says. 'It's a bit overwhelming for Alice, just now. I think she expected to have you home when you first woke up.'

Alice. What have I done to her?

'Don't worry...' More footsteps fade into the beeps and buzzes and hisses.

Don't worry. About what? I don't know what I shouldn't worry about.

Moving shapes. Footsteps.

Stay calm, Rachel. Breathe. Hurts.

'I'm with you.' Beth. Another voice that grabs me, pulling at something deep. Something real. 'Alice has been strong for you all this time, but... It's different. Lately, we've never known what state you'll be in. It's a bit much for her when you take fright. I wish I could cuddle you better.'

'Don't worry, Beth. The fear will pass.' Julie, keeping Beth calm. Keeping me calm.

'We'll go through the awkward bit again, and then maybe Alice will come along,' Julie says.

The awkward bit. Again. What has she told me before? Is Beth leaving me forever? My throat hurts.

'Rachel, it will be confusing, taking in everything at once. I know you've woken up in hospital before, but this time, it's needing all your strength and willpower just to stay with us. Recovering will be a long job. Do you understand?'

I move something. Arm, I think – yes, it must be. Understand? Something serious has happened to me. And Alice is scared.

What have I done to her?

What nightmares have I given her?

I DON'T WANT TO GIVE ANYONE NIGHTMARES.

It's NOT FAIR, what I do to people.

47

LOVE

Rachel

This is the next day. I know it is. I've been asleep, sort of. And days must have passed before the scared-Alice day as well. Lots of days. Time. I can sense time passing. And light – not the scary darkness. Moving light. And voices.

No, I don't want this. I don't want to be this broken person in a bed. I want to be Beth's lovely Rachel. Rachel in Beth's picture. Beth. I want Beth!

'Calm down girl – you'll hurt yourself, see.'

I don't know this voice. A valleys accent. Valleys. Places. Places I've been. Walking up on the tops with Beth and Alice. Walking. With legs. In the wind and sun. Wind and sun. Feeling. Feeling free. Free. Not free. Trapped.

'Calm down. Don't panic.'

Panicking: Rachel does that. Rachel does panic. Me. I screamed and Beth came. Where's Beth? Breathe. Hurts again. I CAN'T SCREAM. She won't come. Beth has left me alone.

No Beth. No. No. No. HURTING.

'Don't try talking, girl. Let it heal, see.'

'Let it heal.' That's what Mum says when I'm a kid and I've bitten my tongue. 'Let it heal.' I'm a kid.

No. This is bigger. I'm bigger.

'Just chill, bach. Just chill. The doctors are doing their rounds. You'll see someone soon.' Light. A blurry face I don't know. 'Relax, bach. You're all het up. She'll be here in a minute.'

Looking. I can see more, now. I'm in… A cubicle? Life support rigs and monitors. What life I have seems to come from the machines here. Or not. No, I'm only hooked up to a few. Nose – never had that. Wrist. Catheter – must be – it itches. Buzzing air mattress. I'm a machine. A cyber-Rachel.

Colours. I can see colours. Blue sky outside the window. And a cloud. Pale, fluffy, with a yellow tinge to one side. Blurred and drifting slowly across. Everything's blurred, and everything's colours. I like colours. Alice colours. Beth colours. Tom colours. Julie colours. Mathilde colours. Singing colours. Remembered colours.

Remembered people. A swirl of mixed-up people. Dazzling bits of life.

I'm here. No need to panic.

Thank you, Mathilde. Don't leave me.

Mathilde. Is she real? I can't think. People – Alice, Beth. Shattered glimpses. Someone dropped the jigsaw.

Mathilde. I need her help. God, am I BRAIN DAMAGED?

I'm always here when you need me. And I'm not the only one keeping you safe.

Julie comes walking in. I can hear her footsteps AND see her. Recognise her shape and her Julie-colour.

'Nice to see you focussing. How's the eyesight?'

My turn to speak. There's a hiss. It HURTS.

'Sorry – don't try to answer. I'll try not to ask questions. But your tracheostomy scar is healing nicely. It won't be long before you can swear at me.'

Love

She touches my forehead, and it feels… I want her to do it again. And she knows, and she strokes my fringe across, and again, and again. Lovely touch. She reaches for something down beside me and tucks it against my cheek. My Molly. More memories. I'm a child. I'm an adult.

'Rachel, I'll explain again. I don't think you've been taking it in. You came out of coma seven weeks ago, but you've been asleep most of the time. Normal, good sleep. You don't need the details yet, but the signs are all pointing the right way. You can recover, but we need you onside. We need your help too. I know it's confusing and frightening, but you're through the worst. You can do it, and we all believe in you.'

Whatever look I give her, she gets the message that I'm scared, but I want more.

'You might not remember, but your epilepsy was going out of control. You were already in hospital when you went out. That lump was disrupting the neurons. A benign tumour in just the wrong place. It's gone now, and it shouldn't come back. We induced the coma to help your brain recover after the operation. All went well, but then, coming round was a problem.'

Her voice is flowing into my head slowly. Do I need slow? My head – they took the lump out. Is there enough of me left?

'You got into a pattern. Seemed to prefer coma after all that time. You added a bit more on the end.'

She steps out of the way, and now I can see Beth's blurry face. Beth's lovely grey eyes. Beth's throaty voice. 'You took your own little holiday. We started to wonder whether you were planning on coming back.' She wipes her eyes. 'But you're well past that – you're on the way.'

Alice's voice. 'Fuck you, Rachel Bothwell. You've taken your time.' And that smile, from the other side of the bed.

Love. That's the feeling flooding me now. Love. Pure love.

Fuck-you-Rachel-Bothwell is loved and loves. Still loves. Still can love. And the relief is like a gentle tide flowing through me. A sea of relief. A sea and Alice. Alice, in the space at my side, and the infinite sea. Memories. Alice said I was her mother, beside the sea. One weird mother. I belong to Alice. I belong. Can I tell her?

'A-a-a-lice,' I manage, and it hurts. But the smile between Alice and Beth and Julie takes away the pain.

Alice cuddles close, and her words vibrate in my ear. 'Love you, my Rachel.'

I get the right signals this time. Face signals. That's the corner of my mouth she just kissed. Can I move it?

'YES, Rachel. Do that again.' She calls out behind her. 'JULIE! She can smile!'

And Julie is back with her arm around Alice, and I perform my new trick.

'It helps to smile with both sides,' Alice says, and I try again.

'Right – smiling practice every day, zombie-face.'

I look over at Beth, and my head moves.

I DID THAT! I don't know how, but I did.

Beth looks… I can't focus, but her hair is shorter, and I don't remember that much grey. I look back at Alice. So much more gravity about her, and short hair, where I remember a big bunch of golden hair.

I keep looking back and forth between them, moving my head a little more each time, and they gaze at me, letting me build their pictures inside me. What have I put them through?

'We won't wear you out now,' Julie says, 'But you won't

miss anything. Alice is keeping a diary of your time here. It helps her see your progress, and it should help you. Recovery will take time, but you're on the way. You can start with the speech therapist now, and we'll soon have you talking easily. Then you can keep the diary together.'

'All about wicked Doctor Julie,' Alice says, and grins, but reaches up and touches Julie's fingers on her shoulder.

'Rachel, what Alice has helped you through... Alice is...'

'Stop it!' Alice says. 'Don't.'

'It's a bit early to do any more explaining, but you are ticking most of the boxes now – well on the way. I'll leave you with Beth and Alice – back in a minute or two. Is that okay with you?

Yes. Smile. Success.

And I wiggle my shoulders and get kisses on both sides for my clever trick.

'You really are coming back, aren't you?' Beth says. 'I was beginning to wonder... Never mind.' She wipes her eyes.

'Oh, Mam,' Alice says. 'Yeah, and Rachel, I've been reading up on the recovery process. Don't fret about making sense of stuff. Your mind needs time: you're going through a stage. Things will join up. You're past the worst of the delirium – that wasn't much fun. And you might have noticed you're off the drips. Moving wards, this week.'

Beth is still wiping her eyes, and I wish I could cry with her, but don't seem to have any tears. 'Be-e-eth,' I manage, and Alice claps her hands.

'This is immense for Alice, Rachel. She's easier now, but when you were out of it, she got upset if she missed a single day visiting. How many have you missed, Alice? Eight or nine in all this time?'

'Eleven – you can't count.'

'Tom has been most days, helping us both. Iestyn, Siân and Joe as well. And your mother, but she finds it hard.'

All these names. Mysterious people someone called Rachel loves. Yes, I know now. They're people I love. I know a lot about them but can't seem to hold all this knowledge at once. It's a struggle to keep on being Rachel. To keep on being.

Beth comes closer, letting me focus on her warm grey eyes. 'Didn't think we'd get you back. Alice has always found something to say to you, and she's written down everything you've missed.'

'Saves getting bored.' Alice grins. 'I'm off for a hot chocolate – I've seen enough of Mam's waterworks. Back in a bit.'

Beth smiles after her. 'Julie told me that without Alice, you might not have made it as far as the operation. Before they got you stable enough to operate, you were fluttering in and out of consciousness. It was Alice's voice that drew your responses. Kept your brain active.'

Alice. Vague memories. The Alice voice. Primrose yellow, and full of life. And against the disembodied essence of Alice that reached me, a hollow, silvery sing-song, pulling me down into oblivion. Into the dark. Enticing and frightening. But also a dusty pink voice tugging me the other way, towards life and light. *Don't let it pull you down!* Mathilde, struggling to help me reach out to the people I love. *Listen to Alice.* Mathilde – with me then in coma and still with me now. I can feel her warm presence.

I try my hardest to think my thanks to her. 'Thank you, Mathilde.'

Thank you for trusting me, Rachel.

It works – I can speak to Mathilde inside my head. 'You're always warm, always loving. Always there when I'm desperate. How could I not trust you, Mathilde?'

Believe me, Rachel, we talked a good deal when you were unconscious.

Beth smiles at something behind my shoulder. 'Having a moment with Mathilde?'

I nod. I can nod. It's something else I can do.

'Thank you, Mathilde,' Beth says.

Julie is back and I know Mathilde has moved out of the way.

'Your recovery is taking a long time, and that's tough for Alice,' Julie says. 'She needs you to help as well. She needs you to work your hardest at getting better – you can do it. You've been retreating, but we need you back in the real world.'

'Alice believes in you.' Beth says.

Alice, with that older, serious face, and short hair. A portrait swims into my mind. Beth, when she was a girl like Alice, with the same hair. And the story. I'm still confused about my own story, but I do know this one. The picture was painted by Beth's father, Gwyn Howells. He died beside her when she was a child. She tried to resuscitate him, but couldn't. Beth is here, with her arm around me, and I didn't die.

I didn't die.

I didn't die. She got me back.

Beth is close. Here, where I want her.

'You… Got… Me… Back.'

'I did,' she whispers, and a little smile crosses her face. 'And you're fucking well staying with me this time, Rachel.'

48

FIDELITY

Alice

Julie told us that Rachel was still at the beginning of a journey, but I never expected it to be such a long one. Rachel fell into a never-ending patient universe, where existing used up her energy.

Mathilde told me that if Rachel didn't bother us and keep on bothering us, she would never get better. But Rachel didn't want to bother anyone. Talking was tough for her, and her new voice was nothing like the old Rachel. She sounded like Dad drunk, deep and slurred, but without the alcohol smell. At least her Rachel-in-coma smell had gone.

Julie got her moved into Rehab, although she wasn't strictly ready for it on her charts. And Julie finally let go. Tom and I had been telling Julie for weeks that now was the time, and at last she handed on Rachel's case to Doctor Evans. Rachel looked hurt about it, but she didn't know what Julie had been through. And Julie kept on visiting just as often.

Doctor Evans was a no-nonsense doctor who expected Rachel to Rehabilitate with a capital R. A kick up the bum. Easy to tell her that was what she needed – ten times harder to watch the despair on her face as she struggled through her exercises.

I had to keep my visits short. Ten minutes, and her eyes would start wandering. Visiting so often would have been impossible without backup, but I had the best backup in the world: Mam, Tom, Mathilde, Nan, Granddad, Dad (most of the time) and Julie – yes, she was far more than a doctor. And at school, Miss Akoto, Kamala and Jake. And Mari, my counsellor.

Rachel and I shared our diary of her recovery. I'd begun this second diary in the scary phase of delirium, when I needed to psych myself up to visit at all. That was the bit Mam handled far better than me. Mam was best at calming her down. Then we had the Sleeping Beauty phase, when my visits meant sitting beside sleeping Rachel with my sketch book. And finally, two whole months after she came back to consciousness, I was able to add some words from Rachel into our diary.

Now it was our routine, and everything we talked about went in there. But Rachel had never asked about the time before she came round. Maybe her mind was protecting her. It was already June when Mathilde said, *She's ready*.

And Rachel finally asked the question on the day before her thirty-ninth birthday.

'My time in coma. I can't imagine how it must… How was it for you?'

'That's in the other book. I'll fetch it tomorrow. About time, I suppose.' I held Rachel by both shoulder and looked into a pair of eyes more awake than at any time since last December. 'We managed – no worries.' And I knew that Rachel was beginning to understand all that had happened. And to realise that there was a great gap in her life.

The next day, we staggered the birthday visitors, and I gave them strict instructions not to tire Rachel out. Eventually, I shooed them down to the café. Mam and Julie knew exactly why.

I took Molly, snuggled her into the crook of Rachel's arm, and took out Rachel's old ring-backed notebook that I had used for the first diary. Or another Alice had. Was I still the same person who'd started the diary in December?

Rachel swallowed and nodded. 'I'm ready for it.' And I began to read.

> *Diary for Rachel Bothwell.*
>
> *30ᵗʰ December.*
>
> *The Wednesday before Christmas, you were in hospital after a seizure at your office party. Tom fetched Mam, but I refused to let her go without me.*
>
> *Doctor Cook did some tests, and you went all panicky, holding my hand, and I could feel you slipping away. Mathilde was with us. You smiled at me, and then started convulsing. Lots of small seizures, and then you went still, and they cleared us out to do the full emergency stuff. You looked very dead, and I was SCARED.*
>
> *Doctor Cook took me back in, to show me you were alive and under control. I'm still a bit frightened each time I see you, but not as bad as Mam. They are keeping you safe and asleep now.*
>
> *I asked Doctor Cook what I could do. She said talk to you, even when you look asleep. And keep a diary, so you don't need to worry about what you've missed.*

This is it. I'm writing it in your book because it feels more you-and-me.

I hope you don't mind, but I've torn your lists out of the front and put them in your desk. They're not to-do lists any more. They're to-done.

Later.

Just been in to see you. No change. There's not much to tell you about Christmas except we cancelled everything, and your mother came. Nine days since your seizure. I can't sleep, so I've been tucked up with Mam writing this. Some doctor I would make.

I hope you like your Christmas present. Granddad Joe found a big old swing, a double one, down the scrapyard. He thinks it's from some park. You always sneak a go on the swings when we walk down that way, and so we thought it would be just right for you. When you get round to waking up, we can swing next to each other. I love you.

31st December.

Still the same. I've been thinking about angels una-wares. Remember I told you what Miss Akoto said? We don't know who our angels are, and they surprise people big time. You need angels now, and so I'm appointing three guardian angels besides Mathilde, who tells me she's with you. Tom Richards, Bethany Howells and me, Alice Howells: we're your angels. Doctor Julie Cook and the other doctors and nurses are sort of healing angels, and so you have a whole

flock of angels. It's school holidays, and I'm missing
Miss Akoto, because I could tell her the angel stuff.

Rachel smiled when I read that. 'I've felt my angels all the way through. Especially you and Mathilde. Even when I was really scared, I knew I wasn't alone.'

I leaned in closer and kept on reading.

1ˢᵗ January.

Your mam came today. She only managed a few min-
utes beside your bed, and Tom had to take her out. You
aren't THAT scary. But you are a bit of a pain, you
know.

2ⁿᵈ January.

I brought Molly and wrapped her hair round your fin-
gers, just the way you like it. Doctor Cook says familiar
feels are good. Molly is with you, and so you don't need
to be frightened. I will wrap her hair round your fingers
each time until you wake up.

3ʳᵈ January.

Dad came with us. Dad and Mam holding hands. Gross.
But he's been good since it happened. Granddad Joe and
Nan have been spectacular. And Tom, even better.

Your mam and I sat on the swing for you, and she
got all emotional. She gave me a picture of you in your
doctor gown, and I have it beside my bed.

You haven't opened your eyes, but you look sort-of
peaceful. Not scary any more. Doctor Cook has asked for
more scans because your results are all over the place.

4ᵗʰ January.

*They called Mam today, and Tom took us in early,
because you were a bit conscious. Just lying there, but
Doctor Cook said you were. Nothing much happened
on the screen until I spoke to you. Then a lot. It's like
your way of answering me. You talk to me in brain
waves, and that's cool. We went away and had lunch,
came back, and you did it again, lots of times, and I
stayed until late at night with Tom.*

5ᵗʰ January.

*Not so good today. I'm writing this in my own bed. I
don't want to write this bit with Mam. This afternoon,
I did the scientific thing you would have done. I took
Doctor Cook away from Mam and asked the probabil-
ity question about you recovering. I said truth. No lies.
She said maybe 60%. Not good. Even lower, I think.
I'm not sure whether she even knows.*

*I told her fuck probability, you are living. Said it a
bit loud.*

*A nurse wanted the rude girl to be quiet. Doctor
Cook said fuck that, hope is what you need, and I've got
it. You will live. THIS is important.*

*Because you are you, and there is only one you.
Because my mother is a pain without you. Because Julie
Cook is the best fucking doctor in history (I hope). And
because you are my mother too. I love you, Rachel, and
you will live.*

Rachel reached out to pull me close, but I had a lot more to read, so I sat back and smiled. 'You did live, nutcase.'

6th January.

More brain activity, and we left Mam to sleep over in the visitors' room in case you need her. Nan is staying with me tonight because your mother has gone back to London. She'll come back as soon as you wake up.

7th January.

Mam didn't go in the visitors' room. Stayed with you and didn't sleep at all. Dad and Granddad Joe took me in this afternoon. No traces jumping. Doctor Cook wasn't there. She left a note saying they've sedated you a bit more to prepare for your scans.

The nurse said there was no point anyone staying overnight. No point. She freaked me big time, saying that. I was Maximum Baby Alice.

I lost it just when Doctor Cook came back. She took me in her room and gave me a cwtch and said I could let it out as much as I liked. Because this is hard for everyone, not just for kids. She loses it sometimes and has to hide it when she's on duty.

Doctor Cook made me feel strong. I said she could cry on my shoulder anytime, and we shook hands, strong. I'm one of the team, that's what she says. And she's my friend Julie now, and I'm Alice. We're Team Rachel. AND WE ALL WANT YOU BACK.

9ᵗʰ January.

*I'm having a day off seeing you and going to school.
Mam says I must. Got too wound up yesterday.*

Later.
*I HATE IT. Shit. I need to be with you. Going back to
school was like a bad dream. I didn't want to talk to
anyone. Miss Akoto was good about it, though.*

*Mam is keeping me away from you, and I bet
there's something wrong. So, I might as well write
about that angel stuff. Everyone smiles when they call
me your guardian angel. Not Julie: she takes me seriously. But they smile. I MEANT IT.*

*I have guardian angels of my own, like Mam and
Nan. And you have Tom, who brings me along, and
is so strong and sure. He doesn't fuss. And Mam, who
is a spectacular angel. Now she's over the shock, it's
like she can carry everyone through it, especially me.
Maybe she knew this would happen and got herself
ready in case.*

*I think EVERYONE has an angel inside them
really, but some people NEVER let the angel out. You
do – you were the first person to make me feel it's okay
to be me.*

*After school, I told Miss Akoto what I was thinking,
and she said the difference between meeting an angel
and being an angel might not be very much.*

11th January.

News. Julie knows now: that lump is triggering small stuff which is triggering bigger stuff. She said it's like a pebble in a stream which isn't a problem until all driftwood piles up behind it. And she thinks the only way to help is to take it out. Julie can't do that work, but she will be there with the surgeons to make sure you are okay.

I gave her a look, and she gave me one back. She knows how fucking scared I am for you. We had a cwtch with Mam and Tom, and I told her she's the best doctor ever, and it's not her fault if it goes wrong. Because Julie wants you back.

12th January.

Watching you sleep. Tom with me. It should be one visitor at a time, but they say I need an adult. Not sure which of us is the more adult. I bring in your book with me each day now. Something to do while you're sleeping, but some days, I just draw pictures.

I don't like it when your beep goes off for them to change the drugs. It's a little shock each time. A good thing Tom is here to hold on to. Operation on Monday.

I turned the book to show Rachel and flipped through some of my drawings. Rachel's sleeping face, empty of expression. Julie, at one of the monitors beside her bed. Rachel's face again. Stanley and Morwenna waiting by the door. Rachel's face. Mam leaning on Dad's shoulder in the hospital café. Rachel's face. Tom and Mrs Jones from your work, talking at the nursing station with Julie and Emmy hanging behind Tom. Rachel's face…

I drew her face in the air and ran my finger down real Rachel's cheek. 'I can draw your face in my sleep.' And I had to wipe my eyes before I carried on reading.

15ᵗʰ January

Watching you with Mam. Operation tomorrow. I don't ever want to let you out of my sight, Rachel. Mam's been here all day. I wish she could sleep. Love you x

All this 'love you' stuff was getting embarrassing, because I'd grown up about ten years in between writing it and reading it to Rachel. But I had to read her every bit of it with no cuts, because I'd been promising myself I would from the beginning.

16ᵗʰ January.

No one slept last night, and I stayed off school. The three of us went and waited in the hospital café forever. We don't like the visitors' room. It's claustrophobic. Another ace spelling, but I can't get happy about little things like that.

I'm happy about something massive instead. You are stable after the operation. They took out the little tumour. They're going to test it to make sure it isn't the sort that spreads. More waiting. Julie says it won't have cured your epilepsy, but you'll be back to normal freak-outs. They'll keep you sedated while you heal. Night-night for now.

18th January.

*Nothing. Just watching the steady waves on your
screen. They are sort of comforting. Not bad stuff, like
before the operation. School is a drag. Kamala hugged
me, and I told her to bog off. I wish I hadn't. I didn't
mean to upset her.*

19th January.

*No one talks to me. Kamala looks at me, but she hasn't
said anything.*

I couldn't help a little smile about this bit. I didn't know
Kamala very well, back then. I was a bit scared of her because
she was so cool. And I didn't know how much she would
help me cope with the next few months.

Rachel noticed my smile. I think she was beginning to
understand how much life changed while she was in hospital. Back then, Alice Howells had no friends of her age.

22nd January.

*I've been visiting, honest, but there's been nothing
much to write. It's lonely, being a guardian angel.*

23rd January

*Rachel. Rachel. Rachel. Rachel. Rachel. I can't get your
name to look right. Maybe when I get it perfect, you'll
wake up.*

More embarrassment. And remembering feeling lonely and desperate. When even stepping on the cracks in the pavement could kill Rachel.

24th January.

My counsellor says it's fine to shout and swear if I'm angry. And Julie says the same, but I don't want to shout at her. I hate this shitty hospital. We had a cry together. That's not like Julie. When I asked the probability question, she just shook her head.

Tom said it's best that I know, so she told me. You're not getting better. They had to put you into a deeper coma because of random brain waves again. Fuck you, Rachel Bothwell, DO NOT give up on me.

Same night.
I told Mam she needs some sleep. She shouted. Now it's me vs Mam. I don't want this. Getting ratty with each other. It's like nothing works without you.

Rachel put out her hand and stopped me. 'What have I done to you? I can't imagine...'

I smiled back at her but couldn't help the tears. 'You've turned me into Alice, your daughter. I don't want to be anyone else.' And I kissed her. 'I'll stop now. It's not all bad stuff – I'll save the best bit to read to you tomorrow.'

Julie appeared round the curtain and took me by the shoulder. 'Enough for now?'

I nodded.

Julie stroked Rachel's arm. 'Concentrate on this. You know you are loved. You know you have been loved all this time. Alice has faith in you making a complete recovery. I have. We all have. You can hear the rest of Alice's story later.'

'Yeah. Been wanting to read it forever,' I said. 'But it's hard, remembering all that stuff.'

'It might be better if I read it,' Julie said.

'Nah – it's a Rachel and me thing. We'll manage together. Tomorrow.'

Rachel gave me real, genuine Rachel smile. 'Together.'

49

GUARDIAN ANGEL

Alice

Rachel had a surprise for me when I arrived next day: one word with just four letters. Not a small surprise: a MASSIVE one.

'Alice, do you know what I've got today? It feels strange. It feels new. It's something I'd forgotten how to feel. I've got hope.'

And I wanted to dance on the ceiling but got reading instead.

25th January.

Kamala asked if I was coping when I stayed in at break. I said no. She sat with me forever and didn't ask. I said thank you. I hope she doesn't mind that time I swore at her. She's the biggest girl in class, so maybe she's just being kind.

26th January.

Your mother wants to move in. She's retired early from school, and it's easier for visiting. I don't want her here. She's too grown-up for me and Mam. I bet Mam thinks so too, but she's being nice about it, because this is your house, not ours.

28th January.

*Mam was talking about how nearly wonderful we
were. We had one special autumn with you, and we
should be grateful. I hate this WERE stuff.*

30th January.

*Phew. Your drawing friend Morwenna needs a new
tenant, and so your mother is moving in with her.
Glad to get away from London, she says. You won't
have noticed, but Morwenna keeps visiting you with
Stanley.*

*Kamala gave a talk in class about being a Hindu.
Lots of exciting festivals and food. The girls groaned
when I asked about the faith part. One divine presence, many gods. Maybe Kamala will be my friend.*

Rachel raised her eyebrows, but I tried to keep a straight
face and kept on reading.

2nd February.

*The girls say I have a zombie mother, and no one
should touch me. You are a sort of zombie, and I think
I'm turning into a hospital zombie. I haunt the place.
I know every fucking corner, sign and toilet. And the
hand gel gives me zombie hands.*

*It's not all bad. Yesterday, me and Miss Akoto and
Kamala talked tactics. I'm ready to fight back and
show the girls I've got feelings. Kamala is my friend,
REALLY. She says I'm the bravest person she knows.
And Jake. I've got two ACTUAL friends.*

Later, in bed.
I want you to be Rachel again and do physics and art
with Mam. She doesn't paint any more. Says she can't,
without you. Makes jewellery to sell at craft places
because she doesn't get too stressed doing that. Mam
talks about getting a regular job because she doesn't
want to live off your money. But Dad had another big
show, and he's paying her something for me now. Rachel,
you've only gone and made Dad SENSIBLE. And we've
started photography together, like he promised.

4th February.

I CAN'T LOOK AFTER THEM ALL.
Tom is down about Emmy picking up all the bad
feelings, as well as over you. And Julie told me she
dreams of playing her cello with you. I said why not try?
So today, she's playing her cello for you, right here
in ICU on her day off, and it's lovely, and sad, and you
aren't even listening. Julie is playing just for you. She's
a special doctor and a special person. And there's tears
in her eyes and I can't write.
Fuck you, Rachel Bothwell. FUCK YOU.

Rachel looked away, but I turned her head back to face
me. 'You need to let Julie love you too. She couldn't carry on
being your doctor. Not now we're all so close.'

'I must have hurt her so much – poor Julie – I didn't
understand.'

'Don't worry. We've been telling her you love her really.
And she knows it.'

Rachel shook her head. 'Poor Julie. And you said…
Beth – painting?'

'You think Mam could ever stop for long?' I turned the page.

5th February.

*I didn't say yesterday because I was angry with you.
Your Cardiff office has closed, so we've got more of
Tom. He lives with us now. He sleeps in the small front
bedroom. Tom is all right. No pretending to be a kid
with me.*

*We talk through the bad stuff, and he's been helping
Mam sort everything. Mam is brilliant in hospital, but
at home, she's one big muddle. And I love her.*

6th February.

*Embarrassing. Yes, double r and double s. I have an
imaginary you to take round with me. I tell you things,
but quietly, so that no one knows. I know my head is
about twenty, but the rest of me is an infant with an
imaginary friend. Fuck.*

7th February.

*At school, they laugh about two mothers, but I see
what Mam has lost.*

*Me and Mam have had our hair cut short. You've got
a shaved patch at one side, where they did the op, but
we've gone for short all over. We stand with you. Kamala
wanted to as well, but her mam wouldn't let her.*

*The best news is that your tumour was benign. It
shouldn't come back. But they still can't wake you up safely.
Shit. Mam sang to you, but you weren't listening. Fuck.*

8th February.

Today, Rachel Sarah Bothwell, d.o.b. 17.06.84, I gave a presentation to Year Six about how it feels to live with someone in a coma. I was nearly shitting myself.

Kamala came and hugged me afterwards, and Shareen, and Leah, and Jake, who's well cool. Not the Evils, but they couldn't be rude because they fancy Jake.

9th February.

Cai and Isabelle came to see you this evening, but you didn't say hi, so I did. Over here on some book business. Isabelle gave me a hug – one with a gap in the middle.

BIG respect at school. Only now they won't talk to me because I'm a top person. No more sweet little Alice.

10th February.

You knew this might happen. Some bills have come, and Tom wanted to know how much rent Cai paid. Mam and Tom looked in your desk, and found the envelope that says, OPEN IF ANYTHING HAPPENS TO ME. You are a genius. Bank stuff. Payments stuff. All the details. And the other one inside, FURTHER INSTRUCTIONS.

Mam cried when she saw you'd put Mam and Nan in charge of care decisions. And your will, witnessed by Tom, and he hasn't said a word. If you die, the house is ours. Mad, you are. And you're not going to die, because we're not going to let you go.

'We didn't let you go,' I said, as firmly as I could. And I had to hurry on to the next bit.

11th February

Often, when I get here, Molly's hair is already wrapped around your fingers, because the nurses see what I do. But I always unwrap it and wrap it back again, because they never do it in just your way. Only Mam and Tom and me know your way.

I've been bringing in your poetry books and reading to you. That shelf in the toilet is stuffed with poetry. I didn't know scientists did poetry. I wish we could talk about it.

'We can,' Rachel said. 'Poems are coming back, in bits. I bet they're the ones you read.'

'Must be. Let's finish this first.'

13th February.

BIG EXCITEMENT. Phone call from Julie and we rushed here with Nan and Granddad Joe. You had a seizure in the night, and it has kicked off more brain activity. You wriggled a lot. Opened your eyes a few times, but Julie says it's normal, and you probably aren't seeing. She said don't get too excited, but we are.

And after last week, Julie has had her hair cut to stand with us. Not as short, and she has red dyed tips. I want that, but Mam thinks school won't allow it. Shit.

Doing photography in the park with Dad. I get better pictures – people don't act stiff when a kid has the camera. They don't know I'm not a child all the way through.

O-o. 'Do I have to read this?' I gave Rachel my best grin and read it anyway.

14th February.

Valentine's day. You're healing up nicely where they operated. I have a boyfriend called Mick. Not Jake, because he's my mate, and he actually thinks. Mick's kisses aren't spectacular. He's a short-term Valentine-only boyfriend.

'TOO RIGHT, HE WAS!'

15th February.

Shit. Shit. Shit. Shit. Shit. Shit. You aren't responding. Gone floppy again. I got told off for swearing in class. Fuck Miss Akoto. Fuck you, Rachel Bothwell. I love you.

16th February.

You had another seizure, and I was there, and there was more stuff on the screen, and more wriggling and blinking. The blinking is spooky. I wish you wouldn't do it.

I've seen a counsellor they got for me seven times now, and she's well cool. But it's easier to talk to Miss Akoto. And Mathilde. She helps me sleep every night.

18th February.

Mam wouldn't paint, and so Tom asked her to do painting therapy because he gets so stressed. I joined in and we ACTUALLY laughed. And we did some body-painting, because Mam said it was fun. Tom got all squirmy painting me and Mam, even though we had our bathers on. And I got to paint round Tom's Celtic knot tattoos on his arms. His arms are massive. I didn't know how much I'd missed hearing Mam laugh.

Later.

No wonder Tom gets stressed. His mam came over for tea (after he had showered the paint off) and she's worse than your mother, Rachel. I don't think she knows he's an adult, and she's dead suspicious of Mam. I bet she thinks they're lovers.

Emmy hid behind her, and her mam helped her eat. Me and Tom grinned at each other, and I got Emmy to help me, just like you did. She buttered my bread and sliced some cheese, laid it on the bread, all neat, and cut it in half. Her mam was well miffed.

We had a swing, and Emmy's smile felt like medicine. She's one of my top angels.

20th February.

Do you know you've been in this coma for twice the time we lived together? Well, you don't, do you? All your knowing is on hold.

Extra for late edition.

*Guardian angel Alice H. told our special correspondent that she never knew it would be a job for life. When asked why she had been an angel for so long, she said, 'Because Rachel B. is a lazy c***.' When asked*

whether this was appropriate language for an angel,
she said, 'I'm the best sodding angel she's got. She'll
have to lump it.'

And we laughed so much that Maria in the next bed looked out of her curtains. 'Sorry,' I said. 'Rachel's a bit mad, you know.'

'You're right, Alice. You're the best sodding angel I could ever imagine.'

And this was the first time I had properly laughed with Rachel since December. It might even have been her first laugh since she came back from nowhere-land.

21st February

WE NEED YOU BACK. Shit. This is the longest wait
in history, Rachel. I like writing your name. Rachel.
And I will wait for you forever.

Trust me to write a bad song lyric. Rachel tried to catch my eye. I looked at the book.

25th February.

Mam has found me a young carers group to talk to,
but they all care for someone at home who talks to
them. I'm frightened I'll forget the sound of your voice.
    Emmy says I'm best sad Alice. But I don't want to
be fucking sad all the time.
    Mathilde helps most. Says she's watching over me,
even when I'm asleep. Says she tells you about me,
deep inside your dreams. I hope she's real.

Rachel sat up. 'Mathilde kept on reaching me – prompting me to listen to your voice – pulling me back to you.'

And just thinking about Mathilde, I felt her warmth. Rachel gave a tiny smile that told me she could feel her too. Real Mathilde, with us both, not just a hope.

I had to shake my head a couple of times before I could go on reading. It's not easy to read when you know an awesome guardian angel is listening.

27ᵗʰ February.

You've been moving and blinking again. And Julie thinks you responded to a command once. Like she said, 'move if you can hear me,' and you did. But it's not definite. And I WILL NOT GET EXCITED this time.

Tom had an interview as a helper at Techniquest a few days ago. You know Tom – all nervous, waiting to hear. It would be a WAY better job than your sodding office. He's great with children. Even me, and I'm ten times more difficult than most kids.

1ˢᵗ March.

St David's Day. Mam made Welsh cakes. Bad idea. Nan is the expert.

Jake and Kamala came round after school. THEY LOVE MY ROOM!

It's the first time I've had friends round that I can remember, ever! And Kamala and Jake are going to join our Climate Emergency group. Miss Akoto has already joined, and Tom. Pity about the Welsh cakes.

2nd March.

Julie played her cello, and you rippled on the screen.
She did it again. You did it again. Complex waves.
Basic awareness, she called it. Tom burst into tears.
And all of us. You didn't even move, you silly sod.
That's what Mam calls you. Because she loves you.
And we all do. YOU CAN GET BETTER NOW.

3rd March.

Not like yesterday. You smell.

4th March.

Same. Shit.
I CANNOT STOP VISITING NOW. It matters.
I heard a nurse talking about persistent vegetative
state. She CANNOT have been talking about you. Tom
is worried they'll talk about bed blocking next.
Julie can't say whether there'll be long-term brain
damage. And that's not fair, because I've been your
fucking guardian angel all this time. WHO WILL
YOU BE?

Later on. In bed.
Tom brought Emmy round to give me a cwtch and
go on the swing with me. All this care is keeping me
going, but Mam doesn't get it so much as me, because
she's not a child. And she looks awful. PLEASE get
better, so you can give Mam a cwtch.

Rachel turned away. 'Beth… What have I done? I don't know… Alice?'

I stroked her arm and got her to turn back and face me. 'Shhh! That's way back. Months ago. Mam's good now. Don't spoil the best bit!'

5ᵗʰ March

Whispers You were conscious today for a very short time. I could only tell from the traces. Julie is going to bring you back ever so slowly.

6ᵗʰ March

Not today. Julie says hang on. We mustn't hurry. Now you are nearly here, we need you to take your time. Your hair is growing back nicely and so is mine, and I'm letting it. Mam's looks like a horror movie, so we dyed it green, but it's fading now.

Kamala and her mam came to see you. Jake wouldn't. Said hospital freaks him. I know that feeling. Kamala said you looked spiritual. Spiritual and a bit smelly.

I showed her a picture of you before it happened. I know what you are going to look like when you're old. You don't look too bad really. But you had better keep away from mirrors when you wake up. Julie says your face will fill out again.

7ᵗʰ March.

After school, I asked Tom to take me to see Mathilde in the museum. I wanted to tell her you were on the way back, but she already knew. She smiled the best smile ever.

Mathilde said I'll need to be patient and she felt all warm and loving. And Tom looked at me like he might have noticed Mathilde talking. Said it looked like I was having an Emmy-moment. And that must be good, I think.

This evening in hospital was even better. Lots of movement. Can you see us when you open your eyes? Julie tried to take away more medication but couldn't take you off one of the drugs. It might be a few days. We must get it right.

Rachel. Rachel. Rachel. RACHEL.

8th March.

Julie cut down one of the suppressants. We talked to you. AND YOU ONLY FUCKING WENT AND WAVED YOUR FOOT AROUND! Julie thinks you meant it to be your hand. Easy mistake for a lazy sod like you.

Doctor Julie Amazing Cook has done it! She's got you back. And she fell to pieces BIG TIME. It's been so fucking long. The other consultant and doctors and surgeons and her students came and hugged her. It got a bit crowded. You're back, sleepyhead.

HELLO, RACHEL!

I held up the fat, ring-bound book. 'That's it, then. All done.' And I don't know how I felt, because I didn't feel anything. All that time I'd held Rachel's story inside me, ready to tell her, and now it had gone, flown off into the air.

I fished in Rachel's locker for our present diary and flicked through the pages, but I couldn't help a sigh. 'No way am I reading through all this stuff again.'

Alice, it's all safe with me. Everything you've shared.

Trust Mathilde to be around at the right moment.

I needed one more glance at the last page in the old book.

HELLO, RACHEL!

I turned it to show Rachel. 'Hello, Rachel.' And she pulled me right up onto the bed and into her arms. I could be her kid again. Was her kid again.

And I can't find words for the feeling we shared when our guardian angel gave us both a cuddle.

50

WHILE I SLEPT

Rachel

I was completely in awe of this girl who had sustained six months of fidelity and bravery. But each time I missed a step towards recovery, the thought of all she had gone through left me feeling profoundly inadequate.

June slipped into July and physically, I still had the abilities of a drunken jelly. I'd got used to my jumble of memories, and knew that most of them could be found, but concentration was beyond me. It was as if my mind forced me to look away.

One evening, Julie appeared on her way home from a long day at work. I tried to thank her for her continuing attention. 'Julie, you've been my rock. If only I could tell you how much…' And, as usual, the precise thought I had lined up slipped away.

'It's time we worked on concentration. Getting your artistic side going would help. How about some painting with Beth? You have enough motor control.'

Beth. I had spent my recovery focused on Alice, frightened to let the thought of Beth enter my head. Julie filled the blank for me. 'You two need some help, don't you?'

I let my eyes do the talking.

'Oh Rachel, you look as guilty as hell whenever she's around. But if you don't talk to her, the pain will just sit there. Is that fair on Alice, after all she's been through?'

'No,' was all I could say. I had caused Beth unlimited pain and stretched her daughter almost to breaking point. And I knew Beth had been in this situation before, patiently attending to her mother and stalling her career in the process.

'Call her,' Julie said.

I did. Yes, I could do that now: I could handle my phone, just about. But we didn't often talk. 'Beth, how about you visiting on your own this evening?'

'Julie bent your ear as well? I suppose she's right. See you about seven?'

Julie didn't go home. She helped me into a hospital wheelchair with head and side supports, and we waited for Beth in a small office next to the sluice room. She carefully tipped the headrest back, and my neck managed the weight of Fuck-You-Rachel-Bothwell's faulty brain. Necks are amazing, and most people ignore them.

'She said seven o'clock, Julie.'

'And Beth ever looks at the clock?'

'You've known her all these months. I've slipped out of phase with everyone, and I still can't get my head around it.'

'You're not the only one. You're my first patient who has been out for so long and come back. Getting you right is a long job, and it is affecting Beth.'

As if to prove the point, it was Siân who appeared. 'I'm here to check Rachel hasn't grown horns. Madam is downstairs with a coffee.'

'Okay, let's go exploring,' Julie said. 'I'm off duty.'

Siân frowned. 'And just why are you here at all?'

Julie tugged a lock of my hair in the way Alice often did. I got the message: it was Fuck-You-Rachel-Bothwell's fault. She put my neck supports back in place.

Since December, my world had been ICU and neurological wards, and now here in the more relaxed atmosphere of rehab. But apart from trips for scans, the extent of my exploration had been cautious trundles to the window at the end, with its view over the playing field. As Julie pushed me out into the main corridor, crowds of people seemed to be racing towards me, and I had to ask her to slow down.

'Wait here a mo,' Siân said, and went back for my trusty shock-stoppers. But they didn't stop the shocks. It was the people. People and more people. I was used to meeting people one or two at a time. Now I was surrounded by them.

'Rachel, you're shaking,' Siân said.

'Out here – it's scary.'

Julie stopped my chair. 'You've been in stagnation. You will get over the shock.'

'It's hard – I am trying.'

'I know.' Julie rolled me forwards more slowly. 'That's why you and Beth need to be strong and good together before you leave. She's waited for you all this time. Kept Alice going. Kept me going as well. And in spite of all that, she feels inadequate.'

Inadequate and Beth didn't fit together in my head, and I let my mouth droop.

Julie rolled me into a lift. 'You have Alice's diary. Other people experienced your coma, too. You scared me shitless, for one. It's important that you hear Beth's story.'

I gritted my teeth as the doors closed and the lift rattled. Ground floor. Cabbage and disinfectant. The smell of the school hall. I was a kid again. Julie rolled me past the kitchens and into the café. Beth was at a table with her head in her arms.

Julie let go of my chair and dashed over to her, leaving me facing a painting of a bunch of pansies. Pleasant and precise. Suddenly, I was festering with hatred for each ordinary, clinical brushstroke. Conformity. Limits on imagination. THIS was what Beth had smashed for me. Conformity through fear of my own imagination.

I had recovered enough memories to understand the barrier we had broken together. But now, for a half-creature like me, Beth was unreachable.

For ten seconds. Then she was here with her arms around me, holding me, weeping into my shoulder. She gulped. 'Seeing you free – out of the ward...'

'We'll be over there in the corner if either of you needs resuscitating,' Julie said, stroking a hand across Beth's back. And the way she put a comfortable, familiar arm out for Siân – what was this thing that had grown around me while I slept?

'Julie said I need to hear your story, Beth.'

Beth settled opposite me, I stretched my arms across the table, and she reached out to touch my fingers. The touch of Beth sent me right back. Before we met, I had built a wall around myself and let my fears rule. And Beth had been slipping into a worn-out shadow of herself. Then, in a crowded street, she was the one person who stopped when I screamed.

We began a process of mutual healing that day. Even with my fragmented patchwork of memories, I knew now that the way I fled from Beth several times over was a part of it, guessing that here was someone who might want to understand me. We did get a chance to feel each other's wounds, but we didn't get a chance to heal them.

I didn't die. The chance was still here, waiting for us. If only we could get over…

I pulled my hands away. I could never get over the pain I had caused by being Rachel in Beth's life. 'I don't know if I'm ever going to manage to…' To what? I'd lost the thread already.

'You alive is all that matters,' Beth said, and caught hold of my hands again.

'Tell me how it was, Beth.'

'Inevitable, I suppose. Dad all over again.' She looked down, and I didn't interrupt as she gathered her thoughts. 'I was just numb at first. Then it started to hurt – Alice, of course – seeing her with you.'

'Memories.'

She swallowed. 'I was barely eighteen months older when Dad died.'

'Beth?'

'You really do not want to know.'

'Tell me anyway.'

She looked across at Julie and Siân, and kept her head turned away. 'I caught myself dreaming about turning off your life-support. Just to get out of the situation. And then I couldn't get over the fact that I'd let the thought enter my head.'

'Look at me – please?'

She hesitated, but turned back to face me, with self-loathing written in her eyes. If I had been Beth, and seen my daughter so crushed, what would I have thought?

'Beth, you gave me life – you didn't take it away.'

'Just sitting watching you could be agony. Knowing you were close beside me, but completely out of reach. I could never tear myself away – other people had to turf me out. Even before Alice got so desperate. I didn't handle it well.'

'Who would? Seriously, it was a bit extreme.'

'I suppose so. When Alice did go down, I was back coping. But it was always hard to leave your side.'

I stroked her hand. 'When was it worst for Alice? There's anger in the diary, but it's hard to tell.'

'She felt it most after the operation: when you didn't come round. And then again when you came back in March and April. The delirium – you didn't always recognise her, and that hurt. Julie had told us what to expect, but it was still a shock.'

'For you too.'

'No – I'd seen delirium before, with Mam. I just went on automatic. But the days dragged on. I told Alice again and again that she didn't need to keep visiting. It was exhausting. Everything was exhausting. Life was exhausting.'

'What happened?'

'We'd got into a rhythm before you came round. The rhythm carried us, I suppose. Sharing the visits – not that Alice missed many – working with Miss Akoto at school. Siân was amazing, and none of us would have managed without Tom.'

'Tom – he was just a friend. Wasn't he? I'm hazy about Tom.'

She smiled. 'A bit more than a friend to you.'

'And he's helped all this time?'

'He was with you when you went out – maybe that's how it started. He had trouble of his own – a lot was happening in his life. Losing his job – needing a new direction. Endless problems with his mother over Emmy.'

'Over Emmy? Is Emmy alright?'

'Tom is trying to find Emmy a home where she can be more independent. But his mother won't let her go. And Emmy picked up all the upset over you.'

'Oh, Emmy.'

'She's been better lately – Alice has helped her a lot – they just sit on the swings and chill together. And I think Emmy has helped Alice – they don't need words. But we still have to persuade her mother for every single visit.'

'Visits – I remember from Alice's book – Tom has moved in with you, hasn't he?'

Beth smiled. 'Rather a long time ago. He's moved on since then.'

'I'm sorry, I'm not keeping up.' Understatement. 'Fuck, what else have I missed?'

She smiled. 'A lot. Tom made everything possible for Alice. Talked with her. Talked with me. Drove us back and forth. Helped me sort out your finances. Handled the corporate solicitors over you. You hadn't worked your notice when you went out. They wanted you in a private facility – state of the art, so they said – one of their companies. No mention that all they offered was palliative care. Julie checked it out: they didn't even have a consultant neurologist.'

'Tom – Julie – how many people have saved my life?'

'A few. Tom did everything, even though he'd been made redundant.'

'Tom.'

'He has gained something for his trouble. A whole new life, actually. You seem to have forgotten.'

'Forgotten what?'

'Yes, we thought it hadn't sunk in. If you remember, Tom used to be down on himself all the time. Looking back at what couldn't be mended.'

That, I did remember. 'His marriage broke up while he was at sea. He looked stressed from the day he started at work. He's at Techniquest now, isn't he?'

'He loves it. Showing children the experiments, demonstrating, answering questions. He takes demonstrations into schools, too – practises the new ones with Alice. And he shares a flat down Mackintosh Place with someone special.'

I knew that twinkle in Beth's eye. Another good recovered memory.

'Go on, tell me!'

'Yes, you have forgotten – I thought so.'

'Beth?'

'He's not alone any more. I knew from the beginning. You knew a while back, but I don't think it really sank in. Maybe we told you too soon after you woke up.' Beth beamed at me and clasped my hands together in hers.

'Come on, Beth.'

'She's sitting over there with Siân.'

'JULIE?'

Beth nodded.

'But…' Confusion. Had I known this? I couldn't find a hint of it.

'Beth, are you sure they told me?'

'I was with them. It was when Julie first thought of handing your case over. She didn't do it straight away, because she wanted to see you through the worst of the after-effects. But she did explain. Her relationship with you and with Tom and with all of us was making it harder. We were all merging into one family around you.'

'Family. That's what I've been feeling with… everyone.'

'A lot of what we talked about back then didn't sink in. You were detached, busy healing yourself. We decided to keep relationships for later. For now, I guess.'

I had known about Julie and Tom in April maybe, or May, or June. For a minute or two, at least, I had known. Once or twice or three or four times, I had known. But now, I knew I would never forget that two of my angels had fallen in love. Julie in all her Julie-ness, and Tom in all his Tom-ness. 'Julie and Tom? That is so utterly…' The right word escaped me.

'Magical? That's what Alice keeps saying. And you're the person who brought them together – you just happened to be asleep at the time. Alice is right.'

'Alice. Alice – I don't know where to start.'

'The things she has seen. Not just you, but the other patients. And the things she has heard.' Beth's hands slipped away. 'And it's gone on so long. I think she expected to have you home when you woke up, even though we told her it would take time.'

'Alice.' Crushing shame. I couldn't look at Beth. 'What I've done to her.'

'Alice,' she said, and paused. 'Scientist. Environmentalist. Photographer. Musician. Skilled carer. Poet. Mystic, even. Oh yes, you've done a lot to her. Alice has been tested to her limit.' Beth drew a breath. 'But never beyond her limit. What you never got to see was the effort everyone – everybody – put into supporting Alice.'

'All those angels.'

'Yes, and having them for you and for Alice supported me. Alice has never, ever been alone in the way Mam left me after Dad died, not ever letting me talk about him.'

'The thought of Alice left like that...'

'It was my deepest fear – that I wouldn't cope and she would end up with no one.'

'Oh, Beth.'

'It never happened. All your angels helped me cope, and Alice has always had people to go to. Julie, Tom. Siân and Joe. Miss Akoto especially. Counsellors when she needed them. And there's Emmy – she draws everything out of Alice. New friends – Kamala is an absolute star, and her mam. Your mam has helped – or tried to. And Iestyn – he's a fully-fledged angel now. A bit of a dark angel, but that's Iestyn.'

'And you.' I tried to hold her eyes as tenderness filled me up.

'After a few wobbles to start with. It did get easier. What matters is that Alice has used the experience. It's a part of her, and it has made her one special person.'

'She needs to be a child again, doesn't she?'

'It might be a bit late for that. But there is still a child inside her. Desperate to play with her favourite human being. She needs you home, Rachel.'

'I want... need...'

Beth's fingers... I couldn't reach.

I didn't have the strength to lean forwards far enough, and my fucking seat belt... I rocked, and I rocked and I rocked the chair. 'BETH!'

And her fingers were back, caressing mine. 'I need you home too, my love – you're the other half of me.' Touch was back. Touch was what we needed: words were redundant. We stayed there, touching fingers across the table while Julie and Siân fended off a cleaner with his mop. Remembering with our fingers.

And when we finally left, I made sure that Julie knew I truly understood that two of my angels were in love. Because I kissed her hand and told her how dearly I loved them both. I tried to remember signs I might have missed between Julie and Tom.

But no, all my angels were so close and understanding that anything short of full-on snogging would have passed unnoticed.

All my angels. All Alice's angels. All Beth's angels. It's a struggle to express how wonderful it felt to be connected again. No, not again. To be more connected than ever before. To be fully, truly among people for the first time in my life.

People. I wanted to feel their presence, their touch, and every sign of life they gave. Every sign of love they gave. I was drunk on people, falling in love again. In love with Beth and Alice and Julie and Tom and Siân and Joe. In love with Mathilde, the angel who kept me in touch with the human beings I loved. In love with sharing my life with them, and the living-ness and lovingness of being alive.

51

A GOOD DAY TO BE NEW

Alice

After all the scares and fears of the year, I got a new one. I was eleven, and ever since September, I had been far too old for primary school. Now, I was far too young to leave. Kamala and Jake were cool kids, ready for high school. I was a mess.

Having one mother in hospital and the other living on edge for seven months didn't help, but the real problem was me. I knew that my body would rush me through puberty without asking my permission. I knew in clinical detail all the changes that would happen. It was a one-way ticket to hormones taking over. To losing control.

I didn't want to grow up.

Biology wasn't the only reason growing up freaked me. I was committed to urgent action on the climate emergency, but every time I opened my mouth, I sounded like an eleven-year-old rabbiting on about her enthusiasm. I was an eleven-year-old rabbiting on about her enthusiasm. Even the letter I wrote to the Senedd, meaning every word, was now embarrassing. I needed to grow up in order to be believable AND I desperately didn't want to. ARGHHHH!

Who would be freaked about growing up like me? Not Kamala – she had already broken the puberty barrier and people listened when she talked. Not Jake – he was far too laid back. Only one person fitted. The problem was, she was already grown-up. Sort of. But she still couldn't dress herself, walk or concentrate for more than a few minutes. Two things I was sure of. She was just as freaked as me about losing control of herself. And she had resigned over a corporate climate whitewash.

I could share my fears with Rachel. When she was ready. If she was ever ready.

When she managed to walk the length of the ward with a frame, I gave her a treat, thanks to Dad's big printer. A poster-sized blow-up of the apple tree covered in bright green, growing apples. Rachel lay back on her bed and gazed and gazed at the picture. Our tree. Mathilde's tree.

After a long forever, she whispered, 'Home.' And tears flooded her cheeks.

'Home's waiting for you, Rachel. I want you back before the apples are ripe.'

'It's beautiful – all these apples, growing while I slept. While you kept visiting.'

'I kept visiting the tree too. Mathilde always met me there.'

'Mathilde… Home… Apples… All that darkness…'

I was used to these moments when Rachel drifted back inside herself and sat back to give her some time. The longing in her eyes reminded me of the time I first saw and touched her apple tree. When she explained that the tree needed time to produce apples. Rachel had needed time, too. But now, she was coming out of the darkness. She was almost ready.

'You can catch up with the apple tree growing in all my pictures.' I said, and stuck the poster to her locker.

'There's more?'

'Your idea. One a week, from winter to apple time, and on to leaf-fall was our plan, but we haven't got there yet. I'll bring Mam's tablet to show you.'

'My idea?'

Obviously one of the many that had gone astray. Rachel's thinking worked, but it didn't work in order. And that was another of her fears. She knew that she might not get all her abilities back. Rachel had spent most of her life as a professional thinker, so that was disorienting for me and Mam, never mind for Rachel.

I chose the date and time of her first adventure beyond the hospital. We arranged for her to be waiting at the school gate after my last day at Primary School. A day I had been dreading for months. I needed the support, and I needed to make Rachel feel useful, even though she would stay in a wheelchair and head straight back to hospital.

*

Rachel

Outdoors. Fresh air. A gentle breeze that felt like a gale on my skin. The heat of the sun and cool of the breeze playing tag, making goose pimples race up and down my arms. My hair seemed about to take flight. And the light – everything drenched in it, even though I was wearing my darkest shades. Noises from all directions. Scents and smells that didn't belong in a hospital ward.

A scarily bumpy taxi ride pulling me in all directions. I needed to rest and settle before I moved, but the driver had another fare to pick up.

As soon as Tom eased my wheelchair down the ramp, a crowd of excited children engulfed us. Tom leant over to protect me, and Beth and Julie shielded me from the worst intrusions. But my senses were heading into overload, and my head was spinning. Seizure coming? Too much was happening to be sure.

Most of the children had dispersed by the time Alice walked outside with her teacher's arm around her. I looked up into caring eyes, and Miss Akoto took my hands.

'Praise the Lord!'

'Thank you for...' I looked towards Alice.

Miss Akoto shook her head. 'Thank Alice.'

'I do. Every day.'

Alice knew she would see Miss Akoto at climate emergency meetings, and Beth would be stepping back from the special needs art club to let Miss Akoto take her place alongside Alice. But today was the end of a shared journey that had carried her. She hugged her own guardian angel for a long time.

Back to hospital, but this time with a sense that the future was waiting for me. Mathilde felt it too. *We'll have you home before the apples fall.*

The third Saturday in August was the twenty-second day since I'd walked the rectangle of corridors unaided, the seventeenth since I'd walked up a flight of steps and the thirteenth since I'd managed down as well: much harder. Alice was keeping count.

That day, I got dressed without help, did my exercises, and managed fourteen times round the corridors at a brisk walk, scattering nurses with my determined glare.

Alice strolled into the ward as if she owned the place. 'How many?' she asked, dispensing with any need for greetings.

'Fourteen.'

'Pathetic. That's only two more than yesterday.'

Alice. So much more relaxed now. So much younger now. Her hair was growing fast and she was wearing little bunches. I soon had plaits, thanks to Alice, one nicely covering the shorter patch where they had shaved the side of my head.

It was time to go home, eight months after an office Christmas party and Ian's death. A death that my exploding memory had chosen not to forget, however inadvertently I had precipitated it.

The idea of leaving my hospital life-raft had grown more frightening with each successive sleepless night. Would I manage any kind of independence? The woman who could once visualise fields simultaneously in several dimensions now struggled to do her shoelaces. What of the woman who casually threw together a bid worth billions and beat three competing global corporations in the process? She couldn't even calculate the number of days she'd been in hospital.

But now, with Beth and Alice two living presences beside me, and the promise of sleeping in my own bed tonight? My condition didn't matter anymore. I was going home.

'Are you ready, then?' Beth said.

'Yes. Yes. Yes. Yes. YES!'

'Yes,' but my yes was tinged with fear. I had breathed hospital air, eaten hospital food, and my whole life had become geared to hospital routine.

Tom arrived with Julie, here to make sure her longest-serving patient got home safely. While I wasn't on her list anymore, I was hers and always would be. Julie had persisted in finding my underlying problem, and she was the one who identified my hidden tumour. My healing angel.

At her most desperate, Julie had played her cello to an unresponsive lump. But she came back, playing again and again, and in another place, kept on playing her heart out to Tom. Her cello became their matchmaker. And one of the first sounds I had identified as I came round was the gorgeous, rich brown tone of Julie's cello.

Now, the moment had come to step out of this haven of safety. And I couldn't. The foyer was busy and chaotic. And that 'yes' inside me shrivelled away.

I had refused a frame because I did have the strength to do this. If there had been no distractions, I would have managed without a stick, but I needed some sort of prop.

I let a little crowd of visitors and a couple of hurrying nurses pass by.

Now – the door was clear.

But my legs wouldn't move. My pulse raced and I gasped for breath.

'Not easy to step over the threshold, is it?' Julie said.

Too right. I had been walking outside for two weeks, and I had been much further in a chair. Ten days ago, I had managed a visit home to dissuade an occupational therapist from installing a stair lift. A new stair rail and grab handles had been the compromise, but I hadn't ventured beyond the staircase.

Today was a different kind of frightening, letting go of months of life-saving care. 'Just give me a minute.'

Beth beckoned to Alice. They walked outside and stood looking up at the sky, doing an Alice-and-Emmy on me. Enticing me.

Sky. I missed the sky.

A little gust of wind ruffled Beth's hair, back in the familiar Alice band, although barely long enough. Beth. She looked back towards me.

Beth was out there. I was in here.

That was wrong.

My body impelled forwards by I-don't-know-what, I rushed outside into Beth's arms, my stick went flying, and we collapsed into some bushes.

Julie and Tom and a passing prop forward called Mel extricated us from the foliage. Alice rescued my stick. Beth rubbed at a couple of scratches on her arm, but she wore biggest smile I had ever seen. 'Apple tree's waiting, you silly bugger!'

'Bloody maniac,' Mel said. 'What you been drinking?'

'Fresh air. I've missed it.'

He shook his head and hurried inside to fetch his wife and new-born baby. They were going home today. A good day to be new.

I had an interrupted life to pick up, and a home to rediscover. Had it changed in my absence? I wanted to see the apple tree first and took Beth straight through the house and outside the back porch. Alice hung back in the doorway, suddenly looking shy. Maybe, like me, she couldn't quite believe this was happening.

Our very own shaded, back-yard-ish garden was waiting for me. The familiar high stone walls patched up with bricks and cement hadn't changed, but the garden looked better tended than I remembered, with beans on poles and herbs that Alice and Joe had planted. And the beautiful, beautiful apple tree was in full leaf, with a good crop of apples beginning to change colour. Alice's tree. Mathilde's tree. Our family tree.

And one extra surprise – yes, it was in Alice's diary, but its magnificence was still a surprise – my Christmas present, still waiting for me in August. In the corner behind the studio was a double swing with a big, old-fashioned metal frame, painted intricately by Siân and Joe.

I saved up the moment of having a swing, and in the doorway gained a companion who had grown beyond her comfortable fit in the space against my side. I led Alice to the piano at the far end of the room, and ran my fingers over the keys. Not yet: not enough stability in my hands. Alice sat down and took over, with a note-perfect Debussy arabesque, played from memory.

And then we had tea in our lovely, cosy kitchen with Julie and Tom. A box of Siân's Welsh cakes was waiting on the table. Julie handed me the inevitable charts and gave us endless instructions. Beth rolled her eyes, and Julie suddenly stood up and wiped her eyes. 'Now I'm fucking up letting go – AGAIN.'

I got up and hugged her. 'You can fuck up anything you like, any time you like.'

She reached for Tom's arm. 'Take me away, before I say something stupid.' And off they went. Family.

Just the three of us. The right moment for my first time on the swing? Alice hung back again when I suggested it, preferring to watch with her arm around the apple tree. I didn't exactly feel stable and rocked myself gently with a foot dangling in the dust. Beth got the other swing flying high, with no grown-ups to tell her to be careful.

No grown-ups, but an indignant child called out, 'BEHAVE, MOTHER!'

And then there were two of us on the second swing. Alice wasn't heavy, but she was no longer the skinny little thing I'd first met drawing an invisible velociraptor on a bus window. Her weight hurt, and I didn't have enough muscle and bulk to support her. She needed this moment. I needed this moment.

It hurt. 'Alice, I'm not very... Not very...'

She leant back against me and twisted her head to look me in the face. Yes, I was very. Very. VERY. I was very enough to hold us steady for a few moments longer. And more moments. And more.

'Don't want to squash you,' she said, and hopped lightly off my lap.

I was a mother again.

Siân appeared, waving from the back porch. 'Just left your favourite curry. See you tomorrow when you've settled.'

Settled? Siân had gone. Tom and Julie had left us and gone... I didn't know where. I wasn't sure whether anyone else lived here. Had I got confused?

'It's us?'

'Us,' Beth said, and put an arm around the apple tree. 'Us with our tree.'

Alice and I joined her, the three of us hugging around the tree. 'Us. Because we are,' Alice said. And I was wrong about the three of us: there were four.

Because we are.

And then we didn't know what to do. I was home, emotionally exhausted, and there was so very much I needed to catch up on that...

We gave up, went inside, flopped on the sofa together, and…

When I woke up, I was wrapped in a rug, it was dark outside, and both Alice and Beth were curled up next to me in their pyjamas, watching one of the Potter movies. The clock said eleven and I was as limp as a jelly, but strangely refreshed.

Alice poked her mother. 'She's back.'

'I didn't mean to fall asleep.'

'It's your home – you bloody well do what you like.' The young girl had been in the ascendant lately, but here was mature Alice, straight from her diary.

'You'll need time to adjust,' Beth said. 'Julie has left some notes, and I've put them beside your bed. What to expect.'

'Julie?' I had to ask. 'Who lives here? Where? I've lost track.'

Alice laughed. 'Not Julie, but that would be AWESOME!' We live here. Us.'

She turned the TV off. 'Past my bedtime.'

'And a half,' Beth said.

'Wheeeee! Got my Rachel back!' Alice kissed us both and skipped out of the room, looking far from sleepy.

Beth shook her head. 'I wish she could be a little girl more often.'

'Seen too much.' Too much of me, unconscious.

'I don't know.' Beth stroked my forehead. 'When I was her age, I'd seen nothing. And I lost everything. Alice has won in the biggest possible way, getting you back.'

She pulled me close, and I settled into her warmth for a while. A gently gorgeous experience. 'I didn't know… God, I've missed you.' Her immediacy, her presence, her warmth, her skin, her everything.

'Cuddles don't come on the NHS, do they? Recovery begins here: recovering you and me.' And we stayed cuddled close until Beth yawned, 'Bedtime.'

Stairs, one at a time using the new extra handrail. I had done a lot of stair practice, but always with a physio and a nurse in attendance. Strangely, it felt easier than in hospital. These were my own familiar stairs.

While I got ready for bed, Beth hovered behind me, making sure I hadn't forgotten any of those details I'd needed to learn all over again in hospital. And she REALLY wanted to be sure I would remember the one detail that had been so hard-wired into me since girlhood that even two-and-a-half months in coma hadn't wiped away the habit: taking my tablets. I even remembered to brush my teeth.

I got into my own bed in my own room in our own home. Alice appeared in the doorway with her rag doll, Myfanwy. Still not too grown up for a story with Molly and Myfanwy. It was midnight, a good time for a story.

52

AS MANY MOMENTS AS YOU LIKE

Alice

Rachel's first night at home was a new kind of scary. No doctors – no nurses – she was in our hands.

I woke up panicking in the middle of the night. But as I fought to escape the duvet, I heard the creak of a door and the shuffle of Mam's feet as she checked on Rachel. After a few moments, Mam headed for the bathroom, and I clambered out of bed. Then the floorboard creaked in Rachel's room below me. Good – Mam was back in with her. I lay back down, but both awake and in dreams, I was listening for Rachel.

At two minutes past six, I heard rustling from below and couldn't stay put any longer. Mam was in the chair by Rachel's window busy with her sketchbook. Rachel was sitting up in bed, looking dazed.

'Alice? You too?'

'Yeah – couldn't sleep – sort of scary.'

Mam played with her pencil. 'It's like when Alice was tiny.'

Rachel dug Molly out of the bed and put her on the shelf. 'You needed…?'

'Needed to check you were breathing.'

'When was that?'

Mam shook her head.

I went and sat up beside Rachel. 'Four o'clock. I heard Mam – knew I didn't need to come down.'

'Both of you?'

'It is scary, having you home. There's only us if stuff goes wrong.'

'I'm fine.'

'Doesn't make it any less scary, Doctor Bothwell. Mam – you sleep in here for now. Go on – it'll stop the worry. You've slept here all this time.'

Rachel looked questions at Mam, and Mam put her hands over her eyes. 'I needed to be here for you, Rachel. To help me believe you would come back.'

Her hands slipped away, and they shared a look I wished would go on forever. The two most precious people in my universe, glued together by care.

Mam keeping Rachel's bed warm for all these months is what I would have done if Mam hadn't got there first – and on some of the worst nights, I had ended up in there with her.

'Oh Beth!' Rachel swung round and struggled to sit upright on the side of the bed.

'Easy there!' I shuffled along and propped her up.

'I would feel safer if you stayed for the moment,' Rachel told Mam. 'As many moments as you like, actually.'

'Well, that went well,' I said. 'Now I can get a few nights' sleep. You do know Mam snores like a foghorn.' I couldn't help my voice shaking. Easy to joke – not so easy to deal with so many different feelings.

'You two! I am so very lucky...' Rachel reached for my hand and burst into tears.

'Rachel, it's not long after six, you're just out of hospital and it's too early for water works. You get back sleeping.' I hugged her, tucked her back in bed, cuddled her, and by the time I'd sat back up again, Rachel was fast asleep.

I went back up to read my book, waited an hour and got dressed. When I slipped into Rachel's room, Mam was asleep in the chair by the window with her sketchbook on her lap. Rachel was awake, cuddling Molly and smiling, although I could still see tears.

I put my finger to my lips and went to make some breakfast on a tray, adding some flowers from the garden in a jam-jar. 'Food, Rachel. You need to eat before you go into hibernation again.' Mam didn't even wake up.

An overflow of emotion followed by deep sleep was the pattern in Rachel's first few days. But as days turned to weeks, she began to cope – and I got less teary. It felt like we were being each other, apart from the doziness. Sleep was hard to find for me.

Rachel could doze anywhere and at any time. Doze. Eat. Doze. Exercise. Doze. Have a go on the swing with me. Doze on the swing, but never quite fall off. Doze with a mug of coffee in her hand and hardly spill a drop – an ace skill. Doze standing looking out of the window. Julie said it was all part of the adjustment process – Rachel was fully occupied with being Rachel.

Mam stayed in with Rachel for three weeks before the promise of spreading out in her own bed won. But I still paid Rachel some unscheduled visits in the middle of the night to make sure. I guess I was the biggest nightmare in the house. I didn't want a weekend away with Dad, and even shopping with Nan got me teary. I couldn't bear to be away from Rachel and was getting scared about managing school at all.

Emmy helped me because she never asked how I was coping. We spent hour after hour on the swings, sharing our own language of glances and wrinkled noses. Now, with Emmy, I began to put down some of my worries.

The Rachel who came out of hospital had a lot more in common with Emmy than Rachel the stressed high-speed thinker I used to know. And she had the slow, slurring voice to match. I could actually see words forming in her mouth, and the struggle she had to put them in order.

At first, it was disturbing, until I realised that words would find their way out in their own time, and that Rachel was just as deep a thinker as she had ever been. The long pauses Rachel used to shuffle words into order made Emmy giggle. Maybe she was proud not to be the slowest person around for a change.

Occasional night-time screeching seizures seemed to be Rachel's new normal, and as always, I was first there. But these were routine and didn't scare me. Rachel's latest traces were back to averagely weird Rachel-waves, according to Julie.

Ah yes, Julie. She didn't have far to travel if I did need to consult her – all the way from the back bedroom. Julie and Tom moving in was my idea, and I don't think Rachel actually noticed until they were here, because they'd been around most of the time anyway. They were family, and they belonged. Even Mathilde was happy about it, although I don't think either Tom or Julie believed she was real.

Julie and Tom were still a new couple, but they had a ready-made family. And Mam was happy with the smaller front room. Her most important space was the studio, where she was painting a series of pictures for the hospital foyer.

I had competition for rehearsal space now, with Julie and

her cello and Tom at least three grades below me on piano. His mam claimed he used to be good, but there was something missing from Tom's playing: music, mainly. Rachel just sat back and smiled at us all as we played. Although I knew she was soaking up the music as deeply as she ever had. Before her coma, she once said she needed music to help her breathe.

And after a few weeks, I persuaded her to join in. She managed her first squeaky arpeggios on the violin while I held it safely under her chin and Julie steadied her bow hand. Playing properly could be years away, but Julie had a better idea.

Rachel used to lead the sinfonietta from her violin, and they'd never had a conductor. But Julie saw no reason why Rachel couldn't conduct. I went along the first time she tried it, in case she needed a box of tissues or a spare pianist. But I was wonderfully unnecessary. Rachel was music-making again.

My first few weeks at High School weren't as scary as I'd dreaded, but I had a new muddle to sort out. What could I safely share at home with four adults and Mathilde?

Sitting beside Rachel on the swings in the twilight, I figured that she had the same problem from the other direction. What could she ask about things I might choose to keep private? Her voice was cautious when she whispered, 'How's school?'

This was better than expected. She was actually being a mother. Which meant I could be a kid and not tell her anything much, and even send her some coded love.

'Fuck you, Rachel Bothwell.'

And that made her laugh. One of those amazing laughs I'd been collecting, because hearing Rachel laugh made her recovery more real.

I needed to say more, but didn't know where to start. I jumped off my swing, picked up a stick and poked at some moss on the wall. 'Okay – nothing to report – it's fine. But I will tell you if I need help, honest.'

'Honest?'

And all of a sudden, I could be honest, and tell her what was really bugging me. 'I've managed you through coma – you can manage me through puberty.'

Rachel shook her head. 'I'll try. I didn't manage too well.'

'I guessed. Reality – I'll get it from you.' And then we were Rachel-and-Alice again, and I knew we could share anything. And I gave thanks to every angel I could think of that she was back here with me.

In late September, my cycle of photos of the apple tree reached the point we had all been waiting for. The apples were ripening quickly – apples that had grown while Rachel slept. And Dad was there to capture my first bite of an apple that Rachel had promised me, long, long ago in another life – almost another universe – when I was a child and she was a scientist. Dad's second picture was a close-up of my wrinkled nose. These apples were definitely better cooked, but I did force myself to eat the whole apple. Because.

Rachel's intensive physio regime bore apples, too. Rachel and Mam walked through the park, round the lake and back almost every day, even in the rain: more than four kilometres with a stop for coffee. Or two. But Rachel did still have days when her mind and body weren't on the same wavelength. On wheelchair days, Mam pushed Rachel to meet us on our way home from school, and the bunch of us took turns pushing her back.

I was working to get Rachel's scientific mind fired up, too. I came up with the plan months ago when she was still struggling around the ward, probably thinking about nothing much more than left foot HERE and right foot THERE. I discovered that the Senedd had a new climate change committee, and surely that was where Rachel should be.

The e-mail I wrote had embarrassed me ever since. It was a message from a desperate child, hoping her closest friend might recover enough to manage SOMETHING.

I didn't expect a reply, but the secretary of the committee had heard Kamala and me speak at a meeting. They had already co-opted some teenagers onto the committee, and now they wanted younger people who would have to deal with the effects of our warming climate. Oh, and Rachel could come too.

Kamala and I had already discovered that sitting in a room for an hour with experts from all over Wales took concentration and a lot of sweet drinks to keep us awake. But it was exciting to be included.

The first time we took Rachel, she nodded her head occasionally and dozed off once or twice. But I didn't care, because she was alive, sitting next to me. Alive in everything we did together.

This Alice found her Wonderland in the wonder reflected from Rachel. Everything seemed to be a wonder to her now. Even when she dozed off, she came back with a smile. Not a smiley-faced emoji. A smile that shone right out of Rachel and right through me.

And through us all, Alice.

53

IN THE DARK

Rachel

Once upon a time, I was alone in this house. So scared of the dark that I needed a nightlight in my room. Both scared of my epilepsy and scared to impose its effects on others. Both ashamed to mention it and ashamed to hide it in a world where disability could be out in the open.

I hid in plain sight, assuming that no one would ever want to share my life. And it took Alice and Beth to show me that my assumption was spectacularly wrong.

With a few setbacks, Alice was recovering from the trauma of the last few months, and Beth... Well, Beth was on a whole new journey.

Back in March, she had sketched my flaccid corpse of a body behind closed curtains in hospital. She captured each stage of my recovery in a series of small abstracts that filled and warmed as my eyes passed from one canvas to the next. No overt human form, but every sign of returning life.

And every sign that this was the same artist her father had been proud of. Beth had re-made that broken connection and didn't complain when Iestyn returned some of her early paintings. We hung them in the hall alongside the portrait of their young artist.

As for the luminous crayoned figure on the wall opposite, I felt good that this was once me. The experience had aged me a few years, but I wasn't too worried, because beauty was all around me. In Beth's pictures, in Beth, in Alice, in Tom and Julie. And in every wonderful human being I met.

Beth's pictures prompted me to visit a pair of family members I hadn't seen since December. Girl in a Green Dress reminded me of Alice worrying about her growing body and fretting over what would come next. Oh, and she was called Agnes, and seemed pleased to meet me again. Embarrassed, but pleased.

Rachel, my friend? Girl in Profile, my angelic companion Mathilde called to me, but I was confused. I couldn't see her. All the paintings had been moved around, and in Mathilde's place was the famous portrait of a girl in a blue dress. The next picture showed Gwen John's attic room in Paris, not unlike our housemaid's room. But Mathilde had disappeared. I sat down and tried to calm my racing heart.

'Where are you, Mathilde?'

Safe. Do not worry for me.

I went and asked an attendant, and yes, they had moved the pictures around weeks ago. The Gwen John collection was too extensive to display all at once. I didn't want to leave Mathilde in her unknown resting place and sat down again.

My picture is safe, and so are you. Back home with me.

'I'm sorry it's been so long, Mathilde. Thank you for looking after Alice – she wrote in our diary that she felt you were with her all that time.'

I'm always with her. She hasn't realised yet. But I think you know, deep inside.

And all at once, I did. That old wallpaper we found in Alice's room. We were privileged to share our house with someone who was far more than a ghost.

Alice talks to me as much as you do, but she imagines a housemaid with no name lived in her room. Not a refugee from the Great War, a working musician who lodged with Gwen's friends for many years.

'We live in your house?'

I moved on later, but that was my happiest time. The years when I first felt truly at home. You share that feeling with me, Rachel. You drew me back, I think. When you first walked into my room, you were already sensing that you had found a home, and somehow, that set me free.

I was too dazed to form sensible questions, but Mathilde answered them anyway.

You talked to me, and I found I could answer, found that I knew you deeply. Far more deeply than I knew myself. I had long felt drawn to Bethany and Alice when they visited dear Gwen's picture of me. And as you let them into your life, so you let me in too. And strangely, into some sense of myself.

'You were there all the time?'

That knowledge is not available to me. But maybe something of me has never left. It's the sense of homecoming that bonds us, and Alice and Bethany too. They needed a home, far more desperately than you imagined, and they have found one with you and me. We belong.

'We do. Truly, we do, Mathilde.'

I left after a brief *au revoir* with Agnes in her green dress. Now I had a strong sense that the appropriate place to meet Mathilde was not here or down in the museum vaults but in the privacy of her home – our home.

How much of this was happening inside my head? Was the question even relevant? She was precious, and that was enough.

And her story added up, particularly her half-French, half-Welsh accent. Had Gwen John helped the girl she once painted in Paris to find a home here? The same refuge I had found? Gwen must have passed through Cardiff many times on her trips between France and her old home in Tenby.

Mathilde. I felt ready to return to modelling, something I could share with her. But Beth wanted me back sketching for my first session in life class, to give my visual skills and coordination a proper workout.

Returning to those upstairs rooms felt like travelling back in time. To a special time, when I had dared let out a self I'd kept repressed. There were some new faces, but Stanley pointed to my old place at the easel on his left. Jade was still here, to Stanley's right, and close enough for me to understand that Stanley wasn't lonely anymore.

Morwenna came and gave me a motherly hug. A woman once shocked by the touch of my hand. I remembered Mum talking about life drawing, but she wasn't here. Maybe she needed a little more encouragement.

Beth walked through from the preparation room with… No!

Not my mother. She couldn't have been thinking of doing that. She was wearing the white robe. And I wanted to be anywhere but in the room with her.

This was inappropriate. WRONG.

My mother was smiling at me, and at Stanley, Jade and Morwenna. She didn't even look nervous. Nothing computed. I didn't know – didn't want to know – what she looked like underneath her clothes.

If anyone had noticed the extreme panic and embarrassment behind my easel, they didn't show it. Maybe they were warned in advance. 'Ignore the zombie. She's slightly mad.' Beth blithely introduced the newcomers without a glance at me, telling them that it's not a competition. No need to worry how their work looks in comparison with the others. She introduced her model, Gaynor, back after last term.

Back after last term. Mum had never told me. Or had the memory leaked away like so many others?

'It's fine if you want to talk to me,' Mum told the newbies, shedding the robe, and sitting, relaxed and upright. At least she wasn't facing me.

People were beginning to draw. I opened my box of pastels. They would notice if I didn't draw anything. I was going to have to look at her.

Mum. Beautiful. Poised. My pose – the pose she taught me – a violinist. Yes, I could look, and wondered what music was playing through her head. Biber's Mystery Sonata, *The Guardian Angel*, perhaps?

My pastel was already sculpting the shape of Mum's back on the paper. I hadn't asked my hand to begin. It was all just… happening. A drawing of my mother, not so much naked as triumphantly without need for clothing.

I looked around. Saw a flash of warmth between Morwenna and Mum. Not yet a year and a half after my father's death, Mum was taking big, big steps into the future.

My drawing had appeared on the paper without effort from me. And now another, and another, and another. I loved drawing my mother, and I LOVED the automatic nature of the process.

Beth was here, breathing in my ear. 'As if you've never been away.'

'I am just so glad to... to be my mother's daughter. Look at her!'

'Her daughter's mother,' Beth said.

Mum, full up with love and humanity, but never with a chance to express it until now. When she changed poses, I mouthed, 'Proud of you, Mum.'

'Proud of you, too. I always was.' And I hurried out of the room in tears.

Morwenna came and put an arm around me, gently leading me back. 'Don't hide this from your mother.' And so, I didn't.

After the session, and a long hug from Mum, I needed some quiet time with Beth to process the evening's events. We cancelled our taxi and caught a bus to town.

By my side on the bus, Beth told me how Mum had joined the class after Easter, drawing with fluidity from the start. Her transition to modelling had been more tentative than mine, dressed at first. But I was out of danger and Mum had Morwenna for emotional support. She soon became the star model, able to sit perfectly still almost indefinitely. 'Never as relaxed as you, Rachel, but she has a different kind of beauty.'

We wandered through town towards the bus stop for home. It was windy, but not cold, and I tugged Beth's arm. 'Walk home?'

She poked out her tongue. 'And give me another panic? Right, I'll go halves. Bus to Albany Road, and then we walk.'

Getting off the bus, we headed up Alfred Street, where Beth had coped with motherhood in that poky little extension. This brave, quiet but endlessly creative woman had never stopped caring for everyone drawn to her, despite a life that was one long struggle. And she had knowingly taken the enormous risk of befriending me.

Beth smiled as we passed the alley. 'Remember the morning Alice brought back your coat – with you in it?'

'And I first stood on a Lego brick? We neither of us understood each-other's barriers. We needed Alice to sort us out.'

'She kept that red coat in her room all the time you were in hospital. Sneaked it back downstairs on the day you came home.'

'Alice.'

We stopped, held hands and let the city sing to us. The same ordinary but intoxicating song every night bird loves. The rumble of a far-off train. Generators humming. A Tom cat's yowl disturbing a dog into half-hearted barks. Drunken shouts far behind us. Thumping bass notes from a passing car on impossibly low suspension. A distant motorbike: a sound of freedom and escape.

Around the corner, we passed Alice's old school, with more memories for Beth than for me. She paused by the gate. 'It doesn't seem long since…'

Further up, a bunch of drunken women had come to a halt against a wall, sporting a tired array of plastic horns, furry ears and tails, and too-high heels. Two were prostrate on the ground. 'You okay?' Beth called.

'Who are you, then? Fucking social worker?'

'I love my city,' Beth whispered. And a series of memories surprised me. My undergraduate years at Cambridge. Always the sober one on nights out, avoiding alcohol and drugs because my body had its own special way of losing it. I'd cut myself off from the home where I'd never felt I belonged but failed to find a safe anchorage. Until now.

A gust of wind blew chip papers along the street, and I looked up. Clouds were racing across the sky, eerily lit from below. I imagined them passing on and on, over sleeping family after sleeping family.

Beth followed my eyes. 'Plenty of angels up there tonight,' she said.

I could feel home drawing us onwards. Home. Heading home to Alice and Julie and Tom and Mathilde. And with the new knowledge that my mother had found her own home at last, with Morwenna. 'Mum's had a real new start, hasn't she?'

'What about her daughter? You've had a few starts interrupted.'

We reached the corner and headed down our street. 'The coma is a part of me now, and the damage. But what can I do with my life?'

FEAR.

I stopped. 'I'll never concentrate enough to…'

Steady now. I'm with you.

I gave Mathilde silent thanks, and let Beth take my arm and mother away my fear. 'Just enjoy being yourself. I have extensive plans for your being.' She stopped me in our front porch. 'You do know that the true, impulsive, loving Rachel is alive and well? Give it time and we'll see what we can manage together. That's what families are for.'

I ran my finger along the wall tiles. 'Being… here… together.' Did I speak the words? It didn't matter because I felt the warmth of home wrapping around us both.

When I looked up, a shadowy figure was standing under

the tree in the street. Her long cloak rippled with ever-changing tints of shade beyond name.

Mathilde smiled. *You fear the dark, Rachel. Good things can be found in the dark.*

'I'll try to be brave,' I called, but she disappeared behind the tree.

Beth followed my line of sight but didn't say anything. I led her through the house and out into the dark of the garden, with the top branches of the apple tree illuminated by a distant streetlight. Alice rushed out to join us. 'Where've you been?'

'Coming home, the slow way,' Beth said.

The slow way. A new feeling settled around me, one I've rarely shared. Real contentment. My cares about my variably disabled state and possible future faded away.

I heard a tap on the window above. Julie and Tom were silhouetted against the light, arm in arm. My family had grown in the dark, while I slept. And Alice had done most of the nurturing and growing.

Alice, my daughter and guardian. I picked up a windfall, slightly bruised and smelling of life. 'Ready to pick some apples, Alice?'

She wrinkled her nose. 'In the dark?'

Somewhere out in the shadows, Mathilde was humming a tune.

'Is that…?' Alice's eyes widened.

I shrugged. Beth smiled.

Alice gave the slightest of nods, reminding me of Granddad Joe. And she scratched her head, reminding me of herself. 'You've been here all along, haven't you, Mathilde?'

I don't mind you sleeping in my room, Alice. I like the company.

'You…?' Alice opened her mouth, thought better of saying anything and fetched a basket from the porch.

And Mathilde sat on the wall swinging her legs while the three of us picked apples in the dark.

The End

Our lives rarely fit into neat episodes,
and often endings contain the seeds of new beginnings.
These friends have more to share in the next book,
Angels and Blackbirds.

AUTHOR'S NOTE

Epilepsy is a condition with many different forms and many causes. Other people may experience it in a wholly different way to Rachel in the novel. Rachel's experience of epilepsy is based on my own, although mine has been fully controlled for many years, and was never so severe. However, the psychological effect it had on me in my teens and early twenties was profound and life changing. Living with epilepsy presents its own challenges, because if you don't talk about it, no one will know you have it until they witness you in seizure, and that can and does shock people.

GWEN JOHN (1876-1939)

The two portraits they talk with can be seen in Cardiff Museum, where the author worked for a short time in his late teens, always stopping to have a word with Gwen John's portraits. They can also be viewed in the National Museum of Wales online art collection, where they have many of Gwen John's works.

Girl in Profile (Rachel's friend Mathilde in the book) and Girl in a Green Dress can be found here, as can the other two pictures mentioned, A Corner of the Artist's Room in Paris and Girl in a Blue Dress.

https://museum.wales/art/online/
?action=show_works&item=408&type=artist

APPLES IN THE DARK 2

Angels And Blackbirds

Every morning, Mam tells Emmy to brush her teeth and not swallow the toothpaste. Until the morning Mam doesn't wake up. And at thirty-six, Emmy steps out of the shadows.

Emmy has always lived with her mother, who has made every decision in her life. Emmy's deep empathy with the people around her often covers her lack of comprehension, and she simply doesn't know how to make choices. But all that changes when she discovers that other people trust her. Emmy tells the story with Rachel, who is still on a slow journey to recovery. Life for Emmy becomes a whole new adventure.

ACKNOWLEDGEMENTS

One of my greatest discoveries when I took up writing unexpectedly at the age of fifty was just how caring and supportive the writing community is. The list of names here could be endless, especially as this series of books has been evolving for a number of years alongside other writing projects.

A special thanks to Mandy Berriman, for criticism, advice, encouragement and smiley emojis on this and so much more of my writing over the fourteen years we've been sharing the writing adventure. Patient beta readers on this book have included the wonderful Janette Owen and the late and much missed Julie Cordiner, fine writers themselves.

Leigh Forbes cast her eagle eye over this book and is responsible for the typography and design. I would like to give a special mention to Dr Stephanie Carty's Psychology of Character course – it was a great help in ensuring the congruence of my characters. Rosie Claverton, doctor and author, helped me with the medical details – particularly with the problems associated with a long recovery. My first mention of Debi Alper is for her editorial work on an early draft of this book, which saved me from pursuing numerous blind alleys!

Amongst my many writing tutors, Debi Alper (again) and Emma Darwin taught me much wizardry and alchemy, both in person and through the amazing Jericho Writers Online Self-Editing course. Julie Cohen taught me most of what I know about plotting (and how to peel a Post-it note). And it was during two successive lectures by Julie Cohen and Allie Spencer that the idea of creating this series of books from the wreckage of an earlier novel took shape.

This was back in 2014 at the Festival of Writing at York, an important date in my calendar since 2010. Many thanks go to Harry Bingham for nurturing so many of us as writers through the Festival, through the late lamented Word Cloud and through Jericho Writers. Many thanks to Anna Burt and all at Jericho. Mentioning the Word Cloud leads to so many inspiring fellow writers that I can't possibly name you all, but you know who you are, and I'm sending you all big cwtches from Wales.

To my wife Fiona go my eternal thanks for her patience with a dreamer. To my offspring Lucy and Simon for inspiring me, putting up with me and badgering me when necessary. To my late father for introducing me to the wonder of the scientific world, for playing the piano with my small ear pressed against the soundboard beside his feet, and for his own sense of wonder.

And lastly to my fellow Weirdlings, Mandy Berriman, Debi Alper and Rachael Dunlop, for being.

ABOUT THE AUTHOR

John Alex Taylor grew up in Cardiff, and he lived in Scotland and then for many years in Wessex before moving back to Wales. He lives with his wife Fiona between the South Wales Valleys and Bannau Brycheiniog with a view of the Black Mountains from his study window. The son of a scientist who was also a fine musician, the brother of an artist and the parent of a scientist and a mathematician, also a musician, John has always been fascinated by the blurred edges between science, all the arts and spirituality.

He worked for over thirty years with people with learning disabilities, Emmy's peers, and you will discover a lot more about Emmy in the next book. Along the way, John became a storyteller, adapting stories for the people he worked with, often to help them make choices. Writing sprung from that, but he didn't start writing until he was fifty. Now, he's busy making up for lost time. He rarely misses a day walking in the beautiful Welsh countryside and giving thanks for the small beauties (and big mountains) all around him.

For more information, pictures of locations and news of future publications, visit

johnalextaylor.com

Dryw bach: the little Wren who shouts at me from the bushes.